THE CONQUEROR'S SHADOW

ARI MARMELL

First published in Great Britain in 2010 by
Gollancz
An imprint of the Orion Publishing Group
Orion House, 5 Upper St Martin's Lane, London WC2H 9EA
An Hachette UK Company

1 3 5 7 9 10 8 6 4 2

A CIP catalogue record for this book
is available from the British Library

ISBN 978 0 575 09861 9

Typeset at The Spartan Press Ltd,
Lymington, Hants

Printed in Great Britain by
Clays Ltd, St Ives plc

The Orion Publishing Group's policy is to use papers that
are natural, renewable and recyclable products and made
from wood grown in sustainable forests. The logging and
manufacturing processes are expected to conform to the
environmental regulations of the country of origin.

To my father, Howard,
without whom I wouldn't have known
Jack (sic) about sci-fi and fantasy
Thanks, Dad

PROLOGUE

Dawn broke across the eastern horizon, seeping into the skies above the ancient city of Denathere, the Jewel of Imphallion. And the ancient city, in its turn, would break beneath the newborn dawn.

Plumes of smoke undulated upward – hypnotic, grey-hued serpents taking great bites from the heavens. Thick and oily, they blackened the air. The clouds themselves grew dark, contaminated, sickly. And the sun did not shine upon Denathere, thwarted by the unending night.

Nor could the sullen and defeated dawn dispel the nightmares of the city's terrified citizens, for on this morning their nightmares were real.

Fires raged unchecked through district after district, devouring homes, possessions, lives. Corpses – bloodied and broken – lined the streets. Crows swarmed thick as flies. Dogs, driven feral by the inescapable scent of blood, snapped and snarled, killing over pieces of meat that might once have fed them dinner rather than been a part of it.

From Denathere's walls – cracked, shattered, and breached, but still intimidating – watched the city's new masters. Most were mercenaries, their faces bereft of pity as they glared over the suffering they left in their wake, fingers idly clenching blood-sated blades. They, at least, were human. Over soldier and citizen alike watched the cyclopean gaze of the one-eyed ogres; from around their feet came the high-pitched giggling of the wild, sadistic gnomes – misshapen creatures delighting in the bloody work they performed.

Across Denathere's surrounding fields stretched a sea of

humanity. Tent peaks formed islands in the rough tides of the assembled horde. Here and there fluttered a brightly coloured banner, the standard of a lord or Guild whose soldiers contributed to the gathered army.

The fields swelled with the dull drone of thousands of voices, drowning out any other possible sound. Animals for miles around fled in terror, diving deep into burrows or taking to the skies, squawking loudly as they flew. Even in the heart of the occupied city, the battered populace heard the steady clamour. 'Salvation!' they whispered breathlessly to one another. But if salvation it was, it came too late for the thousands who lay dead or dying in the carnage-strewn streets.

On a hillock in the surrounding fields, beyond the reach of even the greatest siege engine, stood the largest tent in the assembled multitudes. An enormous pennant, longer than a tall man, flapped dutifully in the breeze, displaying a great bear – standing rampant beneath a broken crown – embroidered upon a field of royal purple.

A man stood now atop that hill, a spyglass pressed to his right eye. His face was rough, weather-beaten, and his rich brown hair was just lightening at the temples. The tabard he wore over his heavy armour displayed the ensign of a red eagle upon a navy field; the same could be found upon the shield lying at his feet. Slowly, he lowered the glass, shaking his head as though to dislodge the image of the shattered city.

'Does it get easier, Nathan?'

Nathaniel Espa, Knight of Imphallion, bowed perfunctorily. 'Good morning, Your Grace.' He turned his head and nodded to the young regent's companion, a soft-featured, dark-haired woman clad in a leather vest over a rose-red tunic. 'Good morning, Rheah.'

Lorum, Duke of Taberness and Regent Proper of Imphallion, smiled faintly. In his mid-twenties, Lorum knew just enough of tactics and war to recognise that he couldn't lead so vast an army. He might give the orders, but every man on the field knew it was Sir Nathaniel who planned the campaign. Self-conscious in polished armour never marred by the sting of an enemy's blade, the regent brushed light blond hair from a youthful, clean-shaven face. 'How you can manage courtesy this early, Nathan, is beyond me. I feel as though I've been sleeping on rocks for a week.'

Rheah laughed softly. 'You *have* been sleeping on rocks, Your Grace. That's the joy of war: the chance to visit places no sane person would wish to go, to meet a great many people who would like nothing better than to kill you in all sorts of revolting and painful ways, and to sleep on rocks sharp enough to hobble an elephant. You should have been told this before you got here.'

'Wonderful,' Lorum muttered.

Nathaniel, however, had seen too much to smile this morning. He merely glared at Rheah, who seemed oblivious to her friend's foul mood.

When it became clear she wasn't about to acknowledge his irritation, he spoke instead to the young regent. 'I believe you were asking me something, Your Grace?'

The young regent gestured toward the columns of smoke dancing in the air above the city they'd come, gods willing, to save. 'I was just wondering about all this. Does seeing this sort of thing ever get any easier?'

Nathaniel turned back toward the city and shook his head. 'Gods, I hope not,' he muttered softly. Abruptly he punched his right fist into his left palm, nearly breaking the delicate spyglass. 'What's that bastard up to?'

Rheah nodded slowly, ignoring for a moment the puzzled look on Lorum's face, 'You think there's more to this than just conquering more territory?' she asked, her voice low, suddenly solemn.

'Absolutely,' Nathan answered. 'He's not this stupid.'

'I don't understand,' the regent admitted, a hand half raised to get their attention. 'How do we know he's not just trying to take Denathere like he did the others?'

'He's moved the bulk of his armies into the city,' Nathan explained, attention fixed on the distant walls. 'Far more than necessary to overrun the defenders.'

'So?'

The knight sighed. 'Your Grace, have you been paying attention to my lessons?'

'Of course,' Lorum insisted, sounding injured.

'All right then. Look around. Tell me about the area.'

'There's the city, of course. The defensive walls. And, well, just open fields. Farmland, basically. A few hills.'

Nathan nodded. 'Good. What does that mean?'

The young regent's eyes glowed with sudden under-standing. 'Denathere's not a particularly defensible city!'

'Very good.' Nathan smiled. 'All Denathere has is those walls. Big and imposing, certainly, but breach them and there's nothing left to stand in your way. If you were taking this city, would you hole up inside?'

'Not a chance!' Lorum insisted. 'I'd be vulnerable to counter-attack. Like . . .'

'Like the one we're about to launch,' the older man con-firmed. 'Exactly.'

'It's one hell of a mistake,' the regent muttered.

This time Nathan and Rheah shook their heads in unison. 'No,' Rheah told him. 'Corvis Rebaine is not a man who makes that sort of mistake.'

'Damn it! I just wish there was some way to learn what he was doing in there!' Nathaniel growled again, waving his spyglass helplessly toward the city.

'Actually,' Rheah said, her expression thoughtful, 'there is.'

In the centre of Denathere, coated in ash, blackened with soot, stood a large stone hall. The banners that once fluttered gaily from the great columns and wide arches were gone, burned to cinders or yanked down by inhuman hands. But even without the pennants of the lords and the Guilds, the looming structure radiated importance.

Soldiers, human and otherwise, milled about in the streets surrounding the Hall of Meeting, mired in that frustrating pause between engagements. The surrounding buildings once represented the finest design and architecture the city had ever produced. Elegant sweeps, intricate murals, lofty peaks: all reduced to smoldering heaps of burned wood and uneven piles of jagged stone. The Hall alone remained largely undamaged.

The noble edifice stood mostly empty. The central chamber, home of constant and convoluted negotiations between Guilds and noble houses, was a wreck. Shattered crystal and wooden splinters littered the floor, the oaken table that had served for two hundred years pounded to kindling by overeager soldiers. The private rooms were in no better shape. From the ground floor to the roof, furniture lay smashed, mirrors and crystalware shattered, anything remotely valuable long since plundered.

Only the basement showed any signs of life. A chamber normally used for storage now produced the oddest combination of sounds: the undertone of frightened whimpers and desperate conversation, but also a series of oddly rhythmic thumps.

Within the walls of the chamber, well illuminated by a surplus of oil lamps, waited the city's elite. Wives, children, and the aged of noble families huddled against the wall, features pale, many sobbing. Mothers clutched protectively at their children. Sprawled beside them were the eldest of the Council of Guilds, too old for the use to which their younger compatriots had been put. Several of the occupying soldiers milled about, paying only marginal attention to the prisoners.

In the room's centre, the stone floor gaped open as though Daltheos the Maker had taken his great hammer to the earth. It was from this yawning pit that the strange thumping issued.

One suspicious eye trained upon the nearest guard, a fellow of middle years pushed himself from the wall and sidled over toward another man, white-haired and older still. The elder of the pair, his face covered in sweat, scowled at the newcomer. 'What do you want, Bennek?'

Bennek, Earl of Prace, scowled right back at him. 'I want, Jeddeg, to know how you could let this happen.'

'I beg your pardon?' The old man's expression changed not

a whit, but his eyes grew cold. He rose, swiftly if unsteadily, to meet his accuser's gaze. Several guards allowed their hands to hover near their weapons, but they made no move to interfere. 'How, precisely, is this my fault?'

Bennek shoved a finger at the other's face. 'All of you! The entire council! We knew he was coming. We all knew! We asked the Guilds – we *begged* you – for the funds to increase our own armies. You refused us!'

'The Guilds did what we could,' Jeddeg insisted, his tone that of a man who'd repeated the same argument a dozen times over already. 'How could we know we'd have so many of them to deal with? Besides, I didn't exactly see the noble families riding at the forefront of the defense, did I?'

'You bastard, I'll—'

'Would the two of you *stop*?'

Silence.

Tyannon, eldest child of the Baron of Braetlyn, blinked in bewilderment, as startled by her outburst as they were. At fifteen years of age, the cusp of adulthood in Imphallion, Tyannon was accustomed to being treated as a child – and normally to keeping her place, as a good child should. Her tongue cleaved to the roof of her mouth at the realisation that she had just raised her voice to two of the most important men in Denathere.

'You've something to say, girl?' Jeddeg asked.

One hand nervously twisted the hem of her dirt-encrusted tunic. 'That is – I—'

Her little brother, Jassion, tentatively stepped forward and gripped her other hand tightly in his tiny fist. 'Tyannon angry?' he asked, his quiet voice even smaller than usual.

She took a deep breath, squeezing his hand once. 'Yes, Jass. Yes, I'm angry. But not with you, sweetheart.' She glanced up, a sudden fire in her eyes. 'At them!'

Bennek frowned darkly. 'Now, see here, Tyannon—'

'I am! And I can't believe what I'm seeing! I can't believe the two of you are still fighting! People are dying, and you still can't leave each other alone!'

'Tyannon,' Jeddeg said, 'we're trying to work out a way—'

'You're doing nothing of the sort!' she screamed, actually stamping her foot in emphasis. 'This isn't about solving anything! This isn't even about them!' She pointed at the guards, who were now grinning openly at the entertainment. 'This is about the price of grain, or trade routes, or whatever damn thing you were discussing the day before last! If you'd put my father in charge, we'd not have lost so quickly.'

Two pairs of eyes went cold, and Tyannon realised she had, perhaps, gone a bit farther than was entirely appropriate.

Before she could stammer out an apology – or the earl or the Guildmaster could let loose with some scathing retort or another – a new voice sounded from behind her. 'Do we have a problem here, gentlemen?'

Tyannon heard her brother shriek and felt his grip tighten in hers; she saw Bennek go pale and his lip begin to tremble; saw Jeddeg fall back against the wall, eyes wide. She knew she ought to turn around, to move, to do *something*, but she found herself frozen stiff. She showed no sign of life at all, save for her accelerated breathing.

To her left, one of the guards reluctantly moved forward. 'We – ah, that is, we were just about to step in, my lord,' he hedged.

'Of course you were. How fortunate that I've saved you the trouble.'

The guard smirked at the trembling girl, watched her eyes grow wider still. *The fight's over!* they all but screamed, even as her voice remained paralyzed. *Why won't you go away?*

'What's your name, child?' asked the voice behind her.

'T-Tyannon, my lord.'

'Tyannon.' The name rolled around in the speaker's mouth, as though tasting it for imperfections. 'And why am I speaking to the back of your head, Tyannon?'

'B-because I'm f-facing the other way, my lord?'

Most of the captives, and indeed several of the guards, gasped in disbelief, and the young woman tensed in expectation of a sudden blow. After a moment of silence, however, a soft chuckle was the only response.

Then, 'Turn around, Tyannon.'

Her shoulders slumping, as if she'd consigned herself to whatever fate the gods might hold in store, she obeyed.

The figure looming before her came straight from one of the fairy tales she read to Jass every night – one of the darker ones. Shorter than his ogre minions, he nonetheless loomed over her, filling the entirety of her vision. A demonic suit of armour concealed his body head-to-toe: midnight-black steel, with thick plates of bone that gleamed unnaturally white in the orange glow of the lanterns. From small spines of bone on his shoulders hung a heavy cloak of royal purple, a coincidental match to the regent's banner on the fields outside. The flickering lanterns sent his shadow dancing across the walls, as though guided by some mad puppeteer. Atop it all, a helm of bone, a skull bound in iron bands. Nothing human showed through the grim façade, no soul peered from the gaping black holes in the mask.

With a desperate surge of will, the young woman pulled her gaze away from the hideous mask, glancing downward instead. Her eyes fixed momentarily on the chain about his neck. It dipped down beneath the bone-covered breastplate, linked perhaps to some pendant or amulet she couldn't see. Her eyes travelled lower still, to the large axe upon which his gauntlet rested. It stood upright, butt of the handle upon the ground. The blade was adorned with minuscule engravings – abstract shapes that gave the impression, though not the detail, of thousands of figures engaged in the cruelest, most brutal acts of war. Tyannon whimpered quietly as she saw that there were worse things to stare at than the blackened eye sockets of the helm. Things like that axe, and the figures engraved upon it, figures that seemed almost to move on their own, independent from the dancing torch-light . . .

'Do you know who I am, Tyannon?'

'Yes.' Her voice never rose above a half-drawn breath. 'You're Corvis Rebaine.'

The iron-banded skull tilted in acknowledgment. 'That frightens you.' It was not a question.

'M-my lord,' Tyannon told him, 'you frighten people much greater than I.' For some reason, that realisation seemed to relax her. Beside her, Jassion cried out softly; she carefully steered him behind her, putting herself between her brother and the monster before her.

'Do I?' For a moment, the man who'd conquered half of Imphallion fell silent. Tyannon's muscles twinged in protest, so rigidly did she hold herself.

A black-and-bone gauntlet gestured abruptly; despite herself, the young woman jumped, a tiny yelp escaping her lips. But Rebaine merely pointed at the arm she held behind her back, fist clenched with a death grip on Jassion's wrist. 'You do your family credit, Tyannon. But your brother is safe with me. As are you.'

Tyannon's countenance shifted abruptly, a surge of anger seeming to drown her fears. 'Are we?' she asked, her voice gone bitter, her stammer gone. She waved, her gesture indicating not merely the people present in the room, but the entire city suffering beyond the thick stone walls. 'You'll forgive me, my lord, if I have some difficulty taking you at your word.'

Whatever response the warlord intended was aborted by a sudden scuffling within the pit, followed quickly by a raised voice. 'My lord! The diggers have found something.'

Rebaine forgot everyone else in the room. He stepped to the rim of the hole, glancing down, past the thick earth, past the mass of nobles and Guildsmen he'd pressed into service as excavators. He peered into the thin, stone-walled hallway they'd uncovered, part of a small complex of rooms buried beneath the Hall of Meeting since before the birth of the city itself.

'It's really here.' It was barely a whisper, inaudible to anyone else.

Or at least it should have been.

/Did you doubt that it would be?/ The voice, as always, was mocking, sarcastic, even when its words were not.

Ignoring the speaker, Rebaine leapt down into the pit, a cloud of dirt billowing upward at the impact. The diggers drew back fearfully – many quivered visibly at his mere presence, including one man Rebaine recognised as the Baron of Braetlyn.

I wonder, Rebaine thought to himself in passing, *where the young woman gets her spark from. I can't imagine she learned from watching any of* these *people*.

At the bottom of the pit loomed another, smaller hole, leading into the ancient stone tunnel that was Rebaine's objective. An inky blackness filled the corridor, but Rebaine had never been frightened of the dark.

He knew what was in it.

Fingers twitching within heavy gauntlets, his mouth formed words that did not exist in any human tongue. Behind the horrid mask, his eyes began ever so slightly to glow, and the blackness parted before him.

'Get these men out of the pit,' he ordered his guards. 'Make certain they have water and food.'

'At once, my lord. Will you be wanting some of us to . . .' The soldier swallowed, unable to finish, as he stared nervously into the black.

'No. I will go in alone. Find Valescienn. Inform him that I expect him to hold off Lorum's armies should they attack before I've returned. Tell him that Davro and his ogres are to fall back from the main walls and surround the Hall of Meeting. They're our last line of defense. The gnomes and the other soldiers should be able to hold the wall for some time without them.'

'Very good, my lord. Best of luck down, um, down there.'

Rebaine nodded, and swung down into the passage.

/We're being watched, you know,/ the unseen speaker informed him idly.

'What?' Rebaine glanced down in annoyance. 'Any particular reason you waited this long to tell me?' His heavy boots landed with a resounding clang on the ancient stones paving the floor. Unhesitating, he set out toward the north.

/*You were having such fun conversing with the young lady, I felt it would be inappropriate to intrude.*/

Rebaine snorted. 'Of course you did.' He brushed an enormous cobweb from his path, then chose the leftmost of three identical passages. 'Watched how? Seilloah assured me she could block any scrying spells sent our way.'

/*Seilloah lacks imagination. It's not a scrying spell Someone – it tastes like Rheah, though I won't swear to that – has sight-linked herself with a fairly large and exceptionally ugly beetle. It was lurking in the corner of the room upstairs, and it is now scurrying along the wall some few feet behind you.*/

Another pause as he glanced at the relatively unmarked walls around him. Which intersection was this? He'd studied the map for days, but it was impossible to be certain.

Right this time, he finally decided. Then, 'How can she see anything? It's rather dark, or hadn't you noticed?'

/*Why, so it is. How foolish of me to have missed that. I surely can't imagine how the little creature might be able to see us down here.*/ A sudden gasp sounded in Rebaine's mind. /You don't suppose she's using magic, *do you?*/

The heavy sigh echoed in the depths of the hideous armour. 'I imagine you think you're funny, don't you?'

/*Well*, I'm *amused.*/

'One of us ought to be.'

/*Shall we kill it already?*/

Left turn, straight ahead twice, left again. 'Deal with it, if you wish. I have no concern but your happiness.'

/*Of course not.*/ The crystal pendant hanging beneath Rebaine's breastplate warmed faintly, and a sudden crunch echoed through the hall behind them.

Rebaine continued, frustration mounting each time he stopped to think about his position on the map. It would have been convenient to have it with him now, but he'd burned it once he'd memorised it to his satisfaction. Despite the chill in the air around him, he lifted his helm now and again to wipe the sweat from his brow.

'Why do I wear this bloody thing?' he snapped finally.

/*Something about fear and terror among all who see you*,/ the voice replied drily. /*Or that was your claim, anyway. Me, I can't picture any of your kind being all that frightening.*/

'Fear.' Rebaine shook his head. 'This would be so much easier if they'd just cooperate. I wouldn't *have* to terrify them all.'

/*The girl didn't seem all that scared, toward the end there.*/

Rebaine once again saw the girl – Tyannon, he corrected himself – the fear in her eyes burned away by her sudden anger. 'She's got spirit, that one.'

/*She does indeed.*/ A pause. /*You should kill her before it spreads.*/

'I don't think so, Khanda.'

/*I'm serious. This sort of thing is dangerous. Let her stand up to you, and others may decide they, too, can get away with it. You need to put a stop to that sort of thing immediately.*/

Another head shake, this one forceful enough to send the helmet clanking against the armour's shoulder spines. 'I don't kill children, Khanda.' Although Tyannon hardly qualified as a child; she certainly showed more maturity than most of her elders in that chamber.

/*Of course not. You just have your armies do it for you.*/

Rebaine swallowed the enraged comment working its way into his throat, choking it back in a tide of bile. There was nothing to be said, no reply he could make, that wouldn't play right into Khanda's hands. Nor was this a topic he enjoyed discussing. He'd decided long ago, when he first set upon this path, that the end results were worth whatever it cost him. Still, he didn't find it pleasant.

Instead, he directed his attention back to the twisting corridors.

'This is it,' he said finally, examining the enormous, rust-coated metal door impeding any further progress. 'We're here.'

/Congratulations. Can we get on with this already?/

'Not much for savouring the moment, are you? All right, fine. Let's do it.'

/Shall I? Or would you prefer to batter it down with that oversised shrub trimmer?/

Rebaine glanced down at the wide-bladed axe. It could do the job, certainly. For this was Sunder, one of the last of the Kholben Shiar, the demon-forged blades. It was said that with enough patience, a man could carve apart a mountain with such a weapon.

On the other hand, why take the risk of sending chunks of steel flying through the chamber? He'd pursued this prize too long to risk damaging it now.

'The fancy way, I think,' he said after a moment of contemplation.

/Very well./

The warlord concentrated, focusing his thoughts. His own skills at magic were unremarkable at best. Never formally tested, he imagined he'd qualify as a mere Initiate of the First Circle, or at best an unskilled Second. Pitiful compared with many of his enemies – such as Rheah Vhoune, Initiate of the Seventh Circle. Of all Lorum's allies, she was the most dangerous: in recorded history, only Selakrian himself, Archmage and Master of the Tenth Circle, had achieved the Seventh at a younger age than Rheah.

On the other hand, Corvis cheated.

So accustomed had he grown to the process that he no longer consciously noticed it. He visualised the effect he desired, thrust forth a gauntleted hand, and drew upon not his own power and skill but those of his inhuman ally. Flakes of rust fell from the door, as though agitated by a mild earthquake, yet the corridor itself held steady. The metal began to glow red, then white, in a very specific pattern of lines, dividing the door into eight sections that met in the middle. The air in the corridor grew acrid, painful to breathe. First one wedge, then a second, pulled back from the centre, in rather the same way a man might peel an orange. The metal fragments plastered themselves to the wall, the floor, the ceiling, and slowly cooled back to their normal state, welded permanently with the stone.

Even before the segments fully cooled, Rebaine stepped through the ring of metal into the room beyond. Yes! There it was, lying upon a table, coated with webs and the dust of ages. It had waited for millennia, waited for him. With this, there would be no more bloodshed. There would be no more *need*. With this, and this alone, he would rule.

Eyes gleaming beneath the nightmarish helm, Corvis Rebaine strode forward, hands outstretched . . .

'Rheah? Rheah, can you hear me?' *A familiar voice. Concerned, worried. Also anxious. More on his mind than just the question.*

'Will she be all right?' *Another voice, also familiar, though not so much as the first. Younger. Far more worried. Fear. The accompanying clanking is probably his hands – gauntleted – wringing together.*

'How would I know? What do I know about magic? I don't even know what happened to her! I—'

Slowly, mentally bracing herself against the stabbing pain she knew the light must bring, she opened her eyes. 'Water,' she croaked. A strong hand slid behind her, helping her to sit, and she felt a glass pressed to her lips. It was lukewarm, made gritty by the ambient dust and dirt, but she drank deeply. With every swallow the burning pain in her throat lessened, and the ogre inside her skull finally ceased the ceremonial dances he was performing up and down her brain.

'Are you all right?' Nathaniel asked. She realised it was he who held her up.

'I will be, given a few moments. Thank you,' she added, directing the comment at Lorum, who'd held the glass for her. The young man stepped back, smiling slightly.

'What happened?' the knight demanded.

Hesitantly, Rheah rose to her feet, leaning only lightly on her friend's shoulder. 'I was detected. My little helper was killed. In a rather excessive display of power, at that.'

'Power?' Lorum asked hesitantly. 'Couldn't they just have stepped on it, or squashed it?'

'I suppose they could have. Rebaine chose not to. The death of a mount is never a pleasant experience.' With a grimace, she rubbed the bridge of her nose with the thumb and index finger of her left hand. Obviously, the ogre wasn't *completely* exhausted.

'Your Grace . . . ,' Nathaniel warned quietly. The young man frowned, but nodded.

'Rheah,' he said tentatively, 'I hate to press you under the present circumstances, but—'

'But,' she interrupted, 'you need to know what I learned.'

Another nod.

She sighed once, forcing herself to straighten up. 'Less than I'd hoped, unfortunately. I know Rebaine has discovered a series of tunnels, a complex or catacomb of some sort, beneath the Hall of Meeting.'

'Tunnels?' Nathaniel asked. 'Where do they lead? Could he move his troops through them? Is—'

An upraised hand silenced him. 'Don't get ahead of me, Nathan. No, they're useless for troop movements. They're small, and they don't seem to lead much of anywhere. He's searching for something down there. Something specific.'

The young regent's eyes grew wide. 'Like what?'

'I'm not certain. But it's something worth trapping his entire army in a nearly indefensible city to find.'

Lorum and Nathan exchanged bleak glances. The regent stepped away, stopping only when he reached the tent's canvas wall. Absently, his left hand dropped to the table beside him, fingers drumming on the tactical map. His eyes unfocused, as though peering into the city itself. 'How close do you think he was to his goal?'

'I can't say for certain, Your Grace. But he definitely gave the impression he knew where he was going. If I had to guess, I'd say fairly close.'

'That's what I thought.' Lorum allowed himself one more endless moment to stare into space, to fully ponder the ramifications of what he knew he must do. Then, with a fortifying breath, he turned around.

'Then we can't give him any more time,' he said firmly. Nathaniel, in the mix of everything else he was feeling, found himself impressed that the young duke was growing into the role required of him. 'Gather the generals and tell them to form up the men. We attack as soon as they're ready. May the gods smile on us all.'

Many of the guards and the prisoners, united in their curiosity despite the loathing each felt for the other, peered intently over the edge of the pit into which Corvis Rebaine, the Terror of the East, had vanished an hour before. No sound emerged from the blackened depths; no flicker of movement could penetrate the age-old darkness.

'Maybe the gods are with us,' Jeddeg whispered softly. 'Maybe the bastard's died down there.'

Tyannon kept her mouth clamped firmly shut for a change. She looked, instead, at the exhausted, despairing faces around her – all but that of her father, who refused to meet her gaze.

The darkness beneath them splintered; a burst of flame rolled down the corridor, cracking the stone walls as it passed. A wave of heat flowed from the pit, stinking of smoke and brimstone, making the watchers' eyes water and blink. And then it passed, replaced by the sound of screaming.

But this, despite the hopes of the gathered prisoners, was not the scream of a man roasting to death in the inferno's heart. No, these were shrieks of mindless rage, of a fury that couldn't be expressed by voice alone. Even as they watched, a second burst of fire flowed down the passage, followed by the sound of shattering stone. Immense clouds of dust poured up from the hole at the base of the pit, and the building shuddered. Guards and prisoners alike exchanged horrified glances at the realisation that Rebaine was collapsing the tunnels.

Tyannon blinked, her eyes tearing again to clear the dust from beneath her lids. When she could finally see again, he stood before her, an impenetrable shadow emerging from the billowing dust. The hideous axe hung from his right hand, flecks of stone and dirt falling from the blade. In his other he held something, boxy, wrapped in mould-covered and moth-eaten red velvet. Rage radiated from him in palpable waves; prisoners and guards alike fell back in fear.

All save one: a large man, tall and broad of shoulder. His hair was a light blond, almost white, and cut close to his scalp save for a single long lock at the back. He wore a hauberk of chain, topped by a black cuirass similar in design to those worn by the rest of Rebaine's men. His square features were marred by a jagged scar running from his left ear to just beneath his nose. He, and he alone, stood his ground, undaunted by his master's fury.

'My lord?' he asked, his voice gruff, tinted slightly by an accent Tyannon could not place. 'Things did not go well?'

'Well? *Well?*' Rebaine spun viciously to face his lieutenant. 'Does it *look* like things have gone "well", Valescienn?'

'Not as such, my lord, but—'

'A godsdamn key!' He shook the cloth-covered object in Valescienn's face, neither noticing nor caring that he would surely have broken the man's nose had he not flinched away. 'All the writings in which he spoke about this, his "greatest accomplishment"! You'd think that just once, he'd have bothered to mention it needs a bloody *key*!'

Valescienn paled. 'You mean—'

'Useless.' Rebaine stepped back, arms falling limply to his sides. 'It's completely useless.'

The blond man's eyes widened, then narrowed in sudden anger. 'And without it? Are you suggesting we'll not be continuing on toward Mecepheum?'

'Mecepheum? Valescienn, we'll be lucky if a third of the army survives to escape the damn city! We—'

'My lord!' Another soldier dashed into the room, his face coated in sweat, skidding slightly on the rubble and detritus near the pit. 'My lord, Lorum is attacking! There are tens of thousands of them! Nobles, Guild soldiers . . .' He croaked to a stop, gasping for breath.

A mutter passed through the soldiers, each thinking the same thing. But it was Valescienn, as usual, who possessed courage to voice it. 'We can't win, my lord,' he said quietly to the back of Rebaine's helm. 'This city is a death trap. It won't hold for us any better than it did when we took it.'

Rebaine's shoulders slumped, an invisible gesture in the confines of his nightmarish armour. He'd failed. He'd gambled everything on the knowledge that victory lay hidden *here*, in the ancient tunnels beneath Denathere. And he'd lost.

He would, at least, deal with it properly.

'Valescienn, tell the men to fall back. Escape by any means possible. I free them from my service. Let them go home, or find employment elsewhere.'

'My lord?' The question was incredulous, almost plaintive. 'You don't wish us to regroup elsewhere?'

'There's no place to regroup, my friend, nor any purpose. Even with luck on our side, we'll not have enough men left once we've escaped to make a proper army. And I'm tired, Valescienn. I'm tired.'

'But—'

'Do it! And tell Davro his people may return to their homes as well.'

Valescienn nodded, steeling himself for his final question. 'And my lord? What of you?' For they both knew the approaching army would happily have let every last man, ogre, and gnome escape unharmed, if they could get their hands on Corvis Rebaine.

'Seilloah's protections will hold for some time. That should shield me from conventional scrying techniques. Nor am I without power of my own, when those fail.'

/Hmm. Not exactly "your" power, is it?/

Rebaine ignored that, and Valescienn remained ignorant of the conversation's third participant. 'I should be able to avoid them for quite a while,' Rebaine added.

'And if Vhoune should send a hunter after you?'

'Hunting spells require someone who has seen the target,

18

closely, within a few months or so, Valescienn. Neither Vhoune, nor anyone else in Lorum's employ, has.'

'No,' the other man said softly, 'but there are those who have.' His eyes, cold as gnome's blood, swept the room. 'Say the word, my lord, and they're all dead.'

Only the enclosure of the hideous helm stifled Rebaine's faint sigh. 'No, Valescienn. There's been enough death today.'

'Then how do you plan to protect yourself?'

'Better, I think, to risk one than to slay them all. I know Rheah Vhoune. She's skilled, she's determined, but she is not near as ruthless as she pretends. I don't think she'll risk a hunter if she knows I've someone who would suffer the consequences alongside me.'

'A hostage, my lord?'

'I see no other alternative.' He examined the hostages, surveying his options – a sham, for Valescienn's benefit. He'd already made his choice.

/*You have no idea the trouble you're courting*,/ Khanda snapped inside his mind.

'Tyannon!' Rebaine barked, ignoring his unseen companion. 'Come here.'

The young woman stepped forward, her face whiter than the bone on Rebaine's armour. He reached out and pulled her near, so near she choked on the scent of smoke and oiled steel.

'Tyannon, listen to me.' He spoke softly. 'Whether you believe me or not, I mean you no harm. Your blood serves no purpose; you do. When that purpose is served, you will be free to leave. You have my vow.'

'You – you could just force me, my lord.'

'I could. But I cannot afford to have you fighting me right now. If you will not come willingly, I will have to choose . . .' The mask inclined, ever so slightly, toward little Jassion, huddled behind his sister's legs. 'Someone who *cannot* fight me.'

Tyannon shut her eyes tight, fighting back sudden tears. 'I will go with you, my lord.'

'Good.' Rebaine, suddenly aware of how close she was,

stepped back abruptly; now was not the time for such distractions. Instead, he grabbed her wrist, pulling her along after him, ignoring the sudden wailing from her baby brother.

'Valescienn, farewell.'

'Until we meet again, my lord.' The clashing and the cries of battle in the streets began to seep into the room through cracks in the stone. 'You'd better go.'

The skull-mask nodded once. Then, too quietly for anyone else to hear, 'Khanda?'

/Yes, foolish one?/

'I believe it's time for us to depart.'

/You realise I could probably protect you from any hunters they sent after you. You don't need the girl./

' "Probably" isn't good enough right now.'

A sudden flash of blinding red light, and they were gone.

Valescienn watched as his lord disappeared, ignoring the growing sounds of battle. Rebaine, for all his skill and power, had his blind spots. It was a flaw Valescienn himself did not share. Catching the eyes of the soldiers who clustered around the pit, he waved a casual hand toward the captives.

'Kill them.'

The chamber erupted in screams then, desperate people trying to flee despite the lack of any possible sanctuary. The sounds of splitting and splintering filled the room, a ghastly symphony played with swords and axes, conducted by a blond man with empty, soulless eyes. The floor grew wet and sticky with blood, and one by one, the screams fell silent.

At the back of the crowd, an old man moved. He sought no escape, for he knew that was quite impossible. And though no less terrified than all those around him, no less frantic to cling to whatever years of life might have remained to him, he knew there was something more important he must do. Heart hammering in his chest, he ducked behind the panicked crowd and lifted a sobbing young boy off the floor. As swiftly as he could, he stepped to the edge of the pit in which dozens of bodies, some still twitching, already sprawled.

'I wish there was a less unpleasant way, my boy,' he said to Jassion, his voice hushed and obscured by the clamour around him. 'But you'll live.'

Jeddeg smiled, then, despite the sudden tears cutting through the dust on his face to vanish into the prickly depths of his beard. 'If – *when* you see your sister again, tell her I wasn't a *completely* selfish bastard, yes?'

The old man let go. Jassion fell from his hands, to land with a painful thump on the uppermost corpses in the pit. He lay for a moment, stunned, until he was covered and almost crushed by the body of Jeddeg himself, the man's head shattered from behind. He wanted to cry, to scream. Mostly he wanted his sister back. But he knew that any sound would let the bad men find him, too. And so he kept quiet, even when the blood of the men above began to coat his arms, his head, and his face, even when their weight threatened to squeeze the breath from him.

And finally the room went silent. The last sounds of the slaughter faded from the farthest corners, but not from the depths of a young child's mind, where they echoed unending, and would until his dying day.

CHAPTER ONE

The most wonderful thing about it was that it was a simple, ordinary house.

Not a large structure, but roomy enough for the comfort of its inhabitants, with a bit of space to spare. The walls were solid, dependable, fitted together over many months by loving hands. The builder had used no magic in the house's construction, though certainly he could have. But that would, in a way, have defeated the entire purpose.

Windows sparsely dotted the structure, numbered and positioned perfectly. They were sufficient to admit the bright sunshine during the day, and the glimmer of moon and stars at night; to cool the house during the warm summer months, yet not so numerous as to make it difficult to warm against winter.

The house sat on the very outskirts of town. It was near enough to be neighbourly, but retained a certain modicum of privacy unachievable in the heart of the small but bustling village. Chelenshire, it was called, a rather weighty name for a community of perhaps five or six dozen souls.

Another advantage to the house's position at the edges of Chelenshire: it kept the inhabitants away from the slow but steady traffic that passed along what was once a major trade route. The odds of a stranger recognising the house's inhabitants were minuscule, but even 'minuscule' was a risk not worth taking.

This morning, in particular, was a sunny one. The air was warm without quite crossing the fine line into hot, the sky a bright and cloudless blue. Birds wheeled above, droves of them, rejoicing in the last of the fine weather before the blistering heat and the rare but torrential storms of summer fell heavily upon them. Squirrels, gophers, and the occasional rabbit dashed across the grass, each on its own quest for fruits, vegetables, nuts, or whatever else might volunteer itself for lunch. An entire garden's worth of food lined up in neat rows on two separate sides of the house. Lettuce, tomatoes, carrots, radishes, tomatoes, onions, squash, and more tomatoes – the lady of the house was abnormally fond of tomatoes – all beckoned invitingly. But though they would occasionally stop beside the garden, perched upon hind legs, to stare longingly at the repast calling to them, none of the rampaging rodents ever set paw into the garden itself. Something about the area itself kept the animals – as well as slugs, snails, and a huge variety of harmful insects – at bay.

There may have been no trace of magic in the building of the house, but the garden was another story entirely.

With a soft grunt of pain, the man currently at work yanking weeds from the bed of squash leaned back on his heels, one hand pressed to the small of his back. He was, he reflected grimly, too old to be spending hours on end hunched over the vegetables.

Hell, he didn't even *like* gardening! It was his wife's passion, she who spent so much of her time maintaining the place day after day. For his own part, he'd have been quite content to buy vegetables at the market. But though the money was not an issue – he'd enough saved from past endeavors to live many years in luxury – she had pointed out that such a lifestyle in Chelenshire would attract unwanted attention. And it was to avoid notice, after all, that they'd moved to Chelenshire in the first place.

Thus the garden, and their occasional hunting, trips, and her embroidery and needlework, and his days spent in town, helping old man Renfro down at the forge or advising Tolliver on matters of policy.

But the forge was silent today, as was most of Chelenshire, in observance of Godsday. And she'd asked him, as a personal favour, to help in the garden. He shook his head, bemused, waiting for the pain in his back to recede. It was many years now since he could refuse her anything.

Of course, he reconsidered as he suddenly stood in response to another back spasm, *maybe it's time to start*.

He wasn't an especially conspicuous figure, not like in his younger days. He was taller than average – taller than most of the men in the village, certainly. In his prime, he'd been mountainous, his body covered with layers of rock-solid muscle; even Xavier, Renfro's large son, was a delicate flower compared with what this man once had been.

Middle age stole that from him, though a combination of strict exercise and natural inclination saved him from going to fat, as so many former men of war inevitably did. He was, in fact, quite wiry now, slender to the point of gaunt. His face was one of edges and angles, striking without being handsome, and the gaze of his green eyes piercing. Hair once brown had greyed; it hung just past his neck, giving him a vaguely feral demeanour. Even now he could do the work of a man half his age, but he wasn't what he used to be.

And his back still hurt.

'Daddy, Daddy!'

The grin that blossomed across his face washed away the pain in his back. Quickly he knelt down, catching the wiggling brown-haired flurry that flung itself into his arms. Standing straight, he cradled the child to his breast, laughing.

'And a good afternoon to you, Lilander,' he said mock-seriously. 'What are you running from this time?'

'Monster!' the boy shouted happily.

Gods willing, he could not help but think, *this will be the worst sort of monster you ever know*.

What he said, though, was, 'Indeed? Is it a horrible monster?'

Lilander nodded, giggling.

'Is it nasty? Is it gross and disgusting?'

The boy was laughing loudly now, nodding even more furiously.

'Is it – Mellorin?'

'Hey!' called another voice from just beyond the garden. 'I heard that!'

Both father and son were laughing now. 'Come on out, Mel. I'm just teasing.'

Her own lips twisted in a disapproving moue, a brown-haired girl, just shy of her teenage years, stepped from around the corner. She wore, as they all did, a simple tunic and breeches of undyed cloth. She was, her parents had decided, far too prone to dashing and racing around to dress her in skirts.

'Well, you don't *look* as though you were chasing him,' the grey-haired man commented seriously. 'You don't seem to have been running at all.'

'I don't need to run,' she said smugly, staring up at the two of them. 'I'll catch him eventually anyway.'

'Oh? And why's that?'

'I'm smarter than he is.'

Lilander stopped laughing and scowled down darkly at his older sister. 'Are not!'

Mellorin sighed theatrically. Her father, fully aware that he would soon have to be stern and fatherly, restrained a grin. She was so much like her mother.

'I refuse,' she said with exaggerated dignity, 'to be drawn into that kind of argument with a child.'

The man's lip quivered, and he coughed once.

'Are not!' her brother insisted again.

Her eyes blazed suddenly. 'Are too!' she shouted.

All right, that was about as far as it needed to go. 'Children!' the man barked, sharply enough to get their attention but not so loud as to suggest he was angry – yet. 'What have I told you about fighting?'

'I don't know,' Lilander said instantly. 'Besides, she started it.'

'Did not!'

'Did too!'

Shaking his head, the children's father gave them both

another sound lecture – one he'd given hundreds of times previously, and fully expected to give hundreds of times more, possibly starting as early as lunch – and sent them both into the house. The windows weren't quite thick enough to keep the recurring cries of 'Are not!' 'Are too!' from invading the garden.

'Louder than ogres,' he mutterd with a trace of a smile as he turned back toward the vegetables.

'More dangerous, too,' came the reply from behind him. 'They broke another window this morning. That's why they were outside in the first place.'

She stood at the edge of the garden, leaning on a rake. She frowned at him, but he'd known her long enough to see the spark of laughter in her eyes. Her hair, a richer brown than his own had ever been, was simply braided. A few rogue strands fell across her face; she brushed them aside reflexively, unaware of the gesture.

'You're beautiful,' he told her sincerely.

'And you're trying to change the subject. I'm too tired to be flattered.'

He couldn't help but laugh. 'Well, I'd be more than happy to look after the children today. Of course, it means. I'd be forced – reluctantly, I assure you – to skip helping you out here in the garden . . .'

'Oh, no! No, you're staying out here with me if I have to stake you up like one of my tomato plants. You—'

A sudden shattering drifted from the general direction of the kitchen, followed immediately by 'Mellorin did it!' 'Did not!' 'Did too!'

Their mother shook her head, sighing. 'As soon as we go deal with whatever disaster just happened in the house.'

'Ah,' he replied, 'normal life. It's what we wanted, isn't it?'

She laughed again, even as they started moving, the garden temporarily forgotten. It was amazing, even after all these years together. 'I love you, Tyannon,' he said simply.

Tyannon smiled back at him, this man who had been her husband for half her life. 'I love you too, Corvis.'

Corvis Rebaine followed his wife back into the house, pondering for just a moment how much things could change in seventeen years.

The celebration wound gradually down, leaving all of Denathere deliciously exhausted.

The westerly sun shed the last rays of the day upon the lingering vestiges of barely controlled chaos. Streamers of bright cloth littered the roads, as though a rainbow had shattered above the city, strewing shards carelessly about. Children, their exuberance not quite worn down by a full week of freedom and too much sugar, ran around madly, laughing happily or shouting at one another, determined to experience the absolute maximum of fun before their parents called them home for supper and bed. Even a few adults still danced in the streets, one hand clenched about a flagon of ale or mead or wine, the other clenched about the waist or wrist – or, in a few of the darker alleys, other parts – of a second like-minded citizen. Vendors shouted hoarsely to passersby, trying doggedly for one final holiday sale.

But most of the city residents, worn out from a full week of revels, were snug in their beds, beginning the painful recovery that all too often follows excessive jubilation.

At the edge of town, Guild-hired mercenaries cranked the handles of a huge wooden wheel. Chains clanked, gears rotated, wood creaked, and the gates of the city ponderously slammed shut. The sound, a solitary clap of thunder, rolled across the city. Drunk men sobered slightly at the sound, and the happiest citizens shivered briefly, for it was a palpable reminder of what they were celebrating – what they had so very nearly lost.

Outside those walls, atop the same small rise on which the regent's tent rested so long ago, a figure stood, watching the city's lights wink out one by one. The people of Denathere would sleep soundly this night, worn out from celebrating their liberation from the Terror of the East, safely ensconced behind their walls. And impressive walls they were, higher and thicker than those that had fallen before Rebaine's assault, topped by guard towers equipped with catapults and ballistae. Even given Denathere's poor position, the new walls alone made the prospect of taking the city a daunting one.

Or they would have, had their enemy not already waltzed in unchallenged, bearing food and drink and gifts for the celebration.

Cold, dead eyes narrowed as a nasty grin crept its way across his face. Even with its violent history, Denathere remained a city of naïve, complacent people.

It was astounding how little had changed in the seventeen years since he'd been betrayed and abandoned within those walls.

'Report, Valescienn.' The voice was hollow, with the faintest of echoes.

Well, Valescienn amended slightly, turning slowly around, *there* have *been a* few *changes* . . .

Valescienn himself had aged little. His hair was still a moonlight blond, his ice-blue eyes still utterly devoid of anything resembling humanity, and the same spiked ball-and-chain still hung at his side. There were a few more circles beneath those eyes, and a second scar – across the right side of his forehead – joined the one he'd sported for years. Otherwise, he showed little indication that nearly two decades had come and gone since his last visit.

The master he faced now, however, was most certainly not Corvis Rebaine.

He was shorter than the Terror of the East, for one; shorter, in fact, than many of his own soldiers, standing several inches below six feet. A flowing black tunic covered his arms, emerging from beneath a set of bracers and cuirass that appeared, bizarre as it seemed, to be made of dark reflective stone. His black leggings and leather boots were similarly guarded by greaves of the same material. Spidery runes were etched in silver into the onyx-like substance. Numerous rings – all of silver, save for one of a simple pewter, with an emerald stone – adorned his fingers, slid on over thin lambskin gloves.

The entire ensemble was topped with a heavy black cloak, slit vertically to create a shifting effect, implying movement even where there was none. It boasted a deep hood, one that only partly hid an utterly featureless mask of stone. Even in the dim light of the rapidly fading dusk, Valescienn looked into the face of his new lord and saw only his own darkened and twisted reflection staring back at him.

'I have been watching the city for some time, my lord,' Valescienn began.

A hand waved impatiently, the rings creating a scintillating silver arc as they moved through the dying light. 'Tell me of the men. Are they in place?'

'They are. I've been sending them into Denathere in small groups for the past week, just more celebrants come to the party.' He smiled grimly. 'I imagine more than a few have forgotten themselves and become quite as drunk as the citizenry, but most should be ready for your signal.'

'They had better be. Any of our men who are found drunk within those walls are to be treated like any other citizen. Is that clear?'

Valescienn frowned. 'Yes, my lord. But I wonder if . . .' He trailed off when it became clear his master was no longer listening. He took the time, instead, to observe the man he'd chosen to serve.

The dark-garbed figure began to pace. The silver runes upon his armour, seen through the shifting streamers of his cloak, danced and wiggled their way across his body. Valescienn averted his eyes. Rebaine had been frightening, but Lord Audriss was *disturbing*. Power radiated from the man like a fever, infecting all who came near with a sense of their own inherent inferiority. Valescienn had feared Rebaine in the same way he feared any man – and there weren't many – who could best him on the field of battle. Audriss, however, scared him to the depths of his soul, made him afraid in places he hadn't known he possessed. And that, more than any other reason, was why he served the man now.

Audriss pivoted, and Valescienn noticed, for the first time, the dagger he wore on his left. A black hilt sprouted from an equally black sheath – little wonder that the weapon was nigh invisible against the outfit and the cloak. But now that he had spotted it, Valescienn wished he hadn't, for as he became aware of the crescent blade, it, in turn, became aware of *him*. A sense of impending violence, of gleeful anticipation, crept into his mind through the cracks and crevices of his soul.

With a ragged gasp, Valescienn tore his eyes from the dagger. He knew what it was that Audriss carried at his side, recognised it as cousin to the axe Rebaine had wielded. But Rebaine, even in the crush of battle or the most depraved depths of slaughter, never unleashed the full power of the Kholben Shiar. Audriss, he was certain, would have no such compunction.

Then, even more uncomfortable with Audriss's silence, he asked, 'My lord?'

The pacing behind him stopped; he swore he could hear even the rustle of the robes as the hood twisted about to face him. 'Yes?'

'If I may be so bold, what are we waiting for?'

'That.'

A low fog appeared at the base of the hill, emerging, so it seemed, from the earth itself. Climbing slowly, it rose until it covered the grass at the top of the hill, and Valescienn's boots to the ankle. And then it erupted, forming a pillar the height of a large man. The currents flowed inward, a spinning maelstrom of white. As the mist disappeared from beneath his feet, Valescienn couldn't help but glance downward. The grass glistened wetly, but the reddish tint, and the metallic aroma flaying at his nostrils, suggested strongly that it was not dew coating the ground around him.

A face appeared in the column of mist, made up entirely of hollows in the fog. The sockets filled with thick, bubbling blood, which coalesced into a pair of red but otherwise human eyes. The rest of the face flushed with blood as well, and then the body beneath it. And just like that the mist was gone, and a third figure stood beside them.

His face, features sharp as a razor, gazed unblinkingly at Valescienn. His hair was black and straight, falling in a loose mass down to his shoulders. He wore a simple white tunic, open to the waist, oddly spotless and crisp despite the damp environs, and grey leggings tucked into black riding boots. His fingers, long and slender, ended in perfectly manicured nails. His lips were full, almost feminine, and his flesh was perfectly smooth.

'An interesting choice,' the new arrival said as he examined Valescienn, his voice melodic.

'He serves my purposes admirably enough,' Audriss replied.

The stranger stared a moment more, then strode over to the black-robed man. As he walked, Valescienn saw that the fog had not entirely dissipated; it still trailed from the newcomer's feet, stretching from his boots to the ground with each step, clinging like watery mud.

'Valescienn,' Audriss said, as casually as though he were performing the introductions at a family reunion, 'this is Mithraem.'

The strange figure bowed once, formally. 'An honour, I am certain.'

Valescienn, who recognised the name with a certain sick horror, was finding it very difficult to breathe.

Mithraem smiled once, a shallow, mirthless expression, and dismissed Valescienn's presence entirely. 'The Legion stands ready for your signal.'

'Excellent.' Audriss beckoned once to Valescienn, who stepped forward, his mind numb. 'That, indeed, is what I was waiting for. Tell the men, Valescienn. I want them ready for battle the instant our people inside take the walls.

'We attack tomorrow.'

*

The final cool gusts of spring faded away, and summer descended upon Chelenshire. Men went about their daily tasks, each assuring the others that the heat bothered him not in the slightest, each frantically wiping sweat from his face and forehead with a shirtsleeve when he felt no one was watching. The weather, merely uncomfortable rather than reaching the blazing levels it would attain in another month, didn't weigh down the children of the village. They went about their own chores or dashed hither and thither (save for the younger ones who remained stuck on 'to and fro' in play, as their whims and circumstances – and mostly their parents – dictated.

For their own part, Lilander and Mellorin had completely abandoned the chores to which they'd been set, choosing instead to chase each other around the yard with a bucket of well water, screaming and shouting and generally soaking anything unfortunate enough to cross their winding and unpredictable path. But Tyannon was in the house working on mending the outfits the children ruined yesterday, and Corvis – hard at work repairing the fence they used to pen their horse, Rascal, and already sweating profusely – decided quite resolutely that it was too damn hot to go chasing after a pair of children who had more energy to spare than he. Let them wear themselves down a bit, *then* he'd go after them.

He grinned, though it didn't quite reach his eyes. *You never could stop thinking tactically, could you, Rebaine?*

'Ho there, Cerris!'

It was the name he'd given when he and Tyannon moved here, a name close enough to his real one that he could explain away any misunderstandings or slips of the tongue. He'd grown as accustomed to hearing it as he was his real name, but he *was* startled to hear it now. Few visitors wandered out to the edge of town in the rising heat of late morning.

Carefully laying down the hammer with which he'd been working, Corvis straightened to his full height. Approaching him on the road was a man perhaps a decade his senior, his pace steady, though perhaps not as quick as it once was. He was round but not quite fat, short but not squat. He wore over his shoulders an embroidered cloth that would, on a woman, have been called a shawl, but which he himself insisted was a mantle.

For just a moment, Corvis grimaced. This visit likely meant news from outside, from the world beyond Chelenshire – news Corvis was never glad to receive. Every time he heard of the kingdom beyond, of the political wrangling and Guild maneuvering and cultural decay, he couldn't help but wonder, ever so briefly, if the world would be better off had he not given up all those years ago, and if it were he who ruled from the halls of Mecepheum now.

Then he would look at his home, or his wife, or his children, and his regrets would fade.

Until the next time.

'And a good day to you, Tolliver,' Corvis called, swiftly gathering his thoughts as the man drew nearer. He breathed shallowly, for the scent of the man's acrid sweat preceded him by several paces. 'Rather a warm day for a stroll, isn't it?'

'You have no idea,' the town mediator gasped at him, leaning one hand heavily upon the fence post between them and gulping in great, heaving breaths. His face was red from the heat and the exertion of what was, for him, a lengthy walk. 'I'm rather astounded that I haven't just melted on the spot.'

'That,' Corvis remarked sagely, 'would be a large spot indeed.'

Tolliver glared at him, panting. 'It's all very well for you to make fun, scrawny as you are. You've little enough to fear from heat, after all. Three or four drops of sweat are enough to cool you completely.'

'I can't sweat,' Corvis told him. 'Scrawny as I am, people mistake it for crying, and then I can't go anywhere for the constant offers of sympathy. I tell you, it's a burden.'

That glare lasted a moment longer, and then the mediator's face burst into a beaming grin. 'That's what I like about you, Cerris! You've a sense of humour!'

'Oh, is that what you like about me? I'd wondered.' He gestured toward the house: 'All joking aside, it is hot out here. Can I offer you something?'

'Most kind, thank you.'

They were perhaps ten paces from the house when Lilander, shrieking happily, raced past them from around the corner. Corvis had just long enough to realise what was about to happen, but insufficient time to do a thing about it.

With a gleeful laugh, his daughter appeared from around the same corner, the bucket of water clenched in both fists. The liquid missile left the bucket before she registered Tolliver's presence, and by then, of course, it was far too late. With a remarkable show of speed and agility, she'd vanished back around the house before either her father or his guest finished blinking the water from their eyes. Lilander, recognising that the game had taken something of an unexpected turn, bolted the other way.

'I see your children are both well,' Tolliver said, his voice dry – the only part of him that was, at that point.

'Only until I get hold of them,' Corvis muttered. 'Mellorin and Lilander. Ha! I should have named them Maukra and Mimgol!'

Tolliver blanched and offered a swift sign against evil. 'I wish you'd not speak those names aloud, Cerris. No point in tempting fate, is there?'

'My apologies, Tolliver. For my slip, and for my children's actions.'

The other man smiled good-naturedly. 'Well, they're hardly as bad as the Children of Apocalypse, for all that. Truth to tell, Cerris, the water's as welcome as anything else. I haven't felt this cool since I left my house this morning.'

'Is there any particular reason,' Tyannon asked from a nearby chair as they passed over the threshold, 'you're dripping so profusely on my floor?'

'Tiniest cloudburst in history,' her husband told her with a straight face. 'Damnedest thing I've ever seen.'

Tyannon smiled, rising to her feet. 'And how are you today, Tolliver?'

'Oh, I can't complain, Tyannon. Well, I could, actually. It's bloody hot out there. But it wouldn't do a one of us any good, so I'll pass.'

She brought towels, and the three of them sat down around the table with mugs of ale and a platter containing a heavy wedge of cheese and a variety of vegetables.

Tolliver looked around him, taking it all in as he did each time he visited. The house was the same on the inside as it was without: plain and simple, homey in a way that his own much larger dwelling could never be. Wooden cabinets lined the walls in the kitchen, simple but comfortable chairs surrounded the thick table at which they sat. This was a place of peace; a family could be quite happy here.

It was Tyannon who broke the meaningless small talk that filled the first few moments of their repast. 'Tolliver, you're always welcome here, and it is a joy to visit with you. But I'm afraid I don't believe you're here for entirely social reasons.'

Tolliver's lip quirked. 'Am I that transparent, Tyannon?'

'Oh, no,' Corvis said, hiding his grin behind an upraised mug. 'Many things, Tolliver, but not *transparent*.'

But this time Tolliver didn't rise to the bait. 'I fear you're quite right, Tyannon. The truth is, I'm here to invite the both of you to a town meeting tonight.'

Corvis and Tyannon frowned as one. Chelenshire held town gatherings on a regular basis to discuss policies or changes in local law, problems with crops, that sort of thing. But . . .

'This month's meeting isn't for another two weeks,' Corvis observed. 'Who called this one?'

'I did, actually.'

'Why?' Tyannon asked, the slightest catch in her voice.

Tolliver sighed. 'Audriss struck again a few nights back.'

Despite the blazing heat outside, the room grew chill. This man calling himself Audriss had appeared some few months before, a great army at his back. Since then, several towns and even a pair of small cities had fallen to his relentless advance. So far, Duke Lorum was either unable or unwilling to send his own armies to meet them.

Corvis himself felt a shiver of fear trace its way slowly, caressingly down his spine. He knew which cities and towns had fallen; he knew, more than any other man alive, what their significance was.

He was fairly certain, too, that he knew what news Tolliver was about to deliver. For the first time in years, he found himself praying: praying, in this case, that he was wrong.

'Is he moving in this direction?' Tyannon asked quietly.

'No, not that we know. It's just . . . he's never done anything of this magnitude before.'

Corvis closed his eyes. He wasn't wrong. He could have spoken along with Tolliver, word for word.

'Denathere has fallen.

'Again.'

CHAPTER TWO

'We've breached the gates, my lord.' The triumph in Valescienn's voice was layered with a thick coating of contempt, like a morning frost that refused to melt away beneath the feeble sun. 'If you want to call *them* gates. Denathere is ours.'

Corvis Rebaine, the Terror of the East, grunted softly and nodded – both acknowledgments utterly lost within the confines of his death's-head helm. For long moments he stood atop a small hillock and stared, almost mesmerised by the columns of smoke that reached tentatively upward as though uncertain how best to reach the clouds above. The screams of the city reverberated in his mind, echoed within his helm. He knew the scent of blood and burning couldn't possibly have reached him yet; he must be imagining it, remembering its like from a dozen prior cities.

He wondered if anticipating it now was worse than the day it had stopped bothering him entirely.

'My lord?' Valescienn prompted. 'This is it, Lord Rebaine. Can I assume that your intricate plans and strategies call for more than standing here staring at it? Because I've got to tell you, we could've done that without fighting first.'

The expressionless skull turned coldly toward one of the few men undisturbed by its gaze. 'How long would you estimate before Lorum's armies reach us?'

'Well, he's *finally* got the Guilds whipped into line, and

they knew we were headed this way. Probably no more than a couple of days, and possibly less than one.'

'Then we'd better make every minute count. Get the men to start searching. And Valescienn?'

'Yes, lord?'

Inwardly, Corvis sighed. 'We can't afford to waste any time on heroes and patriots. Put up the usual deterrents.'

Valescienn grinned, tossed a casual salute, and was gone. And for many moments more, Corvis watched as the heads and the bodies of the dead were hoisted high, raining gore down upon the streets in a foul monsoon, to hang as a warning to any who might still be inclined to resist.

They did indeed attend the town meeting, though there was, as Corvis glumly predicted, a great deal of fear and shouting and little in the way of meaningful results. Frankly, he didn't even hear much of it, for his mind was so thickly swaddled in the stifling blanket of old, uncomfortable memories. Tolliver, his face and voice calm, moderated the gathering, keeping as much order as he could. It wasn't much, but he tried.

'How could this happen?' one hysterical voice in the crowd asked him.

'According to a few who escaped,' Tolliver told them, 'Audriss slipped some of his men into the city during the celebration. They took the walls from the inside.' He didn't feel the need to point out the irony involved: the celebration that opened the door to the city's conquerors marked the anniversary of a previous invader's defeat.

'This Audriss is as bad as Rebaine ever was!' someone shouted.

'Maybe it *is* Rebaine!' suggested a third voice. 'How would we know?'

I know, Corvis thought to himself. *But somehow, I don't think you want to hear* how *I know*.

In the end, the consensus was to wait, to keep an eye on

which way the invaders turned from Denathere, and to prepare. The same thing they'd decided after the previous meeting, and the one before that. The same thing the rest of Imphallion was doing.

Corvis remained silent throughout the meeting and during the walk back home. They shared a late supper, put the children – who'd escaped with only a brief scolding for their stunt with the water bucket – to bed, and Corvis and Tyannon retired as well. And still, he said nothing.

'Sweetheart,' Tyannon whispered to him, some moments after he thought she must have fallen asleep, 'what troubles you?'

He actually smiled, then. 'The news is not bad enough? I need more to disturb me?'

'Need? No. But I know you, Corvis. Something *is* bothering you.'

He sighed, rolling over to face her. 'You're right.' He shook his head faintly. 'I'll tell you if you ask, Tyannon. But it means talking about . . . then.'

She frowned. 'I hate thinking of Corvis Rebaine, Terror of the East, but I haven't forgotten him. Tell me.'

'All right. When I was first planning my campaign, I couldn't know exactly when the Guilds would grow frightened enough to push Lorum into action. I knew I had to fight my way to Denathere—'

'Why?' she asked quickly; it was, after all this time, the one secret he'd never told her. What could he possibly have been seeking in that city that could inspire him to make the worst tactical decision of his career, and lose his army in the process?

As he'd done so often before, he ignored the question. 'But I wasn't entirely certain how I'd get there. It's not exactly easy moving an army across hostile territory, even without organised opposition. I had to be prepared to alter course if Lorum's forces mustered before I was ready.'

'Yes?'

'I mapped out two specific plans, Tyannon. Two campaigns, two routes for my armies to take from our mustering point beyond Imphallion's borders all the way to Denathere. What I did, almost two decades ago, was in line with one of those plans.'

Tyannon's voice dropped to less than a whisper, as though her throat were choked with ice. 'Are you saying—'

Corvis nodded. 'Audriss followed the other. Somehow, this man got hold of the maps and plans I created twenty years ago. The plan he followed to get his army to Denathere was mine.'

She lay back, goose bumps peppering her arms and shoulders. 'So what will he do next?'

'I don't know, Tyannon.' Corvis, too, lay back, staring sightlessly at the ceiling. 'All my plans culminated at Denathere; whatever he does next is his own.'

With the town's decision made – if 'wait and see' could be called a decision – the inhabitants of Chelenshire did just that. Terrifying as the news of Audriss's depredations might be, there was the sense, prevalent in all isolated communities, that it affected them only peripherally. Regardless of which of Imphallion's major cities was next – even if Mecepheum itself was the warlord's ultimate goal – there should be no need to involve Chelenshire directly; there were many routes from Denathere to the other major cities, and Chelenshire was quite some distance from any of them. Certainly, if the rightful government of regent and Guilds was overthrown, there would be consequences for everyone, but the citizens of the village could see no *immediate* threat.

Corvis was rather less complacent. The details of Audriss' plan – of *his* plan – nagged at him, the final clinging pains of a hangover he couldn't shake. He'd possessed but a single copy of his targets and strategies for the war he waged two decades past: one lonely document, penned in his own hand. The idea that it could somehow have made its way to a complete stranger, so many years later, was disturbing in the extreme.

But this alone was not the whole of his concerns. What bothered him beyond the 'how' of the entire situation was the 'why.' Tactically, taking Denathere was a piss-poor move. Corvis himself took the risk in search of a goal far more precious than the city itself, and it was a gamble he paid for with the scattering of his armies and the complete collapse of his plans. Anyone with so much as a student's understanding of warfare could have looked at the details of his campaigns and rejected their end result as militarily unsound.

Audriss had already proved he was no stranger to the ways of battle, no incompetent tactician. Therefore, for him to have chosen to follow the plan despite its tactical flaws implied one of three things, none of which made Corvis feel any better.

One, the man was utterly insane.

Two, he knew far more about Corvis' true objective than any man alive should possibly know. Even his closest lieutenants hadn't been told what he sought in those tunnels beneath the city.

Or three, the warlord was sending a deliberate and personal message to Corvis himself.

All in all, not one of them was a pleasant prospect.

But for all his questions, he could do little enough about it. And though he was distant and distracted for several days, slowly the routine of everyday life lulled him back into the same sense – of comfort, if not of complacency – that he and Tyannon had found in Chelenshire. And so he, too, merely watched and waited, for almost two weeks.

Until the afternoon before the regular town meeting, when everything changed.

'Did not!'

'Did too!'

Mellorin and Lilander clambered over a small rise, each shouting at the other with childish gusto. The argument was half an hour old now and revolved around the earth-shattering issue of which of them had started the *last* argument. For it was the previous conflict that resulted in them both being sent to gather firewood for cooking, allowing their beleaguered parents some few moments of peace. Mellorin had raised the argument – rather eloquently, she thought – that the pair of children, even working together, couldn't haul as much wood as either parent alone.

It had, of course, been utterly ignored.

Grown-ups, she complained silently as she kicked a branch from her path and watched with angry satisfaction as it cracked against a nearby tree, *make no sense at all. If kids ran the world, we'd all be better off.*

She halted, startled, as a second muffled crack followed the first. She examined the stick, but no, only one break there. It occurred to her only then that the rustling of the leaves ahead – which she had attributed to the light breeze blowing past them – ceased the instant the crack sounded, though the breeze was undiminished.

Mellorin was a remarkably intelligent girl, and it took her no time at all to realise there was someone in the wood near them.

Clever as she might have been, though, she had also grown up in Chelenshire, surrounded by friendly, gentle people. 'Hello?' she called curiously. 'Who's there?'

The brush exploded in a sudden flurry of movement. Mellorin leapt back, screaming with shock and the first stirrings of fear. She saw a huge shape, a shaggy beard, and smelled the sour stench of flesh long unwashed. A sudden sharp, blazing pain on the side of her head, and then darkness.

Lilander, eyes wide, watched from deep in the bushes, where he'd fallen as his sister leapt back. He saw the big man pick Mellorin up and throw her over his shoulder, saw him move deeper into the trees, saw the large sword the man wore strapped to his back.

When he was certain the man wasn't coming back, he turned and, carefully retracing his steps as only a determined child can, made his way toward home.

Corvis and Tyannon stood in the doorway, idly watching Rascal dance across the grass, racing from one side of his pen to the other and back again. Corvis' arm rested on the back of her shoulders, her head upon his left bicep, her hair trailing down across his side and his back.

'Quiet,' he said to her, his tone one of utter marvel. 'I'd forgotten what it sounded like.' He chuckled, then, as Rascal skidded to a stop just before the fence, sending clods of dirt to spray across the painted wood.

'Maybe we should build one of those for the kids,' Tyannon suggested. 'It seems to keep the horse happy.'

'No good. The children have fingers and thumbs. They can climb.'

'True. I—'

'Lilander!' Corvis called suddenly. And indeed, there was the boy, trudging tiredly across the stretch of garden that separated him from his parents. His father began to grin, an expression that quickly fell at the sight of his son's face, dirt-covered and tear-streaked.

'Lilander?' Tyannon asked, concerned. 'Sweetie, are you all right?'

'Where's your sister?' Corvis interjected, his heart racing.

'Bad man!' the boy sniffed, his lip quivering. 'A bad man took Mellorin.'

The look on his face left no doubt that this was not just a child's fantasy. 'Corvis!' Tyannon gasped.

'Take Lilander inside. Stay there!'

'But—'

'One of us has to stay with him, Tyannon.'

She nodded, fighting back tears of her own, acquiescing not so much to his words as to his tone. There was fear in his voice, of course, but anger as well; a slow, smoldering anger she hadn't heard in years.

Corvis set out across the garden at a dead run, pausing only to lift a long-handled spade from where it leaned against a fence post. He hefted it once, as though testing it for balance, and then he was gone, his long-legged lope carrying him out of sight before Tyannon could blink.

'Mommy?' At the insistent tug on her pant leg, she stared

down into the serious eyes of her six-year-old son. 'Mommy, is Mellorin going to be all right?'

'Yes, honey.' She picked the child up in her arms, cradling him to her breast and rocking slightly. 'Yes, Mellorin will be fine.'

I don't know! she wanted to scream, to him, to the heavens, to the faces of the gods themselves. *She could be dead, or worse! I don't know if she's going to be all right! I don't know!*

About her – or her father.

And she held him tightly to her, so he couldn't see her tears.

She'd been conscious for some moments by now. But the disorientation, the sudden bouts of dizziness, and the pounding pain in her skull conspired to keep her from forming a coherent thought or from making any meaningful observations about where she was.

She blinked, trying to clear her vision; the side of her face was plastered with something sticky. She felt several strands of her hair on her cheek, apparently glued there by the substance she steadfastly refused to acknowledge as blood.

A deep breath, two, three, and the pain faded ever so slightly. The muffled buzzing in the air resolved itself into voices, and the voices into words.

'. . . a damn idiot!' was the first thing she heard. 'An absolute, undeniable, as-the-gods-are-my-witnesses idiot!'

'I didn't think it was *that* big a deal,' a second voice protested. 'What's your problem?'

'What's my *problem*? Have your eyes gone the way of your wits, man? *She's* my godsdamn problem!'

Mellorin knew full well who 'she' was.

'No one's supposed to know we're here!' the first voice continued, building up steam for a good long rant. 'Now you've gone and grabbed one of them! It'll only be a matter of hours before someone misses her and comes looking! You—'

'Oh, shut up, Brend! Just shut up! It's no big deal! They'll figure an animal got her. Besides, we'll be long gone by the time they start looking. We were about done here anyway.'

'And I suppose you plan to drag her with us?' the other man – Brend? – asked.

'Nah. We'll mangle the body a bit, make it look like wolves or something, and leave it.'

If any of the men heard her gasp, they must have attributed the sound to the wind or some woodland creature, for not a one of them so much as glanced her way.

'So,' a third voice cropped up, 'if we're gonna kill the little bitch anyway, why'd you bother to bring her here alive in the first place?'

'Well, I thought we might get *some* use out of her before we left . . .'

'You,' Brend said, voice cold, 'are a sick man, Varbin. She can't be more than twelve.'

'Doesn't make her any less female, does it?'

'Hey!' the third voice said as a vaguely face-shaped blur appeared in her fuzzy field of vision. 'She's awake!'

Rough hands dragged her to a sitting position; the rest of the world spun in the opposite direction, and the pain in her head flared. Gingerly, she raised a hand to her head, discovering only then that her wrists were bound together.

'What . . . ,' she asked weakly, swallowing around the painful dryness in her throat. 'What do you want with me?'

'That,' the man kneeling before her said sagely, 'is under debate.' A few crude chuckles sounded from behind him – more, in fact, than could be accounted for by the three voices she'd heard thus far. 'What's your name, girl?'

'Mellorin.' She swallowed again. *Don't show fear. They can sense fear.* At least that was supposed to be the case with wild dogs, and seeing as how she had no other experience to fall back on . . . 'What – what's yours?'

The man grinned, the expression seeming to gleam horribly on his unshaven, greasy face. His hair, dark and filthy, fell about his head and danced as he laughed. 'My name doesn't matter, Mellorin.'

Mellorin tried her best to smile. 'Really? That must be frustrating.'

The smile on the man's face vanished as though she'd sliced it off with a knife. This was not the way helpless victims – especially children – were supposed to behave.

A curved blade sprouted from his hand and jabbed forward, coming to a halt just before it drew blood on the side of her throat. He was rewarded with a sudden sob.

'That's better. You shouldn't be so rude to us, young lady. When people are rude to us, it makes us upset. We tend to be rude back.'

'There are no animals around here,' she whispered, fighting back tears. 'No dangerous ones, anyway. If you . . .' Her voice broke. 'If you kill me, they'll know it wasn't an animal!'

The man kneeling before her blinked once and looked back for support. The sweaty, bearded man who'd grabbed her in the first place – Varbin, she remembered – merely shrugged. 'So they'll know it wasn't an animal. We're still not planning to be anywhere near here by the time they find her. So what's the big deal?'

With a small shriek, Mellorin thrust the man's arm, and the knife along with it, away from her throat, beating on his chest with her bound hands. More startled than anything else, he fell back, staring at her. And then he reached out with his other hand and slapped her across the face, just beneath the earlier wound. Mellorin recoiled, agony racing through her skull.

'Please!' she screamed at him as the man's shape loomed over her, knife held before him. 'Please don't hurt me!'

The man took a step closer to her, then another . . .

And then a second shape towered above her, looming tall between her and her attackers.

'She said "please".' Mellorin, though nigh paralysed with fear, sobbed in relief when she recognised the voice. 'You really, *really* should have listened.'

*

To one side, half a dozen men, all large, filthy, and well armed. On the other, a lone figure, long hair wild about his neck and shoulders, easily half again the age of his eldest opponent, armed with only a heavy spade.

It was not a discrepancy that Brend, Varbin, or the others failed to notice. A mocking, contemptuous grin settled upon the features of every man present.

'You seem overmatched, old man,' Brend told him, taking a confident step. The resemblance between the new arrival and their captive didn't escape his attention. 'Her father?'

Corvis nodded once.

'How cosy. You came to die with her.'

These men had worked together for several years, and for all their bickering, they moved and fought as one. Even before he'd finished speaking there was a sudden lunge, not from Brend, but from the man who'd held his knife to Mellorin's throat, intended to quickly end what negligible threat the girl's father might pose. They'd used the tactic many times before, and it never failed to catch the target off-guard.

There is, as the saying goes, a first time for everything.

A blur of movement, a sudden hum in the air, and the spade flashed downward, striking the man's forearm edge-on. A hideous crack reverberated throughout the woods, instantly followed by an agonised scream. The man stared, eyes filled with tears of pain, at his arm and at the two separate ends of what was once a single bone, now protruding through torn and mangled flesh.

His face slack with shock, Brend stepped toward Corvis, his hand dropping frantically toward the hilt of his sword. Corvis met him halfway, jabbing with the butt-end of the tool. Brend, sword dangling from its scabbard, fell to the ground thrashing, a bubbling sound in his throat as he tried to draw breath through a crushed windpipe.

The other four men charged as one, Varbin leading the attack, a cry of rage on his lips. Four swords rose in the air, clutched in hands eager to kill this interloper, to rend him limb from limb and feed the surrounding soil with his blood.

The environment itself conspired against them. One man fell, his boots tangled in a protruding root that he would have sworn was not there mere instants before. Before he could rise to his hands and knees, Corvis' spade landed, point-first, on the base of his skull. Another thug hauled back to take a mighty swing, only to find his blade lodged in an overhanging branch, granting his foe a precious moment to dance aside.

Even as Corvis swung the spade with his right hand, his left darted out and grabbed for the man's wrist. By the time the body hit the forest floor, ribs caved in by the edge of the tool, Corvis held the man's long sword in his other hand.

Varbin was next, falling to his knees as a shrub twisted beneath his feet; as he plummeted earthward, the flat end of the spade rose up to meet him, spreading his nose across the rest of his face. The blow might or might not have been sufficient to kill him. Corvis, growing more tired than he let on, was not about to take any such chance, and finished the fallen man with a quick downward stab of the stolen sword.

That left only one man unwounded. He, fully aware of his fate should he continue to fight, allowed his sword to tumble into the dirt and dropped to his knees. 'Yield!' he shouted, staring upward, his eyes imploring. 'I yield!'

'Very well.' Corvis stuck the bloody long sword into the earth behind him, reached out with his vacant hand, and dragged the first man he'd struck – who stood, sobbing and staring at his ruined arm – to stand beside the one who'd surrendered. Then, keeping one eye upon the pair of them, he knelt down in the grass and hugged his shaking daughter to him.

'Did they hurt you, sweetheart?'

'They . . . they hit me on the head,' Mellorin told him, twisting so he could see the blood matted against her skull, plastering her hair to her face. 'And they . . . they were going—'

'Shhh. It's all right now. Everything's all right. We're leaving in just a few minutes.'

'Can't we go home now?' she implored.

'In just a bit, sweetheart, I promise.' He turned his own head, so she couldn't see the burning in his eyes. 'Daddy has something he has to do first. And I need you to do something for me, Mellorin.'

'But—'

'I need you to rest.'

Carefully disentangling himself from her arms, he rose smoothly to his feet. A short muttered incantation, and Mellorin fell into a restful, painless sleep. It was a shame the spell wouldn't work on an alert subject, one not already on the edge of unconsciousness. But then, Corvis *wanted* them awake. Aware.

Feeling.

The prisoners blanched, falling back before the doom they saw etched across his features.

'You first,' he said, facing the uninjured man. 'Who sent you here?'

'No – no one!' he stammered, edging backward. 'We're just – just wandering bandits! We—'

Corvis nodded once, and then the spade flashed upward. It hit directly between the man's legs; his scream wasn't quite sufficient to drown out the sound of his pelvic bone cracking under the impact.

'As you can see,' Corvis said mildly to the man with the broken arm, gesturing with the bloody tool at the quivering shape on the ground, 'I'm in no mood to have my time wasted. Who sent you?'

'Oh, gods!' The man's broken arm spasmed as he gestured. 'I can't tell you! I can't! He'll . . .' He froze, his lip quivering, as the spade rose slowly to point at him.

'I doubt they'll be able to save that arm,' Corvis told him. 'But you have three other working limbs.' He smiled, though there was no mirth at all in the expression. 'At the moment.'

'Who are you?' the man whispered.

The past seventeen years had failed to rob Corvis of his flare for theatrics. Very deliberately, he allowed the spell that had set the roots and branches against his enemies to lapse.

Murmuring the words of a new incantation under his breath, he released the spell even as he drew breath to answer his prisoner's terrified query.

It was a simple illusion, easily mastered by the youngest apprentice of the First Circle, but it was more than sufficient. For the span of perhaps a dozen heartbeats, he towered over the cringing soldier, encased once more in black steel and gleaming white bone, an iron-banded skull staring down upon its latest conquest.

'I,' he intoned as the mirage faded, the last remnant of a forgotten dream, 'am Corvis Rebaine.'

For long moments after the illusion flickered away and was gone, the injured man stood, frozen, his shallow breathing the only sign that any life remained to him at all. Even the steady patter of dripping blood came briefly to a halt.

And then he laughed. It was harsh, high-pitched – bordering on the manic – an ugly sound. It twisted itself around the trees, insinuating itself between the leaves and through the holes in the trunks. Animals, creatures that had hunkered down and hidden during the clamour of the battle, pricked up their ears, flattened their tails, and fled.

But this was no mocking cackle, as Corvis at first assumed, no last act of defiance. It was flavoured instead with sheer desperation, blind panic, and perhaps the first hint of looming madness.

And still he laughed, until tears ran freely, down his cheeks and his face reddened for lack of breath. Only when he literally lost the strength necessary to keep it up did the fit subside, leaving him standing, fully spent, before his captor.

'Are you quite through?' Corvis asked coldly.

'Corvis Rebaine.' The bandit shook his head, eyes wide, teeth and lips twitching randomly from a rictus grin to a clench of pain to slack-jawed fear. 'Of course. It would have to be.'

'Why are you here? Who sent you?'

'We'd wondered if you were dead, you know,' the man told him, oblivious to the questions he'd been asked. 'After that fiasco at Denathere, everyone figured you'd be back for revenge, but it never happened. We . . .' He froze, the words clinging by their fingertips to the inside of his throat, as Corvis again raised the spade and held it, tip down, over the man's left foot.

'Three limbs. Remember?'

'Audriss,' he whispered, his face white. 'Audriss sent us.'

The ground tilted beneath Corvis' feet. *He wasn't supposed to come here! Chelenshire is useless to him!*

He was supposed to leave us alone . . .

'Why?' Corvis demanded. 'Is he headed here?'

'I – I shouldn't . . .'

The spade dropped an inch or so.

'No! No, please! I don't know! I swear I don't! We were just one of a dozen scouting parties! He's sent us all over Imphallion! Getting the lay of the land, seeing what kind of resistance he might face! But I don't know which way he's going! I don't know! I don't! I—'

'I get it! Shut up!'

Corvis thought furiously in the sudden silence. It didn't quite ring true, yet he couldn't bring himself to believe the man was lying to him. Whatever the case, any illusions he'd harbored that Chelenshire could somehow avoid the whole affair had been brutally shattered into so many splinters.

He glanced around him as though seeing the area for the first time. Four corpses, and one man on the ground, twitching, who wouldn't survive the next few hours without the attention of a healer – attention that Corvis was not inclined to provide.

But that left one man standing.

'The first question,' he muttered, 'is what to do with you.'

'Mercy! I told you everything I know! Mercy, I beg you!'

Corvis nodded once. 'Mercy, then.' He spun about once, his left hand yanking the stolen sword from the earth. Momentum carried him about, full circle, and the man's head bounced across the dirt to fetch up against a nearby oak. The rest of the body toppled sideways, the broken bones of the arm digging furrows into the soil.

'Considering what I want to do to you,' Corvis told the head, meeting its lifeless gaze, 'that's mercy enough.' The sword, coated in blood, tumbled to the ground; the spade followed a moment later. Somehow, he didn't think either he or Tyannon would care to use it in the garden anymore.

Corvis knelt, cradled his daughter in his arms, and slowly made his way home.

CHAPTER THREE

'Are you certain about this?'

Even in the darkened basement, lit only by a single black candle in the centre of the room the irritation was obvious on the younger man's face. 'I'm certain that if you ask me that one more time, I'm going to strongly consider feeding your liver to the gnomes.'

The ancient fellow, his skin desiccated and shriveled almost to parchment, recoiled, one hand nervously rising to stroke the remaining wisps of beard. 'It's just . . . You understand what it is you're trying to awaken here?'

'Better than you. Do it, before I decide to use your soul to awaken him the old-fashioned way.'

The old man muttered something unintelligible, knelt beside the candle with a creaking of tired bones, and began to chant. Three times his old voice wavered nearly enough to break the spell, and three times the younger man reached for his blade, ready to spill the wizard's life.

But there was no need. Faint, so faint that even the lone candle was almost enough to drown it out, the tiny stone that was the object of their attention began to glow.

/Feed . . ./ It was weak, barely an echo of a whisper, but they both heard it in their minds.

'Soon,' the younger man cooed, his tone almost seductive. 'Soon, my friend, you'll have all the souls you could ever wish for. But first I need your help to locate someone, someone who knows some *very* important secrets.'

/Who . . . ?/ It was almost a groan, little more.

'A rather violent fellow by the name of Valescienn.'

'Well,' Audriss said, leaning back heavily in his velvet-lined chair, 'that was unattractive.' He negligently waved a hand through the image hovering over the mahogany table before him: Corvis Rebaine carrying Mellorin from the woods. It scattered like pipe smoke and faded away.

/It's not as though you didn't know what he was capable of,/ the now familiar voice in his mind responded drily.

'Perhaps, but it was surprisingly brutal.'

/Most animals get that way when their young are threatened./

'Indeed.' Audriss rested his chin on an open palm – only here, in the sanctity of his most private chambers, would he dare to remove the featureless mask – and stared moodily across the table. 'He used magic in that battle.'

/Assuming Rebaine hasn't signed any sort of treaty with the local flora, or learned to disguise himself as a suit of armour, I'd say that was a distinct possibility./

The dark-garbed warlord ignored the sarcasm. 'I thought you said he and your old friend had parted ways.'

/Spells that simple, Rebaine can perform on his own. And Audriss, if you refer to Khanda as my 'old friend' one more time – well, I have a truly horrendous genital-rot curse I'm just itching to try out on someone./

'"Itching". Hysterical. Tell me, are all your kind as obnoxious as you are?'

/I have a gift for it./

'Because if they are, I should just stick Rebaine with you and Khanda. Between the two of you, he'd do anything I asked just for a few moments of peace and quiet.'

/Speaking of whom, are you certain we shouldn't be watching him now? Are you so convinced he'll act as you anticipated?/

'Quite certain. I haven't left him any other option.'

/He could run./

'Oh, no. Not Rebaine. I know him too well for that. No, he'll do exactly as I expect him to, you can bet your soul on that.'

/Funny. Now who thinks he's the court jester?/

Audriss's reply was interrupted by a sudden knock on his heavy chamber door. A quick snap of the fingers, and his black mask affixed itself perfectly to his face. Even as he rose, a second gesture sent the door swinging ponderously open, seemingly of its own accord.

'My lord?' the soldier standing without asked nervously.

'I distinctly recall giving an order recently,' Audriss said, tapping one finger against the chin of the mask with exaggerated care. 'Now, what might that have been?'

The soldier, a young man who'd served Audriss long enough to know that responding to the question was not a wise move, swallowed nervously.

'I've got it!' Audriss announced. 'Could it have been that I was *not to be disturbed*?'

'I – I beg your pardon, my lord! But – but we felt you should know—'

'Yes?'

'We've captured another group of refugees attempting to flee Denathere. A large family and their servants, or so it appears.'

'I see.' They weren't the first citizens to attempt an escape from the sudden reign of Audriss – called by some under his rule the Serpent – and they wouldn't be the last. 'It seems we'll require another example. Give the women to the soldiers, have the men impaled alive before the front gate.'

'And the children?'

Audriss sighed; did he have to do *everything*? 'Slaves' quarters. Raise them to be useful.'

'Yes, sir!' The warrior moved to depart.

'Soldier!' Audriss called abruptly. The man froze.

'Y-yes, sir?'

'Those are, you realise, my standing orders. I gave them after the first escape attempt. Why am I repeating them to you now?'

'S-sir, it's just – I thought—'

Audriss sighed again. 'Are you hungry?'

'I . . . no, sir, I . . .' It dawned on the young soldier only belatedly that, just perhaps, his lord had been addressing someone else.

/I could eat./

'He's yours, then.'

The soldier's mouth opened, wide but deathly silent. A faint green glow shone behind his eyes; his jaw gaped wider, and wider still, until muscles tore, skin peeled, bone shattered. The glow faded as quickly as it appeared, and the man collapsed.

/A tad bitter, but not too bad./

'I'm so glad you approve. Tell Mithraem he can have the body.'

/I believe he needs them alive, but I'll ask./

'Fine. Enough chatter for now, though. I've got a long night of planning ahead of me. And I'd like to see if my citizens take the proper lesson from the impaling.'

The chamber door slammed shut.

Night brought small relief from the harsh heat of summer, the best the citizens of Chelenshire could hope for. The moon gazed down on windows left ajar, flung open in a largely futile attempt to banish the day's accumulated warmth. Stars twinkled above a town that restlessly tossed and turned, asleep in its own sweat.

In one house, at the very edge of town, the heat was even greater. For in that house, an entire family shared a single room, as they'd done for three nights running.

The day following the incident in the woods, Corvis and Tyannon described the assault – albeit with certain details judiciously edited out – to a stunned populace at the monthly meeting. Their tale was met with outraged cries, and it was all Tolliver could do to bring the meeting back to order. Clearly, Chelenshire could no longer 'wait and see,' but what their next course of action should be was a matter of no small consternation. For the nonce, Tolliver had promised a regular patrol of volunteers throughout the surrounding area.

It was, Corvis knew, a useless gesture. Were Audriss to

send any more raiders, any of Chelenshire's 'militia' would find themselves overwhelmed before they could so much as pull steel. Still, it made the people feel better, and it allowed Tolliver to feel as though he'd done something to protect his friends and his friends' children. Corvis kept his doubts and concerns to himself.

Now three days later, the town was no safer and the children continued to sleep with their parents. Mellorin woke screaming on a regular basis, her nightmares refusing to abate and permit her to heal.

The children had never known who their father really was. They, like everyone, had heard tales of the warlord Corvis Rebaine, but they'd never once associated him with 'Cerris,' their father. Corvis and Tyannon were determined to keep the truth from them at all costs.

But now that truth refused to stay away, and Corvis found himself too old and tired to outrun the past.

He finally came face-to-face with the decision he'd been avoiding since the instant he saw his beautiful daughter – dirty, bloody, and scared out of her mind – trembling on the forest floor.

Corvis gingerly pushed the thin sheet aside. With a grace remarkable in a man his age, he slid across the room. Boards creaking only slightly beneath his tread, he drifted past his sleeping children, pausing just once to look down at his daughter's face. At the moment, at least, she wasn't dreaming. Her expression was smooth now, at peace. His own eyes closing, he offered up a brief and silent prayer to Shashar the Dream-Singer, asking only that her sleep remain serene, unbroken by nightmares. And then he was gone, pushing the bedroom door shut.

More swiftly now, he moved through the house as though seeing it for the first time. The kitchen and parlour, the first rooms completed, in which they'd slept wrapped in blankets while the rest of the house grew slowly around them. The children's room, largely unoccupied for the past several days; he stared grimly at the toys scattered about the floor, the pretty ribbons hanging from the sill, the purple stuffed horse that Mellorin was 'too old for' but kept 'because Mother made it for me.' All these and more he saw, and his rage swelled once more at the thought of what these men had stolen from his children.

And then he was there.

The door was narrow, sandwiched between two walls that didn't quite converge. The room beyond was not large, and while hardly a secret chamber per se, it was remarkably easy to miss. He and Tyannon used it primarily for storing old things they no longer needed but refused to dispose of.

Corvis pulled the door ajar with nerve-racking slowness, wincing as the hinges shrieked not unlike a cat fed tail-first into a loom. Then, shrugging mentally – either he'd woken someone or he hadn't – he stepped inside.

And promptly tripped over one runner of the cradle he'd spent so many hours sitting beside, rocking first Mellorin and then Lilander into slumber. He caught himself before he tumbled head-over-heels into the pile of miscellaneous clutter, but it was a near thing.

His head shaking in dissatisfaction, he leaned carefully against an old moth-eaten tapestry. Though neither fancy nor particularly valuable, it had been one of his favorite possessions for many years, until the wear and tear, the holes and the smudges, forced him to admit it could no longer be displayed in any tasteful fashion. And thus it lay here, rolled up and stuck in a corner of a storage closet: tattered, irreparable, and too well loved to be discarded.

Rather, Corvis reflected sourly, *like a tired old fool I could mention.*

He was stalling; he knew it even as he looked over the cradle, the tapestry, and everything else that lay in the cluttered room. It was time either to do it, or to give up and go back to bed.

For a long moment, he felt so very tempted to do just that. He had a family. He was comfortable here. And what he now contemplated was quite possibly the most idiotic thing he'd ever conceived.

But there was another part of him that remembered, in graphic detail, the fate of all who once stood in his way, whose only crime had been to have the misfortune of living in a city that he, Corvis Rebaine, had wanted.

Yes, he had a family. And he'd be damned in the eyes of every last god if he'd let such a gruesome end befall them. Audriss must be stopped, before Mellorin, Lilander, or Tyannon could be threatened again.

Cerris, citizen of Chelenshire, couldn't stop him.

Corvis Rebaine, the Terror of the East, might.

He reached downward, pushing aside myriad mementos of past years, until he'd cleared enough space to see it. The handle was old, slightly corroded, and coated with dust and cobwebs. Over a decade had passed since he'd so much as seen what lay within, and he'd never thought he would again.

Then why, he couldn't help but ask himself, *did you keep it at all?*

Shut up, he replied to himself sharply. Getting a firm grip on the handle, he twisted and yanked.

And then he bent over again, rubbed his head where he'd hit the wall behind him, got an even firmer grip — it was easier, now that his first attempt had cleared the dust off the small handle — and yanked once more.

The trapdoor shot open as though spring-loaded. A sudden burst of musty air puffed into the closet, the cloud of dust rising above him, an enraged spirit awakened from what was supposed to have been eternal slumber.

But when the dust cleared, when his eyes adjusted to the darkness within the small alcove, he saw only what he expected to see. A black drop cloth over a large chest. And within that chest . . .

An axe. A suit of black armour, spiked, plated with bone. And a helm formed to evoke an iron-banded skull.

Shaking violently as a newborn calf, Corvis lifted the helm from its place in the chest, where it had lain untouched for years. The jaw gaped open as he lifted it up, as though the skull itself were greeting him. Corvis gazed intently into the sockets, examining the dark strips of iron crossing the face and continuing around the head. He glanced down at the armour itself, saw his reflection, though blurred, in the dusty black plates, saw the thin spines jutting from the cuirass. He pondered, in his mind's eye, the image the entire ensemble must have projected. And though he fought to keep it away, one specific thought kept returning, over and over again, to the forefront of his mind:

What the hell *was I thinking?* I must've looked like a world-class idiot in this thing!

It was a humbling realisation. To look back and realise that he'd been strutting about like a peacock in some grown-up version of a children's costume was a tremendous blow to the ego. For some minutes he could do nothing but stare in abject horror at the thing in his hands. The skull's gaping jaw now appeared to be laughing at him, and he felt a sudden urge to join in.

'The saddest part,' he told the helm seriously, 'is that I always thought I looked so damn impressive back then. It took me almost twenty years to get the joke, and now that I have, it's not all that funny.'

The skull, perhaps having laughed itself out of breath, chose not to reply.

'But the fact is,' he explained to the helm, 'it always had the desired effect. People were scared of me.

'Of course, I imagine people would be frightened of anyone who did what I did, no matter if I'd been wearing a purple kilt and a wimple. I suppose it'll have to do.'

His hands initially fumbled with the buckles, but the old familiarity began to seep back into his movements, washing away the rust and clumsiness of years of disuse, the fingers recalling what the mind had long forgotten. Undersuit, chain hauberk, greaves, thigh guards, cuirass, bracers, arm guards . . .

And helm. Damn, that thing cut down the peripheral vision something fierce! But at least the armour was on.

It was not quite so well as it used to fitting. Some of the straps he tightened to their limit. He'd lost a great deal of muscle mass since he'd last worn this infernal getup, and the pieces were sized for a broader man. It would do, and it fit well enough that nothing should fall off or out, but it felt wrong.

And I'm quite sure, he noted, feeling around at the helm, *that when I wore this last, my hair wasn't long enough to stick out the bottom. I must look like I've got a sheepdog in here with me.*

Corvis clanked from the room as quietly as he could – which wasn't saying much – in search of a mirror.

Tyannon, her arms crossed, her left foot tapping steadily to an unheard drummer and one eyebrow raised in a statement far more eloquent than words could ever convey, awaited him in the hallway.

'Umm,' Corvis explained.

'I was quite sure,' his wife said, her voice level, 'that we were being burgled by the world's clumsiest thief. It's a miracle that you haven't woken the children. May I humbly suggest that stealth is not your chief talent?'

'I – well, that is.' Corvis sighed, the breastplate and spines rising and falling with the gesture. 'It's kind of hard to see in here.'

Tyannon snorted, and though she tried desperately to hold her face in its stony façade, the corners of her mouth twitched.

'Are you laughing at me?' Corvis asked, his voice suddenly suspicious.

Her entire face spasmed as she struggled to retain her composure. 'No, dear.'

Corvis frowned darkly, forgetting that he himself had been struck by the ridiculousness of the whole thing not two minutes before. 'Because I don't think this is particularly a laughing matter.'

Tyannon squeaked; unable for that instant to speak at all, she merely nodded in agreement.

'This was the mark of Corvis Rebaine!' he insisted, his voice rising. 'The Terror of the East! This armour brought fear and horror to an entire kingdom!'

'Of course it did, dear.'

Their eyes locked through the sockets in the helm. Corvis deflated like a spent bellows when Tyannon, unable to contain herself any longer, collapsed against the nearest wall in a fit of hysterical laughter.

'Oh, the hell with it,' Corvis snapped, yanking the helm from his head and letting it fall to the floor. 'This is a stupid idea anyway.'

'No. It's not.'

Corvis looked askance at his wife, his pride stinging, and only then noticed the trembling of one clenched fist, the desperate tone to her laughter. The anger drained from him, leaving him spent.

'It's something I have to do, Tyannon,' he said quietly, sincerely, reaching out to pull her as close as the armour's damn spines would allow.

'I know it is,' she whispered.

'I don't want to go anywhere.' His voice grew hoarse, and he knew that she knew this, but it must be said now. There might be no other opportunity. 'I love you more than anything, Tyannon. You, the kids – you're everything in the world to me now.

'But they came here, Tyannon. They came *here*, to our home. They attacked my little girl.' He smiled through the sudden dampness on his face. Reaching out with a hand, his grip gentle despite the steel gauntlet, he cupped his wife's chin. 'It took me longer than I expected, Tyannon, but I finally conquered the world – or at least the part that matters. I don't know what Audriss wants, but I'll be damned before I'll let him take that from me. From us.'

'I know,' she told him again, tears encroaching on her own voice. Shyly she reached up, brushing his long grey hair away from his eyes. 'And I understand, I really do. I just want you to come back to us.'

'I'm tougher than that, Tyannon, even with a few extra years on me. I won't die that easily.'

'It's not that.' He felt himself falling into her deep, dark eyes. 'I mean I want *you* to come back to me, Corvis. Not – not this.' She tapped a finger sharply on the cuirass that encased his chest. 'I want the man I love, not the man he used to be. And if you go out again, in this, I don't know who's going to be wearing it when you walk back through that door.'

'Tyannon, you know that's not what I want anymore!'

'Isn't it?' she asked pointedly, stepping back and glaring at him, her hands on her hips. 'Can you stand there and swear to me that there's not a single part of you left that *does* want it?'

And Corvis, his face flushing, looked away.

'That's what I thought,' she whispered, barely a breath at all.

Before she even saw him move, though, he was again clutching her to him as tightly as he dared, his mouth pressed to hers. For mere seconds, for long centuries, they stood locked in that strange half embrace. And then Corvis straightened his arms, breaking the kiss and staring intently into his beloved's face.

'Yes, I still think this kingdom would be better off with me in charge, Tyannon. Someone's got to do it, or the damn Guilds and petty nobles are going to tear it all apart. And if someone offered me Imphallion on a silver platter, I'd take it without a moment's thought.

'But I have my priorities straight, finally. I know that going off to wage war on everyone and everything would take me away from here, and that you probably wouldn't be here when – if – I got back. And nothing, not even the world itself, is worth that.'

Tyannon smiled through her tears, her face shining, at least in Corvis' eyes, with a radiance to shame the sun itself. 'Come on,' she said, her voice husky with emotion. 'Let's get you straightened up, at least. Can't have you going off to war all disheveled. Reflects badly on me, you know.'

Carefully hiding his own smile, Corvis bent to retrieve his

discarded helm, and allowed his wife to drag him after her into the sitting room.

Several moments and several revolutions later, Corvis was feeling just a bit dizzy, and Tyannon was intently examining the armour in the flickering lantern light, one finger thoughtfully tapping her chin. 'One more time,' she ordered.

'Again? Sweetheart, my backside hasn't changed in the past thirty seconds, I promise. I—'

'Turn.'

Corvis sighed and spun slowly. 'I feel like a top.'

Tyannon examined him a moment longer and then shook her head. 'The armour,' she said, trying to be tactful about it, 'isn't new anymore.'

'I know how it feels.'

But staring at his dim reflection in the poorly lit mirror, he was forced to acknowledge her point. The armour, while still perfectly serviceable, was past its peak. The bones, magically hardened and preserved, had yellowed; the steel, even after careful polishing and scouring, bore sporadic pockmarks, remnants of the rust that attacked it during its long inactivity. The undercoat of chain would require much oil to make it fully flexible again, and the cloak sported several moth-eaten holes that would take a good bit of mending to close.

'It suits me, really,' Corvis said wanly. 'Older, a bit battered, maybe not as neat as it used to be, but hale and hardy all the same. I think it adds character, don't you?'

Tyannon's eyes blazed alarmingly and Corvis, having been a wise general in most respects, decided it was time to reassess his strategy.

'I'll just grab a cloth and get to polishing, then.'

'You do that.'

The first hints of grey prodded gently at the eastern sky by the time the pair of them, working together, had scrubbed and polished and mended the armour restoring it to a state that Tyannon declared passable. Corvis stood, encased head-to-toe in the armour, staring intently into the mirror. His wife, chewing thoughtfully on a knuckle, hovered off to one side.

It was *almost* exactly as it had once been. Only the most observant witness would have noticed the single tiny discrepancy, the lack of the chain and pendant that dangled always from Corvis' neck during his more violent years.

'It looks ludicrous,' Corvis snapped.

'True. But at least it's clean.' Then, sensing his expression although she couldn't see a hint of it, Tyannon added, 'I think it'll work, Corvis. It seems strange to us now. But to anyone who doesn't know you as I do – well, you're still the Terror of the East.'

Corvis shrank at the quaver in her voice. 'And that bothers you.' It wasn't a question.

'Shouldn't it? I remember the first time I saw this thing, Corvis. However you've changed, it's not something I'll ever forget.'

'I know. I'm sorry.'

She smiled at him, though it was an anemic effort. 'Well, we've been through all that. No sense in dredging it all up now, of all times. When . . .' She swallowed once. 'When are you leaving?'

Corvis took a long look at the sky outside the window. 'Not until tomorrow, at the earliest, maybe the day after. I need to gather some supplies, go over some maps . . .'

'Good,' Tyannon said softly. 'Then we've got some time.'

The children, exhausted by a hard afternoon's work the previous day, slept soundly through the clatter of several large pieces of armour sporadically falling to the floor in the next room – and through the softer, gentler sounds that followed.

The brutal heat of summer blasted the earth as though the gods would reforge it into some brand-new shape. Grass, brown and brittle, crackled noisily underfoot. A few birds, more hardy than most, circled lazily in the sky, blackened shadows against the blazing sun. Occasionally a small animal, driven by need to leave the shelter of the trees, darted across the road. A faint breeze, too weak to offer relief, whispered over the plains.

And other than that minuscule gust, and the occasional squawk of a distant bird, the only sounds to break the tranquility were the steady clip-clop of a set of hooves, the occasional jingle of the animal's saddlebags, and the even more occasional cursing of its rider.

Corvis very deliberately refused to allow himself to look back, even though Chelenshire was now many hours behind him. He feared even that simple act might cost him his nerve to go on. He'd nearly changed his mind that morning, when he knelt and hugged his children goodbye, telling them Daddy needed to go away for a while, but that he'd be back as soon as he possibly could. Lilander bit his lip and sniffled. Mellorin wavered between contending in her most grown-up voice that she was old enough to help her mother take care of the place, and sobs of fear when it occurred to her that he wouldn't be there if more of the 'bad men' showed up. He'd tried to tell her that part of the reason he was leaving was to make certain that no more bad men *would* show up, but she didn't seem comforted.

To Tolliver, he'd simply explained that he thought he knew some folks back home who could help with the 'Audriss problem.' He didn't explain, and Tolliver, who considered himself a polite man, didn't ask. He'd simply wished Corvis luck and godspeed on his journey and promised that he and the rest of the town would see to it nothing ill befell Tyannon and the kids. Corvis, who knew far better than anyone else what sort of ills might befall them, was nonetheless comforted that *someone* was watching after his family.

Sunder, glinting in the sun, swung from a baldric that normally hung from Corvis' shoulder, but for now dangled from one of Rascal's saddlebags. A longsword, old but well kept, hung in a worn scabbard on his left hip. His armour was carefully wrapped in oilcloth and stored in the saddlebags. He wore instead a sturdy suit of traveling leathers that creaked as he moved, the stiffness not yet fully worked from them. They were solid, durable. They would stand up to any travel, any travail, and most of the elements – they'd even function as decent armour, if push well and truly came to shove.

But they were also bloody *hot*, and the journey ahead of him wasn't a short one. Even the great Corvis Rebaine couldn't take on an entire army by himself. Before Audriss learned that a new enemy walked the land, Corvis needed to gather some allies.

Fortunately, he had a pretty good idea where to start.

Chapter Four

'What do you mean, "I have no idea"?'

Valescienn shrugged, no more intimidated by the growing ire in Audriss' voice than he'd ever been by Rebaine's. 'Well, let's see if I can put it into clearer terms, my lord. I *do not know*.'

'You were his lieutenant!' Audriss all but snarled, knocking the map from the table with a gauntleted fist. 'He trusted you with his entire campaign!'

'Not entirely. We never discussed what was to happen beyond Denathere.' Again, the warrior shrugged. 'He kept saying he'd tell me after. Frankly, I'm not sure he thought it mattered.'

Audriss sighed, casually running his finger over the glowing green ring. 'Ah, well. It'll take us some time to reach Denathere. I'm sure we'll come up with something by then.'

'Some time,' as it turned out, had been months. 'Some time,' as it *also* turned out, hadn't offered any insight to make the choice any easier.

A veritable avalanche of papers and parchments covered the scarred surface of the oaken table. Reports and tactical commentary in at least four languages peered from the pile, various and sundry symbols tracing a twisted course across the table.

On the end farthest from the door, a map lay spread across a relatively uncluttered area. Torchlight flickered over the images, the shadow of some mad giant dancing across entire nations. The room echoed with the final screams of the dying fugitives. The houses of the condemned, set to the torch at the Serpent's command, sent a thick, woody smoke across the city, thickening the air even in this lofty chamber.

Audriss hunched over the map, one metal-clad hand spread, palm-down, in the plains to the east of Imphallion.

'Abtheum, I think,' the black-garbed warlord muttered softly into the smoky air around him. 'Yes, definitely Abtheum.'

/'Definitely' as in 'definitely' or 'definitely' as in 'I'm going to change my mind again in an hour'?/

'I do not,' Audriss snapped indignantly, 'recall asking your opinion!'

/You rarely do. It's never stopped me from giving it anyway, has it?/

'Impudent creature!'

/Indeed. I thought you'd decided last night that Orthessis was 'definitely' our next objective. Now it's Abtheum again. I humbly suggest that you come to a final decision sometime this millennium. There's only enough food in Denathere to keep your armies fed for a generation or so./

'It is difficult,' Audriss admitted, crossing his arms and standing straight to glare at the map, as though this entire predicament were the cartographer's fault. 'They're both viable targets. They both lie on routes that will eventually take us to Mecepheum, and neither is particularly better defended than the other.'

/One could always try flipping a coin./ The voice hesitated for a moment. /It's a shame Imphalam the First couldn't have built his capital someplace more convenient. This 'march the armies across hundreds of miles to take Mecepheum' bit makes for some interesting strategising, but it grows old rapidly./

'Aren't you pretty much ageless anyway?'

/That does not, alas, make me any less prone to boredom./

With a grunt of annoyance, Audriss spun from the table and began to pace the long chamber, stopping now and again by the window to breath deeply of the scented smoke. 'It is,' he offered hopefully, 'still possible we won't need to keep up this farce anyway. Perhaps Denathere is as far as we need go. Perhaps—'

/He's here./

The Serpent halted. Even as he watched, a dense white mist began to seep in beneath the door frame, leaving a thick residue of blood on the wood. Audriss idly waited as his ally's features appeared in the pillar of mist, filled in with blood, and flushed solid.

'I'll admit that it's theatrical,' the Serpent said sharply, 'and perhaps even useful in any number of circumstances. But it takes a damn sight longer than it would just to open the bloody door like a normal person!'

Mithraem, smoothing out a nonexistent wrinkle in his pristine white shirt, raised an eyebrow and smiled, revealing a perfectly straight set of gleaming ivory teeth. '|"Bloody door," is it?'

'Bah! What have you learned?'

Mithraem stretched languorously, a great cat in vaguely human clothing, and then strode to the nearest chair, leaving bloody prints on the floor. Unmindful of Audriss's growing impatience, he extended his legs out comfortably before him, crossing them at the ankles, and steepled his fingers together in front of his face.

'Well?' the warlord demanded.

One side of the pale man's mouth quirked. 'You, my friend, should learn patience.'

/He's got a point, actually. You do tend toward the abrupt./

'This is what I get,' Audriss spat bitterly, 'for surrounding myself with immortals.'

'It does,' Mithraem told him, 'tend to influence one's outlook.' Then, 'My agents have spent many nights discussing the issue with the city's leaders, noble and Guildsman alike. They were quite insistent, actually. I'm certain we've learned from them everything we can.'

'And?' Audriss asked, his voice not quite breathless.

'As we expected, I fear. Not one of them has any idea what Rebaine was searching for in the catacombs – and thus, no information of any use to you.'

'Damn!' The table jumped at the impact of the Serpent's fist; papers cascaded onto the floor, and only Mithraem's inhuman reflexes prevented a wine goblet from overturning onto the map.

'Tsk, tsk, Audriss.' He held the drink up before him in toast, sniffed it once – his expression quickly shifting to one of intense distaste – and placed it back on the table. 'Quite careless of you. Besides, it's not as though this was unexpected. I—'

At the sound of spasmodic scratching, two pairs of eyes flickered to the chamber door.

'It appears,' Audriss said, 'that I'm destined for interruptions tonight. Enter!'

Heralded by the creaking door, a misshapen form, garbed in filthy black rags and tatters, shambled into the room.

Little more than three feet in height, the new arrival was painfully gaunt. Its limbs hung in nominally human ways, although select bulges and twists suggested muscle and bone that were not present in any child born of woman. It jerked constantly as it walked, and in motion it became less human still, for its limbs jutted in directions displeasing to the eye, bent at angles to make staunch men squirm. Two eyes, closer together than they should have been, blazed an irritated pink above a maw full of jagged and broken teeth.

'The Audriss is busy, yes, busy with other things,' the creature said to the room in general, its voice the sound of broken bone ground against a rock. 'He wonders, does it want him to come back later?'

Though none could possibly see it, Audriss shuddered once inside his armour. Gods, but gnomes gave him the shivers!

'No,' he commanded; his voice steady enough to belie his unease. 'Give your report.'

The shambling little creature nodded and slid forward a few more steps, pausing to examine the bloodstains Mithraem had left on the ground. Audriss could actually see the thing's nose twitching.

'I said report!'

'Yes.' The gnome looked up from his contemplation. 'He comes from the catacombs underneath, yes, below. Much digging, moving of rocks. Did the Audriss know, he wonders, that many of the tunnels were collapsed, yes, full of rocks?'

'I knew. It's why I've given him – you – so long to search the damn place!'

'Ah, he sees, understands, yes. All the rocks moved, tunnels are cleared, empty. Some will not stand, no, fall again when he moves braces, supports. But the catacombs are searched, all of them, yes.' The gnome rubbed its hands together, the calluses on one palm grating noisily against the jagged nails of its fingers.

'And?' Audriss demanded. 'What did you find?'

'Find, yes. Underground room, below, at the end of corridors. Metal door, yes, but melted, opened, burned away. Not natural, no. Magic. He feels it in his bones, yes, when the magic comes.

'But the Audriss will be unhappy, he thinks, yes it will. He searches the room, yes, all of the room, until there are no more places for hiding, no, not for secret things. Nothing is there, he thinks, no. The Audriss will have to look elsewhere for its treasure, yes, for what it wants. He wonders,' it said abruptly, cocking its head to one side with an audible snap, 'where it will go now? He wonders, will he go with it?'

'Of course you'll go with it – me!' Audriss shouted furiously.

'Can it . . . pay?' There was a soft slapping sound as a thin tendril of spittle dropped from the gnome's lips to land on its shoes.

'We have a bargain, gnome.' Audriss felt his lip curl at the memory of what he'd had to offer. 'You hold up your end of it, I'll hold up mine.'

'He honours his bargains, yes, agreements. He wonders, then, where it wants him to be, yes, to go.'

Audriss sighed and turned back to the map. Abtheum or Orthessis, Orthessis or Abtheum. They were both viable, both tactically sound, both defensible if the armies chose that point to make their own stand . . .

And both, unfortunately, at least three months away at the speed of an army's march. Damn! Imphallion's sprawl was definitely no asset to a would-be conqueror.

It was, thankfully, a decision that Audriss felt he could put off for a while longer. 'The armies,' he told the others, 'will have to travel by the main roads. The supply wagons won't make it through the wilderness. And it's the same road either way up to . . . here!' His finger stabbed downward, covering a small dot on the map. 'Once we take this town here, we'll decide if we're heading northwest to Orthessis or southwest to Abtheum.' He peered closely at the parchment, looking for a name. There. Vorringar.

'You can meet us there?' he asked the disgusting little creature.

'Meet, yes, be there. He can go. He wonders what it wants him to do, yes, when he gets there many walks before it does. The things above the ground are slow, yes, and clumsy.'

'Just wait for us. We'll contact you in the usual manner when we arrive.'

'Good, yes. He goes now to say what the Audriss has told him, yes.' Still muttering to itself, the gnome shambled away through the door.

'Odd little creature,' Mithraem remarked drily. 'Do they all call themselves "him"?'

'Something about their language, or how they think, Or what have you. It's obnoxious.' A sudden thought occurred to Audriss, purely irrelevant but intriguing. His eyes flickered down to the ring that gleamed a sullen green upon his finger. 'Pekatherosh?'

/Yes?/

'Have you ever consumed a gnome?'

/No. Can't do it./

'Can't – but you eat souls.'

73

/*Exactly.*/

So much for curiosity. 'I'd been hoping either you or the gnomes would find what we were looking for here,' he said to Mithraem, 'but I can't say I'm surprised we didn't. Even if he couldn't make use of it, Rebaine isn't stupid enough to have left it here.'

'Still,' the other acknowledged, 'we had to know.'

'We know now,' the warlord snapped. 'I'm leaving a garrison at Denathere, to occupy the city. Can you assign any of the Legion to support them?'

Mithraem rose gracefully from his seat. 'I can station a few of my people here. They won't enjoy being left behind, but they'll obey well enough.'

'Good. Tell them not to gorge themselves while I'm gone; I'd like to have a city left when I get back.'

'What a novel idea. I'll be sure to tell them.'

'Do it quickly. I want the men packing the instant the sun's risen. We're leaving in two days.'

/*And what of Rebaine?*/ Pekatherosh asked once Mithraem had dissolved again to mist and seeped through the open doorway.

'Rebaine will play his part, never you worry. For now, I'm more concerned with the war effort itself.'

/*You don't* sound *all that concerned.*/

'I'm *not* "all that" concerned. The only things between us and our next objective are a handful of small towns – including Vorringar. It's such an insignificant little speck, it barely made it onto the map at all.

'The next stage of the operation is a piece of cake, Pekatherosh. There's nothing between here and Vorringar to slow us down.'

CHAPTER FIVE

Slowly, the world bouncing beneath him and his head pounding with each jolt, Corvis fought his way back toward consciousness. Leaves and twigs appeared before him, just in time to sting his face as he passed. The saddle on which he sat was hard and uncomfortable – the heavy ropes that chafed his wrists and ankles were worse.

Blinking languidly, trying to focus through the pain rattling around in his skull, he peered blearily about him. The dappled horse trod along a wooded path through thick copses of trees, following a broad-shouldered, greasy-haired fellow who clutched the animal's halter. The hem of his cloak and the heels of his boots – all of him Corvis could really see from behind – were worn and frayed, bespeaking a life of constant travel.

His gestures slow and deliberate, hoping to avoid being heard above the clop-clop of the hooves and the faint rustling of the leaves, Corvis fidgeted at his bonds. All he learned, to his chagrin, was that his captor knew what he was doing: his feet were bound together beneath the horse's girth, tight enough that he couldn't possibly kick the beast into sudden movement, and his hands had barely an inch of slack from the pommel to which they were tied.

He learned, as well, that his captor had sharper ears than Corvis had given him credit for.

'You might as well relax,' the fellow said in the gruff tone of a man who loved his pipe. 'It's a long journey back east, and it's not going to get any more comfortable for you.'

He turned as he spoke, and the sight of his unshaven cheeks and heavy-lidded eyes punched through Corvis' remaining haze like a ballista. Images of that morning flickered back into memory . . . The man leaping out at him from where he'd lain concealed in a shallow culvert . . . Corvis drawing his own weapon in a desperate parry . . . His attacker's blade, covered in foreign runes, shearing *clean through* Corvis' sword as though it were made of so much bread crust . . .

And all had gone black, until he woke tied atop this horse. Corvis knew full well that he should be dead now, had his attacker wished it. The man must have struck with the flat of his astounding sword.

'Who are you?' Corvis asked, startled at how gruff his own voice sounded.

'Evislan Kade. Perhaps you've heard of me.'

The prisoner swallowed once. 'Perhaps' indeed! Corvis took a moment, running mental eyes over the list of enemies he'd made in recent years. (It was, though certainly far smaller than the list he would one day accumulate at the head of a mercenary army, already growing uncomfortably large.)

Still . . . 'I can't possibly be worth enough to interest someone like you,' he protested.

'You'd be surprised,' Kade told him. 'As it happens, Colonel Nessarn's family is more than a little rich, and more than a little perturbed at what you did to him. Now be a good little bounty and shut up for a while, or you'll spend the rest of the journey gagged.'

And for four laborious days – days in which Corvis spent all but a few moments tied either to a horse or a tree – that was the extent of their conversation. They traveled along game trails and forest paths, never drawing anywhere near the main highways. Corvis was tired, hungry, and sore, and he was certain that he was nothing but one large bruise from his knees to his hips. Still, he struggled to remain alert, ever watchful for even the smallest opportunity . . .

It came in the late morning of that fourth day, as Kade dragged his 'bounty' off the horse for an all-too-infrequent rest break. Brusquely he shoved Corvis into a stand of bushes in order to answer nature's various demands, and Corvis nearly gasped aloud as a clump of thorns gouged rivulets of blood from the skin of his left hand. And then, instead, he smiled, and snapped off the largest of those thorns between his fingers.

It wasn't much of a tool, but it was more than Kade expected.

When evening fell, and the bounty hunter moved toward the horse to truss his captive up against a tree for the night, Corvis had managed to pick and tear through only about half the individual strands that made up the rope about his hands. It would have to be enough.

A desperate yank against the weakened bonds shredded the flesh of his wrists, but the coils gave way with a vicious snap. Corvis twisted low in the saddle, one hand dropping to the pommel of Kade's sword even as he drove the other forearm into the bridge of his captor's nose. Kade staggered back, blood flowing from both nostrils, and Corvis straightened, the hunter's sword in his hand, ready to bring the flat down against the horse's flank . . .

And froze, mesmerised, for the weapon was *moving* beneath his fingers. Runes danced along the edge of the blade, and as they passed it was a blade no longer, but the haft of a much heavier weapon. What had been the sword of Evislan Kade was now a terrible war-axe, just barely small enough to wield in a single hand.

Somewhere, in a part of Corvis' mind normally accessible only in his deepest nightmares, a voice uttered a single word.

'Sunder.'

Kade lunged, and Corvis – scarcely taking his eyes off the magnificent, malevolent weapon – threw a punch that landed on an already broken nose. Even as the bounty hunter crumpled to the dirt, Corvis reached down with the axe, slit the bonds around his feet, and kicked the horse into motion.

And still he did not look around him, did not look where he was going, but had eyes only for the prize in his fist. He knew what it was, of course, knew well the legends of the Kholben Shiar, the demon-forged blades. For a weapon of such power to simply fall into his hands so easily, it seemed almost a sign from the gods themselves.

Corvis Rebaine moved deeper into the woods, his mind awhirl with thoughts of chance and power, and a growing sense of destiny.

The sun beat down hot as ever, but here, in the foothills of the Cadriest Mountains, there was some measure of relief. The range cast its long and jagged shadow over the hills and valleys below, a curtain against the worst of the sun's wrath. Within that shadow, thick green grasses covered the earth and animals roamed the valleys, feasting upon those grasses – or upon one another.

Not a bad place to live, if one didn't mind a distinct lack of human company. For one trying specifically to *avoid* such company, it was paradise.

In a wide valley nestled between two unusually tall foothills stood a house. Well, perhaps 'house' was a bit generous: it was a single large room surrounded by four crude but sturdy walls. Within lay a pallet of furs atop a pile of hay, to serve as a bed, and a slab of tree to form a chair or table.

The room's only truly notable feature hung on the inside wall, closest to the door: a suit of partial armour, consisting of thick leathers and crude metal plates, accompanied by a long spear with a jagged blade and a single-edged straight sword that grew thicker near the tip. The sword and armour both wore the layers of dust that accumulated through years of neglect, but the spear showed signs of more recent use.

Behind the house was a simple wooden pen containing a flock of sheep and a small herd of fat pigs, and only their bleats and cries broke the stillness of the valley.

The entire scene was utterly pastoral – at first. Only when one of the woolly sheep wandered near the house, munching idly on grass or bleating mindlessly at the passing clouds, would any observer acquire an accurate sense of scale. The house, and everything in it, was built to accommodate a figure more than twice the height of an average man.

Standing on his front porch, little more than a few heavy wooden planks laid flat upon the ground, Davro held a hand to shade his eye from the sun and gazed contentedly at the lands around him.

Although dressed in a simple, nondescript tunic and leggings, he was an impressive figure. Large even for an ogre, Davro towered a full thirteen feet over his surroundings – almost fourteen, if one counted the length of curved horn jutting from his forehead above his single central eye. His skin was a flushed, angry red, and thick brown nails grew from the tips of his fingers, which numbered only four on each hand. Two small tusks protruded from his lower jaw, nestled within a mouthful of large and painfully sharp teeth.

Davro, one of the finest warriors of his tribe, had been expected to become the tribe's next chieftain. Just as soon as he and his brethren returned from fighting alongside the armies of the human, Corvis Rebaine.

His present lifestyle, one he'd lived for many years, would have deeply shamed the other warriors of his tribe. They would, in fact, have been forced by their own code of honour to kill their favoured son.

But none of them knew. And considering how far the ogres dwelled from the Cadriest Mountains, Davro saw no reason they ever should.

A series of snorts from behind the house, concurrent with

the sound of a large snout rooting about in the trough, reminded him it was just about time to slop the hogs. He turned from his contemplation of what he considered 'his' valley, preparing to wander back through the house . . .

And spun back abruptly as a sudden hint of movement caught his eye. Was he imagining things? Had one of the sheep somehow slipped the pen?

No. No rogue livestock, this; the figure resolved itself into the shape of a man leading a horse. He must have spent a great deal of time picking the smoothest, easiest routes in order to get a mount so far into the foothills.

The ogre hadn't set eye on another sentient creature in years, and he wasn't inclined to start inviting guests to lunch now. With a bit of luck, the man was smart enough to let himself be frightened away; and if not, there were other, less equivocal options.

He stepped quickly into his house, pulling his great spear from the wall. The weapon had seen little use over the years, having functioned only to protect its owner's herds from mountain lions or the occasional far-ranging wolves. But it was sturdy as ever, kept well sharpened, and ready as it had ever been to drink the life of two-legged prey.

Davro fixed his face in the most vicious, tusk-bearing expression of mindless rage he could manage, a look that once sent many experienced warriors fleeing in terror. With an earsplitting bellow he knew would carry across the valley, he raised the spear over his head and charged across the springy grass, his long legs devouring the distance with start-ling speed.

The man's horse reared in fright and tried to bolt, but the human held tightly to the reins, speaking calmly to the terrified animal. By the time Davro drew near, the creature was sufficiently calm that it was unlikely to try to break away, though its eyes rolled about in its head and its breath came in heavy gasps.

The human, however, merely raised an eyebrow at Davro's

charge. Not only had he not fled in mortal terror, he showed no real reaction at all.

This man, Davro decided, *must be a lunatic. No honour in killing a lunatic. I'll give him one more shot.*

'Leave this place!' the ogre snarled, his voice deep and rasping, his words slurred slightly by a mouth not meant for the speech of man. 'You are not wanted here, human! If you stay, you are dinner!'

'So theatrical, Davro?' the human asked, the corner of his mouth quirking upward in a tiny smile. 'Is that any way to greet an old friend?'

Davro slowly lowered his spear, growing ever more confused, and peered down at the stranger. 'Friend? I don't know you, human . . .'

'Sure you do. Besides, you wouldn't eat me anyway. You told me once you hate the way humans taste. That's why you always left the cleanup to your lieutenants.'

Recognition began to dawn. The man's face and build were not familiar, but . . . that voice. He knew the voice, even if he couldn't quite place it.

The ogre tensed, spear half raised, as the man reached for the saddlebags on his horse. But rather than grab the large axe, the human dug inside the bag and removed what appeared to be a skull. His brow furrowed in puzzlement, Davro only barely reacted quickly enough to catch it as the human tossed it toward him.

'Perhaps this will jog your memory, Davro.'

Davro stared at the skull – no, not truly a skull, a *helm* – that had landed in the palm of his hand. His eye widened, his breath catching in his throat. Ever so slowly, he felt his fingers slacken of their own accord, and he heard, seemingly from a great distance, the sound of his spear striking the ground.

'Lord Rebaine . . .'

'So you're *not* trying to conquer Imphallion?' Davro asked for perhaps the fourth time. The ogre, it seemed, was having some trouble with the concept.

They sat comfortably inside Davro's house, the ogre perched upon the stump, Corvis on the thick mattress that smelled unpleasantly of untanned hides. Each held before him a mug of broth, Corvis having supplied his own mug from his traveling gear. He'd insisted on letting the ogre take a moment to get over his shock before he'd explained his purpose in coming here, even told him to take a minute to feed the pigs, who were by then squealing angrily at the delay in their dinner.

And then he'd told Davro an abbreviated version of the tale: his escape from the basement of the Hall of Meeting in Denathere, his years with Tyannon, and, most important, the attack on Mellorin.

'No,' Corvis said again, not quite suppressing a smile. 'Shocking as it may sound, I'm not out to conquer anything. I just want to stop Audriss from doing it while I still have a family and a home to protect.'

'You might just make a deal with him,' Davro suggested. 'He must know that you weren't – umm, aren't – someone to trifle with. Ask for . . . What'd you say it was called, Chelenshire? Ask for Chelenshire to be left alone, and let him get on with it.'

'It's not so simple, Davro. I know the kind of person Audriss is. That would just be a challenge to his authority. No, he's got to be stopped cold. And I can't do it alone.'

Davro exhaled slowly; it took Corvis a moment to recognise the sound as nothing less than a hefty, ogre-sized sigh. 'Sorry to disappoint you, after coming all this way. But you're not my lord anymore, Rebaine. Quite frankly, I haven't thought about you or the war in years, and I've got no intention of starting up again now. You'll have to find someone else to help you.'

His eye was set, steady, unflinching. It was evident that the ogre was entirely serious, and prepared to be stubborn about it.

'I never saw you as the farmer type, Davro. You must be bored out of your mind here.'

'Actually,' Davro said, his voice indignant, 'I'm quite happy.'

'Herding sheep?' Corvis asked mockingly. 'Raising pigs?'

'I like sheep and pigs.'

'I need your help, Davro. I can't afford to take no for an answer.'

His eye narrowing further, the ogre looked his visitor slowly up and down.

'I'm not entirely sure,' he said slowly, 'you can afford *not* to. It's been a lot of years, Rebaine. You're not as intimidating as you used to be.'

Corvis rose to his feet. 'I can still take you, Davro. I may not be as strong as I used to be, but I'm as fast as I ever was. And Sunder's just as sharp. Besides, the magics I control—'

'I don't think so. I don't see your amulet anywhere.' The ogre smiled at the sudden consternation on the human's face. 'Your soldiers weren't *all* brainless idiots, Rebaine. I'm no expert on sorcery, but I've seen enough wizards in action to know you never did cast spells the way the rest of them did. And that pendant was the only thing you ever carried constantly that didn't serve any real purpose. I can put two and two together as well as anyone.'

'It could have just been sentimental,' Corvis muttered gruffly.

'On you? Hardly. Besides, if you had your magic, you'd have convinced me already.'

'I know a few spells yet, Davro.'

'Maybe. But not, I think, enough to worry me. And I just don't think you're prepared to attack me head-to-head. No, Rebaine, it's time for you to be on your way. It was nice talking to you again. We should do this again in another seventeen years.'

A shadow fell across Corvis' face, and he took a single, slow step toward the ogre. Davro's hand dropped to his spear.

'I *really* wouldn't recommend it, Rebaine.'

Another step. 'You took an oath of service, Davro. Remember? I don't recall that there was an expiration date on it.'

'An oath in Chalsene's name,' the ogre protested. 'I don't worship him anymore. I've got about as far from him as possible, in fact, in case the pigs and the sheep hadn't told you as much. And from the look of things, I don't think you do, either.'

Corvis smiled harshly. 'Truth be told, Davro, I never did. I only accepted the oath because I knew your people worshipped him. But whether you want to acknowledge it or not, I doubt the Night-Bringer takes oaths in his name so lightly.'

Davro's hand clenched and unclenched rapidly on the haft of his spear, his palms sweating, his expression apprehensive. Still, he shook his head. 'I'll take my chances.'

Corvis all but shrank, the aura of looming violence fading away, until he was again nothing more than a traveller on a long journey, one better suited to a man many years younger.

'Then there's nothing more I can say,' he said dejectedly. 'If that's your final answer, I'll be on my way.'

'It is,' Davro said with a succinct nod. Corvis mirrored it, and moved toward the doorway.

He paused as he pushed the curtain aside, as though a thought just popped to mind. 'You realise that I need the ogres whether or not you're with me. Your people make unstoppable shock troops.'

'You go right ahead,' Davro told him, his mind already drifting to other matters. 'If you've got enough to pay them, I'm sure they'll be more than happy to fight for you again.'

'But if you were with me, they might join up without pay. You could play it up, the return of the great Lord Rebaine and all that.'

'Rebaine . . . Leave.'

'The thing is,' Corvis continued as if he hadn't heard, 'if I *do* approach your tribe without you, and identify myself, they're certain to ask me where you are. I'm sure your family is quite concerned for your well-being. As a sympathetic family man myself, I'm afraid I'd feel obliged to tell them where you are and what you've been doing with yourself.

Purely for their own peace of mind, of course. I'm sure you understand.'

Davro roared to his feet, his spear grasped tightly in both hands. The entire house shook as the ogre pounded across the room, fully determined to skewer his former lord and master like a roast.

But Corvis no longer stood in the doorway; he'd leapt from the house the instant he'd finished speaking. He stood now on open ground, Sunder held skillfully in a two-handed grip, spinning slowly before him. With room to maneuver, his own agility might just counter the ogre's twin advantages of strength and reach. Davro skidded to a halt just outside weapon range, and the two slowly circled. Rascal, ears flattened back against his skull, interrupted his meal of valley grass to watch the drama unfolding, and the sheep set up a loud communal bleat.

'I am going,' Davro informed the human coldly, his voice even deeper than usual, 'to kill you.'

'Do you really think that's your best option, Davro? There's a pretty good chance you'll lose.'

'I'll take that chance.'

'Even if you win,' Corvis pressed, his voice anxious, 'I'll get in a few good shots.'

'I'll heal.'

'Eventually, maybe. But you won't be able to care for your animals, Davro! How are you going to manage?'

The ogre frowned around tusks glistening with spittle, but he kept circling.

'Or you can come with me, Davro. Just until Audriss is dealt with. Then you can disappear again. I'll even help you "die" in front of your tribe, if you want. You can come back home without any fear of being bothered again.'

If anything, Davro's scowl grew even darker. But he stopped circling and slowly lowered his spear to point at the grass. 'You wish to prevent Audriss from destroying the life you've built by destroying the one I have?'

Corvis shrugged and let Sunder drop to his side.

'Hypocrisy, as it happens, is a sin that I find I can live with.' Then he smiled ever so slightly. 'But I've no intention of destroying your life, Davro. Just interrupting it for a little while.'

'I could just as easily be wounded or killed doing what you're asking.'

Corvis shrugged. 'Come with me, that *might* happen. Take me on here – with my magics, with Sunder – or make me tell your tale to your tribe, and it *will* happen. Better odds,' he added with a smile as forced as it was friendly, 'if you co-operate.'

'You're really not going to give me a choice in this, are you?' Even in the ogre's rumbling tone, it sounded almost plaintive.

'Not as such. If it makes you feel any better, I don't really have much of a choice myself.'

'Amazingly enough, Rebaine, it doesn't.' The shaft of Davro's spear quivered, a hound anxious to be let off its leash, but Corvis was right – helping him was the least risky of the options he had left, and they both knew it.

'Fantastic,' Corvis said as Davro's shoulders slumped with a frustrated grunt. 'I do need you to do something for me, though.'

'And I've so been looking forward to repaying you for all the favours you've done me. Whatever can I help you with?'

Corvis ignored the ogre's sarcasm. 'I need you to take an oath that you won't run out on me the first chance you get. That you'll stay with me, fight alongside me, and in general do your utmost to help me complete my task. And most of all, that you won't kill me in my sleep.'

It was a vow that both could trust, should Davro willingly take it. There were few ogres alive – indeed, few members of *any* race or people – who would risk the blasphemy of breaking an oath in their own god's name.

'Not the trusting sort, are you, Rebaine?'

'As it happens, I'm not a complete idiot. You can't risk fighting me at my best, but sleeping men tend not to defend themselves all that well. If you're coming with me, I have to know that you're *really* with me.'

Davro shook his head. 'I don't worship Chalsene anymore, I told you that.'

'I know. So swear by whichever of the gods you *do* honour now.'

Davro flushed, looked down, and muttered something.

'What was that?'

'I said,' the ogre grumbled, 'I now offer my prayers to Arhylla.'

Rebaine raised an eyebrow. 'She'll do.'

'Fine. I swear by Arhylla Earth-Mother that I will aid you in your task to the best of my ability until that task is complete, or you release me from this vow.' He frowned. 'Will that do, or do you need it carved in stone and signed in blood?'

'That works. Thanks.'

'Who's going to care for my animals?' the ogre demanded.

'Can you leave them enough food to last for a week or two?'

Davro's brow furrowed in thought, causing his horn to quiver. 'Some of it'll go bad by the end, and the bugs will be horrific, but I think so. This is going to take a lot longer than two weeks, though. Hell, it would take longer than that just to reach my tribe!'

'Indeed. But we're not going straight to meet with your people. There's another stop we've got to make on the way.'

'Oh? Are we hiring a shepherd?'

'We are going,' Corvis said with exaggerated patience, 'to find Seilloah.'

'Oh.'

'Once she's with us, I'm sure that, with her abilities, we can arrange something for your animals.'

'Assuming,' Davro said darkly, 'she's got any interest in joining with us. Or were you planning to blackmail her, too?'

Corvis laughed. 'I don't think that'll be necessary. Why don't you go get your stuff, Davro. We need to get moving.

And polish that sword, for the gods' sakes! There's enough dust on that thing to choke a wyvern!'

'I'm helping you because you haven't left me a choice,' the ogre growled. 'It doesn't mean you go back to being my superior officer, and it doesn't mean you get to pull rank. You let me worry about polishing my own sword, thank you very much.'

'Always sound advice,' Corvis said with a smirk. 'I'll just wait for you here then.'

Grumbling, Davro stormed back into his house.

CHAPTER SIX

The mounted lancers charged across the shallow fen, weapons bristling and protruding like a steel hedge – or perhaps the back end of an armoured porcupine – and the towering ogres set their feet and their spears to meet that charge.

Fantails of watery mud plumed from the horse's hooves, blotting out the world beyond the attacking knights, and the young ogre called Davro wondered again what could possibly be driving them on. The sucking mud clutched greedily at the horses' hooves, slowing their advance, and the humans outnumbered the ogres by less than three to one: suicidal odds by any reckoning. Yet still they had come, into reaches well known to be part of ogre lands, as though determined to throw their lives away.

Lances and spears met armour and flesh with a deafening crash, and then there was little time to think at all. Davro thrust about him, his spear plunging through human and horse alike – and sometimes both at once. To his left, a knight stepped within his reach, swinging a broadsword with both hands, and Davro casually kicked his attacker with enough strength to buckle both the armour and the bones beneath. Another, still mounted on his wide-eyed charger, stabbed the jagged end of a broken lance at the ogre's midsection. Davro plunged his spear point-first into the earth, caught the lance with both hands, and used that grip to literally fling the knight from his saddle. Before the fallen fellow could even hope to rise, Davro had recovered his spear and – a paean to Chalsene Night-Bringer on his lips – plunged it through the knight's chest.

Still, though the ogres had no doubt of their eventual victory, the battle was not going quite so easily for others as it was for Davro. More than one lance had found a home in ogre hide, and the humans' swords were sharp, their armour sturdy. Much of the blood spilling onto the fen was not human, and not every corpse to fall that day was possessed of two eyes.

From the thickest knot of fighting, Davro heard the voice of Gundrek – the tribe's chieftain, an old ogre tough as saddle leather – raised in a fearsome war cry. Swiftly, the younger ogre moved toward his revered leader. He would never have insulted Gundrek by calling out to ask if the chieftain required aid, but neither would he let the venerable warrior be borne down by sheer weight of numbers.

From beyond the gathered knights and warhorses, Davro's spear flashed. Hot blood sprayed across Gundrek's face and horn, and the wrinkled ogre's face split in a savage grin. His own jagged sword lashed up and out, cleaving through the torso and the mount of a knight who had spun to face the sudden assault from behind.

Penned in from two sides, the humans attacking the chieftain had lost the advantage of mobility – and against the ogres, mobility was the only advantage they had.

The rest was not battle, but butchery. With neither need nor desire for prisoners, the ogres moved through the battlefield, slaughtering those who had fallen but survived. Not even the horses were spared. And then, too, were slaughtered those ogres whose wounds would have proved crippling, allowing them to die a warriors death on the battlefield rather than returning home as a burden to their tribe.

Only then, when the ogres had fed death its fill, did some of the uninjured tend to the wounds of those who might yet recover, while others set about efficiently carving the edible meats from the bodies of fallen horses and men.

'Its peculiar, though,' Gundrek mused in the harsh tongue of the ogres as he examined the last of the fallen. 'What could have driven them to such folly?'

Davro could only shrug. 'Who understands the ways of humans? I certainly do not.'

He and Gundrek – indeed, all the surviving ogres of the band – froze as one as the morning haze of the swamp finally burned away beneath the rising sun. There, at the edges of their lands, waited another human force, far larger than the first. A dozen clashing styles of dress and armour made them appear almost slapdash, but there was nothing haphazard in how they held their blades.

'An advance force?' Davro asked, gesturing at the corpses around them even as he straightened and readied his spear once more. 'To test our strength?'

'Perhaps,' Gundrek conceded, 'but I think maybe not. There is something . . .'

As if to confirm his guess, a single figure rode forward from the assembled throng. He towered high upon a mighty charger, and his armour was a monstrosity of blackened steel and polished bone.

'I drove my enemy into the marsh,' he called, though only Gundrek, Davro, and a few of the other ogres could understand his words, 'in the hopes of slowing them down, so that I might run them to ground. That they have led me to you is greater fortune than I might have hoped. Otherwise, I'd have lost many days searching for your home.'

Gundrek stood tall and stepped forward, Davro a mere step behind. 'And who are you,' he asked in heavily accented Human, 'that you should seek us out?'

'I am Corvis Rebaine. And you,' the human added, with an expansive gesture that encompassed the vast array of broken bodies, 'are precisely what I need.'

'Are you sure you can keep up?' Corvis asked, concerned.

'As long as you don't have the poor beast galloping the entire way, yes.' Davro actually huffed. 'The day a healthy ogre can't outlast a horse is the day I hang up my sword for good.'

'Umm, Davro, you tried that already. That's why I found you herding pigs.'

'Oh, shut up.'

Corvis, his head bobbing slightly with Rascal's methodical gait, watched around him as the ground passed beneath their feet. The grasses glowed with a jade sheen in the light of the afternoon sun, and the grazing animals watched them pass with a minimum of alarm. Clearly the beasts of this place had few worries or concerns. The trees, though sporadic, were tall, their leaves thick in the full bloom of health. A few white clouds drifted over the mountains, casting enormous shadows upon the valley.

'This is a beautiful place you picked to live,' Corvis admitted. 'I'm surprised there isn't a settlement here.'

'Don't get any ideas, Rebaine. I like it nice and empty.'

'Relax, Davro. I'm not moving in, just commenting. And I promise you, I'll do my best to get you back here just as soon as possible.'

'Why, how kind of you. That's so considerate, I could just squat.'

'I'm trying to make conversation,' Corvis protested. 'To make the journey go faster.'

'I see. You know what's even better than trying to make conversation?'

'What?'

'*Not* trying to make conversation.'

'Perhaps I'll be quiet, then.'

'Miracles do happen.'

Corvis, deciding he wasn't apt to get the better of this particular conversation, chose to watch the miles and the scenery pass in silence.

It was Davro, in fact, who finally broke the hush. Just as they reached the edges of the foothills, where even the tiny knolls tapered off into sprawling flatlands, he asked, 'Rebaine . . . How by all the reeking hells did you even *find* me?'

The former warlord grinned down from his perch atop Rascal's back. 'I didn't have to find you. I cast a locating spell on each of my officers and advisers at the start of my campaign twenty years ago. Never saw any reason to dispel the enchantment, so it's still active. All I have to do is concentrate on you, and I've got an exact direction and approximate distance.'

Davro scowled, his tusks quivering. 'Didn't trust us?'

'Hell, no!' Corvis laughed briefly. 'I didn't trust anyone at the time, though, so you shouldn't take it personally.'

'Fine. So you can find me. Seilloah and – what was that reptile's name? Valescienn. You know how to get to them, too?'

'Well . . .' Corvis frowned briefly, an expression not lost on the ogre stomping along beside him, flattening the flora as he walked. 'Seilloah, yes.'

'Not Valescienn?' Davro asked in mock sympathy. 'Did the poor widdle sorcerer overestimate his spelly-welly?' He grinned wickedly at the disgust sliding across Corvis' features.

'Something's disrupted the spell on Valescienn. Not sure what it might have been, or even if it was deliberate or not.'

'Someone broke one of your spells by accident? My admiration grows by leaps and bounds.'

'It's an old spell, damn it! And a small one! It's entirely possible—'

'I bet one of Rheah Vhoune's spells would have held up.'

Corvis glowered. 'You're not planning to make this journey pleasant, are you?'

Davro looked at him seriously, his single eye glaring straight into the human's own. 'Not in the slightest. Why should I be the only one who's miserable?'

Another mile passed in silence. The terrain flattened,

broken only by grasses waving in the wind and an occasional copse of fir trees.

'So where *is* Seilloah, O Master Wizard?' the ogre said abruptly. 'You still haven't told me where we're going.'

Corvis, who'd hoped his companion might forget the issue for a while longer, squared his shoulders.

'Well, you know her fondness for – umm, sylvan surroundings, right?'

'Rebaine . . .'

'And we know that, being who and what she is, she doesn't have a lot of the innate prejudices and superstitions a lot of the common folk are prone to.'

Davro's jaw was beginning to twitch. 'Rebaine? *Where?*'

Corvis sighed. 'If I'm judging the distance right . . . Theaghl-gohlatch.'

The ogre drew back, his eye widening so far his entire face stretched. He hissed, little more than an indrawn breath, and the hand that wasn't already clutching his spear dropped instinctively to the hilt of his newly polished sword.

'You're mad! You've gone absolutely, stark-raving insane!'

'I'm as sane as I ever was,' Corvis said mildly.

'Oh, *that's* reassuring! No! Not a chance! We might as well just have it out right here! I'll have a better chance of getting home that way than I ever will in Theaghl-gohlatch.'

'I doubt it's as bad as all that.'

'Go to hell. You humans think of my people as savage – and maybe we are – but one of the first things we ever learn, before we set a single finger on a spear or a sword, is that death should accomplish something. You want me to face a few hundred soldiers armed only with a ladle and a live turkey, well, there's honour to be gained dying in battle, so I might at least think it over before telling you to go rut yourself. But there is no way I'd even consider throwing my life away for no purpose at all! No. I'm not going.'

'I seem to recall an oath, Davro.'

'That was before I knew about *this* lunacy! I said I'd help to the best of my ability. Dying impaled on a bloodsucking tree by some forest demon is *not* the best of my ability.'

'Fine,' Corvis snapped, exasperated with the entire affair. 'Walk with me as far as the edge of the forest. Then you can make camp and sit with Rascal while I go in and find Seilloah.'

'And what am I supposed to do while I'm waiting?'

'I don't care! Sing campfire songs, tell the horse ghost stories – whatever!' Corvis kicked Rascal into a brisk trot, unconcerned with any reply the ogre might make.

And that, with the exception of essential observations such as 'We'll camp here,' and 'Snore like that again and I'll shove a rabbit up your nose,' was the extent of the conversation for the next five days. The miles passed at a crawl – the plains alone stretched on for almost three days, draining a surprisingly large portion of the rations Corvis carried.

Fortunately for the travellers' stomachs, the plains gradually gave way to a thin wood that, according to Corvis' map and the tug of his spell, would eventually thicken into the nigh-impassable forest of Theaghl-gohlatch. The wood was benign, at least initially, not to mention teeming with deer, wild rabbits, and a plethora of other edible creatures – including the occasional owl, which Davro insisted was a delicacy among his people. Upon entering the woodlands, Corvis retrieved a short recurved bow from his saddlebag, and set out to kill something a bit meatier than a shriveled apricot or flattened fig. He hadn't bagged anything larger than a rabbit on their first night in the woods, but it took only a few tries the second evening before he put a steel-tipped shaft into the side of a large buck. Davro broke several thick branches from the nearby trees and whittled them into something approaching Y's. One sharpened sapling later, they were sitting beside a cheerful fire, watching the animal slowly roast.

His tongue loosened and his attitude mollified by the prospect of a real meal, Davro condescended to speak that evening. 'I suggest you smoke as much of this as possible and take it with you. You won't want to shoot anything once you actually enter Theaghl-gohlatch.'

Corvis smiled around a mouthful of venison, trying to catch the juices before they rolled down his chin. 'I think you're being just a bit paranoid, Davro. Legends and superstition.'

'You'll change your tune quickly enough when some banshee's sucking your soul out through your pupils.'

Corvis' only immediate response was a muted chuckle – but when he woke Davro for watch sometime around midnight, the ogre couldn't help but notice the heavy scent of smoke mingling with the succulent aroma of the meat.

It was roughly four hours after noon the next day when Davro's steady pace jerked to a sudden halt, Corvis pulling Rascal up alongside him. They stared in silence at the sight rising from the earthen floor to greet them.

'I'm going to take a wild stab at this,' Corvis said quietly, 'and say that we're here.'

It appeared as though the gods had decided, on a whim, that the forest needed a wall to spruce it up. Thick and heavy, consisting primarily of trees far older than those through which the travellers had passed, it formed a solid barrier. Between and around the ancient moss-covered trunks sprouted a variety of bracken and brambles, rough-edged leaves and needle-tipped thorns visible even in the dim light. If Corvis had half a dozen men with axes, he might have carved a man-sized passage in time to do any good. As it was, it appeared impossible for even a lone man, unmounted, to make his way into the thickets of Theaghl-gohlatch.

No way except for one perfectly clear path cutting through the impenetrable mass of trees, a mountain cave transported to the forest depths. It gaped open, an ovoid orifice that Corvis firmly insisted to himself did *not* look like a mouth, just as the overhanging branches that protruded into the tunnel did *not* look like fangs. Moisture, possibly dew or collected rainwater, trickled from some of those branches to drip irregularly onto the dirt below.

'I hate this,' Corvis said simply.

'Can't imagine why,' the ogre told him. 'Legend and superstition.'

'Yes, but it's an awfully *dark* legend and superstition.'

'Can't say I'd recommend carrying a torch in there, either. Some of those branches are pretty low hanging.'

Corvis shook his head and then determinedly slid down from the saddle. 'I'm not entirely without magic, Davro. I can make light enough to see.' Brusquely, he adjusted the sword at his left side to a more comfortable angle and slung Sunder's baldric over his left shoulder to rest at his right hip.

'Armour?' Davro asked.

'Not in there. I'd rather be able to move.'

The ogre shrugged. 'Your call. If you're not here in two days, I'm calling you dead and going home. Any later, and I won't get back to my animals before the last of the food runs out or goes bad.'

'I told you, Seilloah will take care of that.'

'Only if you're alive to ask her to.'

'Fair point. All right, Davro, wish me luck.'

'Why?'

Taking a deep breath to steady himself – after all, there was nothing to be worried about (and that gaping, slavering hole did *not* look like a mouth, damn it!) – Corvis stepped inside.

If someone had simply tossed a heavy cloth over his head, it could not have grown more instantly dark. Even though the passage loomed open behind him, the light itself seemed to lose its nerve, refusing to enter the depths of Theaghl-gohlatch. Corvis wondered if it was possible for light to be afraid of the dark, and then quickly gave up the notion.

All right, Corvis, focus. Evil warlord. Terror of the East. Not about to let a forest stop us, are we?

Shaking off his doubts, Corvis muttered the words to a minor incantation. His surroundings began, barely perceptible at first but with growing rapidity, to brighten. He kept the illumination down to a muted glow, little more than a moderately sized lantern. He wanted to see, but he also wanted to disturb as few of the denizens of this place as possible. Somehow, the thought of flooding the surrounding hundred yards with daylight didn't seem even vaguely inconspicuous.

Now that sight was more than a memory of happier moments, Corvis studied the environment, one hand hovering within a hairbreadth of Sunder.

The earth beneath his feet was a thick, tightly packed soil that clung tenaciously to the soles of his boots as he braved the darkness. Here and there, a small sapling, a hint of brush, or a far-ranging root would intrude into his path, but by and large he seemed to tread upon a road deliberately cut through the heart of the wood. On either side, reaching into a canopy of leaves too dark to make out, the trees lined up, soldiers of a relentless, disciplined army. Only a handful were visible at any given time, briefly touched by the light he cast as he walked, and just as rapidly fading back into the permanent gloom that was their entire world.

And if the branches quivered where the light touched them, if the leaves and twigs drew back from the gleaming, well, that was just a trick of the breeze and the rustling of small animals. Right?

The roof above, interwoven branches and heavy leaves, was lost in shadow beyond the range of his meager light. Corvis felt that even had he cast his spell with all the power at his command, the weight hanging over his head would still appear as nothing more than a dark, threatening veil.

The rustling of the trees grew more violent. Corvis could hear the gentle whisper of leaf upon leaf, the scraping of twigs and branches. The shadows cast by the looming trees danced across his face and arms, phantoms that threatened to claw at his eyes, his mind, his soul.

Shadows? On his face? Corvis suddenly swallowed, his throat dry as if he'd gulped down a mouthful of desert sand. *He* cast the spell; *he* was the only source of light! The shadows should be falling *away* from him.

Yet the flickering and dancing continued before him. And even as he glanced in growing apprehension to either side, determined to spot the shadows he knew must be stretching away from him into the forest, his eyes could pick out nothing but a wall of gloom, a curtain of darkness hanging, impenetrable, behind the first of what must have been countless rows of the ancient forest giants. He felt each of the hairs on his neck slowly stand up, and the Terror of the East barely repressed a shiver.

Slowly, Corvis looked back the way he came. He'd walked only a dozen steps or so into the heavy, unnatural night of Theaghl-gohlatch. Still, he was not even remotely surprised to discover the passageway sealed behind him; it was simply too apropos. Where before there was a portal – menacing but perfectly functional – into the forgotten world of light and life, there stood now only more of the implacable forest: layers upon layers of trees standing between him and whatever was out there.

With little other option, then, Corvis went forward.

I'll admit this much: If – when – I do get out of here, I'm going to pay a damn sight more attention to Davro's legends and superstition!

Only when he'd maintained his steady pace for several moments, and had grown as accustomed to the alien surroundings as he was ever likely to, did further details penetrate his numbed mind. Sounds – quiet, distant, muted, but present all the same – slowly worked their way into his ears. The call of an owl, the chitter of a squirrel of some sort – they were all there, and more. For all the fear that lurked in this place like another hungry predator, the wood apparently contained all the requisite woodland life of any other forest. He found that oddly comforting. Hell, if a squirrel could live here, the place couldn't be *all* bad, could it?

But this ephemeral respite proved just another taunting phantom, as he realised that the sounds never changed. No matter where he walked or what noise he made, the calls of the animals remained unaltered, neither drawing nearer nor rushing away in sudden fear. What briefly seemed a comfort was now mocking him, mocking his foolishness in daring to hope. It seemed as though all he heard – all he would ever hear – were the echoes of life that had not existed in this place for untold ages.

There! A sudden flash of movement on the path before him, barely within the last flickering inches of his light spell's range. Nothing tangible, nothing identifiable, just motion where before there was none, and then back to the same, featureless trail.

Corvis, one hand upon each weapon, had all but convinced himself it was merely his imagination when he spotted it again, this time vanishing into the woods on his right. With lightning speed Corvis drew his sword, sending it whistling through the air. There was no sound of impact, no blood upon the blade. Somewhere, in the depths of Theaghl-gohlatch, the chittering of one of the squirrels slowly twisted and warped itself into a hair-raising cackle of malevolent glee.

It – they – were all around him now, darting in and out on the fringes of his light: ghosts and shadows, movement without form, never remaining long enough for him to make out any detail but the simple presence of – presence. Laughter echoed from the trees around him, cloaked in the call of the hunting owl or the rustling of the leaves. Another blur of movement, nearer than before. Corvis gasped at the sudden touch of fire across his left arm. He stared in shock at the wound – three perfectly parallel gashes, deep, bloody, and already swelling with some unnatural infection – that marred the surface of his skin.

Fighting the urge to lash out blindly around him, Corvis carefully returned the sword to its scabbard, and drew Sunder from his right hip with a quick, fluid motion. The Kholben Shiar flared at the feel of flesh and blood against its grip, exulted at the sense of fear and pain and, most delectable of all, the burning fury in its wielder.

The laughter ceased in a sudden hiss of indrawn breath from among the nearest trees. '*Enemy!*' It was a whisper, but it carried clearly across the unobstructed path. It cradled within itself the voice of legions, though it was spat forth as a single word, from a single source.

A heartless grin settled across Corvis' face. If they feared, they could be killed.

'Enemy, is it now?' he called back, his voice steady, his tone challenging. 'So what was I before?'

Again, an infinity of hisses breathed as one. *'Prey . . .'*

'Ah. Given the options, I prefer my current status.'

Silence from the trees. Even the distant sounds of animals had faded.

'What's the matter?' he called, taunting. 'Not the way prey's supposed to act? Not an enemy you'd care to face? Maybe you should have thought of that before you tried taking a piece of—'

The path, indeed the entire forest, slowly tilted upward before his eyes. He pitched forward, half catching himself with an ungraceful stagger that brought him to one knee. He glanced around wildly, fully expecting a sudden rush of . . . whatever he was facing.

No attack came, but the simple movement of his head set the entire world to spinning. The butt-end of Sunder smacked the ground, its steadying influence the only thing keeping Corvis even remotely upright.

What's happening to me? The wound isn't that bad! It doesn't even hurt any – oh . . .

Though difficult to see through his blurring vision, the gashes along his arm had swelled horribly, spewing blood and a noxious-looking pus into the soil around him. There must have been some anesthetic in the poison, or infection, or whatever coursed through his flesh.

Fueled by spite as much as anything else, Corvis dragged himself to his feet, leaning on Sunder as if the ancient weapon were a simple cane. Then, though every muscle in his body protested, he lifted the axe and dropped unevenly into a ready stance.

'You think I'm impressed?' he shouted, his voice grown hoarse as his body battled the raging contagion. 'I'm not!

Poison or no, I'll take you with me!' He didn't know what he was shouting anymore, only that the words needed to keep coming, that defiance alone kept him on his feet. 'Come on! One at a time or all at once! I'll drag you into hell with me!'

And he thought, for an instant, that his unseen tormentors might oblige. Several trees at the illumination's edge began to writhe and shift, as though something large moved through the branches. Unable to see straight, scarce able to stand, Corvis faced the coming threat.

Nothing emerged from the madly thrashing trees. Instead – or so it seemed to Corvis' failing eyes – the branches of the wooden behemoths stretched and split, lacing their ends together at obscene angles, until the abstract suggestion of a face appeared, woven from bark-covered tendrils. Though no eyes hung in those empty sockets, Corvis was convinced that the thing was glaring down at him.

'I . . . ,' he began unsteadily, but the face in the trees gave him no time to speak.

The leaves shuffled in wildly uneven patterns behind the artificial visage, the branches scraped together. And, impossibly, the random cacophony of sound resolved itself into a raspy, but fully intelligible, voice.

'Follow,' it scraped down at him. Then the branches fell limp, the face dispersing back into its component branches.

Corvis wondered if the entire thing was some twisted hallucination. But no, the trees leaned aside, branches sweeping back, clearing a second, smaller trail that diverged from the main path. Corvis thought he heard a scream of rage from deep within the trees behind him, but no one and nothing appeared to stop him from taking the newly offered route.

Head spinning, chest and legs burning, Corvis stumbled onto the smaller trail. He leaned heavily on Sunder, which quivered in disappointment as the battle and blood were left behind. More than once he stumbled and would have fallen, and more than once a heavy branch protruded into the path where it was most needed, presenting itself to steady him. The trail stretched on forever, though Corvis' poison-racked senses had lost all track of time and he hadn't the first notion how long he'd wandered this endless darkness. The passageway twisted and turned randomly. He wondered, with what coherent thought remained to him, if the damn place was just leading him in circles, waiting for him to lie down and die.

Once, in a lucid moment, he removed a length of bandage from his pack. Shearing off the end, he tied the sliver tightly around the tip of a branch. That, at least, would tell him if he was retracing his own path.

When he came across the strip of bandage some minutes later, tied tightly around the branch of what was blatantly a different tree, Corvis abandoned himself to whatever force guided his steps.

For an eternity he stumbled on. His spell of illumination slowly faded, until the feeble glow could barely show him where the trail left off and the endless trees began. He felt himself drenched in sweat, and he cycled regularly from the heat of fever to the chill of the grave as his body tried to burn out the infection. All feeling drained from his arm and it no longer responded to his commands, moving only occasionally as it spasmed without apparent cause.

He was forced, ever more frequently, to stop and rest, leaning against the trunk of a tree or huddled by the side of the road, vomiting up the few contents of his battered and abused stomach. He thought once of the smoked meat in his pack, realising much time must have passed since his last meal, but the very notion sent him to his knees, dry-heaving.

Finally, he stumbled one time too many, and he lacked the strength to catch himself. The taste of soil coated his tongue, dirt caught in the back of his throat, and he found himself blind. He became aware of a faint tickling on his upper lip, decided it was probably an ant, and wondered deliriously if he could rotate his eyes far enough around to see it if it crawled up into his skull. Maybe if he could make himself sneeze hard enough in the right direction, he could catch an updraft and land the little bug in Davro's dinner. Assuming it was anywhere near dinnertime. Corvis laughed hysterically, choking on the soil, and flipped over like a landed fish. No sense in choking to death while he waited for the infection to kill him. He laughed again.

And then, as his vision cleared for just a moment, he saw it. Not fifteen feet from him, visible only as a vague shape in the last sputtering remnants of his light spell, was a building. Nothing more than a simple hut, but it meant *someone* was here.

Or had been here, at any rate. If nothing else, it offered a more comfortable place to die. With the absolute last of his reserves, Corvis drove himself to his feet and staggered through the front door.

'I see you got my message,' Seilloah told him.

Everything went black.

CHAPTER SEVEN

Nathaniel Espa – Knight of Imphallion, and currently Duke Lorum's eyes amid the growing turmoil in the east – knelt at the bedside of the torn and broken shape that had once been an old friend, and willed the tears not to come.

The Lady Alseth, wife of Sir Wyrrim, laid a hand on Nathan's shoulder. 'It would've meant a lot to him that you came,' she whispered through a throat torn ragged with sorrow. 'It means a lot to me, too.'

'I wish it had mattered,' Nathan said softly. 'I tried to get here sooner, Alseth, I truly did.'

'You couldn't have done any more,' she offered gently. 'Not even the great Nathaniel Espa could have snuck or fought his way into Rahariem, not with so many of the invaders still inside.'

'Maybe I could've had you smuggled out faster,' he protested limply. 'It's just, by the time I knew Ivriel might prove a safe haven . . .'

'You saved me, Nathan. You saved my son, and you allowed Wyrrim to die in a bed, rather than in some dungeon. We're grateful.'

Nathan nodded once, placed a palm upon the forehead of his dead friend, and rose. 'What was he doing on the battlefield at his age, anyway?' he asked.

'Come, Nathan, you've known him longer than I have. You know he'd never sit by while his city was attacked. Besides,' she added darkly, 'it wouldn't have mattered.'

Nathan frowned and escorted her into the next room,

where they both sat and pretended to sip at goblets of wine that neither of them really tasted. 'What do you mean?'

'It was horrible. Even once the walls fell, and the city surrendered, that wasn't good enough. Every noble who had more than a few household soldiers to his name, and every ranking Guild leader – they were *all* rounded up and herded into the keep. I don't know what went on in there, but some of the men who went in unwounded came out looking worse . . .' She choked briefly, but continued. 'Worse than Wyrrim. And many didn't come out at all.'

Despite the redness and the tears, her eyes remained steady as she stared into the knight's widening gaze. 'I've learned enough about war from Wyrrim to know that this wasn't about interrogation or military secrets. This was about fear – and maybe punishment, though the gods alone know for what. Whatever rare civility is normally to be found in war, you'll find none here.'

'And you're certain this isn't a Cephiran invasion?'

'Quite. Some of the mercenaries were foreigners, certainly, but many more were Imphallian. This is someone else, Nathan.'

Nathaniel Espa allowed his eyes to hover once more over the body of his old friend – a corpse that, even hours after death, still soaked the sheets with bloody wounds. Then, slowly, he turned his gaze outward, and wondered grimly what new terror had emerged from the east.

'Idiots!' Lorum, Duke of Taberness and Regent Proper of Imphallion, slammed a fist into the gold-trimmed wardrobe. It rocked dangerously and would have crashed to the floor if one of the servants hadn't dashed to steady it. 'Those bloody, unthinking idiots!'

'In all fairness, Your Grace, they're just defending what they see as their own interests.'

The regent's neatly trimmed beard actually bristled as he

scowled at his companion. 'And when the Guild halls have been reduced to rubble around their ankles, and there's a monster on the throne who won't put up with their damn pouting? How'll those "interests" fare *then*, do you think?'

Nathaniel Espa, former hero of Imphallion and now adviser to the regent and a respected landowner, raised an age-greyed eyebrow, though he refrained from letting the grin he felt actually show on his face. The Lorum of old never had the nerve to speak that way, not about the Guilds, and certainly not to his old mentor. But the regent, having led the kingdom through the hard years of reconstruction after Rebaine's defeat, was made of sterner stuff. In attitude, if not in build, he'd almost come to resemble the enraged ursine adorning his noble crest.

A damn good thing, too, since the appearance of Audriss seemed destined to lead Lorum, and all Imphallion, into yet another war.

Since the Serpent first appeared, Lorum had lobbied with the Guilds for a consolidation of power. The division of governmental responsibility was all well and good during peacetime, he argued vehemently, but an army without a single commander could not prevail against a well-prepared foe. He cited precedent, pointing out that Imphallion's armies fell before Rebaine's advance almost twenty years ago, until all the nobles and the Guilds fielded a unified force. They would have to do so again if they hoped to repel this new enemy, this Serpent, Audriss.

But the Guildmasters were obstinate, and most resisted any such idea. 'Audriss is not as big a threat as Rebaine,' they insisted. 'Denathere got careless; the other cities are more than capable of defending themselves. Let the Guilds field their forces as needed to protect their interests. There's no need to overturn a system that has worked for hundreds of years.'

'It *hasn't* worked for hundreds of years!' Lorum had argued, over and over again. 'It didn't work seventeen years ago!' But most refused to listen, and those few Guildmasters farsighted enough to see the wisdom in his proposal were afraid of speaking out too loudly in his support for fear of alienating their brethren. And so the resistance to Audriss's advance continued: piecemeal, sporadic, and utterly ineffective.

'If this entire kingdom were flooding, Nathaniel,' Lorum continued, his voice a shade calmer, 'they'd rather let the lot of us drown than swallow even a mouthful of pride.'

Nathaniel could only nod. 'True. But if Your Grace will recall, after the war, it was nearly three years before you restored the Guilds to their full authority.'

'It was necessary for the rebuilding, Nathaniel. They weren't cooperating.'

'Oh, I agree, it was your only choice. But it made you few friends in the Guilds, and they'll think twice before allowing you the same – as they would say – opportunity.'

'Damn. Damn! They won't have a kingdom left to exercise their "authority" in if we don't do something now.'

'I say we just *take* the damn armies.' Lorum and Nathaniel both turned to face the speaker, who had remained so abnormally silent that they'd all but forgotten his presence. His face was twisted in its accustomed scowl. 'They can whine all they want, but if you've got most of their men fighting for you, they can't do anything about it.'

Tall, thin, and wiry, he was the image of suppressed energy. Brown hair, cut short, matched equally brown eyes on a face incapable of smiling. His outfit was black, darker even than Lorum's own formal attire, but then he never wore anything else. His tabard sported an odd symbol indeed: an abstract shape suggesting the image of a fish, crimson-hued, on a field of ocean blue.

Not an imposing symbol, but Braetlyn was a coastal territory, grown strong from its humble beginnings as a thriving fishing community. And this young man, now in his early twenties, was Baron of Braetlyn. His name was Jassion, and it was said he'd not laughed once since Lorum's officers dug him, silent and trembling, from the pit of corpses in Denathere's Hall of Meeting.

As he grew to manhood, he'd remained determined, angry, and cold. He was not a cruel lord, no harsher of rule than any other noble; but if there was no malice in his treatment of his subjects and his fellows, neither was there kindness. To Jassion, the world held only three sorts of people: those who could be useful and were to be cooperated with, those who were useless and were to be ignored except where his responsibilities dictated otherwise, and those who were dangerous and were to be killed.

Lorum, Nathaniel, and the others put up with him because he was a relentless fighter and a skilled tactician, and because his rank demanded it. Jassion, as best they could tell, had been gracious enough to place them in the 'useful' category. Not the start of a lasting friendship, but a functional alliance, at least.

'My lord,' Nathaniel began, trying his best to sound tactful, 'I'm not convinced that's the best option at the moment . . .'

'That's fine, Espa. You're not the one I need to convince.'

Two pairs of eyes – one determined, one resigned, both angry – turned on the regent. Lorum sighed shallowly.

'Gentlemen, the enemy is out there, remember? Not inside these walls. And that includes the pair of you, understood?'

'The enemy,' Jassion shot back, 'is anyone who'd keep you from defending your kingdom and separating Audriss's damn head from his shoulders! And if the Guilds are standing in the way of that, then you'd better damn well believe you *do* have an enemy within these walls!'

The old knight stepped up beside Lorum, shaking his head sadly. 'My lord, were we to attempt to seize the Guilds' soldiers by force, Audriss might as well go home. He'd no longer have need to conquer us, because I doubt there would be much of Mecepheum left to conquer. We'd destroy ourselves long before he got here.'

Jassion scoffed. 'They wouldn't have the stones to fight back against a determined force! Once they realised their options were joining with us or dying as traitors to the Crown, they'd—'

'Die as traitors,' Lorum interrupted, 'and take a lot of our men with them. Besides, even if we could somehow pull it off, the political ramifications—'

'Political ramifications? Gods, you're talking about the survival of the kingdom! The Guilds and their politics be damned!'

The two men glared at each other, the air between them threatening to ignite. And then, as casually as if he were reaching out to open a door, Nathaniel cuffed Jassion across the face.

The young baron staggered, one hand reaching for his bloodied lip in shock, the other dropping to the pommel of his sword. 'You – you . . .'

It was, Lorum noted with some small amount of satisfaction, the first time he could remember Jassion at a loss for words.

'You have the right to disagree with His Grace,' Nathaniel informed him calmly. 'You are here, after all, for your input. But Duke Lorum is your regent, and you *will* treat him with the respect due him and his station. Am I quite clear?'

Jassion's black-gloved fingers clenched, inches shy of his weapon. He nodded once, sharply, though his eyes burned. 'Quite. My apologies if I spoke too forcefully, Your Grace. But I still feel you're making a terrible mistake in even trying to cooperate with those bovines who call themselves Guildmasters.'

'Perhaps, Sir Jassion. But I've no other option available. And do not forget yourself again. It is *my* mistake to make. You are not in command here.'

'No,' the baron spat back, his voice bitter. 'I'm not. And we may all suffer for it before this is over.' And with that pronouncement hanging between them, he strode stiffly from the room.

'He should have asked your leave to go,' Nathaniel said mildly.

Lorum didn't seem to hear. 'He's been doing this a lot recently. Storming off and vanishing for hours on end. I wonder where he goes?'

The older man shrugged. 'No place in particular, I'd wager. Jassion would never admit to it, but this is a rough time for him. This situation can't help but bring back memories of his sister. He's probably just spending a great deal of time alone with his thoughts.'

'Yes,' Lorum agreed slowly. 'That's probably it.' But he continued to gaze into the empty hallway, long after Jassion's rapid footsteps faded into memory. Absently, he fingered his signet ring, his badge of Imphallion's highest station, and he frowned. Then he shrugged.

'Come, Nathan. With or without our hotheaded baron, we've got planning to do, and little time in which to do it. Wherever Jassion's gone, I'm sure it's no concern of ours.'

CHAPTER EIGHT

'So?' Tyannon called as Corvis trudged back over the low rise. 'How does it look?'

She stood leaning against a tall, scraggly tree that offered precious little in the way of actual shade, one hand absently clutching her belly where it was just beginning to swell. Leaves crackled under her feet as she shifted her weight, and the air smelled strongly of autumn.

'The property's a steal,' Corvis said, stopping next to her and taking a moment just to inhale the scent of her hair; it had changed, ever so slightly, in recent months. Ever since . . .

'Corvis? You're doing it again.'

'Sorry. Uh, where . . . ? Right. The inn's not exactly the loveliest place I've considered staying, but it's affordable enough. We'll have a roof until the house is done. And there are a few folk in town willing to help with the carpentry for some extra coin. I don't know if we'll have the whole thing done in time for the baby, but there'll be enough to live in.

'That is, if you're still sure *this* is where you want to live? Chelenshire isn't precisely the pinnacle of civilisation . . .'

'That's why I like it,' Tyannon told him, running her free hand across his jaw. 'Are you changing your mind? You promised me—'

'No! No, not at all. Just wanted to be sure.' Corvis frowned thoughtfully, glancing back the way he'd come. 'You know, Chelenshire doesn't have much of a government, really. An official town mediator for disputes, an informal council of elders to make decisions, and that's about it. I bet with someone to teach them a better way, they could—'

'Corvis?' Tyannon's hand dropped away from his face. 'If you so much as *think* it, I promise you you'll wake up one morning with something very, very large lodged somewhere that's *really* not equipped to handle it.'

'Ouch,' Corvis began with a grin. 'Then maybe I . . .'

The words caught in his throat as he turned, nearly solid enough to choke on. Her tone had been light, her lips still turned upward in the faintest wistful smile, but her eyes were harder than Corvis had ever dreamed possible. And he heard, without either of them giving it voice, Tyannon's *real* ultimatum: *if you so much as think it, you'll wake up one morning . . . alone.*

'Maybe I'll just go and arrange for the lumber,' he finished softly.

'Why don't you do that, then?'

'Corvis?'

Tyannon? Is that you? Oh, thank gods! I'll never leave home again, Tyannon, never leave you and the kids, never . . .

'I know you're awake, Corvis. I can hear it in your breath.'

No. He recognised the truth, heard it in the words that penetrated his cocoon of pain and exhaustion. *Not Tyannon.* The voice, though unmistakably feminine, was deeper, flavoured with an accent that hinted coyly of unknown lands.

Corvis kept his eyes firmly shut, hiding tears he refused to shed. 'You always were observant, Seilloah,' he slurred, forcing a smile he did not feel.

'Hmph. Observant enough to know you're still feeling the effects of that damn infection. And observant enough to recognise your voice when you began shouting earlier. Fortunate for you that I did, too. What possessed you to try to battle the sidhe?'

'It seemed,' Corvis told her, the fuzziness fading from his voice, 'to be a good idea at the time.' Painfully, he forced open eyelids that felt glued together with tree sap, and sat up.

'Careful. You're weak.'

'I'd noticed.'

With silent thanks that his vision, at least, had fully recovered from his ordeal, Corvis examined his new surroundings and found exactly what he would have expected from a forest hut. A stone hearth took up one entire corner, a merrily crackling fire warming a kettle of something that emitted a foul, bitter bouquet. Plants cluttered the room – potted, hanging, roaming free, and in one case growing directly through a gap in the floorboards – through which Corvis saw small forms dashing back and forth.

And there, sitting on a stool beside the bed, was Seilloah.

He had always thought of her hair as batwing in hue: black, save for those certain oblique angles from which it was deepest brown. Her eyes were the same mischievous green he remembered. The years had etched a few extra lines into her face, taken a few pounds from her flesh, but she still possessed what Corvis had always thought an ageless beauty. She wore a dark brown dress of the simple style she'd always favored.

And he remembered her well enough not to be taken in by her harmless image and apparent concern, genuine as it may have been.

'Thank you,' he said simply.

She snorted. 'I wasn't about to let you pass on without finding out what you were doing here. Damn it, Corvis, this isn't some gentle wood you can just wander through to commune with the animals! This is Theaghl-gohlatch, for the gods' sakes! What were you thinking?'

'Come now, Seilloah. You don't think this is coincidence, do you?'

She nodded. 'I figured as much. You were looking for me.'

'But of course.' He grimaced at the sudden shock of pain through his left arm. He glanced at it, seeing only blood-soaked bandages that exuded a hint of the same bitter aroma emanating from the kettle. 'Though admittedly, I didn't intend to do it by practically dying on your doorstep.'

'You battled the sidhe, Corvis. That you only *practically* died is astonishing.'

'The sidhe.' He shook his head, then caught himself, expecting a sudden wave of vertigo that never came. 'They've got a pretty nasty bite for myths and legends. I'll have to tell Davro he was right.'

'Davro?' Seilloah asked sharply. 'Davro was with you? Corvis, I didn't find any trace of him. I'm afraid—'

'No, Davro's quite safe. Smarter than I am, apparently. He refused to come into the forest at all. He's camped in the woods, outside of – Seilloah, how long have I been here?'

'You were out for a day or so. Before that, I think you followed my trail for, oh, three hours, give or take.' She scowled as her guest struggled to stand. 'Lie down, Corvis. You need a while to recover.'

'Can't,' he mumbled, casting about for his equipment. 'Davro's going to leave by day's end. Said if I wasn't back in two days, he was calling me dead and going home.'

Seilloah rose, placed a hand on Corvis' chest, and casually shoved. He toppled, much like a felled tree but with less grace, across the mattress and furs. 'I'll send him a message, let him know you're alive. Besides, you're not really dressed for the forest.'

Noticing for the first time that more than his gear and weaponry were missing, Corvis flushed and yanked the covers back over him. Seilloah laughed.

'It's not as if I haven't seen it before, Corvis.'

'That was a long time ago, Seilloah. I'm married now.'

'Really? *This* is a tale I've got to hear.' Her eyes locked on her guest, she sank back down on her stool. 'Davro was just planning to leave, was he? That's not the ogre I remember.'

'He's less thrilled about helping me this time around. Quite frankly, he didn't want to leave his sheep farm.'

'His *what*?'

Corvis shrugged. 'Apparently, all that time he was

travelling with me and squishing people in my name, he was also watching how people other than ogres lived. You know, farming, herding, and otherwise not waiting on Chalsene Night-Bringer to deliver victims to be raided. Seems he decided it was nicer than a life of further bloodshed back home.'

Had the witch's jaw gaped any lower, it might well have been lost in her cleavage.

'I think,' Corvis exhaled, 'I'd better start at the beginning.'

'And I think,' Seilloah replied, 'that I'd better put something on the fire a little more potable than this healing salve. It sounds as though this might just take a while.'

It did. Over multiple cups of an odd but refreshing herbal tea, the entire tale emerged. He spoke of his years with Tyannon – as hostage, companion, friend, and finally lover. He shared, as best mere words allowed, his happiness over the past years, his joy at the birth of his children, and the peace he'd never imagined he could have. He spoke of the rumours of Audriss's campaign, and his fury at the men who'd dared attack his daughter. The recitations finally drew to a close with Corvis' entry into the darkened passage. 'You pretty much know what happened after that. Interesting home you've got here, Seilloah. The décor's nice, but I can't say much for your neighbours.'

'We've got an understanding,' she muttered absently, her eyes distant. Then she frowned. 'I think you went too easy on those men near your home. You know what they would have done to Mellorin.'

'I know,' he said flatly. 'I suppose getting there in time to stop them put me in a better mood. If I'd been too late, I assure you they'd *still* be screaming.'

'I don't doubt it.' Abruptly as it appeared, her frown flipped upward into a large, cat-and-canary grin. 'I can't believe you put poor Davro in that position,' she laughed. 'Gods, he must have been furious!'

'Tried to skewer me with a big spear, actually. But he's a

smart ogre. He knows this is his best option. Which reminds me – I sort of promised him you'd find some way to see that his animals are taken care of until we get back.'

'Oh you did, did you?' Seilloah's eyes flashed green – in anger or mirth, Corvis wasn't certain. 'Were you so very certain that I'd be willing to help you in your endeavours? Were you planning to blackmail me, too?'

'You know, Davro asked me that exact question. No, Seilloah, I'd never do that to you.'

Now those green eyes went cold. 'Because you'd never do such a thing, Corvis, or because you don't have anything on me?'

Corvis grinned sheepishly. 'Admittedly, if I *did* have something on you, I might have to consider it. But I'm glad I don't. I don't want to pull that sort of thing with you. Davro was a good lieutenant, and his help will be useful. But you were a—'

'If you say *friend*, I may seriously consider poisoning you myself.' Her gaze grew heavy, oppressive. Corvis felt it as a pressure on his chest, a catch in his breath. 'You didn't have friends, Corvis. Not Davro, not Valescienn, and not me. You had people you could trust enough to let you use them. Nothing more.'

'That's not true, Seilloah. With you, I . . .'

Her unblinking gaze would not allow him his feeble denial. Defiantly, Corvis drew in a breath. 'Seilloah, whatever we were or weren't in the past, I'm asking you now: will you help me?'

'Corvis . . .' She rose gracefully from the stool and sat beside him on the bed, one hand resting on his own. 'If I told you that I'd only help if we returned to what we were – along with a promise, of course, that Tyannon need never know – if that was the price of my aid, would you accept?'

He stared at her for a long moment, the blood draining from his face. And then, finally, 'No. Some things have to be sacred, even to me. I'm sorry.'

'Good,' she said, rising once more to her feet. 'Then just let me gather some supplies, and we'll go when you're up to it.

Your clothing and weapons are under the bed.' She began puttering about the room, collecting this and arranging that.

'You'll help me?' he asked, confused by the abrupt change in mood. 'Just like that?'

She stopped and straightened up, staring into the fire, her back to the man she knew so well and not at all. 'Not for your sake, Corvis. For hers.'

He blinked several times, puzzled, before comprehension finally dawned. 'For Tyannon? Why?'

'Because,' Seilloah told him, hair gleaming in the flickering firelight, 'I thought once, long ago, that I might have been her. And I'd have wanted someone to help me and *my* children.

'Rest now,' she said abruptly, returning to the task at hand. 'We should get a move on as soon as you're able. Can't keep Davro waiting. Ogres are notoriously impatient.'

Corvis watched as she packed, pondering. Then, with a mental shrug, he reached beneath the bed for his possessions. They lay within easy reach: his pack, his sword, his clothes, and, bizarrely, a short spear, scarcely the length of his arm, covered in ever-shifting runes.

Even as his fist closed around it, he felt the Kholben Shiar taste his soul, as it did to all who dared heft it. He watched Sunder shape itself accordingly, melting down, forming once more into the axe with which he was as familiar as his own skin. And he wondered, thinking of the spear it had briefly been – the weapon of a hunter, not a warrior – what it had seen inside Seilloah.

They remained unmolested as they traversed the darkness of Theaghl-gohlatch. The path seemed less claustrophobic this time around, though whether the cause was Seilloah's light spell (substantially brighter than Corvis') or the extra company, or the simple fact that he wasn't feverish and dying, Corvis couldn't say. He heard rustling in the surrounding foliage, but whatever paced them remained content to watch.

'Seilloah, why would you want to live in this place?' he finally asked.

'What's wrong with it?' she responded innocently.

'Seilloah . . .'

She smiled. 'I've always preferred forests, Corvis. You know that. And with this one, I don't have to worry about the stray hunter or woodcutter wandering too close to my home and getting away before I can, ah, invite him to dinner. People leave this place alone – everyone except you – and that's what I wanted.'

'You and Davro both. Did everyone I knew go on to become a hermit?'

'Quite possibly,' she told him. 'People were oddly suspicious of strangers at the time. I think most of the kingdom was struggling to rebuild from something or other. Some catastrophe. Can't recall offhand what it was.'

'Cute. So if you didn't believe in my cause, why'd you help me?'

'Who said I didn't believe? I still think you'd make a better ruler than anything else we've got available. Doesn't mean I'm blind to the consequences. Corvis,' she added abruptly, 'you know full well that my sphere of influence is somewhat limited. If Audriss has at his command anything approaching the level of sorcery that you used to have, I can't counter it.'

'You'll do fine,' Corvis responded stiffly.

'Corvis—'

'No.'

She bulled on. 'Where's Khanda?'

'Someplace safe.'

Corvis' tone didn't make it entirely clear whether he meant someplace safe *for* Khanda, or *from* him. 'It's your decision, of course, Corvis, but shouldn't you at least consider—'

'No.'

She sighed. 'Fine. Have it your way.'

'That's the plan.'

They emerged into the diffuse light of the surrounding woods just after midday. Davro, his back stiff and his spear clenched tight, stood some twenty feet from the gaping passage. Rascal, his ears flattened, waited behind the ogre, tugging at his tether.

'I knew you were coming,' the ogre said stiltedly. 'The trees grew a mouth and told me.'

'The trees around here,' Corvis said casually, 'do seem unusually verbose.'

'Davro,' Seilloah greeted the ogre with a smile.

'Seilloah.'

'It's been a long time, my large friend. You're looking quite well.'

'As are you. Did he blackmail you, too?'

'That's starting to get just a little old,' Corvis interjected.

'So are you,' Davro spat back. Corvis raised an eyebrow, which the ogre chose to ignore.

'My animals—' he began.

'Corvis already asked me. It'll be a strain from this distance, but I can put the entire herd into a hibernation, of sorts. They won't need food or drink – they'll barely breathe, for that matter – for at least several months, probably a couple of seasons. If we're not done by then, I'll try to think of something a little more long-term.'

'Thank you.'

'That's a handy trick,' Corvis commented. 'Why didn't you ever do that on the armies we faced?'

Seilloah sighed. 'Because sheep and pigs are docile. Trained warhorses are too ornery to cooperate, and as far as humans go, it's *far* more difficult for witchcraft to manipulate anything with a soul. Why don't you concentrate on how to deal with Audriss, and leave the witchcraft to me, all right?'

Corvis untethered Rascal from the tree and set off to the northwest, leading the horse and followed by his companions. Seilloah assured him that a suitable mount would await her at the edge of the woods, so they need not walk all the way to ogre territory. As they marched, snatches of conversation drifted through Corvis' hearing.

'. . . any humans lately?' the ogre was asking.

A deep sigh. 'No, that's the one disadvantage to living in

isolation, I'm afraid. And it means some of my best recipes are going to waste. You?'

'Nah. I don't care for the way humans taste, remember? I thought I told you that.'

'You might have. It's been a while, Davro.' Another sigh, this one more hopeful. 'It'll be nice to get out in the world again, at least for a little while. Maybe we can find a vagabond or two no one will miss. They tend toward the stringy, but if you can mix them with the right kind of vegetables and a good helping of potatoes, they make the most fabulous stew . . .'

Corvis shook his head as the breeze picked up, blotting out the low tone of the discussion behind him.

They reached the wood's end just before dusk some four nights later, and Seilloah's mount indeed awaited them. Corvis stopped and frowned, trying to find some tactful way to object. Rascal's ears flattened, while Davro just snickered.

For her own part, Seilloah smiled and sidled up to the creature, gently caressing its throat and patting it on the head. The creature rumbled, a sound that might have been a purr had this been anything resembling a cat. The massive tail slapped back and forth, sounding like window shutters flapping in a storm.

'Umm, Seilloah . . .' Corvis began hesitantly.

'Isn't he beautiful?' she cooed. 'That's a good boy, yes he is!' She continued scratching vigorously at the rough skin.

'Seilloah, it's a lizard.'

'How observant of you, Corvis.'

'It's a lizard the size of a cow.'

'Yes.'

Corvis felt he wasn't entirely making his point. '*Why* is there a lizard the size of a cow?'

'Because a lizard the size of a lizard wouldn't make for a very good mount, would it?'

Corvis blinked. 'Well, no, but . . . Seilloah, a giant lizard isn't exactly the most inconspicuous travelling companion.'

'Are we being inconspicuous? I thought we were raising an army.'

'Yes, but I'd rather not draw too much attention until we actually *have* the army.'

'Oh, relax,' she said, laughing at him. 'You're wandering down the roadside with an ogre. How inconspicuous is *that*?'

'Hey,' Davro protested.

'But—'

'If we have to go through any towns or cities, I'll have him wait outside, all right?'

Corvis sighed. 'Have it your way.'

Seilloah grinned evilly. 'That's the plan.'

Grumbling something unintelligible, Corvis seated himself on Rascal's saddle. Seilloah heaved herself onto the lizard's back, and the animals set off at a steady pace, Davro marching alongside. Rascal, though he kept one eye on the strange creature beside him, made no overt objections.

'I suppose I better get it over with,' Corvis muttered. 'What's his name?'

'Rover.'

Corvis shut up.

Indeed, they drew some astonished looks from fellow travellers and were forced to circle around a handful of small towns they might otherwise have passed through, but their journey remained largely uneventful.

Davro remained surly, Corvis defensive, and Seilloah vastly amused by both of them. The sun passed above their heads, the miles beneath their feet. The heat of summer grew heavier and more oppressive, and they knew it would only get worse. As they continued northwest, the air grew thick, heavy, and sticky. It was, Corvis remarked, akin to marching through a thin coating of jam. Throttled violently by the savage humidity, the dirt became mud, sucking greedily at Rascal's hooves and Davro's feet. Between the heat, the humidity, and the terrain, their progress slowed to a sickly crawl.

It was just about noon, the sun beating down upon them

through a sky as much moisture as air, when a few gnarled and twisted trees appeared on the horizon.

'The road ends about a hundred yards farther on,' Davro told them, unbothered by an environment that was quickly sapping the strength of his companions. 'We go north there, and follow the waterline.'

'Wonderful,' Corvis rumbled, wiping vainly at the sweat pouring from his hairline with an equally drenched hand. 'Tell me something, Davro, whose brilliant idea was it for your clan to live in a swamp?'

'We're a tribe, not a clan,' Davro said haughtily.

'Oh, well pardon me bloody.'

'And the heat doesn't bother us much. Living here, neither does anyone else.'

'I thought most ogres *liked* fighting everyone in sight,' Seilloah said, her tone sharp. Even the witch was miserable in the sodden atmosphere of the nearby swamp.

'We *do* like fighting,' Davro told her, apparently forgetting that he'd distanced himself from 'we' for nigh unto two decades. 'But we want it on *our* terms and in *their* homes, not the other way around.'

Corvis sighed. 'So where are we going, exactly? The last time, I met you halfway, remember? I've seen maps, but I've never actually been there.'

'As I said, we follow the edge of the swamp north, and then for about a dozen miles once it turns to the west. My tribe's territory begins just a few miles north of – why are you staring at me?'

'Follow until the swamp turns back toward the west?' Seilloah asked in a strangled tone.

'That's what I said. So?'

'Davro,' Corvis explained, his voice beseeching; almost, an unkind observer might have said, whining. 'That swamp must stretch fifty miles before it tapers off! At the rate we're travelling, that's four or five more days in this godsforsaken place!'

'Closer to six,' the ogre conceded with a shrug. 'Remember, it's another twelve or so miles after that.'

'Are you *trying* to kill us?'

'You're the one who wanted to come here,' Davro snapped at him. 'This is your doing. You deal with it.'

Corvis sighed, then, and took a moment to cast an apologetic glance at Seilloah, who was glowering darkly at him. 'All right,' he said, resigned. 'Let's get this misery over with.'

'In a minute,' Davro said, sudden glee evident in his voice. 'I just thought of something.'

'Arhylla help us all,' Seilloah muttered.

'Not us all, Seilloah. Just him.'

Corvis' eyes narrowed. 'What are you talking about, Davro?'

'One of the reasons you *requested* I accompany you,' the ogre reminded him, 'was so I could help you talk to my tribe, get them to accept you as the Terror of the East, returned from obscurity, to lead them all into glory. So you wouldn't have to pay for their help.'

The former warlord frowned. 'Not quite how I'd have put it, but—'

'If that's the plan,' Davro continued undaunted, 'they have to see you as the great warlord, Corvis Rebaine, from the very start. A lanky, grey-haired human won't impress them.'

A voice began to scream in panic in the rearmost chambers of Corvis' mind, but he couldn't quite make out what it was saying. 'So?'

'So, my people guard their lands well. Carefully. The scouts and guards will probably have their eyes on us as early as tomorrow.'

Corvis suddenly understood exactly what his companion was suggesting. 'Davro, you can't possibly be serious . . .'

The ogre was openly grinning now, his entire face stretched, his horn jutting obscenely from above his eye. 'I am indeed. And you damn well better do it, too, or even I may not be able to convince them.

'Besides, what's a little heat to the Terror of the East?'

With a groan that came all the way from his toes, Corvis swung down from his saddle, made another futile attempt at scraping the sweat from his face, and began, with obvious reluctance, to open his saddlebags and unpack his black, heavy, stifling armour.

Seilloah skillfully directed her lizard to step beside the ogre as they watched Corvis, grunting and swearing, buckle on the first pieces of the bone-and-metal contraption. Davro glanced at her and smiled.

'Yes?' he asked, his tone chipper.

'Are you happy now?' she asked him, her own voice hovering somewhere between sympathy, anger, and amusement.

'Not by a long shot,' he told her seriously. 'But a damn sight closer than I was ten minutes ago.' And then he settled in to watch, determined not to miss a minute of Corvis' suffering, and began – badly and out of tune – to whistle.

His name was Urkran. One of Davro's tribe, he was in fact a cousin of the long-lost warrior. Put a good sword in his hand, and he could take the head off a live snake, blindfolded. Give him a solid spear, he could put it halfway through a tree trunk at fifty paces.

Today Urkran stood watch, eye constantly alert, scouring the edges of the tribe's territory. In all living memory, no enemy had ever caught the ogres by surprise, and this, with an unknown army conquering anything and everything it came across, was not the time for that traditional diligence to lapse.

From his post by a gnarled cypress on a small knoll jutting from the marsh, Urkran spotted a trio of figures moving sluggishly but steadily along the waterline. It was difficult to make out any details at this range – the swamp frequently belched up a film of sticky mist – but he determined that two were mounted, while the third, much larger, walked beside them.

Urkran squinted, peering intently through the mists. The larger figure in the group *might* be an ogre, but it was impossible to be certain. His fists clenched on his spear, the sentry slogged into the swamp, moving rapidly and with surprising silence. Three strangers didn't seem to pose any great threat, but duty demanded he make certain.

The marsh gasses and surrounding miasma swirled as he moved through them, eddies forming around his legs. It was a common phenomenon in this fog-shrouded fen, so it was only when Urkran felt a sudden chill on his thighs and saw the sheen of blood coalescing on the water's surface that he realised something was terribly wrong.

The raucous call of a carrion crow was the only audible sound as Urkran vanished beneath the murky, sludgy waters. The liquid rippled outward, mist swirled and spiraled as though agitated. Slowly, a thin trickle of blood rose to the surface, pooling and twisting as it gradually mixed with its environment – and then, with far greater rapidity than it had appeared, the crimson stain shrank, vanishing once more beneath the murk.

The travellers, unaware of the drama playing out twenty yards to their left, continued on their way, the faint sounds of bickering drifting through the miasma to vanish into the swamp.

Smoothly, two forms broke the surface of the water. The first was Urkran; his eye was stretched wide with shock, his breathing shallow, his formerly red skin a sickly shade of pale. Here and there, a few stubborn spots of blood clung to his limbs or his clothes. His weapons were gone, embedded in the mud, not that they'd have done him any good. He was too weak even to turn his head, much less raise a hand in defiance of the creature slowly murdering him.

The other form emerging from the heavy murk was his killer. Less than half the ogre's height, it appeared almost human. A face that didn't quite qualify as round – *puffy*, perhaps, was a better word – was topped by a matted mane of black hair, plastered to his scalp by the surrounding waters. His eyes were cold, piercing, and tinted with the faintest hint of crimson. His lips, fish-pale and thin, gaped open to reveal perfectly white and straight teeth.

The thing leaned over the ogre, those narrow lips a hair-breadth from Urkran's ear. Placing his mouth against the ogre's cheek, it inhaled. Urkran moaned in revulsion as he felt the pores of his skin stretch wide, felt his own blood flow through the newly opened gaps. He shuddered as the creature's tongue danced over his face, determined not to miss a single drop of the ogre's draining life.

He tried to thrash, to fight, to prove he wasn't dead yet, that this hideous thing hadn't killed him, that he was still an ogre. A loose flopping of his limbs as they hung in the water was the best he could manage. When the air in his lungs was finally depleted, he lacked even the strength to draw another breath. His chest burned, and yellow spots danced at the edges of his vision.

'Oh, my,' the thing beside him said, its tongue quickly flicking over its lips to lap up the last few dewdrops of blood; the faint slobbering would have made Urkran shiver, but his body lacked the energy for even that. 'I seem to have taken a bit more than I intended.'

It bent once more toward Urkran's ear, as though confiding a dark secret to an age-old friend. 'I don't think Mithraem would be happy with me if I let you die before I accomplished my assigned task,' it said, its voice little more than a whisper, a breeze of wind reeking of rancid blood. 'It's a shame, too. I'd grown accustomed to this form. I'll miss it. Ah, well, such is life . . .' It giggled briefly. 'Such is life!' it repeated, cackling. 'Oh, that's rich.'

A dark mist gathered around the creature's head, as though it was returning to its prior insubstantial state. But this was different; even Urkran, on the verge of blacking out, could see that. For rather than shifting into mist the thing appeared to be *exuding* it. From its mouth, nose, eyes, ears – even from beneath its fingernails – the mist flowed; and even as it emerged, the body it left behind began to putrefy, rotting from the inside out. The face sank inward, splitting apart as things inside bubbled rapidly to the surface. Thick, noxious fluids drained from the shiveling corpse, pouring into the marsh. Gobbets of putrescent flesh – literal pieces of the corruption that had infested the body – rained downward, bobbing about on the water.

And then nothing remained but the nauseating smell of decay and a vaguely man-shaped stain, slowly dispersing into the stagnant waters. The body, and the mist, were gone.

For long moments, 'Urkran' floated benignly, limbs splayed to provide buoyancy. He allowed himself a full five minutes to recover from the ordeal; that sort of thing was always immensely tiring. Then, with a swift jerk, he was upright, his feet planted firmly in the mud.

He'd have to retrieve the weapons; it would look bad if he returned to the tribe without them. Large as they were, it took but a moment of digging about in the muck to locate them. Once equipped, Urkran resumed his original task of slogging toward the shore. He must get back before the new arrivals spoke with the chieftain at any great length.

His feet once more on solid ground, Urkran peered after the travellers, his single eye gleaming a deep red in the diffuse light of the day. Then, his first few steps awkward as he gradually accustomed himself to his new proportions, he set off after them.

CHAPTER NINE

'Gods damn it to every curdled, lice-ridden hell!' The Terror of the East shoved his way through a mob of civilian prisoners overseen by several of his guards – not too difficult, really, since they cringed away even as he neared – and stalked across the open courtyard. His boots alternately rung out on the bloodstained cobblestones and squelched on the flesh of the fallen – many of the enemy, yes, but far more of his own soldiers than there should have been. 'What were you thinking, you idiot? Do you actually use that head of yours for anything other than keeping your horn out of your throat?'

/ You tell him, you raging font of fury, you! /

'How many times do I have to order you to shut up, Khanda?'

/ At least one more, obviously. /

Corvis clattered to a halt, the expressionless skull staring up into the faces of multiple ogres, all of whom snarled down at him with varying expressions of fury.

'Watch your tongue, little human,' Davro barked first. 'You will *not* speak to—'

Gundrek raised a hand. '*Davro! Uld tharosh vir! Nem Rebaine akka.*'

'*Che, szevok.*' Still scowling, the larger ogre retreated, leaning back against a wooden wall coated with the smoke of distant burning neighbourhoods.

The ogre chieftain nodded. Then, 'What's your problem, Rebaine?'

Corvis crossed his arms and snarled, a sound audible even from behind the helm.

'Lord Rebaine,' Gundrek corrected, with only a hint of reluctance.

'My problem, Gundrek? My problem is that I'm standing in the middle of a field of bodies that includes over a hundred of my own men!'

'This is war,' the ogre said with a shrug.

'Oh, is it? I'm so bloody glad you noticed! And do you know what soldiers like you and your ogres are supposed to *do* in a war?'

'You mean besides kill the enemy?'

'You're supposed to *follow orders*, you half-wit! And you were very *specifically* ordered to head off the defenders over at the temple of Kassek to keep them off Commander Ezram's flank!'

Again, the old ogre simply shrugged. 'This force looked like the larger threat.'

'This force *was* the larger threat! I'd taken that into account! You left us open, Gundrek!'

'Honour demands—'

'No. Honour demands that you abide by your agreements.' Corvis stepped away. 'Swear to it, Gundrek. You and all your lieutenants.'

'Swear to what?'

'To obey. You, swear to obey my orders – swear in the Night-Bringers name! – or you're out of this war.'

A rumble of anger rose like thunder from the assembled ogres. 'And how are you going to make us leave, exactly?' Gundrek challenged, his voice suddenly low. Instantly Corvis' own soldiers tensed, bristling suddenly with freshly drawn blades.

'Soldiers,' Corvis said simply. 'And Sunder. And a demon who, to the best of my knowledge, hasn't ever tasted an ogre's soul before and might relish the opportunity.'

/ *Actually, they're really pretty rancid. I—*/

'Or,' he continued, 'you swear to do what you've already agreed to do, and you continue to enjoy as much fighting as you could possibly ask for.'

Long was Gundrek's stare. The courtyard was utterly silent, save for an occasional prisoner's whimper. Until, finally . . .

'Very well.' First Gundrek, then the other ogres, and finally Davro bowed their heads. '*Kvirriok thenn, Chalsene voro*—'

'In Human, if you don't mind,' Corvis interrupted.

Gundrek's scowl deepened so far it was a wonder his horn didn't droop over his eye, but he nodded. 'Fine. Witness our oath, Chalsene, called Night-Bringer. I, Gundrek, swear that I and my tribe shall obey the orders of our general, Corvis Rebaine, for the duration of the war – *to the extent*,' he added, with a quick glare, 'that any soldier could be expected to do so.'

'It'll do,' Corvis said. He turned, cold eyes sweeping the courtyard.

They can't be allowed to spread rumours of dissension in the ranks . . . He honestly couldn't tell if it was his own thought, or Khanda's.

'Kill them.'

Gundrek's scowl flipped itself into a nasty grin. The sudden terrified screams, and the wet impact of steel on flesh, drowned out the staccato ring of Corvis' departing steps.

Davro and Seilloah both picked with absentminded distaste at the chunks of undercooked meat their hosts had provided. Definitely reptile, Seilloah noted, probably alligator, or perhaps a large snake. She'd have literally killed for something tastier, but when one ate among ogres, one ate whatever they'd managed to hunt.

It was the first rule of their society: Chalsene provides for those strong enough to take it. To grow or to raise one's own food, rather than to hunt it or win it in battle, was an insult to Chalsene himself. It was why the ogres remained so war-like a people, even as their numbers dwindled and their fortunes failed. And it was why Davro, whatever happened, could never let his brethren learn what he had become. It was more than a violation of tradition; it was blasphemous.

The unlikely pair started in unison, the meal forgotten, as the heavy wooden door drifted open. In the doorway stood Corvis Rebaine, the flickering fires of the community casting him as some hellish fiend. For an instant, the past seventeen years were swept away, dust on the wind of memory. Black-clad, covered in plates and spikes of gleaming bone, there remained no trace at all of the man they'd travelled with for the past days. There couldn't possibly be anything remotely human about this looming thing before them.

And then he stepped into the small (by ogre standards) hut, yanked the iron-banded skull helm from his head, and tossed it into the nearest corner with a resounding crash. 'Get this monstrosity off me before I roast!'

Seilloah immediately stepped forward, only to recoil from the pungent aroma emanating from the armour, filling the hut with a palpable effluvium. Her eyes watered, and it was all she could do to keep from choking.

'By the gods, Corvis!'

He glowered up at her, his hair plastered to his forehead by sweat and encrusted dirt. 'Don't you dare complain to me! It was *his* bright idea that I wear this thing for six straight days in this hell-spawned swamp!'

Davro shrugged, unapologetic.

'Your spells helped a bit,' Corvis continued. 'They may even have kept me alive, as much moisture as I've lost over the past few days. But they didn't make it even remotely comfortable.'

'So I can smell,' she said, cringing. 'How did you breathe in there?'

'Carefully. Would you give me a hand now?'

Between the two of them, they did indeed manage to

remove Corvis' armour, though it might have gone quicker had Seilloah used both hands, rather than keeping one cupped over her mouth and nose. Finally, though, a heap of black metal and bone lay in the corner alongside the helm.

'Watch out with those spikes,' Seilloah said, wincing as a shoulder plate dug a furrow into the wooden wall beside it. 'This is a borrowed hut, remember.'

'Whatever.' With a groan, Corvis collapsed onto one of the straw-filled mattresses the ogres provided them for the night, lacking the energy even to change his underclothes.

'Two suggestions, Corvis.'

'What?'

'One, bathe. Two, burn those clothes.'

'But burn them well away from the village,' Davro added. 'I didn't bring you here to poison my tribe.'

'Oh, you're a riot, Davro.'

'So I've been told. All right, what happened? We've been waiting for three hours, now.'

'Well . . .' Corvis sat up with another faint groan. 'They've agreed to join us. They'll need time to mobilise their warriors and make preparations, but once our army's ready to march, they'll be a part of it.'

'Congratulations,' Seilloah told him.

'From me, too,' Davro said, his tone neutral.

'How did you talk them into it?' the dark-haired woman asked him.

'Oh, that's easy,' the ogre interjected. 'He blackmailed them. Right?'

Corvis scowled. 'Anytime you feel like giving up that particular habit, Davro, you go right ahead.'

Davro's brow furrowed in contemplation. 'No,' he decided a moment later, his voice thoughtful, 'I'm not going to be doing that.'

'The agreement?' Seilloah prodded gently.

'Hmm? Oh. It seems Davro was right: the armour made an impression.'

'I was right? And he *admits* it? Heavens be praised.'

'Shut up, Davro. Anyway, they were astounded that the "great Lord Rebaine" – their words, not mine, Davro, so stop snickering – had returned. Turns out many of the older warriors, including the chief, were part of my army all those years ago.'

'Turns out?' Davro asked. 'You didn't know?'

'Come on, there were, what, over a hundred of your people in my army. I'm supposed to know them all personally?'

'Besides,' Seilloah said with a smirk, 'you cyclopes all look alike to us.'

'*Anyway*, it also meant a lot to them that – umm . . .' Corvis glanced askance at Davro, his fingers drumming against his palm.

'What?' the ogre snapped suspiciously.

'Well, seems your chieftain assumed that the reason you didn't come home all these years was that you were serving me. Your – ah, that is, your "undying loyalty" to me made a large difference in his decision.'

'They're helping you,' Davro growled, 'because of *my* "undying loyalty"? To *you*?'

'Well, that's part of it, but—'

'And you didn't feel the need to correct him?'

'It's a useful misconception, Davro. And I could hardly tell him the real reason, could I?'

'But—'

'Besides, if you think about it, it's true in a way, right? I mean, you *are* loyal to me. Oaths and all.'

'You,' Davro spat, 'are *really* pushing it.'

'You're a big guy, Davro. You can take a little pushing.'

'So the ogres just up and joined you?' Seilloah asked skeptically. 'That doesn't sound right.'

'Well – not *quite* that simply . . .'

'Oh, gods,' Davro muttered, 'here it comes.'

'The chief sort of assumed that I was coming out of obscurity to retake the kingdom,' Corvis told them. 'Let Audriss soften them up, and then come in and take everything while everyone's weak and recovering.'

'And?' Seilloah asked.

Corvis exhaled slowly. 'I sort of promised the ogres a quarter share of all conquered territories.'

Seilloah and Davro stared at him as though he'd sprouted an antelope. Davro's mouth worked soundlessly, and Seilloah's own jaw was hanging substantially closer to the floor.

'You did *what*?' she finally squeaked.

'I promised them—'

'I *heard* what you promised them! How could you *do* that?'

'With remarkable ease, actually.'

'Do you have any idea,' Davro asked him, 'what they'll do to you when they find out you lied to them?'

'I didn't lie to them. I fully intend to give them one-fourth of all the lands I conquer.'

'But you're not conquering anything!'

'Then it shouldn't take too long to divvy it up, should it?'

'We're dead,' Davro told them succinctly.

'Look,' Corvis said, his voice sharp, 'it's not as though they're getting nothing from this. Over the course of the war, I'm quite certain there'll be plenty of opportunities for looting and plunder, so they're not going home empty-handed. I'll just – I don't know, I'll make it look good. We won't have enough men to go on once Audriss is defeated. Or I'll mysteriously vanish. Or make them think I'm dead.'

'I'll help with that one,' Davro said darkly. 'I'll make it *real* convincing.'

'In any case, we'll deal with it. What matters is, we've got the ogres on our side, and they count for a great deal. And they'll come out ahead, even without conquering Imphallion, so everyone winds up happy.'

'Why not?' Seilloah asked, her tone thoughtful.

'Huh?' Davro inquired.

'I agree,' Corvis said. 'Huh?'

'Why not conquer Imphallion?' A pause. 'I see it's my turn to be stared at.'

'Seilloah, what the hell are you talking about?'

'Corvis, if this works, Audriss will be dead, or at least

135

defeated. A good-sized chunk of Imphallion will be without leadership. Most of the armies are going to be scattered, if not decimated outright. Plan this properly, you can step in and assume control with a minimum of additional conflict.'

'Seilloah's got a point,' Davro conceded. 'Not so sure I like the idea of you being in charge anymore, but from a purely tactical standpoint, it's the perfect opportunity. Better than you had twenty years ago, certainly.'

Corvis shook his head. 'Look, that's not what I want anymore. I . . .'

Seilloah's expression tightened. 'Corvis, pretend we're meeting for the first time, so many years ago. Tell me why I'm supposed to help a man with bones on his armour conquer the kingdom.'

Corvis' back straightened, and as he spoke, his voice grew strong. 'Because we live in a world gone stagnant. The so-called regent is a puppet figure, some pseudo-king the Guilds allow to occupy the throne because Imphallion is still *officially* a monarchy. The regent himself can't do a damn thing without the Guilds' say-so, and they never say so unless it's good for business. They're merchants, not leaders, and they have no business governing. Imphallion hasn't accomplished anything for more generations than I can count, and a kingdom that isn't growing is dying.'

Abruptly, Corvis opened his eyes, and he actually blushed beneath the disbelieving eyes of his companions.

'Yeah,' Davro said snidely. 'Well, it's clear you don't believe *that* anymore. I'm convinced.'

'Corvis,' Seilloah told him, 'you have a family now. Ultimately, you're doing this for them. I know that. But why does it have to be one or the other? Think of the kind of life you could make for them if you were king! Think of how much safer they'd be if Imphallion had a strong leader again! Of the sort of world you could build for your children in a kingdom in ascension, rather than decline.'

'I – I don't know. I'll think about it.'

Seilloah's eyes narrowed in a look that Corvis recognised

from days of old, and he knew he'd not heard the end of this. Apparently having decided that she'd said enough *for now*, however, her next move was away from her companions and toward her mattress. 'Just be sure to bathe before you go to sleep. I refuse to wake up to that awful stench.'

Corvis glanced over at Davro, who merely shrugged.

'Don't give me that,' Corvis demanded. 'I've never in my life known you to lack an opinion on anything!'

Davro smiled flatly, 'Oh, I've got my opinions. But you, Rebaine, don't want to hear them.'

'Oh? Why, pray tell?'

'Because no matter what I say, it's not going to be the answer you want.'

'How can you possibly know that?'

'Because this question only has two answers, Rebaine. And you hate both of them.' And he, too, stomped to the other side of the hut, flopped down, and went to sleep.

Corvis, exhausted as he was, lay awake and watched the ceiling for a long, long time.

'Where to now?' Seilloah asked as she placed a foot upon the lizard's knee and swung herself up. Corvis – mercifully free of his armour – was already seated on Rascal's back, eager for another day's travel into cooler climes. After that swamp, even the blazing heat of summer in other lands seemed a relief.

'I've been thinking about that since we left Davro's village,' Corvis said softly.

Davro, his mood pensive ever since his brief family reunion, glanced down sharply. 'My *people's* village. I live on a sheep farm. And I'd like to get back there before I die of old age, so squelch the damn preliminaries and answer the question!'

'All right. The ogres are a good start, but they're not an army by themselves. We need soldiers. Lots of them.'

'Great,' Davro spat. 'Know anyone with a few spare battalions lying around? Maybe you should blackmail a Guild.'

'Davro, if I have to hear that word one more time—'

'Gentlemen!' Seilloah barked. 'Focus!'

Corvis, his face flushed, glowered at the ogre for another moment, then nodded once. 'Fine. No, I don't know of any spare battalions. We need mercenaries.'

'You have to pay mercenaries,' Davro pointed out, also forcing himself to stay calm. 'Unless you have a few chests of gold hidden someplace I don't even want to think about, we're short on funds.'

'There are ways to get money,' Corvis said. 'The problem is getting the soldiers. I've been away too long; I don't know where to go to gather men quickly. We can't exactly just start putting the word out. Audriss is sure to hear of it, and it takes too long.'

'Can't help you there,' Davro told him.

Seilloah shook her head. 'Nor I.'

'I know. But I know someone who can.'

'Valescienn?' Seilloah asked.

Corvis nodded. 'I seriously doubt *he's* retired. War was all he knew. And I know he's got connections. He helped me acquire a pretty sizable chunk of my army last time.'

'So what are we waiting for?' Seilloah asked. 'Where is he?'

Corvis glanced downward. 'Umm, about that . . .'

The ogre grinned. 'What the Terror of the East is too embarrassed to admit to you is that he doesn't know. Seems the spying spell he cast on us didn't stick to Valescienn.'

'The spell on Valescienn failed?' she asked with some surprise. Davro's face fell when he realised she'd already known about the spell, and there was therefore no forthcoming explosion.

'It worked fine at first,' Corvis insisted.

'So when did it cut out?'

'I'm not entirely certain,' he acknowledged. 'Truthfully, until I needed to find you and Davro, I hadn't tested the links in years. Never thought I'd need them again.'

'So how are we going to do this?' she asked.

'The old-fashioned way. I know where Valescienn lives, or

at least where he used to. Kervone, a small village not too far from Denathere. If he's there, great. If not,' we ask around until we find someone who can tell us where he's gone.'

'You realise,' Seilloah told him as they guided their mounts southward, 'that if he *has* moved on, this could take a while.'

'You have other plans?'

Davro snarled darkly, but wisely chose not to comment.

Chapter Ten

The past couple of decades had not been kind to Evislan Kade.

Oh, he'd managed to make a halfway decent living, continuing his career as a bounty hunter and occasional assassin even in the wake of his embarrassing encounter with the young fugitive Corvis Rebaine. But it hadn't been remotely the same, not without Sunder hanging at his side. Kade was good, and always had been – but it had been the Kholben Shiar that made him *great*.

Now? Now, Kade was nearing the far border of middle age, reaching the point where no amount of constant practice and brutal exercises could keep his arm from slowing or his chest from aching after exertions that would, in the past, have scarcely winded him. A few more years, and he wouldn't be able to keep working at all, and he hadn't accumulated nearly enough coin to retire. Only the *great* bounty hunters ever struck it *that* rich, and of course, Kade wasn't great anymore.

But all that was about to change.

It had taken him years of searching, of squeezing in what research he could between the various commissions that paid for his room and board. He had delved into libraries deep in church basements, perused the private collections of a dozen nobles, purchased many a drink for village elders who might just remember a tale with the tiniest smidgen of truth behind it. There were times, many times when the quest seemed hopeless, but giving up had never been even remotely an option. Not for someone like Evislan Kade.

And finally, those tales had borne fruit. His heart hammering in his chest, Kade had wound his way into a great stone ruin, a half-buried ziggurat beyond the farthest borders of Imphallion. There, legend had it, was entombed the great Emperor Sahn Vakraad, one of the last rulers of an ancient nation that had fallen generations before the time of Imphalam the First. And there, too – those same legends claimed – was buried alongside him the blade he wielded in every battle, a blade capable of cleaving through the thickest shields or most well-forged armours.

Many a pitfall and trapped portal strove to take Kade's life, but throughout the many winding corridors of Sahn Vakraad's tomb, he persevered. And in the end, he had prevailed. Standing in the sepulchre of the fallen king, he hefted overhead that ancient weapon, watched it reshape itself into his familiar longsword, and heard it speak deep in the recesses of his mind, even as Sunder had done.

Evislan Kade would be great once more. He had a few good years remaining, and in those years, his name would again be whispered in taverns and throne rooms. He would once again be paid the riches he deserved and which would keep him content through his twilight years.

His inner celebration lasted just as long as it took him to stumble exhaustedly back through the upper passageways and out into the surrounding wilds. There he stopped, blinking not so much at the brightness of the sun, but at the assembled throng awaiting him – and the dozens of crossbows that aimed their deadly projectiles his way.

From the heart of that gathering stepped a man without a face, clad in a peculiar stone armour.

'I appreciate you doing all the hard work,' the faceless man told him, 'but I believe you have something I want.'

The great bounty hunter – well, the *good* bounty hunter – Evislan Kade had to fight down the urge to whimper.

Once more, Audriss and Mithraem sat beside a parchment-laden table. It stood within the Serpent's personal tent, an enormous pavilion sufficient to house a dozen men comfortably. Within were all the comforts of home: the table, several capacious chairs, a down mattress, and, finally, an iron maiden, just in case the warlord felt the need to deal with any prisoners personally. A marvel of engineering, it possessed levers to control the length and angle of its inner spines with pinpoint accuracy.

At the moment, the black-clad Serpent was seated in one of those comfortable velvet-lined chairs, his feet propped up on a matching footstool, one armoured hand wrapped carefully around the stem of a silver goblet. He glanced passively at the thin vessel, swirling it slightly and taking a long drink, lifting his face mask just enough to reach his lips.

Mithraem paced in the centre of the tent. His face was tense, and his eyes flickered on occasion to the third figure in the room, the large ogre who now knelt before them. (It was more than merely a gesture of respect. The tent, large as it was, wasn't tall enough to accommodate his height, and no one wanted to deal with Audriss's reaction if a carelessly placed horn was to rip open the roof.)

'Sit down, Mithraem,' Audriss offered magnanimously, his attitude blunted ever so slightly by the wine he'd consumed. 'Relax. He's not going to be able to tell you anything now that he couldn't five minutes ago, is he?'

Mithraem ignored him, focusing instead on the ogre. 'You were sent,' he spat coldly, 'to keep an eye—' Audriss chuckled once at the unintentional pun; Mithraem continued to ignore him, '—on Rebaine and the others. Was there some misunderstanding? Did you find your task too difficult?'

'No, Master,' the thing said in Urkran's voice.

'So tell me again why you've brought an incomplete report.'

'As I said, Master, there was a great deal of commotion when they first reached the ogres. Between the return of Corvis Rebaine and the homecoming of the one called Davro, there was little to be done. When Rebaine and the chieftain finally decided it was time to negotiate, they went off into the chieftain's own home. There was no opportunity to get near.'

'So then, of all times,' Audriss asked from his seat by the table, waving the goblet gently for emphasis, 'you chose *not* to fade into mist? You do it so often, I can't keep track of you lot as it is.'

The other three eyes in the room glared at Audriss and then turned back to regard one another.

'Well?' Mithraem said simply.

'I'm afraid that wasn't possible either, Master. While Rebaine and the chieftain were in discussions, most of the tribe gathered to celebrate Davro's return. It seems this one . . .' He gestured down at the body he currently wore. '. . . was known to look up to Davro, to emulate him, as do many of the warriors. There was a great deal of tale telling and drinking.' He shuddered in barely suppressed horror. 'I had to eat *food*!' he spat. Then, more calmly, 'There was no opportunity to slip away, not without arousing a great deal of suspicion.'

Mithraem shook his head, his dark hair glinting in the torchlight. 'It would, I think, have been worth it. I doubt we'll have need of this particular vessel again – but I suppose one never knows, does one? Very well, so what, precisely, *do* you know?'

'I know that Rebaine *did* come to some sort of agreement with the chieftain. I've no idea what offers or guarantees might have been made, but the tribe is preparing for war. When Rebaine is ready to march, the ogres will be with him.'

Mithraem glanced over at the Serpent, distractedly examining one of his maps. 'You heard?'

'Of course I heard, Mithraem! I'm aggravated, not deaf.'

'And do you not feel something should be done?'

'Eh.' Audriss waved a dismissive hand at him. 'This was to be expected, given Rebaine's past alliances. The ogres are a problem, but not an insurmountable one.'

'You're dismissed for now,' Mithraem told the not-quite-ogre. 'We'll continue this later.'

Urkran nodded once and faded into mist, seeping out through the tent flap and leaving a bloody swath on the floor as he passed. Mithraem snarled after his absent minion, then he, too, departed.

/*These people*,/ Pekatherosh complained with an exaggerated sigh, /*are absolute murder on carpeting.*/

'This is a tent, Pekatherosh,' Audriss replied under his breath. 'I haven't got any carpeting.'

/*That's because they murdered it.*/

'I wonder,' Audriss muttered, 'what sort of arrangement Rebaine came up with?'

/*Worried about the ogres? I thought you said they weren't an issue.*/

'Not substantially. They're dangerous, and they'll cost us some troops if it comes to direct conflict, but we can handle them. I'm more concerned with Rebaine. He's raising his army, but so far he hasn't taken any more dramatic steps.'

/*I told you it wouldn't be that easy. What you're trying to get him to do is, in his mind, a last resort. He'll need some additional motivation.*/

'Fine. Let's motivate him.' Audriss grinned behind the mask. 'And I think I know just the man to do it.' He clapped once, his stone gauntlets producing a dull cracking sound on impact. Instantly one of his soldiers stood in the tent's entryway.

'Yes, my lord?'

'Find Valescienn. Bring him here.'

'Commander? Sir, you'd better come with me.'

Garras Ilbin, a career soldier in the Regent's Army of Imphallion, muttered darkly under his breath as he turned away from the current object of his attentions. The young woman only scowled in response to his apologetic grin, and wandered off.

He squeezed his eyes shut for one brief moment – gods save him from fools and small villages – and ran a leather-gloved finger across his red-brown mustache. *Can't face the boys with ale in the facial hair; wouldn't be proper.*

Then, his hauberk clinking as he rose, he dropped a handful of copper coins on the countertop. He picked his helmet up off the stool beside him and bulled past the young soldier who stood, fidgeting, in the doorway.

'What in Kassek's name were you thinking, boy?' Garras demanded as he stepped into the street. His subordinate flinched, accustomed to hearing the war god invoked only in the heat of battle. His commander, on the other hand, was an old soldier, known to invoke Kassek for a spilled drink or a stubbed toe. 'Shouting across a crowded room? Is that how we communicate these days?'

The young man stared intently at his commander's leathery, weather-beaten face, his eyes wide. 'My apologies, Commander! But—'

'No discipline today, that's your problem,' Garras continued, paying little real attention to the boy he was lecturing. 'In my day, we respected our commanding officers! We had something to report, we walked up to them, told them to their face. None of this screaming like a housewife and fluttering about, oh, no. We . . .' His eyes hardened at the youth's expression. 'Anxious, are you? Have something better to do than listen to your commanding officer?'

The soldier swallowed. 'As a matter of fact, I do, sir! And so do you.'

'I *beg* your pardon. Are *you* telling *me* what I should or should not be—'

'Sir! You *really* need to come see this.'

It finally sank in, and Garras nearly groaned in self-disgust. The ale must have gotten to him more than he'd realised. But what could you expect, assigned to a patrol as mind-numbingly dull as the village of Kervone?

You'd think, Garras often griped, *there'd be some action in patrolling a town so near to Denathere. Hell, the entire city is enemy territory, now. But no* . . . Kervone, two days south of Denathere, was apparently far enough out of the way that the Serpent felt no need to bother with it. And that left Garras and his unit stuck guarding a town worth absolutely nobody's time to attack. It wasn't as if he *wanted* Audriss to raid the place; he was just so *bored*.

Well, maybe it was finally time for a little excitement.

The soldiers jogged through the dusty roads of Kervone, making enough of a racket not only to wake the dead, but to send them complaining to the landlord.

They finally arrived, Garras puffing ever so slightly, at the Sleeping Vagabond, where the soldiers barracked. Rather than approach the door, however, the soldier made a beeline for the rear of the building, whistling sharply. In response to his signal, someone dropped a rope ladder to roll down the wall. The young man climbed, Garras following, cursing softly, a moment later.

He felt better once he'd reached the flat-topped roof of the inn. The man currently on watch, keeping an eye on the various roads into town, was a dark-haired, dark-complexioned giant of a man named Tuvold. Garras and Lieutenant Tuvold had served together for years. If he'd sent for the commander, Garras could be damn certain there was a valid reason.

'All right, then,' Garras barked. 'What's so bloody urgent?'

'This, sir.' The soldier passed a brass spyglass, the unit's most valuable piece of equipment, to his commander. 'I was making a regular sweep of the roads,' he said succinctly, his deep voice clipped, measured. 'Watching for advance scouts or what have you.'

Garras nodded. 'You found something?'

'Not in the way of an attacking force,' Tuvold said, 'but look for yourself, sir. In that copse of trees, just west of north. No, farther over, in the other thicket. Yes, about there, sir.'

Garras scowled, one eye shut, the other pressed, squinting, against the spyglass. 'I see a bit of movement, Tuvold. Maybe a lone figure and a horse, but I can't make out much more than – good gods!' He choked as the 'horse' moved about, apparently seeking a spot of sunshine amid the shadows of the trees. 'By Kassek, that thing's the size of a pony!'

'Bigger, sir,' Tuvold told him calmly, as though giant

lizards were the sort of thing he saw twice before breakfast. 'It gets better.'

'Oh? And how could this possibly get better?'

'Look at the figure standing beside it, sir.'

Garras shifted the spyglass and then started, the colour draining from his face.

'A bit tall to be your average wanderer, Tuvold.'

'I'd noticed that myself, sir.'

'Ogre?'

'Can't think of anything else it could be, sir.'

Garras nodded sharply, trying, to no avail, to bring the ogre into focus through the obscuring screen of greenery. 'He's not scouting,' he muttered. 'He's just sitting there, like he's waiting for something.'

'Should we expect an attack, sir?' the young soldier asked, eyes wide.

'I shouldn't think so. We're a long way from ogre territory. No, he's here on his own, or with a few companions, at most.'

'Companions, sir?' Tuvold asked.

'Indeed.' With a loud pop, Garras snapped the spyglass shut and handed it back to Tuvold. 'Keep an eye on our large friend there, would you?'

'Certainly, sir. Where are you going?'

'I'm going to see if any travellers have entered town in the last few hours. I'm very interested in meeting anyone who'd keep company with an ogre.'

'And if they're a threat, sir?'

Garras just smiled, and stepped to the ladder. 'Assemble the men,' he ordered the younger soldier. 'Have them ready to move, but don't go anywhere until I get back. I'd hate for us to gang up on an innocent traveller by mistake. Makes us look bad, and that makes the baron look bad.'

Not that they were supposed to be there at all. Kervone was weeks away from Braetlyn. But Lord Jassion refused to sit by while the regent and the Guilds argued. Garras' squad was but one of many he'd dispatched throughout the kingdom to guard against Audriss' advance.

If the regent should learn that one of his lords had assigned troops to neighbouring territories, things could grow ugly indeed. The townsfolk wouldn't say anything, as they were happy to have the extra protection. But Garras wasn't about to risk exposure by mobilising his entire unit until he was *certain* these strangers posed a threat.

A few questions asked at the edge of town brought some interesting results. Two travellers had indeed come to Kervone, not two hours previously. A tall, lithe, grey-haired fellow, he was told, with an axe and a sword slung at his hip; and a woman, shorter, black of hair. Both were older – probably about Garras' own age, one astute merchant specified – but in excellent shape. The man led a horse, a fine animal but not large enough to have carried the both of them any great distance.

It was the third person to whom he'd described the strange pair – a young boy, no older than twelve or so – who pointed him in the right direction.

'Aye, sir, I seen 'em just a while back. Gave me a copper to show 'em to the empty house over yonder.'

'Empty?' Garras asked. The house the boy indicated was a good, solid dwelling. Nothing fancy, but a nice enough home for any man or family who'd choose to occupy it. 'Why is it empty? It looks fine to me.'

'That house, sir? 'Sbeen empty long as I can remember. Nobody wants to move in. They're afraid the old owner might come back an' want it.'

'Old owner? Who would that be, son?'

The boy glanced down at his feet, muttered something under his breath, and dashed off down the nearest side street.

Garras let him go, his eyes narrowing. 'Valescienn,' he muttered, turning it over in his mind. Why did that sound familiar . . . ?

Carefully, one hand clenched on his sword belt just beside the scabbard, Garras moved closer, ducking into a shadowed doorway as the pair of strangers stepped from the abandoned house and moved toward a small but sturdy horse tethered nearby.

'Damn! Damn it all!' That was the man.

The woman put a calming hand on his arm. 'It's not as though this is a surprise. We knew he might not be here, Corvis.'

The woman froze even as the words passed her lips, and the man snapped something in response – something about his name – but Garras, the blood pounding in his ears, barely heard a word of it. He felt his chest grow tight, and he found himself gasping for breath, leaning against the doorway to hold himself upright. Any one of the details could have been coincidence, any single fact was meaningless. But added up, they could only lead to one conclusion.

He remembered now who Valescienn was.

He knew who the ogre was waiting for, remembered who used to travel in their company.

And gods help him, he knew who 'Corvis' was.

His face covered in sweat, his head pounding with fear, Garras ran down the street as fast as his legs would carry him, all thoughts of stealth or caution thrown to the winds. There was no time! He needed to reach his men, to warn them, to send a message to Lord Jassioh. Everyone had to know! They . . .

Oh, gods!

Garras attempted to skid to a halt, caught one foot behind the other, and tumbled facedown into the dusty road. He looked up, moustache caked with dirt, to see two pairs of legs – one leather-clad, the other hidden behind a shifting curtain of brown fabric – standing over him.

'Well, Seilloah,' Corvis said, his voice even, 'you were right. Someone's been watching us.'

Corvis retreated a step as the mail-clad soldier rolled smoothly to his feet, unsheathing his blade. Though the man's jaw was clenched beneath his fox-hued moustache, and his eyes were anxious, the grip on his broadsword wavered not at all, and his stance was steady.

With a faint nod of respect, Corvis slipped Sunder from its own baldric.

'Make it quick,' Seilloah hissed from behind. 'We've no time for this nonsense!'

'Tell *him* that!' he shot back.

'I know you!' the soldier shouted at him. 'I know who you are, Rebaine!'

'Well, that's done it,' Seilloah muttered.

Corvis agreed. Bad enough if Audriss learned that Corvis Rebaine was raising arms against him. He didn't even want to contemplate the sheer chaos that would result should the nobles or the Guilds learn that the Terror of the East was back among them.

He lashed out with Sunder, the strike of a steel scorpion, hoping to end the duel before it began. Other than another of the Kholben Shiar, no weapon could survive the demon-forged blade.

But the soldier made no attempt to parry. Instead he leapt backward, his mail clattering, and let the weapon slip harmlessly by. He dropped then into a desperate lunge, determined to skewer this living nightmare like a pincushion.

Corvis twisted his wrists, spinning the ancient weapon. Sparks flew as Sunder's end-cap knocked the incoming blade off-track, nicking the edge. The soldier recovered swiftly, though, and for a moment the two opponents stood, once more crouched and ready, sizing each other up.

Corvis didn't doubt he could win this fight, but could he win it fast enough? Behind him, he heard Seilloah whispering, her fingers drifting in beautifully alien patterns. Apparently she had decided to speed up the process.

Not a bad idea, at that. Already, faces appeared in windows up and down the street, and figures in doorways. Unlike the soldier himself, the citizens of Kervone didn't know who they were staring at, but they knew him to be a stranger, and the other man to be a friend. Someone had surely gone for help . . .

'You there! Drop your weapon!'

The call came from behind the soldier, some distance down the street. Corvis cursed as he saw them, a squad of perhaps six, led by a huge man who twirled a massive ball-and-chain as if it were a toy. It was he who shouted.

'Drop the axe!' he yelled again.

'Tuvold, take care!' his commander called back, his eyes flickering over his shoulder for just an instant. 'It's Cor—'

Corvis lunged, desperate to shut the man's mouth. The old soldier saw the blow coming, and to his credit he very nearly dodged aside. Corvis followed, redirecting his attack, and felt Sunder shudder with the impact – but so awkward was the blow that it was the flat of the blade, rather than the razor-edge, that landed.

The soldier staggered abruptly, eyes wide and visibly glazing over. For a moment he stood, hesitantly raising a hand to the side of his head, just above his temple; he seemed puzzled by the blood that came away on his fingers. And then he collapsed, the impact sending a cloud of dust to swirl around Corvis' ankles.

Bellowing to shame the thunder, Tuvold redoubled his pace, his squad hot on his heels.

'We're too old for this,' Corvis muttered.

Seilloah shook her head, her own eyes fixed on the rapidly advancing soldiers. 'You're never too old to run away.'

Corvis slashed Rascal's tether with a quick flick of Sunder as he hurled himself into the saddle. A quick yank lifted Seilloah behind him, and his heels dug into the horse's side with rib-bruising force. With a startled grunt, Rascal leapt forward, easily outdistancing the enraged soldiers. It wasn't a pace he could maintain for long, but it would get them out of town. Once they'd got back to Davro and Rover, they could put a more comfortable distance between them and their pursuers.

Finally satisfied that any possible pursuit had fallen behind, Corvis reined the panting horse to a brisk walk and circled around toward their hidden camp. 'Going back isn't really an option at this point. If the man survived, then he survived. Not a damn thing I can do about it.'

'This,' Seilloah noted glumly, 'is going to come back to haunt us.'

There was little enough Corvis could say. As they neared the copse of trees, he dismounted, motioning for Seilloah to do the same.

Seilloah lifted a hand to brush her hair from her face, opened her mouth to say something – and froze, her arm half raised, as the sounds of faint conversation floated to them from the copse of trees.

Corvis nodded sharply – he'd heard it, too. With a bare whisper of noise he once again drew his axe, gripping it one-handed, Rascal's reins in his left fist.

The conversation continued, and Corvis' brow furrowed in bewilderment as they crept closer. He recognised one voice as Davro's, and the ogre sounded neither pained nor angry. But if the other speaker wasn't hostile, who the hell was he?

Deciding they were near enough, Corvis draped Rascal's reins over a low-hanging branch, and then leapt into the clearing, Sunder at the ready. Seilloah followed a step behind, lips already mouthing an incantation.

Davro jumped to his feet, hands reaching for his spear. The other figure moved not at all, except to allow an amused smile to cross his face.

'Gods below, Rebaine!' Davro exclaimed. 'You startled me out of at least ten years! I . . .'

Corvis paid the ogre no attention at all, fixing his gaze, instead, on the campsite's new visitor. His jaw fell slack at the sight of the one man he'd least expected to find.

'What's the matter, Lord Rebaine?' Valescienn asked, rising smoothly to his feet. 'Weren't you here to see me?'

CHAPTER ELEVEN

Ivriel was a nothing little flea-speck of a village, one that should've had absolutely no value to anyone whatsoever – except that it sat right on the edge of a line that existed only on a map. And which *side* of the line it sat on depended pretty heavily on whose map you were looking at.

None of the border skirmishes between Imphallion and Cephira had ever *started* over the worthless village, but with the talks over the trade city of Rahariem on the verge of breaking down – again – nearby Ivriel almost couldn't help but be caught up in any coming struggle.

So, just in case they proved necessary, several squads of Imphallion's army – the *real* army, the *loyal* army, not the mercenary (if better-equipped, better-paid, larger, and possibly better-trained) forces of the Guilds – wandered the tiny roads of tiny Ivriel, occupied every tiny room in the towns tiny inn, and bitched to one another about how tiny the place was.

Off-duty and not *quite* drunk enough to earn their commander's ire, two young officers wandered the earthen roads through the centre of town (which looked rather remarkably like every other part of town). They examined the wooden hovels, many only a single room that played home to families of nearly a dozen, and saw rag-clad children playing in the yards, chasing cats and rats that might, if things got even a *little* more desperate, quickly find themselves reassigned from playthings to meals.

'I don't get it, Valescienn. I really don't.'

The straw-haired officer, slightly taller than his companion, glanced contemptuously around. 'It's a pretty vile way to live, isn't it?' he agreed.

'No, that's not what I meant. It's . . . Why are we fighting for this place?'

'Just maybe because Cephira wants it? You weren't already drunk at the briefing, were you?'

'Valescienn, we don't *want* this place! Look at it! If it actually meant anything to the kingdom, to the regent, would we really have let it get this bad? Hell, the people here probably *welcome* this sort of conflict! At least it brings in a little outside coin when we rent out the inn.'

'We're not renting it. We've commandeered it.' Valescienn continued on several steps, only slowly realising his companion had stopped short.

'What? What is it?'

'Commandeered?' The tone was incredulous, and Valescienn honestly hadn't realised the other's voice could *get* that high. 'Why? These are our own people we're starving!'

'No money. You know damn well that if this flares up into a war, the regent's going to need the Guilds to pitch in. The army's not spending one coin more than it has to. We're lucky we're still getting paid at all, and you know it.'

'So we're perfectly happy spending the money to defend the place, but not to keep it alive?'

Valescienn shrugged. 'It costs the Guilds and the regent – in reputation, if not in money – to let Cephira conquer the place. Doesn't cost them a damn thing to let it fade away into the dust.'

'That's *astoundingly* shortsighted, Valescienn.'

'Fine. You go tell them that.'

'I just might,' Officer Rebaine replied.

Corvis, axe dangling from fingers gone slack, gazed numbly at the man he'd come to find. Seilloah stared at Corvis. Davro watched them both, still on edge. And Valescienn's face remained locked in that quirky grin. Neither tapestry nor sculpture could have been more lifeless, more static, than that frozen tableau.

Almost languidly, Davro's eye blinked, and at that signal life resumed. Corvis, grinning abruptly, tossed Sunder to his left hand and extended his right. Valescienn did the same, and the two men clasped arms, one warrior to another.

'I found Valescienn,' the ogre said. 'You can blackmail him now.'

'Davro,' Seilloah spat, 'hush!'

Fortunately, Corvis seemed not to hear. 'What are you doing out here, damn it all? We've been all over town looking for you.'

'So I've heard,' Valescienn told him.

'Heard from whom?'

'As for what I'm doing out here,' the scar-faced man continued, ignoring the question, 'Davro's been asking me that same question.'

The ogre nodded. 'He wouldn't answer me, though. Kept telling me to be patient.'

'But of course,' Valescienn told him. 'I wanted you all together for this.'

It was a cue if ever there was one. The clearing grew chill, a low-lying fog pouring from the earth. It moved in waves, wisps darting this way and that. Tree roots, bushes, and boots reflected a dull crimson in its wake. The air grew thick with a salty, coppery scent.

Rascal whinnied, dancing as he strove to keep his hooves from the haze, and Rover ambled awkwardly into the trees. Davro and Seilloah backed away from the centre of the clearing, the witch, a glimmer of recognition in her saucer-wide eyes, already whispering an incantation.

Valescienn, too, moved to step back, only to find his arm locked in an unyielding grip. Corvis' fingers dug into his flesh.

Even through the thick leather, the warrior knew he must already sport deep bruises.

'Corvis, what—'

'Has it been so long, Valescienn, that you take me for a fool?' A furious scowl wiped all traces of the grin from Corvis' face. 'Have I supposedly become such a dullard that I'll walk into any trap some half-wit lays before me?'

With his free hand, Valescienn grabbed for the flail at his hip, but Corvis proved the quicker, twisting with every bit of strength that middle age had left him.

Valescienn was the stronger man, and well trained, and thus escaped the worst of the injury. Rather than snapping like a twig, his arm simply slipped from its socket with a moist pop.

Swallowing his agony, Valescienn turned completely about, his injured arm hanging behind his back as no healthy limb could have done. He lashed out with his left elbow, a brutal, bone-crushing strike. Corvis dodged the blow, avoiding a broken nose, but lost his grip in the process.

'You – you . . .' Left hand clutched to right shoulder, his arm hanging flaccid beneath it, Valescienn retreated. His jaw was clenched, his eyes burning.

Corvis smoothly shifted Sunder into his favoured two-handed grip. 'You picked the wrong side, traitor.'

'Traitor? I haven't served you for seventeen years – and when I did, it was *you* who abandoned *us*!'

Corvis merely shrugged and raised his blade.

'Corvis!'

He spun at Seilloah's call. She herself was unharmed, for her spell of protection held the creature at bay. But she'd been unable to do the same for their large companion.

The last wisps of fog coalesced into a man-shaped pillar, the features flushing with roiling blood, congealing into a corporeal creature. A wiry hand clasped the towering ogre, forcing him to his knees. Corvis, gorge rising, watched as the creature placed fleshy lips upon Davro's face. The ogre fell limp as the pores on his cheek widened and began to pump blood into his attacker's mouth.

Shouting, Corvis hurled Sunder across the clearing. The blade glinted in the light, finally sinking deep into the enemy's back. The creature reared in pain, its face aimed skyward. It screamed, an inhuman wail of agony, and Davro's stolen blood erupted from its mouth, showering the campsite in gore.

Even as they watched, the body rotted into a sodden lump of refuse, mouldering flesh sliding from bone to form a growing pool. Mist poured from the skull and whipped away into the forest, an undulating serpent of poison. The residue in its wake was thin and sickly, nigh undetectable. Sunder landed with a dull thump in the putrescent mass.

Before the body rotted completely away, Corvis spun to face Valescienn once more, drawing the sword from his left hip.

The enemy was nowhere to be seen. Brief examination of footprints left in the soft soil suggested Valescienn had taken two steps and simply vanished. Corvis knew well that his former vassal had no head for magic, and that someone else must have been waiting to teleport him to safety.

He allowed himself a single shout of anger, lopping the nearest branch from an inoffensive tree. Then, sheathing his sword with a vicious snap, he crossed the gore-encrusted grass to stand beside Seilloah.

'How is he?'

'Weak,' Seilloah replied from beside Davro's stricken form. 'He lost an astonishing amount of blood. But given a few days, I think he'll recover.'

'What . . .' Davro's hand rose feebly from his attacker's remains, dripping a crimson sludge. 'What was it?'

'It turned into mist and sucked your blood out through your skin, Davro,' Seilloah said. 'What does that sound like to you?'

Davro's shudder ran from horn to heels. Even the ogres had their horror stories of the Endless Legion. 'But it's dead?'

Seilloah knew well that it might not be. Dwelling on the border between life and death, the creature could survive only briefly without a mortal body to inhabit. Having that body ripped out from under it was, legend told, a terrible injury. Still, if it found someone sick, or sleeping, or otherwise vulnerable to inhabitation before it starved, someone whose body it could use to feed off others, it might survive.

Davro needed know none of this, just now. 'Yes,' she told him. 'It's dead.'

The ogre grunted.

'Corvis,' Seilloah said, rising to her feet and striding away from the resting ogre, 'we have to talk.' Bemused, Corvis retrieved Sunder – it repelled the surrounding blood, rising clean from the fluids in which it lay – and followed.

'It's daytime,' he noted, almost to himself. 'Those things are weaker during the day, aren't they?'

'Very good, Corvis. And what does that tell you?'

'They're desperate. Or they want us to think they're desperate.' His voice was thoughtful. 'I wish I'd killed it properly.'

'Next time,' she barked at him. 'While you're waiting, you've got a choice to make.'

'Seilloah . . .'

'Our enemies are teleporting people around, they're sending the undead after us. Corvis, my magic won't be enough!'

'Seilloah, I told you, I won't even consider—'

He reared back, face stinging from her sudden slap.

'What the hell was *that* for?'

'I'm trying to knock some sense into you, you imbecile! We need him!'

'Seilloah, you've no idea what you're asking.'

'I'm asking no less of you than you are of us, Corvis. No less than you *demanded* of Davro. We can't do you, Tyannon, or your children any good if we die out here. What if Audriss had sent five of those things instead of one? What if he'd sent a dozen? I can't fight that many, and I can't prevent him from finding us.'

'Then why aren't we dead already?' Corvis challenged.

'I don't know. Maybe we're not enough of a threat. Maybe Valescienn was keeping an eye on his old stomping grounds and saw us nosing about. Maybe Audriss *didn't* actually arrange this, though I find that hard to believe. But we've been stupid lucky so far, and you know it! I'll fight for you, Corvis, but I won't throw my life away because you're too stubborn to accept the truth.

'We need him, Corvis. We need Khanda.'

And Corvis, suddenly as weary as he could ever recall, fell back against the nearest tree, at last admitting to himself that Seilloah was right.

Gods help them all.

'You're what?'

'I said,' Corvis repeated as he double-checked the heavy winter clothes they'd recently acquired, 'I'm going alone.'

They were currently ensconced in a copse of trees some ten miles from their previous camp. The aroma of thick soil permeated the air, and the plants, other than those trampled by Davro's stumbling gait, bloomed brightly in the summer warmth. The weakened ogre wasn't easy to move, but all three agreed that they'd little choice. Kervone's soldiers still sought the strangers who'd assaulted their commander, to say nothing of the distinct possibility of Valescienn's sudden return.

Food was no issue: Corvis and Seilloah had waylaid a farmer driving a few cattle into town. The animals provided sustenance for Corvis and the ogre (who consumed a whole cow at one sitting), while Seilloah made herself a meal of . . . Well, Corvis wasn't certain *what* the meal was, but he did notice, without making any comment, the absence of the farmer's body. He'd have preferred to let the man go — he'd shed too much blood, brought back too many memories — but nobody could be permitted to report on their where-abouts.

It was also from among the trunks carried by these

unfortunate folks that Corvis acquired a bundle of furs, blankets, and other cold-weather apparel. When Seilloah asked him if those were necessary for retrieving Khanda, Corvis had answered in the affirmative. That was also when he'd told them the other part of the plan.

'I'm going alone.'

'You're insane!' Seilloah shouted at him, actually waving her hands over her head. 'You're going to get yourself killed!'

'Weren't you just telling me that we needed Khanda so I *wouldn't* get us killed?' he asked mildly.

'Yes, but I didn't mean for you to go traipsing off by yourself to Arhylla-knows-where to do it! You need us!'

'I do not now,' Corvis protested lamely, 'nor have I ever, "traipsed."'

Davro, back to his old self save for a slight pallor in the face, nodded once. 'Got to agree with him here, Seilloah. I think, even at his most carefree, the best I've seen was a semi-frolic, with maybe a half skip.'

'I *do* need you, Seilloah,' he told her, briefly wondering why he'd bothered to save the ogre. 'I need you to keep working while I'm gone.'

'Working on what?'

Corvis sighed. 'Audriss is moving, the ogres are assembling, and we still lack an army. I need you to tell the ogres where to assemble, and I need there to be an army waiting for them when they get there.'

Seilloah and Davro stared blankly.

'I made a point of listening for any news while we were hunting for Valescienn. Rumour has it Audriss' army is continuing west. The next major cities that way are Orthessis and Abtheum, and unless he's foolish enough to take his army off-road, he's got to pass through Vorringar.'

'How the hell do you remember all this?' Davro asked sourly.

'Years spent studying every map I could find. You might recall that I made a fairly serious effort at conquering this damn kingdom?'

'You seem to be forgetting,' Seilloah interjected, 'that Davro and I don't know the first thing about finding mercenaries. It's why you wanted Valescienn to begin with. And even if we managed, what would you have us pay them with? Our winning smiles?'

Davro offered his best toothy grin, replete with dangling bits of cow sinew.

'We don't have the option of doing things the traditional way anymore,' Corvis said flatly, placing one booted foot in the stirrup. 'You're a witch, Seilloah. Come up with something.'

'But . . .'

He overrode her. 'Once you've got my army, assemble at Vorringar. If you gather most of your soldiers from farther west, you should get there before Audriss does. It's, what, midsummer now. My best guess is, he won't reach Vorringar until the frost. If I'm not back by then, Seilloah, you're in command.'

She froze, mouth agape, and then laughed at him.

'Well,' Corvis muttered, 'that's certainly encouraging.' He settled Sunder more comfortably at his side and made one last check to ensure the saddlebags were secure. 'Davro, if I'm not back by then, you're free to go home.'

'And if you do come back?'

'Then you're stuck with me awhile longer.'

The ogre's mouth twitched. 'So you'll not be surprised if I don't wish you the best of luck.'

'Of course not. Why start now?'

'Corvis,' Seilloah tried one more time. 'What if—'

'No "what ifs". I'm counting on you.' Corvis put his heels to Rascal's flanks and was gone.

'Well,' Davro said philosophically, 'this is interesting.'

'What do we do now?' Seilloah shouted. 'I don't have the first notion of how to raise an army!'

'Seilloah,' the ogre said, his voice thoughtful, 'if he doesn't come back, do you really intend to take command? Or will you up and go home?'

'Probably go home,' she admitted, seating herself upon a long-dead stump. 'We don't have a chance without him. I know as much about tactics as I do hiring mercenaries.'

Davro nodded. 'And no human army would take orders from me, even if I went mad and decided to stick around.'

'What are you getting at, Davro? That we should just give up?'

'Much as I'd like to, no. I took an oath, and I'll abide by it. But since neither of us intends to remain if he *doesn't* show up, then you wouldn't be opposed to a solution that only works if he *does* show up, would you? After all, if everything breaks down because he fails to appear, we won't be there to suffer for it.'

Seilloah blinked. 'I'm not entirely sure I followed that. What do you have in mind?'

He told her.

'*A lot* of nasty people will be upset with us if this doesn't work,' she commented afterward.

The ogre shrugged. 'Doesn't bother me. As I said, I don't intend on being there to see it.'

'Nor do I. All right then. He wants to give us an impossible task, he gets to deal with the impossible solution. Let's move.'

CHAPTER TWELVE

The axe blade fell with a savage crunch, almost loud enough to drown out the explosive grunt emitted by the fellow wielding it. Wood split beneath steel, and then petulantly closed around it, refusing either to release the tool or to cooperatively split down the middle.

'Cerris' grunted a second time, glared furiously at the log that *should* have been firewood by now, and released the handle so he could massage his aching palms with his fingertips. The wood wasn't going to chop itself – though that'd make for a useful spell, come to think of it – but there was plenty of time yet before the autumn turned to cold, and when Corvis realised that he was seriously contemplating going to fetch Sunder to use on the stubborn lumber, he decided that it was probably time to call it a day.

As he turned back toward the house, seeking a cool drink and respite from the sun, he clearly heard from the far yard what he had initially thought were mere echoes of his own futile axe-work. Since it hadn't ceased when he did, however, he wandered his way around the corner to see what was happening. And had to stifle a laugh as Lilander – clad in what was his best outfit, beneath at least three layers of dirt – leapt and careered through the vegetable gardens with a boisterous abandon found only in young boys or men in love. The child was armed with a good solid stick and was mercilessly engaging the weeds in close combat. (He had, thankfully, sufficient sense even at his age not to behead his mother's vegetables.)

Mellorin, her own tunic and flowing skirts spotlessly clean, was playing with her younger brother – that is, following behind him with frequent eye-rolls and remonstrations at what he was doing.

For long moments, Corvis stood beyond the corner of the little house and simply watched, a peculiar grin hovering about his lips. When the boy's constant dashing about threatened to trample a row of tomatoes, however, Corvis decided it was time to play Responsible Parent.

'Its Kingsday, isn't it?' he asked, stepping into view of the cavorting children. 'Shouldn't you be in town?'

Kingsday in Chelenshire was the one day of the week when the village elders and priests gathered the children of the community for schooling in letters, history, and religious doctrine. It was, so far as the *parents* of Chelenshire were concerned, a greater day of thanks even than Godsday proper.

'Father . . .' Mellorin sighed, somehow drawing the word out for the span of at least four extra syllables. 'Lessons were over *hours* ago.'

'Ah.' Corvis glanced up at the sun once more. 'I suppose they were. So what exactly are the two of you—'

He grunted, more in surprise than pain, as a thin stick whapped him across the shin. Lilander stood beside him, his 'sword' held out very seriously before him. 'I'm Nafnal!' he announced proudly.

Corvis raised an eyebrow and glanced at his daughter. 'Nafnal?'

Mellorin sighed, clearly vexed at the adult's inability to translate Lilander-speak. 'He means "Nathaniel", Father. Goodman Ostwyr taught us about the Battle of Denathere today.'

'Did he, now?' Corvis hoped the ice that had suddenly formed in his chest wouldn't harden his words or shine through suddenly narrowed eyes.

'Yes, and now Lilander wants to be Nathaniel Espa and won't stop his stupid sword fighting!'

As if in punctuation, the boy once again made a concerted effort to slay whatever evil beast had taken the shape of his father's knee.

'And where's *your* sword?' Corvis asked her, still struggling to keep his voice steady.

'I,' she informed him loftily, 'do not need a *sword*. I'm Rheah Vhoune. Everyone knows that magic's better than swords any – *eep*!!'

Mellorin could only struggle, mortified beyond belief at her father's sudden display of affection, but escape was impossible. Corvis all but crushed his daughter to his chest, determined to hold her so that she wouldn't see him cry.

Through most of Imphallion, the leaves had begun their annual blush, greens fading into deep reds and rich golds. Sensing the earliest stirrings of the winds, animals began gathering food stores in preparation for the snows that would come in but a few short months. Some of the northernmost territories, farthest from the lands where winter slumbered throughout the year, still sweltered under the tarrying caress of summer. There, people wiped sweaty hands across sweaty brows and impatiently awaited the relief that autumn had already brought to their southern neighbours.

But here, south of Imphallion's lowest borders, many weeks beyond the reach of the regent and the Guilds, stretched lands where winter never relaxed its icy grasp, where snowless summers were a myth of foreign climes. The drifts were already knee-high, the winds mighty enough to stagger a careless traveller and sharp enough to bite through the thickest furs and cloaks. Here, at the feet of the mighty Terrakas Mountains, where even the valleys sat far above the level of distant seas, there was nothing but deadly cold.

A trade route, scarcely used but vital to a select few, wound through the mountain range. Though it rarely rose from the foothills or stretched high into the peaks themselves, it proved a hazardous, arduous path. Still, a steady if minuscule flow of traffic moved along that path. For the exhausted, frostbitten traveller, it even offered a place to rest.

The village, a feeble collection of huts scattered across a vale in the highest foothills, was called Ephrel. Home mostly to trappers and hunters, with a native population of less than thirty, it held but two claims to distinction. One, it was the highest permanent community in the Terrakas Mountains, not counting the villages of the Terrirpa clans. Two, it was the home of the tavern.

The tavern had no name. It had never needed one. Among those merchants who traversed the treacherous road and those hardy few willing to brave the icy slopes and powerful storms of the Terrakas, it was as well known as the mountains themselves. It was the only place a man could find a good drink, a hot meal, and possibly a nighttime companion before trudging once more into the snows. It offered rooms for rent and stables for any animals that survived the trek – all the comforts that could possibly be expected in such a desolate place. And all at prices a mere four or five times those common to Imphallion's greatest cities.

Today was a fairly typical day at the tavern. The barkeep, also the owner, was remarkably well groomed. His hair, tied in a series of tails, was relatively clean, and he'd lost only a small number of teeth to rot and barroom brawls. Standing behind the thick oaken bar, he occupied himself wiping a heavy wooden tumbler with a rag even cleaner than he was.

Slumped at several tables was a motley collection of men, all wrapped in furs, and most grown rather pungent over the course of time. Many folks believed that bathing during winter was an unhealthy practice, and the winter was long indeed in the Terrakas Mountains. Gathered around them, or fluttering through the large common room, were the tavern's other 'employees.' Business for them was slow today. Only one of the whores had managed to drum up any custom, and the sounds of that transaction, emerging from an upstairs room, irritated the other patrons.

The grumble of conversation filled the room, bouncing from table to table, careering off the oilcloth windows, and swirling about the shoulders of the stranger who sat alone in a corner, a mug of bitter ale perched before him. He was tall; that much was clear even through his heavy layers of fur. His hair reached past his shoulders. He wore a matching beard, a thick growth more likely the result of neglect than any conscious choice. The angry red of his face and the rough chapping of his skin suggested a man unaccustomed to the bitter environs.

With the exception of a single word – 'Ale' – he'd spoken not at all since he'd appeared in the doorway, snow-encrusted, three hours past. One of the whores, dark-haired and slender, made as if to proposition him when he first sat down. She might, in another life, have been pretty, but the years had smothered her spirit long ago, and her eyes were dull. The stranger shook his head and sent her on her way, and then he'd simply waited.

The door swung open to bounce loudly against the wall, the latch gouging another chip from the scarred wood. Framed against the snow stood a man whose grandfather must have been a grizzly. Though well over six feet tall, the breadth of his shoulders made him appear squat. Shaggy brown hair sprouted from every visible inch of his head, face, and his arms. It was impossible, without close examination, to determine where the furs he wore left off and his own coat began.

'Beer!' the man roared with a voice like an onrushing avalanche.

'Right away!' the bartender squeaked. 'One beer!'

'Didn't say "one" beer! I said "beer"! Keep 'em coming till I say otherwise!'

The smaller man nodded and all but attacked the nearest tap. The bear-man stood impatiently, scanning the room with brown, beady eyes as he waited. Apparently, he didn't care for what he saw.

'Hey, you!'

The grey-haired stranger glanced up to see the bear making a bee-line toward him. No surprise, that. It had, he decided, been inevitable.

He did not tense. He did not rise. Instead, he leaned back just far enough from the table to provide a clear view of the wicked axe that lay beside him.

'If you even try to tell me I'm in your chair,' the stranger said, 'I'll kill you.'

Caught with his mouth half open, the mountain man bristled – looking rather more like a hedgehog than a bear at that instant – and then deflated. Something in the stranger's eyes suggested that, just maybe, he ought to be taken seriously.

With a nod and a sickly grin, he pivoted to go back to the bar.

As soon as the bear's back was turned, the stranger stood up and clocked him over the back of the head with his mug. The building shook to the rafters as the trapper toppled, unconscious, to the floor.

At the incredulous stares, the stranger could only shrug. 'He'd just have come back after he'd gotten drunk,' he explained.

'You can't do that to Grat!' one of the fur-clad men protested, starting to rise from his own seat.

Grat? That was Grat? Crap.

'I just did.' The newcomer raised his axe for all to see, then set it very softly on the table. 'Is that going to be a problem?'

'No!' the barkeep shouted, waving frantically at the man who'd spoken up. 'No problem! We're all happy here! Everyone's happy!'

A few snarls and scowls suggested everyone was *not* happy, but there was no further trouble.

The stranger resumed his seat, sparing a single glance for the unconscious giant who now lay snoring in the centre of the taproom. 'Well, this is great. What the hell do I do now?'

'Perhaps, good Master, I may be of some small assistance?'

From behind the stranger appeared another fellow, clad in furs bleached an ugly off-white. He was slender, a far cry from the barrel-chested trappers around them. His skin was a shade darker than theirs, and there was a foreign cast to his eyes. His long black hair hung in a single tail, and his smile, an unctuous expression, showed a mouthful of yellowed teeth.

'You shouldn't sneak up on people, friend,' the stranger said to him, slowly loosening his grip where it had dropped instinctively to the haft of his brutal weapon. 'That's a good way to get yourself killed.'

'I humbly bow to your superior wisdom, good Master.' The new arrival gestured toward the table. 'May I have the honour of joining you?'

'Why not?'

For several moments they sized each other up. Finally, the man in white deigned to speak. 'I watch you for some while, good Master. You were waiting for this man Grat, were you not?'

'I was,' the stranger admitted. 'I was given his name in the last village as a man I might hire to guide me into the mountains. Unfortunately, even if he wakes up anytime soon, I don't think he'll want to talk to me.'

'Indeed? But this is to your good fortune!'

The stranger frowned. 'How do you figure?'

'Grat is a competent trapper, good Master, but he is not the man to be your guide into the Terrakas peaks. It is a treacherous place, very dangerous. A man of purpose and importance, such as yourself, should have only the best and most skilled of guides. You, my good friend, must have one of the Terrirpa as your escort.'

Native to the Terrakas, the Terrirpa were said to thrive in the mountains as no one else could. They possessed not only an astounding resistance to cold, but the ability to breathe comfortably at elevations that would cripple most people. Add to that a nearly infallible sense of direction, and they did indeed make excellent guides.

'You have a point,' the grey-haired man admitted. 'I hadn't expected to find any of the Terrirpa in this place. But,' he added, before the other man could speak, 'it seems, by the great fortune you so shrewdly mentioned, that I have just such a one sitting before me. Is that not so?'

'It is indeed, most astute Master.' The other man's eyes twinkled. 'For a modest fee, if you will condescend to allow one so unworthy to travel beside you, I will be delighted to take you wherever it is in these magnificent lands you need go.' He stuck forth his right hand, palm upward in the local custom. 'I am called Sah-di, good Master.'

The stranger placed his own palm above the other. 'Very good, Sah-di. And I am called Cerris.'

The Terrirpa nodded. 'Cerris. It is well. Let us get past the distasteful task of negotiating my humble fees, and we shall be off.'

The haggling took well over an hour, and at the end, all Corvis managed was to drag a truly appalling figure down into the realm of the merely distressing. Yes, he possessed more than sufficient funds, but it was the principle of the thing that galled him.

While his new guide went to his room to gather his equipment, Corvis sauntered to the bar, glaring down at the proprietor, who was trying his absolute hardest to keep a simpering grin fixed to his face.

'Can I help you, m'lord?'

'Yes. I've a horse resting in your stables at the moment.' Poor Rascal, who'd barely made it this far through the cold, couldn't possibly have gone one step farther. At the moment, he was shivering under three or four layers of blankets and probably wishing dreamily, in the way only homesick horses can, for wide-open grasses and fresh apples. 'I need to leave him there until I return. Possibly as long as several weeks.'

'I see, m'lord. Of course.' Already, Corvis knew, the bartender was thinking over a list of the men who would be willing to pay good money in exchange for good horseflesh.

'And the cost for stabling a horse for two weeks, friend?'

'Ah, I believe two silver pennies should cover it, m'lord.'

An outrageous price, but no less inflated than the rest of the costs in this tavern at the edge of nowhere. Corvis removed a small leather pouch from beneath his coat and plunked it down onto the bar. The barkeep's eyebrows rose at the solid clank, and Corvis could swear he saw the man's lip quiver. With a smile, he upended the bag. The fellow's breath caught in his throat at the sight of the small glinting disks – gold, not silver – piled before him.

'Three half-nobles,' Corvis told him steadily. 'There are three more in it for you when I come back to claim him.'

The bartender gaped and gasped as though something obscene was happening beneath the level of the counter. 'I – that is, yes, m'lord! Of course.' He began scooping the proffered coins into the strongbox, and moved as if to hand the empty pouch back to Corvis.

'Keep that.'

The other man frowned. 'Keep the pouch?'

'Indeed. You might need it.'

'I'm not certain I follow you, m'lord.'

Corvis' smile widened, splitting his recently acquired beard. 'You see,' Corvis explained, casually examining the edge on Sunder, 'if the horse *isn't* waiting for me when I get back – and in perfect health – you're going to spend the rest of your life carrying your testicles around in your hands. So a pouch might come in handy.

'Do you follow me now?'

'Yes, m'lord!' The other man gulped. 'Quite well!' And then he was gone, having suddenly decided that something on the other side of the bar needed his attention *right away*.

'I'm so glad,' Corvis called after him. With a satisfied nod, he strode back through the front door, moving around to the stables to bid Rascal farewell.

His lungs burned from the icy air within his chest. Even with a thick cloth wrapped about his nose and mouth, and another tied over his eyes to blot out the worst of the light reflecting from the endless white, his face felt as if it would soon fall off the front of his skull. It was an all-consuming task to keep placing one foot in front of the other. His only signs of progress were the crunching of ice and snow beneath his boots, and the endless trail of footprints he and his guide left snaking along the mountainside.

With the butt-end of Sunder, Corvis tapped Sah-di on the shoulder. The Terrirpa stopped and turned about. Corvis was certain he'd said something, but his voice was lost in the howling of the winds.

Apparently seeing his employer's confusion, Sah-di practically shouted in his ear, 'You wish something of me, good Master?'

'I just . . .' Corvis coughed twice, attempting to regain some feeling in his numbed throat, and tried again. This time his voice, though rough as coal, was intelligible. 'I just wanted to know if this really is the easiest route,' he shouted.

'To all intents and purposes, good Master.'

Corvis pursed his cracking lips. 'What do you mean, "to all intents and purposes"?'

'You tell me you seek the way up Mount Molleya. This is the way we should go. But there are other ways, if the Master prefers. Ways of a more shallow incline than this.'

'Then why the godsforsaken thrice-damned hell are we taking *this* one?'

'Because the other routes, most patient Master, would add considerable time to our journey.'

'Translate "considerable" for me.'

'Oh, at least a week in each direction.'

Corvis fought the urge to whimper. 'This would probably be our best route, then.'

'As the wise Master suggests.'

And so it went, for several millennia-long days. The hours blurred together, smearing into a single, bleary tunnel of bright white below, bright blue above, hideous cold, winds threatening to hurl him over the edge of the precarious trail, and exhaustion so all-encompassing that even his teeth and his hair were tired. And thus, it was with no small amount of dumbfounded astonishment that he happened to glance up past the shoulders of his guide one afternoon to discover several thin plumes of smoke wafting into the air beyond the next ridge.

'One of the villages of my people, good Master,' Sah-di yelled back to him. 'From that point on, the slope grows steeper, I'm afraid. But it may provide us a place to stop and rest up beforehand.'

'May? I don't care for the ambiguity there, Sah-di.'

The Terrirpa shrugged. 'It shames me, forgiving Master, that I cannot give you a certain answer. But I do not know this village. Though I have passed by, I have never before felt the need to stop. I know not what clan they claim, so I cannot know for certain if they will be well disposed toward me.'

Corvis followed his strange companion toward the edge of the ridge, then down into a small hollow – a valley in the very side of the mountain itself – in which sat a circle of crude huts.

A log palisade, scarcely more than a thick fence, blocked the path before them, and the mountains themselves guarded the village from most other angles of approach. Two men, clad in thick furs and with the same unusual cast to their features as Sah-di, flanked a swinging gate bolted into the logs. One stepped forth as Corvis and his guide approached, a hand on the hilt of his mace, while the other sentinel wrapped his own grip around a pull-rope that would, no doubt, set alarm bells tolling at the slightest tug.

The foremost sentry spoke, but whatever he said was completely lost on Corvis. His language was somehow beautiful and repulsive at once, lyrical yet harsh to the unaccustomed ear.

'Please, my good friend,' Sah-di implored him, hands clasped together at waist level. 'In the language of the north. It would not do to insult our guest by speaking as though he were not here.'

'I don't know you,' the guard grumbled in a gruff voice, 'or your friend. What have you done to earn my courtesy?' But he said it in the language of Imphallion, albeit heavily accented.

'Courtesy, good friend, is something to be given without question,' Sah-di chided him. 'Not a prize to be won.'

It was not a debate the sentinel was inclined to continue. 'Who are you,' he demanded sharply, 'and what do you want?'

'My name is Sah-di, of the Pa-ram. The gentle lord behind me has been gracious enough to allow this humble traveller to guide him through the peaks. We seek merely to beg shelter for the night, and perhaps a morsel or two of food. Tell me, good friend, what clan claims this village?'

The soldier – whose shoulders, Corvis noted, visibly slumped at the name 'Pa-ram – muttered, 'Sho-rin.'

The clans of the Terrirpa, Sah-di explained to his employer over a hot dinner that night, were bound via a veritable webwork of boons, favours, and influence. Every clan had several other clans required, often by debts many generations old, to submit to their authority. They, in turn, had others to which they must answer. It was not unheard of, in fact, for one clan to hold supremacy over a second, which held supremacy over a third, which held supremacy over the first. It was a confusing, muddled system, one that an outsider could never hope to fully understand.

But the practical upshot of it all, Sah-di told him – and the only aspect concerning them – was that the clan Pa-ram currently held a multigenerational debt over the Sho-rin. 'In essence, good Master, for the duration of our stay we are as kings in this tiny village.' He grinned. 'I find my territorial borders perhaps a bit confining, but I suppose it is a place to begin.'

Corvis, who'd briefly dominated half of Imphallion, found himself underwhelmed.

But at least they had a warm room for the night, in the home of one of the villagers. The man and his family had been volunteered, as their house's location near the far gate would allow the travellers the earliest possible start the next morning. That he owned one of the largest houses, and that his wife was one of the town's best cooks – both details Sah-di pried from the sullen sentries – were simply fringe benefits.

Their supper, consisting of roast mountain goat and steamed vegetables (grown gods alone knew where) smothered in various sauces, was surprisingly good. Terrirpa culture being what it was, the two visitors sat and discoursed on various unimportant topics with the gentleman who owned the house, while the man's wife and daughter prepared and served the meal.

Over the course of dinner, Corvis noticed his guide's eyes settling more and more frequently, with a certain ungentle gleam, on the girl: a young thing barely scratching the border between adolescence and adulthood. She was, Corvis estimated, not much older than Mellorin herself. That particular thought, once unleashed, ballooned outward to fill his brain until he could think of nothing else. Sah-di continued to leer, and Corvis grew angrier by the minute.

Finally, though, the meal was concluded with nothing untoward, and the day's exhaustion swooped down on Corvis like a striking raptor. He barely had sufficient energy to excuse himself from the table and bid his host a polite good night before he collapsed unconscious onto the thick pad he'd been provided.

He slept soundly and undisturbed, dreaming over and over again of home, of the laughter of children, of Tyannon's gentle eyes.

Chapter Thirteen

'I don't think I pronounced that right,' Corvis admitted.

'Ah, no. Had you actually been casting the spell, I think there's a very good chance you'd have just melted something off. If you were *lucky*, it would've been your face.'

Grunting, Corvis leaned back against the wall and allowed himself to slide slowly to the floor until he sat limply, limbs splayed out like a jellyfish washed up on the beach. Dark circles marred the flesh under his eyes, and both his forehead and bare chest were soaked with sweat.

Seilloah, of course, looked perfectly composed, not a single hair out of place or a wrinkle on her dress. But then, Seilloah *always* looked perfectly composed.

'This isn't going to work, Seilloah,' he muttered finally.

'Of course it is. You just need a few minutes to rest.'

'No, I—'

'We'll start with a different incantation,' she insisted, sorting through the pile of scraps and cracked leather bindings that covered the room's only table. 'Something a little less complex, maybe.'

'Seilloah, there *aren't any* that are less complex.'

'Oh, nonsense. That incantation was Second Circle. And you've already mastered so much of the First.'

Corvis glared, fingers tapping on the wooden floor.

The witch sighed and gracefully lowered herself to sit across from him.

'You can't give up, Corvis. You said it yourself when we met: you can't make this work with force of arms alone.

You need magic – and modesty compels me to admit that I'm probably not enough on my own.'

'Right. And if I had a few decades to study, we might make this work. But I don't, and we can't.'

'So what do you . . . Corvis, no.'

'Why not? You and I both know they exist, Seilloah. I read about them before I even met you.'

'Corvis, the power those icons grant *isn't your own*. The discipline required to control—'

'Do you really think I have a problem with discipline, Seilloah? I can handle it, and you know it.'

Seilloah took a deep, steadying breath. 'Corvis, where do you think the power of those icons comes from? Why do you think that every tale you've read of them ends badly?'

Ignoring the twinge of exhausted muscles, Corvis leaned away from the wall. 'So tell me. What's inside them?'

'Demons, Corvis. The icons you're talking about contain bound demons.'

Long moments of silence. Then, 'Oh.'

'That changes things, doesn't it?' Seilloah suggested.

'No, it actually doesn't.' Corvis licked his lips, dried and chapped from the constant exertion of his failed spellcasting. 'Where do I start looking?'

The agonizing climb took another five days, an eternity of cold and ice that made damnation to the thickest flames of hell seem pleasant. All his life, it seemed, became an endless repetition of footsteps breaking the icy snow, struggling to move just one more stride.

On the fourth day beyond the village, the air grew noticeably thin. Sah-di adapted without difficulty, but Corvis found himself gasping at the exertion of merely lifting a foot from the snow. He was forced to stop at regular and rapidly increasing intervals, to rest and catch what he could of his breath. His chest burned, his skull pounded behind his eyes, and he grew light-headed. By the dawn of the fifth day, Corvis drifted in and out of coherence constantly – he spent half his waking moments in the misty befuddlement of a waking dream, the other half in the living nightmare of the Terrakas Mountains. At one point he regained his senses just after telling an amused Sah-di, very emphatically, 'I already *moved* the furniture, so you cook the dog while I purple.'

The peak of the mountain had drawn slowly nearer, but so had the white wall looming before them, a cresting tidal wave of ice and stone. 'This is the final stretch, good Master,' Sah-di assured him. 'But I fear the remainder of our journey must be made with rope and spikes. I would not insult you or question your capabilities for all the gold in Daltheos's earth, good Master, but I worry you may not be up to completing this journey.'

Corvis nodded breathlessly, leaning against an outcropping of snowy rock. 'I'm too old for this sort of thing, Sah-di,' he gasped.

The Terrirpa's lips tightened. 'You are not an old man yet, good Master. It would be a shame if you never have the opportunity to become one.'

Somehow, Corvis couldn't help but think that Sah-di's reluctance to continue was less concern for his employer's well-being than it was an excuse not to have to make the arduous climb himself.

He allowed himself another moment of rest, hoping against hope and reason that *this* wheezing breath would somehow prove more productive than the last. He muttered to himself, casting every strengthening spell he knew, rudimentary as they were. It was enough to get him moving again. Whether it would be enough to *keep* him moving was another question entirely.

'No,' he said then, standing up straight. 'I have to finish this.'

Sah-di frowned. 'Good Master, I think perhaps that—'

'This isn't open to discussion, Sah-di. I hired you. I'm paying you. That makes me the boss.'

'And it would be poor business sense, not to mention dishonorable, for me to allow my employer to perish. You've come farther already than most men would ever dare or dream, good Master. It is no failing of yours that you cannot make the top.'

Corvis, despite his exhaustion, actually smiled. 'Is that what you think this is, Sah-di? Some personal fixation? You think I'm here for the glory of conquering the great Mount Molleya?'

The Terrirpa shrugged. 'I have seen men do it before, good Master. I have even guided some of them. In truth, I cannot think of any other reason for such an arduous journey. There is nothing at the top worth climbing to.'

'That's where you're wrong, friend,' Corvis told him. 'There is a cave, near the very peak. And hidden within is something quite valuable to me. *That's* what I'm after.'

Sah-di blinked. 'Good Master, you have been led astray. There are no caves in the heights of Mount Molleya.'

'There's one, Sah-di. It's just damn well hidden.'

'But—'

'Look, it's very simple, Sah-di. I'm going on. If you plan to head back now, go. But you won't get the second half of your fee, and you'll be coming back to town having lost your employer. That won't be good for your reputation as a guide, will it?

'And just think. On the off-chance I'm not an idiot and actually know what I'm talking about, you'll have helped me achieve something I desperately need. I'm very free with my rewards when I get what I want, Sah-di.'

The guide chewed the inside of his cheek in contemplation, finally nodding. 'Whatever you may be, good Master, I think you are not an idiot. Moreover, however lowly I may be as compared with so august a personage as yourself, I am a man of my word. I will not turn back now, if you will not.'

Or he wants to get his hands on whatever's so valuable. But that's just fine with me. I want him to get his hands on it . . .

What Corvis *said*, however, was 'I'm glad to hear it, Sah-di. I'm as rested as I'll ever be. Let's get started.'

The remainder of that hellish day, their ascent up the wind-blasted, ice-encrusted rock, became little more than a blur in Corvis' memory. The entire day metamorphosed into an endless labour of fear and pain. Had he been asked even a day later, he could never have described an individual moment of the climb. He recalled nothing of the rough and abrasive rope; the bruised and blackened fingers as they sought, numb with cold, for a ledge wide enough to grip; the hammering on the pitons that echoed back louder than when they'd begun; his nails, torn and bleeding even beneath his heavy gloves, the blood pooling and sticking to the tips of his fingers. It was, in the truest sense of the word, a timeless experience; it took forever, it took no time at all. After an eternity of sheer hell, in the blink of an eye they were there.

By the time the slope levelled out, just a few hundred feet shy of the peak, there was no rational thought left to Corvis; he was an automaton, moving by rote. Sah-di was forced to drag him to the slight shelter provided by an outcropping of stone, and Corvis only watched emptily as the Terrirpa hustled about, setting up something a little less crude. He'd barely erected the small tent when Corvis crawled inside and collapsed into oblivion.

Sah-di watched him, idly rubbing his hands on his own arms, and knelt down to start a small fire, well shielded from the winds by a bulwark of rock and snow. He considered abandoning this madman in the night and returning home, but just as quickly dismissed the idea as a poor one. If he'd planned to go back, the place to have done so was at the base of the cliff, not here at the top. The worst of the ascent was over, and he wasn't sure he possessed the strength to tackle the cliff again without sleep and food.

And this one called Cerris, assuming he wasn't weaving

tapestries out of moonbeams and spiderwebs, might provide substantial reward for those efforts. Carefully, Sah-di rose to his feet. The only sounds coming from the alcove were the crackling of the cheerful little fire and the faint crunch of the native's boots breaking snow, and both were well obscured by the screaming winds. His eyes gleaming with something more than reflected firelight, Sah-di went in search of Cerris' supposed cave.

Corvis awoke the next morning to find the guide standing over him, his expression far less simpering than it once was. 'You've dragged us up here for nothing, you madman!' Sah-di snarled, his usual obsequiousness apparently having been lost in the snow at some point the previous evening.

Corvis peered at him, bleary-eyed. The night of sleep, secure in the tent and warmed by the fire, had done him great good. Though just a few steps shy of frostbite, and so sore that he wasn't certain he'd ever move again, he was again fully aware.

Not that his guide's ranting was helping matters. 'Sah-di, I don't have the vaguest idea what you're talking about.'

'I'm talking about your cave of treasures!' the Terrirpa raved at him. 'I've taken you all this way, and it doesn't even exist!'

Slowly, ignoring the screaming protests from muscles he'd never knew he possessed, Corvis rose to his feet and squinted the sleep from his eyes. 'Sah-di,' he said, 'first off, I'm in a considerable amount of discomfort, and I'm colder than a yeti's backside, so I'd appreciate that you not add yelling to my list of Things That Are Really Irritating Me Right Now. Second, it makes no difference to *you* if the cave's here or not. You agreed to guide me for a set fee, of which I've already given you half. So I have not in any way, shape, or form wasted your time.'

'But—'

'And third, what makes you think the cave doesn't exist?'

'Because I spent all last night searching for it!' Sah-di

shouted at him, practically spitting in Corvis' face. Only after the words left his mouth did he realise that, just maybe, this wasn't something he should have admitted.

Corvis raised an eyebrow. 'Oh? And why would you do that?'

'I . . . I thought I might scout it for any further dangers or impediments to our progress, good Master.'

'Right. Pull the other one, Sah-di; I'm getting lopsided.'

Sah-di blinked. 'You what?'

'Forget it.' Corvis sighed. 'Sah-di, if the cave was easy to find, someone might have stumbled across it years ago. Certain steps were taken to prevent that from happening.'

'Steps?'

'The cave's hidden, Sah-di.'

'What? How do you hide a cave?'

Bracing himself against the cold, Corvis tightened the furs around him and stepped from the tent. His guide, face twitching in puzzlement, followed.

'There,' Corvis said finally, after a few minutes, just as the Terrirpa began to grumble. He pointed to a solid face of rock, liberally sprinkled with icicles. 'The cave is there.'

Sah-di threw up his hands. He'd been right the first time: this man was a full-fledged lunatic. 'There is nothing there!' he screeched, once again dropping the boot-licking servant bit. 'I know you're not blind, so I have to assume that you're either crazy or prodigiously stupid, and I will have nothing more to do with any of this!' And having made his declaration, he retreated swiftly, as though to break camp and begin the treacherous descent just as soon as he possibly could.

Corvis took a deep breath, braced himself just in case he'd misremembered the spot, and walked through the rock wall.

When he re-emerged a moment later, Sah-di was staring incredulously at the spot where he'd vanished, hands loosely clasping one of the tent poles. Muttering irritably to himself, Corvis trudged back over to the tent, pushed past the immobile Terrirpa, and then stepped out into the cold once more, this time with his equipment pack. He stopped by the insubstantial stone, dropped the pack, and removed a torch. Flint struck steel, sparks flew, and the brand ignited. Corvis drew Sunder in his right hand, holding the torch aloft in his left.

'So? You coming with me?'

Sah-di approached warily, trying to keep his eyes on Corvis, the wall, and the tent all at once. He lit a torch from his companion's, clutching a crescent-moon saber in his other hand. Then, though his face blanched as he looked at the rock face that wasn't there, he nodded once.

Corvis returned the nod, and they stepped through.

The cave was deep, extending an enormous distance back and down into the mountain. The ceiling, however, was a claustrophobic eight inches over Corvis' head, and it was narrow enough for both side walls to reflect the flickering torches.

'How is this possible?' Sah-di breathed.

'Well,' Corvis began, 'when the mountains formed, the rocks shifted and cracked, and that left large gaps in the stone. Over the course of time . . .' He stopped, doing his best not to smile at his guide's withering glare. 'Or were you referring, perhaps, to the illusionary wall?'

'I might just have been, good Master,' Sah-di said through clenched teeth.

'Ah.' Corvis moved ahead. His boots echoed endlessly, his pace slowed by the need to avoid the stalagmites jutting from the floor. The flickering torchlight danced happily across the walls with the shadows of the two men, moving in a frenetic waltz. Occasionally, a single drip reverberated through the cave.

'The item I seek was placed here magically, Sah-di,' Corvis told him, keeping his voice hushed as most people seem to do in dark and ancient places. 'It was essential to protect it. Hence, the illusion.'

'It is truly so valuable?' the guide asked, enough avarice dripping from his voice to eventually congeal into a brand-new stalagmite.

'Sah-di, I can assure you that you'll never see anything more valuable in your life.'

Only the presence of the torch in one fist and the saber in the other prevented the Terrirpa from literally rubbing his hands together.

Glad to be out of the biting winds, Corvis moved briskly through the cave, dodging the various impediments, and passing side passages with little more than a glance. Sah-di lost any remaining doubt that his employer knew exactly where he was going.

Until they rounded a sharp bend in the passage and were halted by a looming wall of ice.

Solid, impossibly smooth, it radiated a sense of overwhelming age. No simple sheet of frozen water, this, but a remnant of the all-encompassing glaciers that marched across the lands in ancient days, when winter held dominion for ages without end. Unimaginably thick, the sheet before them reflected black in the feeble flickering of the torches.

'By all the gods!' Sah-di whispered reverently. 'In all my years, I have never even suspected . . .' He shook his head slowly. 'How is this possible?'

'You're starting to repeat yourself, Sah-di,' Corvis commented.

'Yes, good Master.'

Corvis smiled tightly. 'It is fairly impressive, isn't it?' He shrugged. 'Shall we get started?'

'Started with what, good Master?'

Corvis waved a hand toward the ice. 'Where do you think the treasure is hidden?'

'What!'

'Magic, remember?' Then, 'Relax, Sah-di. It's not much more than ten feet in.'

'You expect us to carve our way through ten feet of solid ice?'

'Unless you have a better idea. Our torches wouldn't melt more than a few drops off this thing, and I doubt there's enough wood nearby to build a larger fire. And let's not forget that we've got no idea what would happen to the cave if we softened too much of that wall. It *probably* wouldn't affect the stability of the surrounding rock, but . . .'

Sah-di shuddered. 'I have picks among my tools, of course,' he told Corvis. 'But even if we make our tunnel narrow, such a task could take us weeks! Ice this thick and this old will not easily yield to outside pressures.'

'Surprisingly enough, I'm aware of that. Your job now, Sah-di, is to hold the torches so I can see.' Corvis held his own torch out to the startled guide, who sheathed his blade so he might carry both. The older man then hefted Sunder in both hands.

'No, good Master, you will blunt your weapon. You should use a pick.'

'You might be surprised, Sah-di.'

The Terrirpa shrugged. 'It is your axe, good Master. If you wish to turn it into a blunt instrument, that is entirely up to you.'

Corvis just smiled. 'I suggest you stand back,' he warned. 'Splinters.'

'As you say.'

The cave rang when Sunder bit into the primal ice, quickly followed by a deafening, earth-shaking series of cracks. Shards of ice indeed sprang from the point of impact, ripping a few small holes in Corvis' furs.

When Sah-di glanced fearfully over the arms he'd rapidly crossed before his face – his hair and coats kept from the burning torches by sheer luck – he observed with amazement that Corvis' single blow had created a fissure six inches deep. Far from the weeks of hard labour the task should have demanded, it looked as though his employer would achieve their goal in hours!

'Sah-di,' Corvis suggested, glancing over his shoulder, 'I realise it's cold in here, but I think setting your shoulders on fire might be pushing it a bit.'

The Terrirpa straightened out the torches; he also made a

point of stepping as far back from the ice wall as he could without depriving Corvis of the torchlight.

It was a strange thing to contemplate, but as the hours crept by, Corvis noticed that the chips of ice piling up around him exuded the most unusual scent. It was a dry sort of smell, slightly sour, with hints of minerals and dried meats. And it occurred to him, as he worked, that these could be odours and emanations captured hundreds of thousands of years ago, locked for eons in the immortal ice. Corvis found himself awed by the realisation, silly as it might seem, that he might be the first human being to smell this particular aroma since before the dawn of civilisation.

The demon-forged blade could have finished the job before nightfall, but Corvis needed to take occasional breaks for rest. His arms burned, his back ached, and his fingers cramped. He might have asked Sah-di to take over, but he wasn't about to hand Sunder over to just anyone – especially considering that, in the Terrirpa's hands, it probably wouldn't even be an axe anymore.

By day's end, Corvis – already past the halfway point – decided to spend the night in the cave and complete the job in the morning. Paranoid about what his supposed employee might attempt now that he knew where the treasure was, Corvis kept his hands wrapped around Sunder's haft and slept very, very lightly.

The night passed without incident, though, and Corvis doggedly resumed his thankless efforts after a cold break-fast. Sah-di's own excitement waned under the monotony of watching his companion work, and he was beginning to grow concerned regarding the amount of torchwood remaining.

It was nearing midday, and the Terrirpa was just pre-paring to voice his concerns when Corvis uttered a cry of triumph. All objections fled from Sah-di's mind instantly. He was forced to squeeze a bit to get into the icy passage – it was narrow and squat – but he drew near enough to peer over his companion's shoulder.

There, protruding from the ice, was a dull red crystal,

vaguely tear-shaped. It appeared to be attached to a bracelet or armband of some sort, though as most of the bauble remained in the wall, it was impossible to be sure. Sah-di thought he could just barely make out the form of something else in the ice, hidden even deeper than the ornament Corvis had unearthed – something vaguely rectangular.

But if there *was* something else, Corvis didn't seem interested in it. 'This is it, Sah-di!' he crowed triumphantly. 'This is what we came for.'

The Terrirpa's features twisted skeptically. It looked valuable, yes, but not nearly so much as he expected from Corvis' descriptions. 'A treasure fit for kings, good Master,' he said, trying to muster a modicum of enthusiasm.

He failed. 'You sound less than impressed, my friend,' Corvis told him.

'I must admit that I anticipated something a bit more substantial, good Master.'

'Why don't you do the honours, then, Sah-di?' Corvis suggested, squeezing past the startled Terrirpa. 'It's not lodged in there very tightly anymore, and my arms hurt from all that hacking.'

Sah-di shrugged once and passed Corvis a torch. He knelt beside his own pouch and removed a hammer, a chisel, and a small pry-bar. Then he stood, staring intently at the crimson gem sitting just below eye level. 'Hello, my lovely,' he said softly. 'You have indeed made so arduous a journey worthwhile.' Affectionately, he placed two fingers against the facets.

Corvis watched, expressionless, as Sah-di's mouth gaped in a silent scream. The guide's ears burst in a shower of blood, his eyes bubbled, and the flesh of his cheeks tore apart as his jaw separated from itself. A faint ripping noise sounded, above and beyond the sound made by shredded flesh, and a red glow leaked from his eyes, his nose, his tattered mouth. With a quiet pop, the man's skull crumbled, and his body fell to the icy floor. The red glow subsided from his features, only to take up residence elsewhere. Corvis glanced once at the crystal in the wall, now surrounded by a faint aura. He felt no real pity for the man before him, but more than a small amount of apprehension regarding the next step.

'Hello, Khanda,' he said softly, his voice all but lost in its own echoes.

/Well, well, well. Good to see you, Corvis. It's been a long time./

'Not long enough.'

/And you even brought me breakfast in bed. Uncommonly decent of you. And here I thought you didn't care anymore. I mean, you never wrote. Would a letter now and then have killed you?/

'Khanda, something's happened . . .'

/Well, obviously something's happened. I figured when you entombed me in the middle of a glacier that you weren't planning on retrieving me anytime soon./

'I wasn't planning on retrieving you at all!' Corvis snapped, his patience worn. 'I'd hoped you might spend the rest of eternity sealed up in here!'

/No, you didn't./

'What?'

Khanda chuckled softly. /If you'd wanted me gone permanently, Corvis, there were ways to do it. You could have released me, for one./

'Like hell!'

/Funny. I see you've developed a vestigial sense of humour while I've been away. But look at your choice of 'prisons', Corvis. You could have sent me to the ocean floor, or the heart of a volcano. You didn't. You chose an ice-ridden cave in the ass-end of the world because you were pretending I was gone for good. But part of you knew. Part of you knew from the beginning that you'd be back for me. That's why you chose someplace remote, but not so remote you couldn't reach it. You knew./

Corvis' mouth worked in silence. He'd had doubts since he dug his old dusty armour from the closet at home, and a great many more when he'd finally admitted that he needed the terrible sort of aid only Khanda could provide. But he had never, until that very moment, doubted himself.

/*So,*/ Khanda continued, /*you need me for something. You entomb me in ice for seventeen years – although I must admit that it was a nice twist, using my own power to banish me here. Very poetic. You entomb me in ice for nearly two decades, and now that things have got too big for you to handle, you come crawling back? Is that pretty much accurate?*/

'Do you see me crawling, Khanda?'

/*Not yet. Would you be here because of Audriss, by any chance?*/

Corvis' breath froze halfway up his throat. 'How do you know about Audriss?'

/*Really now, Corvis. You think imprisoning me in this waste-land means I can't keep an eye on things? I've been trapped inside this stupid crystal for close to a millennia and a half; I've learned a few things about circumventing my limitations.*/

'All right, fine,' Corvis said, straightening. 'I've wasted enough time here. If you can see what's happening in the world outside, it means I can save myself the bother of explaining it all to you. Let's get moving. Even with your help, it's a long way back.'

/*My, but we're presumptuous today. What makes you think I'll help you at all, after what you did to me?*/

Corvis' jaw clenched. 'We've danced to this tune already, Khanda. You lost.'

/*That was a long time ago, old man. Some things change.*/

'Fine, if you insist, let's get this over with.' Two long strides brought Corvis to a stop before the protruding crystal. He gazed deep into its facets, watching the hypnotic glow of the entity pulsing within. Then, snarling, he slapped his palm against the gem.

Time froze in the cave. Above Mount Molleya, winds raged, ice and snow pummeled the mountainside. But deep within, there was no motion of any sort, no sound but the slow, shallow breathing of a man locked in a struggle, not merely for his life, but for his soul.

A ragged gasp shattered the silence, and the mounting tension vanished from the room. Corvis, face flushed and chest heaving, staggered away from the crystal, his right palm curled as though he'd just burned it on a stove.

'So,' he said, spitting the words between deep gulps of air. 'Some things *don't* change, do they?'

/No./ Khanda's 'voice' inside his head was strangely subdued. /No, it appears they don't./

'So now that we're past our requisite battle of wills, can we move? It's cold here.'

/Give yourself a decade or so. You'll get used to it./

'Cute, Khanda.' Corvis reached out again, grasped the jewel, and yanked. It slid easily from the ice, a simple ornament on a plain silver armband.

Corvis frowned. 'I've taken to using the armour again,' he told the crystal, 'at least occasionally. Let's go ahead and keep the image as it was.'

/Very well./ The red light from the crystal pulsed, and the metal writhed obscenely about Corvis' hand, embracing him like a living thing. The band lengthened, narrowed, and reshaped itself into a series of tiny links. A moment, no more, and Corvis now held the pendant dangling from the end of a lengthy silver chain. He scowled distastefully at it and then, before he could think twice, slipped it over his head.

'Did the chain used to be this long?' he asked as he glanced down at the pendant now hanging against his chest. 'I remember it being shorter.'

/Heh. You may be as stubborn as ever, but I see your memory's starting to slip./

'Khanda—'

/The chain was always that long, you lackwit. Your neck was thicker./

'Um, right. We need to get back to Ephrel. I've left Rascal and some of my equipment there. Then we've got to get a move on. I need to rejoin the others by the start of winter.'

/Have you looked outside?/

The warlord sighed. 'The start of winter *in Imphallion*, Khanda.'

/*Say what you mean, then.*/ There was a pregnant pause. /*Rascal?*/

Corvis nodded as he strode toward the cave entrance, casually stepping over the husk that was once Sah-di. 'My horse.'

/*You don't need a horse anymore.*/

'Maybe, but he's been a good horse. Besides, Tyannon and the kids would kill me if I came home without him.'

/*You know, this is really disgusting. You sound so domestic. What happened to you?*/

'I got rid of you, for one thing.'

/*And look where that brilliant decision led you.*/ Another pause. /*You kept me up here for seventeen years, Corvis. Your lusty little guide was a nice wake-up, but he won't hold me long. Especially if you want me to start bouncing the two of us – not to mention a* horse, *of all things – across the countryside.*/

'I've thought of that already,' Corvis told him with a frown. He'd been hoping not to take this next step, but then, it wasn't as if the place were filled with the cream of humanity's crop. Sacrificing themselves to help stop Audriss was probably the only worthwhile thing any of them would ever do in their life anyway. 'There's a tavern in the village. There should be enough people there to keep you going for a good while.'

Despite his lack of a physical form beyond that of a small pendant, Khanda exuded a sensation that Corvis could only interpret as a raised eyebrow. /*So generous, Corvis? That's unlike you. You used to limit me to one or two at a time.*/

'This is important.'

/*I see. And of course, it's quite all right for the families of* these *people to lose them, just so long as* your *family stays safe.*/ Khanda chuckled scornfully. /*And you want to believe you've changed? You're the same person you always were, Corvis.*/

'I *have* changed,' Corvis insisted as he stepped through the illusionary wall and moved to break down the tent. Even with Khanda's aid, the journey would take some time, and Corvis didn't plan to abandon his only shelter. 'I'm doing this for my family. Nothing more.'

/That may work for dear sweet Tyannon. It might work for Lilander and Mellorin, it might work for Davro and Seilloah, it might even work for Corvis Rebaine. But you can't lie to me, Corvis. Remember what I am./

'Oh, I remember what you are, Khanda. That's why I left you in a glacier for seventeen years.'

/And I remember what you are, even if you don't. You're vicious, you're violent, and you're absolutely convinced of your own superiority. You've got no idea how gratifying it is to find that you're still the Terror of the East we all know and love. And if you wish, I'll be more than happy to prove it to you./

'What I *wish*,' Corvis snapped between clenched teeth, 'is for you to get us to the village before I freeze my ass off!'

He found himself angrier at Khanda than he'd ever been, so enraged it was all he could do not to shove the damn gemstone back into the ice. The blood beat in his temples, behind his eyes, a scream coiled at the base of his throat, demanding to be released.

But it wasn't the demon's words that galled him, that stoked the fires of his soul. It was, instead, his own fear that, just perhaps, Khanda was absolutely right.

Getting off the mountain, Corvis knew, was not as easy as it sounded. Khanda's abilities at teleportation were closely linked to the memories of his master, and Corvis wasn't terribly familiar with the village through which he'd passed. Furthermore, Khanda was weak from his years of deprivation. The journey to the tavern, therefore, was a series of brief jumps – never farther than line of sight – between long stretches during which Corvis walked while Khanda rested. It was an unpleasant three days, but far preferable to the nine it took to get *up* the mountain.

/You know that I can't do this if these people are at all on their guard,/ Khanda reminded him as they stood in a snow-covered doorway a few dozen yards from the tavern. */You wouldn't be teasing me, would you?/*

'I remember your limits, Khanda,' Corvis told him, trying

not to think too hard about what he was about to do. For whatever reason, the simple fact that a human was expecting danger prevented Khanda from feeding upon his soul. Only people totally unprepared for any sort of harm made viable meals. 'The only danger they face is the possibility of a barroom brawl or a nasty social disease from the whores. And most of them are drunk, at that. They should be easy prey.'

/Let's find out about that, shall we?/

Ten heartbeats passed, twenty, thirty . . .

And the tavern erupted in a concert of agonised shrieks. Had the tavern's floor opened up into the depths of hell, the damned themselves could not have raised so hideous a cacophony. It was followed swiftly by a wet ripping noise, as though someone had crumpled and then shredded a sodden mass of parchment. The screams ceased as abruptly as they'd begun, followed by a series of loud thumps as a dozen bodies fell lifeless to the floor.

'We should probably get Rascal and go,' the warlord said, his voice grim. 'It may take them a few minutes to work up the nerve, but *someone's* going to come see what the screaming was about. I'd just as soon be gone before that happens.'

/Ahh,/ Khanda breathed, completely oblivious to his master's concerns. /Oh, I haven't dined like that in eons! I always enjoy a good feast, don't you?/

'Khanda . . .'

/The children were particularly tasty, I thought. My compliments to their parents./

Despite the cold, Corvis could literally feel the blood drain from his face. 'What children?' he asked in a hoarse croak.

/The whores', of course. They kept the little brats in one of the back rooms while they plied their trade./

'How many?'

/Why, you sound sick. Are you feeling——/

'How many?'

/Hm. Four, I should think. It definitely tasted like four./

Corvis sank into a crouch upon the icy, snow-dusted

ground. 'Four children . . .' he whispered, his eyes locked on nothing at all.

/*It's not as if you – forgive me, your people – haven't slain children before.*/

'You didn't kill them, you monster! You ate their souls . . .'

/*Why, so I did. How observant of you.*/

'I should have left you in that damn cave!' Corvis screamed, trembling in fury. 'What by all the gods was I thinking?'

/*You* were *thinking of yourself, Corvis. Just like you always do.*/ Khanda chuckled again, unmindful of his master's hateful glare. /*If nothing else, I'd say this quite handily proves what I was saying: you haven't changed in the slightest.*/

'What?' Corvis leapt to his feet, snagging the pendant in one hand as though he would rip it from his neck. 'How can you say this proves anything about *me*? You didn't bother to tell me about the children!'

/*And you, Corvis, didn't bother to ask.*/

All that Corvis heard in his dreams for many, many weeks was the sound of Khanda's mocking laughter.

CHAPTER FOURTEEN

'Oh.' Seilloah drew up straight even as the tent flap fell shut behind her, surprised to find the canvas chamber occupied. 'So sorry to interrupt.'

'No prob'em.' The massive figure waved at her from the corner where he sat hunched amid various barrels and crates. His eye was bloodshot and unfocused, the entire tent reeked of drunk ogre breath – not, incidentally, all that different from regular ogre breath, save for the addition of its vaguely disorienting properties – and Seilloah could have sworn that even his horn was drooping. 'C'mon in.'

'I was just looking for a touch of spirits to put a patient at ease,' she said even as she began perusing the cases, unsure why she was bothering to explain herself. 'Going to have to amputate a finger, I'm afraid,' she continued sadly.

'That bothers you?' the ogre asked at the tone in her voice.

'The amputation? No. It's just . . .'

'Jus' what?'

'It's already gangrenous,' she complained. 'It won't even make for good flavouring.'

The ogre blinked. 'Oh.'

'It's Davro, isn't it?'

The ogre snorted. 'I thought we all looked alike to you.'

'Not at all. Most of you are only bigger than a hill. You're bigger than a mountain.'

'Heh. Yeah, I'm Davro.'

'Seilloah.'

'If you say so. You humans all look alike to us.'

'You know,' Seilloah said carefully, 'you really aren't supposed to be here. Lord Rebaine is quite strict about apportioning out the alcohol.'

'He can dismiss me if he wants.'

'Not happy with your service, Davro?'

The ogre's eye narrowed, but he slowly shook his head. Seilloah never was certain, after that, whether Davro had actually decided to trust her, or was just too drunk to watch his tongue.

'This war isn't what I expected, Sei . . . Sheilloo . . . Lady. I've been raiding since I could walk,' the ogre told her. 'We *all* have. I had a brother who died because he was learning to wield a knife at the same time he was learning to eat solid food, and forgot which hand had the drumstick. We're fighters; it's *all* we are. But it's been generations since we've had a good, full-on *war*. I grew up on stories of 'em, but I've never been in one before.'

'And now that you have?' she prodded, her voice strangely sympathetic.

' 'Snot what I expected,' he said again, belching once in punctuation, 'Raidin' for food and cattle and goods, killin' warriors who stand against you, that's all fine. But he's got us burning neighbourhoods and not takin' anything from them. Stringin' up body parts like flags, executin' chained prisoners. What's the point in that, Lady? Where's the honour in it?'

'It's not about honour, Davro. It's about fear. You see, if—'

'Don't care. War was suppose' to be the purest form of fightin' – that's what I grew up believin' – but its not pure at all. And I have to wonder, if this is what Chalsene wants of us . . . How pure can he be?'

'So maybe your devotion belongs to another god, Davro.'

'Oh, right.' Another snort, which turned into another drunken belch. 'And what other god would have an ogre?'

Seilloah only smiled.

The sky was iron that day. The horizon remained cloaked behind a curtain of grey, and the sombre clouds lurked low and heavy, weighing down upon the air.

Autumn had supposedly begun some weeks ago, but summer wasn't yet prepared to draw its extended visit to a close. Throughout most of Imphallion, the pounding heat abated only somewhat, and while the temperatures might have cooled, the humidity rose so high that merely opening one's front door seemed to pose a risk of drowning. The vast majority of the kingdom was, to put it bluntly, miserable.

Misery, however, is relative. In Vorringar, the supply far outstripped the demand, and it didn't show any signs of letting up.

It wasn't the heat, though the townsfolk muddled through their day in clothing as light as decency would allow. It wasn't the humidity, though every individual in Vorringar wandered about in a miasma of unevaporated sweat and droning mosquitoes. The roads through town refused to dry, and every footfall tracked thin mud across the town's many floors; the scent of unwashed bodies, persistent perspiration, and rotted vegetation blanketed the community in an aura nearly visible to the naked eye. But the citizens of Vorringar would have happily borne all of this – and a great deal more besides – if the soldiers would just go away.

Every room at the town's two small inns, every spare room in the private homes, even the floor space of the roomier shops – anyplace one could conceivably billet – one of the assembled mercenaries could be found. And still it wasn't room enough. Vorringar was surrounded on all sides by the tents, campfires, and bedrolls of thousands of warriors. The town was very near to running completely out of livestock, to say nothing of their fast-dwindling supplies of alcohol.

Seilloah, her eyes red and bleary, her brown dress rumpled like an unwashed bedsheet, sat slumped at the end of a long table in the town's largest tavern. It was named the Prurient Pixie, presumably the result of a fit of whimsy, or perhaps drunken stupor. The tavern had become the unofficial command post from which she and Davro did their damnedest to control the anarchy they laughingly called a 'marshalling of forces'. They'd figured that setting up shop in a tavern would make them most easily accessible to the gathering mercenaries.

That had been, they now realised, something of a strategic blunder. Seilloah and Davro had spent the past weeks dashing around town putting out fires – and not always figuratively. Any problem the mercenaries had, they went to their own individual company commanders, and the commanders came to Seilloah. Any problems the townsfolk had with the soldiers, they brought to Seilloah. In the last seven days, the witch managed less than twenty hours of sleep.

'What am I doing here, Davro?' she asked him, shouting to be heard over the dull roar of the taproom. 'I'm not any good at dealing with people! Why do you think I made a practice of eating them, and then moved to the woods?'

The ogre, using one of the tavern's largest ale barrels as a stool, shrugged. 'I've been trying to figure that out for a while myself. I know why *I'm* here; I wasn't given a choice in the matter. You were.'

Seilloah's expression rode the line between anger and despair. 'I can't believe I was stupid enough to get involved in this.'

'I don't think you're stupid, Seilloah.'

'No?'

'No. Crazy as a frog on a hot stove and maybe experiencing the early stages of senility, but not stupid.'

'Davro, please stop comforting me.'

For a few minutes, they listened to the hubbub around them, enjoying the rare opportunity to just sit.

'A frog on a hot stove?' she asked finally.

'Hmm? Oh. Just an ogre expression. See, if you drop a frog on—'

'I get the image, Davro. No need to paint it for me.'

'Beggin' your pardon, m'lady, have you got a minute or so?'

'And here we go,' she whispered. Then, forcing her mouth into something approximating a polite smile, she looked up.

'What can I do for you, Teagan?'

The man before her was hulking and broad-shouldered, though not tall. He wore a thick beard, brown with occasional rogue highlights of red, and his hair was tied back in an ornate braid. He wore several plates of armour haphazardly strapped atop a saffron-yellow tunic, and a small round shield with a wicked spike protruding from its centre on his left arm.

'Nothin' you can do for me personally. I'm here on behalf o' my boys. We all are.'

'We all' referred to the other two people standing one each to his right and left. Seilloah didn't even have to look to know they were there; recently, they always were.

The soldiers she and Davro had gathered belonged to an uncountable number of mercenary companies. Some were tiny, a handful of men who'd gathered for mutual profit; others claimed hundreds of men at their disposal. Of them all, three were considered preeminent, kings in the fraternal order of mercenaries. The leaders of those companies had appointed themselves spokesmen for the soldiers en masse. Teagan was one; the two who lurked behind, content to let their boisterous comrade open the conversation, were the others.

One was a woman, a fact Seilloah found shocking. Female soldiers were by no means unheard of, but she was startled that an entire mercenary company would accept one as their commander.

But however she'd done it, the woman called Ellowaine proved worthy of the position. Her company thrived under her command, and by now she'd instilled a fanatic loyalty in her soldiers. She was gaunt nearly to the point of emaciation, yet strong enough to toss an armoured man over her shoulder and carry him for miles – something she'd actually done when her lieutenant had taken an arrow in the stomach. She wore a chain hauberk and cap, under which she normally tucked her uneven blonde tresses. A heavy crossbow hung at her back, and her favoured weapons – a pair of razor-edged hatchets – swung at her waist.

And finally, Losalis, the third member of the impromptu triad. The man was an ebon-skinned boulder, seven feet in height and wider even than Teagan. He was bald, though he, too, wore a full beard, and his left eye was a lighter shade of blue than his right. At some point in the past, he'd lost his left hand, about halfway up the forearm. Losalis compensated by bolting a triangular shield to his armour; it extended a dagger's length beyond the stump, and he'd honed the edge into a brutal blade. He wore an unusual combination of metal plates and heavy leather, and in his good right hand he wielded a frighteningly long saber.

Losalis, despite his bulk, was the most soft-spoken of the three commanders. Oh, he laughed and joked with his men often enough. But Seilloah noticed that he never spoke on matters of any import without taking a moment for contemplation, and she never once heard him brag of his prowess. Either he didn't care if anyone knew of his accomplishments, or he assumed they already did.

'Have a seat,' she offered them all, gesturing at the chairs surrounding the table.

Teagan shook his head. 'I prefer to stay on me feet, if it's all the same to you. Makes our talkin' look more official to the boys, see.'

Seilloah raised an eyebrow. 'The rest of you?'

Ellowaine frowned. 'I'm quite all right here, thank you.'

'I'll stand,' Losalis said, his voice deep but quiet. 'Not meaning any discourtesy, you understand.' He waved his shield in the direction of one of the chairs. 'A man my size simply grows tired of pulling splinters from his rear end.'

Davro chuckled softly from behind Seilloah, thumping a fist lightly on the barrel. 'Don't I know it!'

Seilloah nodded once. 'Very well. What is it this time?'

'Well,' Teagan said, 'you see, m'lady, there's a few unpleasant thoughts goin' round the boys right about now. Unfortunate rumours, and so forth. You know how soldiers can be.'

Seilloah forced her smile to grow wider. 'A soldier once said to me, "Gossip's the only thing what can move through a barracks faster'n a cheap whore".' Internally, she shuddered. The man who'd said that had been slime of the worst sort, and he hadn't tasted very good.

Teagan guffawed, and Losalis allowed himself a brief smile, but Ellowaine merely crossed her arms.

'Aye,' the chestnut-bearded soldier said, wiping tears from his eyes with the back of a filthy hand, 'that's the right of it.' He allowed himself another chuckle. 'The problem, m'lady, is the nature of these rumours.'

'Some of the men,' Ellowaine interrupted, 'are starting to wonder about the money. Revenge is all well and good, but it doesn't fill the purse or the belly.'

Seilloah nodded, praying silently that these people never learned the truth about the slights they planned to avenge. 'As I've said, our commander ought to be arriving anytime now. Once he's here, the money can be dealt with.'

'Dealt with?' Ellowaine parroted, her eyes ablaze. 'We were promised gold! In advance!'

Teagan nodded sadly, 'You see how it is. And I fear most o' the boys share Ellowaine's feelings on the matter. You've been promisin' us that this commander o' yours ought to arrive "shortly" for well nigh a week. We're gettin' tired o' hearin', m'lady. We'd like to move on ahead to the seein' and the spendin'.'

'There's been some talk,' the large one-handed warrior interjected, 'of leaving. Not all the men, or even most of them, but a few here and there. That sort of feeling spreads. Not to mention that we've eaten this town almost barren. We'll have to start purchasing outside supplies soon.'

'He'll be here,' Seilloah said simply.

'Aye, he'll be,' Teagan said, his eyes narrowed ever so slightly. 'But whether we'll be here when he arrives is the real question.'

'There is another matter,' Losalis interrupted quickly, heading off the brewing argument.

The witch glared at the thick beard across the table for a moment longer, and then turned her attention to the larger man. 'Very well, Losalis. What might that be?'

'Well, my lady, it seems a few of the men have, well, disappeared.'

Ellowaine snorted contemptuously. 'Can't even keep track of your own boys, Losalis?'

Seilloah, however, leaned forward, suddenly intent. 'Disappeared?'

'Yes, ma'am. Not many, but enough that a few of us have noticed.'

'Us? Then it's not just your company.'

He shook his head sharply. 'Not at all. Two from my company, that I know of at least.'

'How many?' Ellowaine asked, her tone softer.

'Near as we can tell, about twenty over the last three days.'

Davro stood, looming darkly over Seilloah's left shoulder. 'And we're sure they haven't just passed out drunk in a corner somewhere?' he asked them.

'We're sure,' Teagan insisted. His expression grew thoughtful, absently scratching at his thick beard. 'I've found a few o' my own boys missin' as well – one o' them my own lieutenant, third in command. I know better'n to put a drunkard in charge o' me people. I can assure you, if he's missin', you can look to find some cause other than a few drops o' the bitter.'

The ogre appeared ready to comment further, but Seilloah stood so abruptly her chair toppled to the ground behind her with a resounding thump. 'Thank you for bringing this to my attention,' she told the three mercenaries. 'I assure you, we'll look into it.'

All three looked startled at the abrupt dismissal, and Ellowaine and Teagan both appeared to be on the verge of saying something impolite. Losalis, however, had seen the witch's eyes flicker toward the door and briefly grow wide as eggs. He nodded once and left the table. His two companions, bereft of his support and wondering what he knew that they didn't, tossed a pair of nasty looks at Seilloah before following their dark-skinned friend.

Davro blinked twice. 'Seilloah, what—'

'Look!' she hissed, pointing briefly at the man working his way toward them through the packed and bustling crowd.

The ogre looked, his brow furrowed. It was a tall human, dressed in travelling leathers. His hair was long and grey, his face mostly hidden by an unkempt beard . . .

His jaw dropped as he finally saw past the impediment of the man's facial hair. Sadly, he shook his head. 'As if the man wasn't ugly enough before now.'

'Davro, hush.' She waited pensively as the man approached, until he'd neared the table. 'Cor—'

A gesture silenced her in midword. 'Not here,' he grumbled, his voice not entirely recovered from the arctic temperatures. 'Private room.'

She nodded once, debated whether to brave the crowd herself, and then said to Davro, 'Tell the innkeeper we need one of his rooms.'

'Why don't you tell him? The man's scared of me.'

'Rabid dogs are scared of you, Davro. Go tell him.'

The ogre frowned sullenly and then bulled his way across the tavern, shoving people and furniture out of his path with equal facility. Though there was a substantial amount of muttering and griping behind his back – from the people, primarily, not the furniture, though one particular table seemed surly about the whole experience – no one had the brass to say anything to his face.

No rooms were available, of course, as they all currently hosted at least four soldiers each, but the terrified innkeeper was only too happy to provide them one of his storerooms for 'as long as Your Lordships require its use'. He even begged off when Davro offered a smattering of coins for his trouble, insisting that he was only too pleased to serve, enjoy the room, and you really ought to be certain that it meets your needs so won't you please go way over there and inspect it *right now*.

'I see the fellow wasn't in the mood to chat,' Corvis said sardonically when the ogre returned.

'He seems a bit nervous around me for some reason,' Davro told him.

'Really? But you're such a puppy.'

Davro scowled at him. 'You know, I enjoyed our conversation yesterday a lot more than I do this one.'

'I wasn't here yest . . . oh. Funny.'

It wasn't much of a room. A damp, musty chamber filled with old barrels and crates, it appeared to suffer from a profound quantity of neglect. It did, at least, possess a few rickety chairs and a writing desk, granting Corvis and Seilloah someplace to sit. Davro gingerly poked and prodded at the crates and barrels until he found one that *probably* wouldn't buckle under his weight.

'So,' Corvis began, 'I see you've managed pretty well, given that you lacked the first notion how to go about finding mercenaries. How'd you do it?'

'No,' Seilloah said with a resolute shake of her head. 'You first, Corvis.' She glanced meaningfully at the dull red pendant about his neck. 'I see you found your tame demon all right.'

/What? *That's* truly *insulting!*/

'Well, aren't you?' Corvis asked him; Seilloah, who could hear only half of the conversation, raised an eyebrow questioningly.

/I *should think not! Tame demon, indeed!* I'm *imprisoned. That's not the same thing as being housebroken and taught to roll over and play dead. You tell her to apologise!*/

'Do you mean you're *not* housebroken?'

/*Corvis . . .*/

'What's he saying?' Seilloah asked.

'Just how absolutely thrilled he is to bask in your radiant beauty after so many years, Seilloah.'

/Oooh, but you're pushing it./

Corvis leaned back, ignoring the protesting creaks beneath him, and emotionlessly gave them a succinct – and somewhat abbreviated – account of his experiences in the Terrakas Mountains.

/But Corvis,/ Khanda told him in a false whine, /you're leaving out the best part./

'Shut up, Khanda.'

/Every story is better with children, Corvis. Everybody loves children./

'Shut up, Khanda!'

/You're so squeamish./

'Anyway,' Corvis concluded, 'I'm – we're – here now. And that means it's your turn, Seilloah. How'd you manage all this?' He gestured in the direction of the door. 'There's got to be several thousand men out there.'

She smiled benignly, then, as did Davro, and Corvis grew nervous. 'I'm not going to like this, am I?' he asked.

'It's your fault, sweetie,' she told him. 'When you ask the impossible, you have to assume some unorthodoxy in your results.'

'What did you do?' It was almost a whimper.

'Well, it wasn't too difficult to find some of the larger companies and mercenary Guilds, after all. They have to make their presence known, if they want any business. Once we found them, Davro got a few of his tribesmen – tribes-ogres, I suppose – and we killed a few of them.'

'You what?'

'It got their attention. We didn't leave any witnesses, and we planted a few ranting and rambling messages about this being the penalty for not joining up with the Serpent when he offered them the chance. Got them pretty riled up.'

Corvis groaned.

'Once they'd stirred for a while, Davro and I approached them and told them we represented someone planning to move against Audriss. They were practically climbing over each other to sign up.'

'For free?' Corvis asked incredulously.

'Of course not. You'll owe them a substantial amount of money.'

Corvis sighed. 'Well, I suppose Audriss has to have a pretty hefty treasury behind him. I'll just pay them from his own stores if we win.'

Seilloah coughed delicately. 'There's an advance involved. And they want to see *all* the money beforehand.'

'An advance?' Corvis asked plaintively. 'How much did you promise them?'

'The numbers were a little vague on that score. Enough to whet their appetite for the rest of it, certainly.'

'And where the hell am I going to get the gold, Seilloah?'

'Why don't you just make it appear?' Davro asked from the corner. 'You've got your magic thingamabob now.'

/*I am* not *a thingamabob.*/

'Save it.' Corvis glared at the ogre. 'Davro, why do you think I was looting the cities we passed through on my last campaign? For fun?'

'Well, it *was* fun . . .'

'I was funding my army, you numbskull! I do *not* have the power to pull gold out of the air, and I can't transform enough of anything else into gold to be worthwhile.'

'In that case,' Seilloah said blandly, 'it appears that you've got a problem.'

Corvis cursed vilely for several minutes. Davro's eye grew wide with shock, and Seilloah blanched.

'Wow,' the witch said when Corvis finally wound to a halt. 'Can you even *do* that with a chicken?'

'Here's what we're going to do,' the warlord said abruptly, glancing up from the floor he'd stared at while pacing and ranting. 'Khanda and I *can* turn enough of this junk into gold to make up a *portion* of an advance; I'll pay the remaining advance from my own pocket.'

'And the rest?' she asked him. 'What do you plan to show them?'

He told her. Seilloah and Davro added a few improvements, and Seilloah strenuously suggested, among other things, that Corvis sit down for a quick discussion with a razor.

'I don't know,' Corvis said slowly. 'I'm starting to like the beard.'

'That skull helmet's going to look pretty goofy if it coughs up a hair-ball every time you open your mouth.'

'You may have a point. Give me about half an hour to clean up and change, and we'll begin.'

Corvis decided to make his appearance from outside. Enshrouded in a cloak of shadows, he crept, all but invisible, from the spare storeroom and snuck from the Prurient Pixie through the back door. Only when he'd circled back to the front did he allow the spell to fade. A single mercenary, leaning up against the doorjamb as he downed his umpteenth flagon of ale, choked as that towering horror stepped from the darkness before his eyes.

Sparing the gasping, gaping soldier not so much as a second glance, Corvis lifted a black-gauntleted hand and shoved the door as hard as he could.

The noise was even worse than before. The iron-banded helm captured the ambient sound, bouncing it back and forth like the inside of a church bell. As if to make up for the excess noise, however, the helm did a passable job of filtering out the worst of the scents. The stale beer, unwashed bodies, and old vomit that were overwhelming before were merely nauseating now.

/Here's a novel idea. Why don't you keep your mind – or what passes for it – on what you're doing?/

'Why don't you do something about that noise, so I can hear myself think?' he whispered back.

/I don't think that'll be an issue./

Starting nearest the door and rippling through the room, a

wave of stunned silence settled over the clientele of the Prurient Pixie. Eyes made bleary with drink suddenly went clear and sober, and the features surrounding those eyes twisted themselves into a variety of emotions, most of which bore at least some relation to fear.

Corvis crossed his arms over his chest and simply stood, waiting for the last lingering pockets of conversation to flicker and die, waiting for the oblivious few in the corners to notice him.

His eyes fell upon the lengthy brass mirror that hung behind the bar. He had lingering doubts as to the true impact of his armour – he couldn't quite shake the nagging suspicion that anyone who took two minutes to contemplate it would find the whole thing silly – but he admitted it was certainly imposing.

Over dozens of reflected heads, the iron wrapped skull gaped back at him, its empty sockets as soulless as he remembered. The blackened steel and plates of bone were newly polished. A brand-new cloak of royal purple hung from the spines atop his shoulders, and Khanda dangled beneath his breastplate on a deceptively delicate chain. At his side hung Sunder, fully revealed for all to see; the array of figures and engravings on the blade capered madly beneath the gaze of Corvis' stunned audience.

/You can't tell me that a part of you hasn't missed this,/ Khanda taunted him.

And for once, Corvis knew that his infernal companion spoke nothing but the absolute truth.

'I think they've waited long enough,' he whispered, ignoring the comment. 'You know what to do.'

/Of course./

Purposefully, inexorably, Corvis began a long, slow stride across the room. Mercenaries scrambled madly to clear the path of the nightmarish juggernaut that had just stepped from the pages of history through the door of their tavern. Khanda swept the room with undetectable waves of power as they passed. The effects of the alcohol the men had consumed were washed completely away; Corvis wanted no doubts lingering after his arrival, and he needed these men stone-cold sober to bear witness.

Only when he'd reached the oak bar did he come to a halt, pivoting smoothly to face the sea of humanity he'd just parted. The skull turned casually, majestically, to survey the common room. Dozens of eyes gazed back at him, filled with fear – but also growing more and more expectant as the seconds staggered by, long-fettered ghosts dragging chains of heavy silence behind them.

'Are any of you here,' the Terror of the East demanded, his deep voice resonating from the farthest wall, 'uncertain as to who I am?'

No one spoke.

'Good. That saves time. You have suffered recently at the hands of that sniveling creature Audriss.'

A low mutter swept the crowd, and a number of expressions grew angry. 'The Serpent, he calls himself.' Corvis allowed just a trace of scorn to insinuate itself into his cold and emotionless voice. 'Hah! The Worm, I call him!'

The muttering of the assembly grew louder, darker, and a few muffled shouts of agreement drifted to the front of the room.

The warlord nodded at the crowd. 'Revenge is pleasant.' He paused deliberately. 'Gold is better.' Another pause. 'I offer both!' he shouted, his hands raised high. 'You know who I am! You know what I have done, what I am capable of doing! And you have now before you the chance to be a part of what I *will* do. You men, and others like you, will be the soldiers of a new order. My order!'

It wasn't just a few of the braver men in the tavern now. The entire crowd cheered his every statement, the fear they felt for this living legend before them having been blown away by a more pressing sense of greed.

'I offer power!'

The cheering grew louder still. Corvis shouted at the top of his lungs to overcome it.

'I offer gold!'

The roar was deafening. Men shouted, boots stamped, mugs and flagons and fists beat upon tables with the rumble of a growing storm.

'I offer the head of Audriss the Serpent!'

The tavern shook with the groundswell of sound. Corvis would scarcely have been surprised to see dust drifting from the rafters, or bottles falling from the shelves.

Smiling beneath his inhuman helm, he again waited, allowing the warriors' enthusiasm to wind down. Then, just as the volume began to fade, he raised a single black-and-bone hand. The room fell into an expectant hush.

Imperiously, the warlord gestured at the storeroom in which he, Seilloah, and Davro had set up shop. 'I will meet with the company commanders in there,' he declared, his voice booming. 'They will line up outside that door, and I will see them one at a time. We will plan . . .' Here, once again, he allowed himself a notable pause. '. . . and perhaps we will see about distributing a bit of the promised gold!'

He spun, cape swirling dramatically, and swept regally through the crowd that had once more burst into shouts and cheers. By the time he reached the converted storeroom, a line of company commanders was already forming.

'Abide another moment,' Corvis said as he passed the first man in line, a broad-shouldered warrior with a thick beard, a braid, and a saffron tunic. 'I will summon you shortly.'

'Whatever you wish, m'lord,' he said respectfully.

Corvis stepped into the other room, slinging the door shut behind him.

'Well,' Seilloah said, 'that was loud.'

His boot heels ringing on the floor, Corvis swung around the desk and collapsed into the chair. He removed his helm, grabbed a nearby rag, and dabbed at the excess moisture plastering his hair firmly to his cheeks and temples. He was clean-shaven now, and his locks had been shorn off at the chin. 'This damn thing,' he complained bitterly, 'is astoundingly hot.'

/I'm *perfectly comfortable, Corvis,*/ Khanda told him snidely.

'Give me a brief summary,' he said to Seilloah and Davro. 'Company commanders. I need a new lieutenant now that Valescienn's clawed his way onto my "Needs Killing" list. You've known these people longer than I have. I want suggestions.'

Seilloah shrugged. 'I'll let Davro handle this end of it, Corvis. I can tell you which ones impressed me the most, but I think you want the opinion of a soldier on this.'

'Seems reasonable. Davro?'

The ogre frowned, his horn quivering a bit as his muscles tensed. 'There's only three worth mentioning,' he said slowly. 'They've sort of elected themselves spokesmen for the rest of the happy mob we've got gathered out there, and they're some of the most respected. It should be one of them.'

'I still have to meet with all of them, you know.'

'That's entirely up to you, Corvis. You wanted my recommendation, so I'm giving it to you. You can't imagine how little I care whether you take it or not.'

'My sincerest and most humble apologies, O wise ogre. Pray continue.'

Davro glowered for a solid fifteen seconds, then shrugged. 'Teagan's a strong man, probably a good fighter, and his people like him. But he doesn't strike me as entirely the most dependable type.'

'All right.'

'Hmm. Ellowaine is damn good at what she does. She's about as cold as they come, except where her men are concerned, and she's efficient. But she's a little temperamental to lead an army, and anyway, I'm not certain most of the men out there would accept a woman as their commanding officer.'

Corvis nodded blandly, ignoring Seilloah's dramatic eye-roll. 'And the third?'

'Losalis. Big man. Calm, collected, and, from what I understand, something of a genius when it comes to tactics. Probably the best man out there for the job, Corvis. *If* he wants it.

Losalis is a little odd, and I'm not sure he's in this for the same reason as most mercenaries. He doesn't seem terribly interested in his reputation, which may just be why he's got such a damn huge one.'

'He's smart, too,' Seilloah added.

'All right. I'm not making any decisions yet, but I'll keep this all in mind.' He looked with no small amount of distaste at the heavy helm, and then took a deep breath and slid it back over his head.

/You didn't ask my opinion, Corvis./

'Noticed that, did you?' Then, after fastening the helm securely, he nodded to Seilloah. 'All right, send the first one in.'

CHAPTER FIFTEEN

'Here you go, Sergeant.' The bag of coins clanked and cluttered weakly as it struck the scarred wooden desktop. 'Tell your men they did an outstanding job, and congratulate them on surviving long enough to return home. Hopefully, it'll be years before Cephira tries anything like this again.'

Corvis Rebaine, relatively new to the rank of sergeant in Imphallion's army – and the only surviving officer of his squad – blinked once and looked meaningfully at the leather bag that sat quivering, rather like a weak pudding, on the desk.

'Sir . . .' he offered hesitantly, unsure how to proceed.

'Is there a problem, Sergeant?' Colonel Nessarn leaned back in his chair, idly stroking one end of his drooping moustache.

'Well, sir, it's just that, unless that bag is full of really small emeralds and rubies, there's no way there's enough in there for me to pay my men a quarter of what they're owed.'

'No, there's not,' the older soldier agreed.

'Uh, and why is that, sir?'

'Not enough funds.' The colonel's voice was utterly flat. He might as well have been discussing such vital concerns as the phase of the moon, or which pair of socks were best on a cold morning.

'I . . .' Corvis actually had to work to force the words through a jaw that seemed somehow determined both to clench in anger and fall limp in surprise. 'Sir, you assigned me to escort duty when the payroll arrived, remember? I *saw* the size of the chest they unloaded!'

'Are you questioning my orders, Sergeant?'

'I'm questioning your *assertion*. Sir.'

The colonel rose slowly to his feet, cheeks reddening in a growing anger behind his moustache. 'The rest is for the Guild soldiers, Rebaine!'

'I see. They're to be paid while my men go without, sir?'

'They won the war for us. Sergeant. I may not be a great admirer of mercenaries, but frankly, it's far more important we keep *them* happy and content with us than it is for us to fill the grubby fists of a few conscripted peasants with coppers.'

Corvis felt his entire body trembling. 'That's your final decision, sir?'

'It damn well is! You take what you've got, and you go and tell your men that they're lucky to be going home at all!'

The guards found Colonel Nessarn the next morning, the tendons in the back of his knees and ankles slit, a dagger pinning his body to the earth through his throat. The payroll chest, which had remained hidden in a false bottom in the desk, was open and held not so much as a single coin.

None of Imphallion's officers saw Corvis Rebaine again – not until years later, when he would face them from beyond their fortified walls, behind the visor of a skull-shaped helm.

But before he vanished that night, every one of Sergeant Rebaine's soldiers was paid in full.

The day grew monotonous, each and every meeting proceeding in exactly the same way. A commander would enter, sit before the desk, his gaze drawn in morbid contemplation of the iron-banded skull and the advisers who stood – or in the case of Davro loomed – behind it. And each and every time, Corvis went through the exact same sequence.

'Name?

'Age?

'Size of company?

'Combat experience?'

That last one achieved some intriguing results. A great deal of them had been involved in the most recent border clashes between Imphallion and the nation of Cephira to the east that had threatened, perhaps eleven years back, to erupt into a full-scale war. What Corvis found surprising, however, was that Ellowaine had been an officer in the private army of the Merchants' Guild until she finally got bloody sick and tired of watching less-skilled warriors promoted over her simply because, as she herself put it, 'they dangle in different places than I do.' Even more interesting was the fact that Teagan, as a young soldier, actually fought during the warlord's original campaign.

'Although,' the thickset warrior had admitted during his interview, 'it was the other side I was fightin' for at the time. Is that a problem, m'lord?'

'Not at all,' Corvis told him flatly. 'You fought for the side you were paid to fight for. That's what mercenaries do. Just remember that this time, I'm the one paying you.'

'Of course, m'lord.'

'Then why don't I show you the gold, and we can move on to your colleagues? Can't keep them waiting.'

'Of course, m'lord!' Teagan repeated, his eyes bright.

The bar that Corvis gave him – which had, until Khanda fiddled with it, been an amorphous lump of iron retrieved from the town blacksmith – was fairly small. Transmutation was an exhausting process, even with a demon's power, and it would have been utterly impossible to generate the precious metal in large quantities. But then, mercenaries were commonly paid in silver pennies, and a single gold noble would pay an average sword-for-hire for a month. Even a bar of such modest size, then, was a sufficient advance to hold on to Teagan's company for some time to come.

'And the rest, m'lord?' Teagan asked shrewdly. 'I don't mean to pry, but yer lovely lass promised us a look at the goods to come.'

'Of course, Teagan. Right over here.'

Concealed beneath the thick metal of Corvis' breastplate, Khanda began to glow. A brief rush of magic swept through the chamber, and a sudden shiver galloped like a frantic gelding down Teagan's spine.

'A wee bit chilly in here,' he commented with a grin. But the sorcery did its job: when Teagan left the storeroom, he was absolutely convinced that he'd seen half a dozen gleaming stacks of gold bars, hidden away inside the tavern's empty crates.

'Think you can do that fifteen more times?' Corvis asked Khanda.

/Please. I'm just manipulating the human mind. It's not as though I'm dealing with anything complex./

'Thanks. All right, send in the next one.'

And so it went. As the hours trudged by and the task grew nearer to completion, Corvis was forced to agree with Davro's assessment. Teagan was a good man to have on his side, but too unreliable and unfocused to lead an army. Ellowaine would have been a good choice, except he didn't quite trust her to keep a hold on her temper. Most of the others were equally unsuited.

Finally, as evening drew near, all the company commanders had paraded through. All but one.

'Name?'

'Losalis, my lord.'

'Age?'

'Thirty-four, give or take a year.'

'Size of company?'

'It's more of a small Guild, my lord. About nine hundred men.'

Corvis glanced up. 'All under your command?'

'Assuming you don't count delegation, yes.' He placed his arms on the desk in front of him, the shield resting awkwardly atop the wood.

'I see. Combat experience?'

'In general, or with the company I lead now?'

'In general.'

'Hmm. A few Guild feuds and guard duty for more merchant caravans than I care to count.' He grinned ever so slightly. 'Was doing that when you last appeared, so I'm afraid I didn't have the pleasure of fighting in your first war.'

'Of course.'

'What else? That border dispute with Cephira, obviously. I think damn near everyone who knew which end of a spear to hold was involved in that one. Oh, and I was a battalion commander in the war against the Dragon Kings.'

That brought Corvis up short. The Dragon Kings of the north had sent a small invasion force against the southern nations perhaps eight years earlier. It was the only time in recorded history that Imphallion and Cephiran forces fought on the same side. That Losalis had commanded an entire battalion said more for his skill and tactical experience than the rest of his history combined.

The low whistle from behind him indicated that Davro, too, realised the significance of what was just said.

'As I understand it,' Corvis said deliberately, 'they only put the best on the front lines against the Dragon Kings' armies.'

Losalis leaned back, his gaze level. 'I *am* the best,' he said, with no trace of braggadocio. 'Whether you choose to acknowledge that fact or take advantage of it is entirely up to you. You're the man in charge, after all.'

Davro snorted over Corvis' shoulder. 'I see that modesty isn't one of your virtues,' the ogre observed.

The dark-skinned warrior shrugged. 'A false modesty is just another sort of lie, isn't it?'

Corvis tried to glance sidelong at Seilloah to gauge her reaction, only to find himself staring at a big curved blur that was the front edge of his helmet. The damn thing allowed nothing in the way of peripheral vision. Repressing an exasperated sigh, he said, 'And what would you do if I were to designate you my first lieutenant, Losalis?'

'Pretty much just pass your orders on to the men, like a trained parrot. Isn't that what lieutenants do?' A large white grin appeared within his night-black beard. 'Of course, in most armies, higher rank means higher pay.'

Corvis laughed out loud. 'I think, my friend, that we can arrange that.' Deliberately, he reached up and removed that abominably uncomfortable helm, then stretched forth his right hand. 'Welcome to the war, Losalis.'

His expression bemused, the large soldier clasped the war-lord's hand. 'Amazing,' he said drily.

'What?' Corvis absently brushed away a few strands of hair dangling in his eyes. 'Are you shocked that the Terror of the East is a human being?'

'My lord, if you listen to all the myths, you're iron-skinned, twenty feet tall with claws and fangs, eat steel, spit poison, and bleed acid.'

'It's all true,' Corvis told him. 'I'm in disguise.'

Losalis chuckled.

'All right, Losalis, here's what we're going to do . . .'

'So, my girl, what d'you think o' our new employer?'

Ellowaine's eyes gleamed over the rim of her tankard. Teagan sat with his chair tilted back and his dirt-encrusted boots propped up on the table. He held in a greedy fist the largest mug Ellowaine had ever seen, and he was constantly reaching out to grab the harried barmaids – by whatever piece of anatomy might be handy – so they might top it off.

'I think that if you call me "my girl" one more time, you're going to shit teeth for a week.'

'Why, darlin', such language!'

'As for Rebaine . . . he *seems* impressive. He's got one hell of a reputation and he certainly *talks* a good fight. But I'm withholding final judgment until I see him on the field.'

'Have you no respect for anyone you've not seen in battle, then?'

'No.' One tiny corner of her mouth quirked upward in the first trace of a smile. 'Of course, for the amount of gold I saw in that room, I'll follow a man I don't respect to the gates of hell.'

'Aye, isn't that the truth?' Teagan sighed lustfully. 'I—'

A massive fist smashed into the table with a veritable thunderclap. The thick-bearded warrior's chair crashed backward as Teagan shot to his feet with a startled oath. Ellowaine rose smoothly as well, her hands clutching the twin hafts of her hatchets.

'What the bloody hell are you doin', Losalis?' Teagan screamed, red-faced. 'You scared me half to death!'

'Just getting your attention,' the taller man said calmly. 'Have I got your attention?'

'I've got half a mind to give you more'n that, you daft—'

'Good.' Losalis shifted his gaze from Teagan to Ellowaine and back again. Then, in an earth-shaking voice that cut through the tumult of the common room and carried to the far walls, he said, 'Lord Rebaine wants the men organised. He wants camps set up by division, he wants them orderly, and he wants them ready to break camp and march at a moment's notice. We're an army now, not a mob, so start acting it. He's called a meeting with all company commanders in exactly one hour, right here in the taproom. It'll be quiet enough, because everyone else damn well better be out getting organised. There'll be an inspection of the camp at dawn tomorrow; any shortcomings will be the responsibility of the company commander.'

'What are you blabbin' about?' Teagan demanded angrily. 'Who bloody well put you in charge?'

'I did.'

The door to the storeroom stood ajar, and Corvis Rebaine, helm clutched under one arm, surveyed the room with eyes even colder than the empty sockets of the skull.

'I'm naming Losalis my first lieutenant,' the Terror of the

East announced. 'As of right now, he is your general. He speaks with my voice, and you will obey him as you would me. Are there any questions?'

Perhaps unsurprisingly, neither hand nor voice was raised.

'Good. Losalis has his instructions. I trust you'll all accept yours.' And with that, Corvis took a single step back and dragged the door shut once more.

Losalis turned his attention back to the occupants of the table. 'From the mouth of Lord Rebaine himself. If you've got a problem, take it up with him. I'm sure he's just sitting in there, anxiously awaiting your personal approval of everything he does.'

Teagan, with a slight flush, looked away. 'All right, Losalis, I didn't mean anythin' by it. Just talkin', you know.'

'Talk later. And it's "sir" now not "Losalis." Are we clear?'

'Aye, Lo— sir. Quite clear.'

'I'm so glad. Why are you still here?'

Muttering under his breath – very, *very* far under his breath – Teagan filed toward the door, Ellowaine walking thoughtfully beside him. As they moved into the street, a grin slowly crept across her face.

'Could you see your way to sharin' the humour with me, darlin'?'

'I think Losalis should make an interesting officer, that's all,' she replied distractedly.

'Interestin'? The man's never expressed one whit o' ambition in his life, an' *he's* the one Rebaine puts in command?'

'And I find that interesting.'

Teagan's beard rustled as he frowned. 'I just don't see why Rebaine chose him. Surely there must've been better choices!'

'Who? *You*?'

Teagan shrugged. 'No, probably not. I don't know that I'd be suited to leadin' that big of a mob. But there are others. Yourself, maybe.'

The slender blonde did something then that Teagan had never seen since the day they'd met: she threw back her head and laughed. 'Me? Teagan, you're crazier than I thought you were. I—' She froze, her hands once more dropping instinctively to her weapons. 'Teagan, there!'

'I see nothin', Ellowaine.'

'No. There! In that doorway.'

Teagan leaned forward, staring intently, then drew back with a muffled oath. 'Is he one o' the men who disappeared?' he asked, his voice gone quiet.

'I don't know him, but I wouldn't wager against it. You'd better go get Losalis. Now!'

Corvis, clad in his armour but minus the obnoxious helm, leaned over the heavy writing desk. His fists were clenched tightly, and he rested on knuckles pressed against the flat wooden surface. His eyes blazed above an infuriated scowl.

Seilloah and Losalis stood before him, Davro looming over them from behind. All of them, even the ogre, looked just a bit contrite.

'I am *not* happy about this!' Corvis barked, as though it were somehow news that he might be upset. 'And I'm even less happy that I'm only hearing about it now!' His fists tightened even further, his metal-clad knuckles grinding into the wood. 'Would one of you care to tell me *why* I'm only hearing about this now?'

Losalis stepped forward. 'Actually, my lord, we only became aware of the issue yesterday, and it was just this morning that we brought it to Seilloah's attention.'

'You only realised yesterday that someone's been murdering my soldiers?'

'My lord, this is the first body we've found. Up until now, they were just vanishing. One man from this company, another from that squad . . . It took us this long to realise there was anything unusual. A handful of men, it could simply have been desertion, off whoring, or maybe drunken stupor. We didn't pick up on a pattern until I happened to discuss it with a few of the other commanders.'

'I see. It should still have been brought to my attention the instant I arrived.'

The witch frowned. 'Corvis, you were—'

'Silence!'

Seilloah flinched as though struck. Davro scowled.

'Losalis, as soon as the men are organised, this is your first priority. I want you to find out who's killing the men, and I want it stopped.'

'Of course, my lord.'

'You're dismissed.'

Seilloah stood rigid until the door clicked shut behind the departing warrior. Then, stiffly, she said, 'If you're quite through with me, I'll be retiring to my own quarters. Or have I not been dismissed?'

The warlord opened his mouth to retort and just as quickly snapped it shut again.

'Seilloah, I'm sorry. I didn't mean to bark at you. It's just, I've been here less than a day, Audriss isn't even here, and I've already got people dying on me.' Wearily, he pulled the chair from the desk and fell into it. 'This is a lot more stressful than I remembered,' he admitted. 'I don't know if I'm cut out for this anymore.'

/If you can't handle it, Corvis, I'll be more than happy to assume command./

'Over my dead body, Khanda.'

/That's a thought . . ./

Seilloah forced her expression to thaw. 'It's all right, Corvis,' she said calmly – so calmly, in fact, that Corvis was quite certain it was anything but. 'I understand.'

'Maybe,' Davro growled, 'but I don't. You know what you are, Corvis?'

'No, Davro,' Corvis said, rising again to his feet. 'Why don't you tell me?'

But the ogre never did tell him. The door to the room crashed open and Losalis hurtled back in, his expression bleak.

'What is it?' Corvis said, his blood running cold.

'I think you'd better come with me, my lord,' Losalis told him grimly. 'Some of the men were looking for room to set up more distant encampments. They spotted what appears to be an advance guard coming down the main road from the east.

'You'd better have a fairly spectacular plan to give the unit commanders, my lord. If his advance scouts are this close already, the main body of Audriss' army can't be more than three days away.'

Those three days were frenetic. Vorringar sat at one of the largest crossroads of the King's Highway, and it was designed to encourage travellers, not keep them out. It simply never occurred to the original settlers that Vorringar might ever be required to withstand a siege. Corvis' soldiers did what they could to rectify the situation, but it wasn't much.

The men placed heaps of rubble at regular intervals around the perimeter of the town, piled between four and six feet high, made up of stone and wood 'conscripted' from the town's larger buildings and furniture. (They cut down only a few of the nearby trees, as they provided good natural protection to the south.) These sad bulwarks, intended to provide some degree of cover from the advancing horde, were marginally better than nothing but didn't remotely make up for the lack of a defensive wall.

They'd quickly excavated a ditch, shallow but steep, around the town just beyond the makeshift barriers. Jagged wooden shafts jutted from the earth within the moat, and local bracken and thorn bushes were draped across the stakes and scattered throughout the trench. A man on foot could easily pick his way through, but it would slow him down enough for Rebaine's archers to have their way with him, and it made a cavalry charge unthinkable. Vorringar's citizens grudgingly allowed themselves to be pressed into service as messengers and porters. They carried arrows and bolts by the bushel, for use by the defending archers. They carefully positioned barrels of pitch, in case the defenders felt the need to start fires, and barrels of water, in case they needed to extinguish any. Any spare iron – rusty nails, old horseshoes, rakes and hoes – was melted down into twisted and jagged bits that should function as crude caltrops. Hundreds of these were promptly scattered across the width of the highway.

Corvis bitterly lamented the lack of siege weaponry, but he knew that no catapult or ballista could be built from raw materials in the time available.

Their position, he admitted to himself, was untenable. Vorringar was hideously vulnerable, and while Davro and Seilloah had done a remarkable job in finding men to fight, they were outnumbered five to one. The ogres would help to even those odds a bit, but even they were too few to tip such a massive imbalance.

'It could be worse,' Corvis muttered on the evening of the third day.

'That so?' Davro grumbled irritably. 'Enlighten me.'

The warlord, along with Davro and Seilloah, was standing atop the town hall, with a good view of the eastern edge of town. They watched as the men strove to finish the last of the defenses. The reek of sour sweat and wood dust enveloped them all, made bearable only because the temperature had finally dropped to more autumn-appropriate levels. Corvis, his shadow stretching out before him as it was rudely shoved by the rays of the setting sun, stared at the approaching tide of flesh and blood and sharpened steel.

The Serpent had arrived.

The enemy made camp less than half a mile from Vorringar, outside the effective range of the archers but not beyond the reach of siege engines. Even now, in the last light of dusk, Corvis heard faint sounds of trees being felled and wood being sawed in the first stages of construction. By the end of the week, boulders the size of yaks would rain down on the unprotected town unless something happened to stop it.

'I wouldn't question your judgment for the world, my lord,' Losalis said softly, appearing on the rooftop, 'but choosing Vorringar as our staging area might not have been the most tactically sound option.'

Corvis grinned a hollow grin. 'Is that a political way of telling your employer that he's an idiot?'

'Not at all, sir. I don't believe for one moment that you're an idiot.' He paused. 'You may have done something idiotic, but that doesn't inherently make you an idiot.'

It would probably have been in character for the Terror of the East to grow furious at that point, but Corvis decided that he didn't have the patience for posturing. 'All right, maybe. I wasn't familiar with Vorringar's layout or defensive position – or lack thereof. I underestimated the time it would take Audriss to get here. I'm sorry. It's been almost twenty years since I've done this, you know.

'On the other hand,' he continued before anyone could get a word in, 'it's not quite as bad as it looks. Audriss can't afford to just swarm us under. Even with such crude fortifications, the advantage in a short-term siege goes to the defender. He'll suffer a hideous number of casualties trying to take this town.'

'Will that stop him, though?' Seilloah asked pointedly. 'Audriss doesn't strike me as all that concerned with the health of his men.'

'No, Lord Rebaine's right,' Losalis said thoughtfully. 'If Audriss is trying to conquer Imphallion, then regardless of what else happens, he's got to take Mecepheum.'

Corvis nodded. 'Exactly.'

'I'm afraid I still don't follow,' Seilloah admitted.

'Audriss is already fighting a war of attrition,' Losalis explained. 'Every city he takes, no matter how efficiently, costs him lives – the soldiers he loses, and the garrisons he has to leave behind. And the closer he gets to Mecepheum, the more organised his opposition becomes. Even if Lorum hasn't whipped the Guildmasters into cooperation yet, that's going to change when an invading horde appears near the capital. The army of Imphallion itself isn't that large, but put it together with the soldiers of the individual lords and the Guilds, you've got an impressive fighting force.'

The witch nodded, comprehension dawning. 'Which means Audriss can't afford to fight us here, right? Even if he wins, he'd lose too many men to have a chance later on.'

'Exactly,' Corvis said, his eyes once more going eastward,

where only the campfires of the enemy were now visible in the growing darkness. 'Stalemate.'

'For a week,' Davro added. 'Then they start dropping small mountains on us.'

'And we've still got someone murdering our soldiers,' Seilloah pointed out. 'We can't afford to grow complacent.'

'Do I look complacent?' Corvis asked with a scowl.

/*No*, Khanda interjected. /*Just ugly.*/

'That's another thing,' the warlord continued. 'Magic.'

'Are you and I taking on the armies by ourselves?' Seilloah asked sardonically.

'Not exactly. Tell me, can you manipulate the forest out there the way you did in Theaghl-gohlatch?'

Losalis's eyes widened slightly. 'You've been through Theaghl-gohlatch?'

'I live there,' Seilloah said. 'I'd be there now if someone who shall remain nameless hadn't found it convenient to drop by uninvited.'

'I'd hardly call it convenient, Seilloah,' Corvis objected.

'You're the witch, then?' the warrior asked. 'The one who kills all those who enter the forest?'

'I don't know that I'm *the* witch. I'm *a* witch. And most people foolish enough to venture into Theaghl-gohlatch are slain by the natives long before they get anywhere near my little stretch of property.' A sudden suspicion washed over her. 'Why do you ask?'

'I think you may have eaten someone I know.'

'I don't suppose anyone would care to talk about the imminent war?' Davro snapped.

'Probably a good idea,' Corvis said blandly. 'Seilloah, you didn't answer my question.'

'Hmm?' She thought back a minute. 'Oh, that. Not as well, I'm afraid. I'm not familiar with those woods out there, whereas I know Theaghl-gohlatch like the back of my hand. Plus, my home has a certain – propensity – toward magic to begin with. But I could probably work some fairly impressive tricks with the flora, if that's what you were asking.'

'It is indeed. I want accidents to happen while Audriss' people are gathering firewood and cutting lumber. Lots and lots of accidents. I want wood to warp while they're building with it. I want the wolves and owls to decide those men taste better than the local rodent population.'

'You don't ask much, do you? I can't give you all that, but I'll do what I can. I can slow them down a little, at least.'

'Every little bit helps. As for—'

/Corvis!/

'Is this really the time, Khanda? I—'

/This is important, you gibbering baboon!/

Sigh. 'Fine, Khanda, what is it?'

/Audriss has magic equal to yours. In fact, he's got a demon-inhabited talisman very much like me./

The Terror of the East felt the blood congeal in his veins. 'How do you know?' he asked tightly.

/Because it just delivered a message to me./

By now Corvis' companions had all fallen statue-still, staring at the expression on their leader's face. 'Corvis,' Seilloah began, 'what—'

Corvis shook his head. 'What message, Khanda?'

/Probably the one you already suspect, O bony one. Audriss wants to meet with you. Alone./

CHAPTER SIXTEEN

It wasn't remotely the fanciest place she'd ever stayed, even on the road, but it was certainly comfortable enough. Clean rooms, fresh linens, a minimum of scuttling insects in the corners, and the sawdust on the common room floor was fresh enough to hide all the other, less appetising aromas of the tavern. It was the . . . What? Sixth inn they'd stayed at? Seventh? She'd lost track, thanks in part to her 'companion's' urgent desire to keep moving.

Tyannon sank down to sit on the straw-stuffed mattress and stared blankly at the far wall, trying to make even a little bit of sense of the past days.

She was clad in a brand-new blouse and skirt, an outfit that thankfully did *not* smell of the smoke and blood of Denathere's agonised death throes. A plate of cold venison sat beside her, a mug of ale on the floor at her feet. She was clean, she was well fed, the incidental scrapes and abrasions she'd picked up in that basement had been carefully, even gently, tended. Were it not for the manacle around her ankle and the attached chain that allowed her full run of the room but not to step across the threshold, she might almost have thought of this as a normal night away from home.

Well, the manacle *and* the man who was even now laying a blanket on the floor across the room, having insisted – again – that she take the only bed.

He looked so normal out of that horrific suit of armour. Just another fellow, his dark hair speckled with bits of premature grey, his face sprouting the first shoots of what might, if left unchecked, blossom into a full beard. Only his eyes, pools as deep as any sea, suggested he was anything more.

'Not hungry?' Rebaine asked, gesturing at the untouched plate. He'd been strangely solicitous – almost shy, even – since he'd taken her. Tyannon was all but positive that the warlord really hadn't the slightest idea of what to actually *do* with her.

'No.' She flinched, drawn from her thoughts, to stare at the – man? Monster? – across from her. 'I'm still full from lunch.'

'You barely *touched* lunch.'

Tyannon shrugged.

'As you like,' he sighed, not so much angry as resigned. 'I'll make sure we get a big breakfast before we head out in the morning.' He watched her, his mouth occasionally twitching as though to say something more, but whatever words he carried got lost somewhere on the way to his lips.

/ *Maybe she's trying to starve herself to death,* / Khanda offered. / *She'd be doing you a favour, you know.* /

Corvis ignored him. Again.

'All right.' He began the litany that had been their lullaby since leaving Denathere. 'No noise. No calls for help, no hidden messages. Anyone you attract—'

'Yes, I know!' Tyannon's fists suddenly clenched. 'Anyone I attract, you're going to have to kill! Anyone who realises who you are, or that I don't want to be with you, is a threat! And no, I don't want to get anyone else killed! How many bloody times do you think I have to hear it?' It was more words than she'd strung together at any given time since she'd confronted him beneath the Hall of Meeting.

Corvis blinked twice. 'I, uh, just want to make sure we understand each other.'

'Oh, I understand you, Rebaine.' And then she

straightened, her face all but lighting up. 'I *do* understand,' she said, her voice suddenly soft but far more firm than Corvis had ever heard it. 'You're trying to keep me afraid.'

/*Kill her.*/

'That's it, isn't it? That's what you're all about.'

/*Kill her, Corvis! Kill her now!*/

'What do you mean?' Corvis asked, almost despite himself, rising to stand before her. She rose, too, though of course she could not match his height.

'Your armies, your monsters, your armour – it's all about fear. It's how you keep control.'

'Well . . . Yes,' he admitted. 'It is.'

/*Have you gone* completely *insane?! Don't talk* to her *about this!*/

'You may not believe it, Tyannon, you may think I'm a monster, but this was never about hurting anyone more than I had to.'

The girl actually laughed, though it was a brittle, bitter sound. 'You hung body parts along the streets where their families lived!'

'As you just said: fear. Tell me something, Tyannon. How many people *didn't* rise up to fight me because they were too afraid of what I'd do to them? How many more lives would I have had to take?'

'You can't rule a nation that way!'

'Not indefinitely, no. But you can *take* one.'

'Can you? Funny, I don't see a crown on your head.'

/*Corvis, this is getting dangerous . . .*/

'It was for the best, Tyannon. If you're with me long enough, maybe you'll under—'

The room literally echoed with the report of her slap. Corvis Rebaine, Terror of the East, actually staggered back, one hand rising to his stinging cheek, and damn if tears didn't come to his eyes! Oh, he'd have liked to shrug it off, to pretend he'd just been startled . . . But it would've been a lie. Damn, the girl could *hit*!

'What was . . . What did . . . What?' he stammered.

'You're a fraud. A pompous, deluded fool trying to convince himself he did the right thing.' Tyannon wasn't sure where the courage had come from, any more than she'd known why she'd suddenly mouthed off to the black-armoured warlord back in Denathere. But she knew she had to ride it while it lasted. 'What do you do when someone's not afraid of you anymore? What then?'

Rebaine's eyes narrowed. 'I'd be careful, if I were you, Tyannon. I—'

'You'll what? You need me, Rebaine. That's the whole reason I'm here, remember? Maybe I can't afford to draw attention to us, because I don't want to get anyone else hurt – but you can't afford to hurt *me*, either.'

'I won't need you indefinitely,' he growled. 'Remember?'

'I remember. And then you'll either let me go, like you promised you would, or you'll kill me because I irritated you. And that'll pretty much put the lie to who you pretend to be, won't it?' Tyannon didn't even wait for a reply; she simply shoved the plate of meat to the floor and curled up in bed, facing away from her open-mouthed captor.

/Damn it, Corvis! I warned you about this! I warned you! For hell's sake, kill her!/

But Corvis could only dress slowly for bed. For many hours he lay awake, the floor pressing on his back mercilessly through the blanket, and stared upward at nothing at all.

/If this turns out to be some blatant trap you're about to saunter into, and you get yourself killed, I'm going to be greatly disappointed./

'Why, Khanda,' Corvis said, voice reverberating hollowly through his helm, 'I had no idea you cared.'

/What are you, stupid? I'd shed more tears over a diseased rat *than I would you. I just don't want to be left on a putrefying corpse out in the middle of some field for the next few centuries./*

'Ah. My mistake.'

/It usually is./

The dirt and gravel of the winding road crunched beneath the warlord's tread. Shimmering moonlight bathed everything in a dancing glimmer of faerie fire, creating a landscape of flitting ghosts and flickering dreams. Most travellers would have found it disorienting, but to Corvis, his night vision enhanced by a simple spell, it was merely distracting.

Sporadic trees lined the roadside, and these he spared a passing glance, alert for any hint of ambush. He didn't need Khanda to tell him this was almost certainly a trap. But Corvis, over the strenuous objections of his companions, chose to accept the invitation nonetheless. He might have made arguments about assessing the strength and nature of the enemy forces, but in truth Corvis was intensely curious to learn exactly what sort of man he was dealing with.

And so he neared the 'neutral area' Audriss's messenger conveyed to Khanda, his right fist stuck to Sunder's hilt as though welded there. His eyes were wide and watchful, the searing power of Khanda's magic tensed and gathered at his fingertips.

/You realise,/ Khanda remarked, */that Audriss probably expected you to meet with him tomorrow. His messenger seemed a bit taken aback when I told him we were on the way./*

'That's the point. I wanted to throw them off a little.'

/To what end?/

'It makes me feel better.'

/Ah, How petty./

'Is there any particular reason,' Corvis asked irritably, 'that you're unwilling to go more than two minutes without making some useless, sarcastic, and, above all, annoying remark?'

/Does it bother you?/

'Excessively.'

/That's the reason./

The grating of the gravel beneath his boots ceased abruptly

as Corvis froze, scanning the road before him with senses both human and infernal. 'Did you hear something?'

/I did, and it sounded close./

One of the shadows before them extruded itself into the light of the moon. A small, misshapen form emerged from that shadow. Corvis could hear the shallow, abrasive breathing and the clicker-clack of the creature's claws as it dragged itself into the light.

'He thinks this is the one he waits for, yes.' The sound – for it could not be termed a voice in any human sense of the word – didn't emanate from the creature in any normal fashion. It *crawled* forth, skittering across the intervening space and washing over Corvis, tickling horribly, a tide of twitching spider legs. 'He thinks that this one he cannot have, no.'

'Oh, gods!' Corvis hissed. 'Gnomes!'

'He thinks you are wrong,' came a second voice, crawling from the shadows. 'He thinks this is not the one. He thinks this is just another human. He wants it, yes, to have. He wonders, yes, if it will taste like the last one.'

'I have a friend you ought to meet,' the Terror of the East told it calmly, determined to show these abhorrent monstrosities no fear. 'You can discuss recipes.'

'He will have it now, yes, take it,' the second voice grated. 'Before it can try to run, to hide.'

'You will not,' Corvis said firmly. 'I'm here to see Audriss.'

'You see!' It was the first gnome again, the one who'd partially emerged into the light. 'He knew! He knew it was the one he wanted.'

'He thinks you are wrong, still, yes. He hungers.'

'And he wonders,' the first mewled impatiently, 'what will happen when Audriss learns you have killed the wrong one, eaten it?'

'He is not afraid, no, not of Audriss, not a human.' But the tone was sullen.

'He will take it to Audriss, yes, and learn. If it is not the one, no, he and he eat it then.'

'Agreed.'

The first of the gnomes shambled farther into the light, granting Corvis an unwanted view of its deformity. Limbs bent not only in the wrong directions, but in an excessive number of those directions at once. Even aided by his night-vision enchantment, Corvis could make out nothing of the creature's face save a pair of gleaming, feral eyes and a gaping, jagged maw.

'He will take you to see Audriss, yes, to speak with him. You will come, yes, follow.' The eyes gleamed. 'He wonders, does it understand? Does it know that it should not attempt to flee, no, nor to hit and harm? Does it know, he wonders, what he will do to it if it tries?'

'It has a pretty good idea,' Corvis said drily. 'It used to work with gnomes.'

'Good. Then it will follow quietly, yes, in peace.' Pivoting grotesquely, the gnome meandered back into the shadows, not even bothering to check if Corvis followed. He did, staying on the creature's heels as it followed an unseen path through tall grasses and trees.

When they finally reached their destination, Corvis was reluctantly impressed by the sheer ostentation of the place. Atop a wide, flat rise had been assembled a pavilion-sized tent, made of thick black canvas and staked out by iron rods. A black pennant, lined in silver and displaying an emerald snake half risen to strike, flapped and kicked loudly from the center pole. A thin tendril of smoke undulated upward from a narrow tin tube functioning as a portable chimney. The ground around Audriss' mobile headquarters was blanketed by a thick but low-lying fog, probably the result of the nighttime condensation dewing the surrounding grass; it added an eerie, surreal aura to the scene.

The only piece missing was the unit of grim, black-clad guards that would normally have been an aesthetic require-ment for so arrogant a scene. Apparently, Audriss was taking his promise of safety on neutral ground to surprising lengths – or else he was so supremely confident that he felt no need for added protection.

/Cosy sort of place,/ Khanda noted.

'I'm so glad you approve.'

/Well, it's nothing a good bonfire wouldn't improve . . ./ There was a momentary pause. /Be very careful. He's got his demon with him./

'So do I.'

The gnome came to a halt, impatiently glaring back over his shoulder – literally – as Corvis examined the tableau. 'There could be a small army in that damn tent,' he murmured.

/Could be, but there isn't./

'Are you sure?'

/No, Corvis, I accidentally overlooked three hundred soldiers hiding behind the tent pole. Yes, I'm bloody well sure!/

'Sorry.'

'He wonders what it is doing,' the gnome grumbled. 'He thinks that it should hurry, yes, keep moving.'

'In a minute,' the warlord snapped, refusing to be rushed. Then, more quietly, 'So what can you tell me about what is inside that tent?'

/Audriss, for one thing. At least, I assume it's Audriss. It's someone I can't probe, because he's shielded. Have you pissed off any other demon-wielding world-conquering madmen of late?/

'No,' Corvis said sourly, 'I figured I'd start small and work my way up. What about the demon? Can you tell me anything about him?'

/Hmm. Let's see . . . He's strong. Not stronger than me, but then, who is? Imprisoned, much as I am. You know, Corvis, I'd be even stronger if you freed me, and I'd be grateful enough to—/

'Don't even start.'

Khanda sniffed. /All right, be that way. What else? I – well, I'll be damned./

'A bit late for that, isn't it?'

/Oh, you're hysterical, you know that? Pekatherosh./

'Excuse me?'

/It's Pekatherosh. I was wondering whatever happened to that son of a bitch./

'Old friend of yours?'

/In the 'I'd love to stake him out on an abyssal plain and feed his living entrails to the parasites' sense of friendship./

The gnome appeared directly under Corvis' nose. 'It must come *now*!'

'Of course. Lead the way.'

The gnome glared suspiciously but stumped toward the heavy leather flap, muttering to itself and twitching.

If the tent's exterior was excessive, the interior was downright opulent, in a sick and twisted sort of way. A banquet-sized table of a heavy oak dominated the cavernous canvas chamber. It was bare, save for a haphazard heap of maps and parchments on the far side, and a pair of ornate wine goblets and glass decanter on the near. In one corner of the tent, directly below the tin skirt of the chimney, sat a firepit large enough to roast a deer (and was, in fact, currently doing so). The spit rotated despite the lack of attendants, but so accustomed had Corvis grown to magic that he scarcely noticed. A four-poster bed with a thick, downy mattress occupied one far corner, along with a towering wardrobe and what appeared to be—

'An iron maiden?' the Terror of the East asked incredulously. 'He travels with an iron maiden?'

/Obviously, this is a man passionate about his hobbies./

'Fantastic. So where is he?'

/I'm not sensing him in here anymore. He probably stepped out so as to make a suitably impressive entrance./

'Probably. I might have done the same thing,' Corvis admitted. 'I bet he'd come running pretty quick if I started poking through his notes.'

/I imagine he would./

'So how come you didn't know it was this Pekatherosh when he contacted you the first time?'

/Distance, Corvis. All he did was send a message; there wasn't enough of his essence for me to identify. Once we got near, though . . . Corvis, you'd better hope that Audriss has a pretty good leash on Pekatherosh. The results are going to be very

236

*unpleasant if we end up confronting each other directly, and that's
exactly what'll happen when one of us gets free./*

Corvis grunted thoughtfully as he made a brief circuit of
the tent. 'I take it there was a special enmity between you
two?'

*/You've no idea at all. Have you ever seen two enraged, rabid
dogs going at it?/*

'I can imagine it.'

/Like that, but ugly./

Corvis was spared the necessity of a response by the sound
of the flap opening. With a deliberate effort, he kept his hands
away from Sunder as he slowly faced the Serpent.

Audriss stood in the doorway, framed in moonlight
reflected by the low-lying mists. For the first time, Corvis
saw the dull black armour, impossibly carved of stone, the
grotesque silvex runes, the gaping hood containing nothing
but a featureless expanse. He appeared unarmed save for a
long, curved dagger at his left waist. Silver rings adorned
every finger save one, the middle finger of his left hand, which
bore one of dingy pewter, topped with an emerald stone.

They stood and assessed each other, these two men who'd
dreamed of domination. Corvis realised that the Serpent
was not a tall man; even without the benefit of armour, he
had more than half a foot on his counterpart.

Finally, his voice echoing behind the mask, Audriss spoke.
'Corvis Rebaine. The Terror of the East. Believe me when I
say that this is one of the greatest honours of my life.' He
bowed from the waist. 'Welcome to my home, Lord Rebaine,
transitory as it may be.'

Corvis inclined his head politely, the jaws of the skull helm
clacking together. 'You are too kind, Lord Audriss. I've been
looking forward to meeting you as well. You and Pekatherosh.' He gestured absently toward the emerald ring.

/Show-off./

'Ah, Pekatherosh. One of my greatest assets in this humble
endeavor. I'd introduce you, but you wouldn't hear a word he

237

has to say, and I doubt seriously that Khanda would feel inclined to be cordial.'

Inside his helm, Corvis scowled.

'But come, Lord Rebaine,' Audriss said, waving magnanimously at the table, 'make yourself comfortable. It's late, and you've walked far to get here. A man of your age should never be kept waiting.'

/*Ouch,*/ Khanda said appreciatively.

'Indeed,' Corvis said, biting off the sharp retort that initially came to mind. He strode to the waiting goblets, selecting a chair at random. Audriss stood directly opposite.

'Before we talk shop,' Audriss said, keeping his feet. 'Would you permit me a moment to satisfy a bit of idle curiosity?'

'That depends on what you're curious about, I imagine.'

'Sunder.' Audriss raised his hands, palm-first, in a gesture of helplessness. 'I've always been fascinated by the Kholben Shiar.'

'If you think there's any chance . . . ,' Corvis began hotly, but he paused. For the first time, he truly looked at the dagger the Serpent wore at his side, truly felt the cold – not a physical but spiritual chill – emanating from the unassuming weapon.

'Well,' he said with forced levity, 'I'll show you mine if you show me yours.'

Audriss laughed. 'Fair enough.' Very slowly, each drew his weapon and extended it haft-first across the table. A tense heartbeat, and then both weapons were snatched simultaneously.

The dagger writhed even as Corvis' fist clenched around the hilt, twisting and flowing; across the table, Sunder did the same. The weapon in the Terror's grip lengthened, widened, sprouted a heavy blade. A cry filled his mind, a faint wail that didn't suggest pain so much as it did the *expectation* of pain. And somewhere in the sound that wasn't sound at all; Corvis heard a name, just as he'd heard the name of Sunder so many years ago.

'*Talon.*'

And then it was done. In his hands, Corvis now held a massive battle-axe, similar in many respects to Sunder itself. The blade was thicker, more squared along its cutting edge, and it lacked Sunder's signature engraving, but it felt identically balanced.

Corvis glanced over to see Audriss holding a thick, single-edged dagger with an ornate filigree running up both sides of the blade. It was a wicked weapon, one clearly designed for murder, not battle.

'You,' Corvis said disdainfully, 'have the soul of an assassin.'

Audriss gestured at the massive axe. 'And you of a brute.' He turned back to the weapon, holding it up as though to catch more of the light. 'Fascinating things, the Kholben Shiar. They know us, I sometimes think, even better than we know ourselves.' Then, with what might have been a sigh of longing, he held Sunder back toward Corvis, who in turn extended Talon. Once again the weapons flowed and shifted until they resumed the forms they'd worn before.

'And the point of that?' Corvis demanded, refusing to accept 'curiosity' as an answer.

For the moment, the Serpent ignored his question, once again sheathing the dagger at his side. 'Wine?' he offered.

'I believe I'll pass, thank you.'

'Why, Lord Rebaine, you don't believe I've summoned you all this way just to poison you?'

Ignoring Audriss' choice of words – summoned indeed – he shrugged. 'Have I any reason not to believe it?'

'Tsk, tsk. You clearly don't understand me at all. You see, my friend, I'm a man with a vision.'

'Of course you are.'

'A vision you helped inspire. I've built my campaign upon the model of yours, though I – if you'll pardon my candour – will succeed where you failed. But Lord Rebaine . . .' Audriss leaned forward, his hands clenched tightly against the table. 'Lord Rebaine, Imphallion is a large kingdom, and there are other nations, even larger, beyond our borders. Surely this land is wide enough for two men to rule.'

Hard as he tried to show no reaction, Corvis was taken aback. 'You want me to *join* you?'

'Why not? Nothing could stand against us! Imphallion would topple like a house of twigs! Cephira would be just as easy. Even the Dragon Kings couldn't stand up to our combined might! We could own this entire continent in less than a decade, Corvis. Think of it!'

'I am thinking of it,' the Eastern Terror said coldly. 'I think it's a fool's dream. I think that you – if *you'll* pardon *my* candour – are a madman. And I think I preferred you calling me Lord Rebaine.'

The air between them threatened to freeze, then eased just as quickly. Audriss leaned back in his chair and chuckled softly. 'That's direct enough, I suppose. Tell me, *Lord Rebaine*, if I'm both a fool and a madman, how have I gotten this far?'

'Sheer luck and weight of numbers,' Corvis told him, also leaning back. 'You've started your campaign based on someone else's plans, and you're slavishly following them like a parrot squawking poetry it can't possibly understand. Beginning at Denathere made no strategic or tactical sense whatsoever, as any first-year student of warfare would have known. If Lorum had mobilised even a fraction of the Guilds, you'd have been completely cut off.'

'Yes,' Audriss said mockingly, 'you'd know about that, wouldn't you? I can't imagine what came over us, Lord Rebaine, to end and begin our respective campaigns at Denathere. Can you?'

'Oh, shit,' Corvis said under his breath, so quietly that only his demon could hear him.

/*Corvis, you don't think—*/

'Yes, I do. He knows, Khanda.'

/*We have a problem.*/

'Since we're being so open and honest with each other, Lord Rebaine, let's get to the point, shall we? It's not at Denathere anymore. I knew it wouldn't be, but I had to make certain. You'd never have left it behind, even though you obviously couldn't use it. I want it. Do that, and half this kingdom, this continent, even this world could be yours with no further risk to you. Surely you couldn't ask for a better offer.'

'I'm afraid I've no idea of what you're talking about, Lord Audriss.'

'Oh, I think you do. But we can play that game, too, if you wish. I'll get it from you eventually.

'Our exchange of the Kholben Shiar,' Audriss continued, 'brief as it was, required at least a modicum of shared trust. I'd hoped it would prove to you my sincerity. Are you quite certain I can't convince you to join me?'

'Quite.'

'Ah, well. I had to try, you understand.'

/Corvis,/ Khanda shrieked, /something's happening outside!/

'I understand completely, Audriss!' the Terror of the East shouted, lunging to his feet and vaulting the table. Sunder flashed outward in a mighty blow that should have ended the conflict then and there.

A shock ran through the weapon as it slammed into Audriss' armour. The smaller warlord hurtled across the room to land with a deafening clatter against the iron maiden; it tottered precariously, righting itself only at the last second. But there was no rent in the armour, no sign of injury as Audriss dragged himself to his feet. A spiderweb of cracks showed on the stone breastplate, but even as Corvis watched, the runes flared briefly into incandescence. When the blinding light faded, the armour was undamaged.

'Magic,' Corvis spat bitterly.

'Well, of *course* magic,' Audriss shouted, steadying himself. 'Stone armour is a pretty stupid idea without magic, isn't it?'

His face grim beneath his mask, Corvis advanced. 'But it's human magic, Audriss. I doubt it can stand up to the Kholben Shiar for long.'

'No, probably not. But Lord Rebaine, you don't *have* very long.'

/Corvis, the tent flap!/

The thick fog cloaking the surrounding grasses now flowed *into* the tent, seeping in beneath the flap. It left in its wake a trail of blood, a thin coating that painted the canvas a thick, rich crimson.

'I'm disappointed in you, Lord Rebaine,' Audriss told him. The Serpent moved farther into the tent, putting distance between himself and his contender. He had once again drawn Talon and he held the infernal weapon before him, his poise and posture bespeaking his skill with the blade.

'How's that, Lord Audriss?' Corvis asked, backing cautiously away from both Audriss and the new arrival, who had assumed the form of a tall, gaunt figure with jet-black hair. He stopped only when his back brushed against the canvas wall.

'You attacked me, Lord Rebaine. After I was generous enough to grant you my promise of safe parley. In my own home, no less! Have you no sense of honour?'

Sunder weaving a sinister pattern in the air before him, Corvis glanced meaningfully at the formerly insubstantial figure. 'And your bloodsucking friend here just happened to be in the neighbourhood? I'm no more dishonourable than you, Audriss. I'm just more honest about it.'

'You've got nowhere to go, Rebaine,' Audriss snapped, finally losing his last tattered shreds of patience. 'Even if Mithraem can't catch you, the surrounding terrain is crawling with his people, not to mention, my own guards and a handful of gnomes. Not even the great Corvis Rebaine can take on those kinds of odds.'

'Why, Audriss, I do believe you're absolutely right.'

Despite what he thought was an obvious cue, nothing happened. Mithraem drew nearer.

'Khanda, now would be an excellent time!'

/What's the magic word?/

His face, already red with exertion, purpled with rage and he shouted something garbled and incoherent at the pendant around his neck.

/Hmm. Close enough./

A flash of searing heat, followed by perhaps three or four heartbeats of pervasive, soul-numbing cold – and then they were in the storeroom at the Prurient Pixie. With a startled oath, Corvis tumbled into, and over, the writing desk, collapsing the furniture and toppling to the ground with a resounding crash.

CHAPTER SEVENTEEN

'Are you certain about this, Corvis?'

'As certain as I've ever been.'

'So not really, then.'

The warlord and the witch stood amid a grove of trees, less ancient perhaps than those of Theaghl-gohlatch, but older still than Imphallion itself. They towered above, aloof giants with beards of leaves and tears of moss, oblivious to the scurrying of the tiny creatures below.

It was a place of power, Seilloah had claimed – a power that they were about to desecrate, to poison for generations to come. Around the perimeter of a rough circle, not a clearing but simply a relatively even growth of trees, thirteen men and women sat on the earth, tied securely to the unyielding boles. The begging and pleading had long since run its course, leaving nothing but frightened sobs and quickened breath to break the night's still silence.

Criminals, most of them, and soldiers the remainder, people who had chosen a life of violence and known that their deaths might well prove the same. Corvis wasn't self-deluded enough to think that it actually made a difference, though.

'Maybe I'm *not* ready,' he admitted at last, wiping the sweat from his palms on the dark leathers and woolen coat that were far more appropriate for forest travel than the black armour he'd recently had forged. 'But it still needs to be done, doesn't it?'

Seilloah only shrugged. 'You know there's no going back after this.'

'Seilloah, there was no going back a long time ago.' He knelt and began striking flint to steel over a loose heap of tinder and twigs.

'Have you chosen one?'

'I have.'

'Based on . . . ?'

'Based on the fact that I had to choose one. We only have a few names, and any's as good as another, I suppose.' A tiny ember sputtered, faded, sputtered once more, sending a thin plume of smoke up into the leaves. The forest began to smell of incense. 'Chant,' he ordered.

And chant she did, her voice taking wing into the nighttime sky, inhuman words and unnatural sounds frightening even the bats and the owls from the air. Thirteen times she circled the fire, each time repeating syllables that should have shredded the flesh of her throat. And with each revolution, Corvis raised an iron dagger and slit the throat of one of the bound and once-more-screaming sacrifices, shaking the blade clean of blood into the faintly crackling flames.

'Now, Corvis!' Seilloah hissed, her voice scraped hoarse by the words of power. 'The name, before the power fades!'

'Khanda,' Corvis growled, his own throat clenched tight. 'Find me the one called Khanda.'

Fortunately for what little remained of Corvis' dignity, he regained his feet before the door slammed open and Losalis charged in, saber drawn, followed by half a dozen men.

The large warrior frowned in puzzlement as he skidded to a halt, surveying the wreckage around him. 'Lord Rebaine?' he asked tentatively. 'Is there a problem?'

'Does it look like there's a problem?'

'Uh . . .'

'Go find Seilloah and Davro. Bring them back here. Now.'

'Right away, my lord.' And once more, Corvis was alone with a pile of tinder that was once his desk.

'Go ahead, Khanda. I'm sure you've got some snide comment to make about all this.'

/Hardly,/ the demon snickered. /There's not a thing I could say that wouldn't detract from the magic of this moment./

'I'm so glad I provide such amusement for you. I wonder if Pekatherosh is blessed enough to glean the same enjoyment from Audriss.'

Khanda's laughter abruptly ceased. /That was really unkind, you know that?/

'What *is* it between the two of you, anyway?'

/A long and sordid history you don't need to know about. This little squabble's been going on for millennia, Corvis. You're just the most recent lucky stiff to get dragged into it./

'Corvis?' Seilloah called as she pushed the door open before her. 'Are you all right?'

The warlord merely shook his head and waited until Losalis and Davro arrived. Then he took a few steps back, selected one of the larger crates, and dragged it over where the desk had been. He sat in the chair, clasped his hands on the surface before him, and tried his damnedest to pretend he didn't so utterly look the idiot.

'So did you see Audriss?' Davro asked without preamble, scratching idly at his horn.

'Oh, yes. And Pekatherosh.'

The ogre blinked. 'Bless you.'

'Very funny. Pekatherosh is Audriss' tame demon.'

/Now haven't we talked about that already?/

Corvis ripped the heavy helm from his head, slamming it down onto the crate. 'He's got every advantage that I do, people. He's got a demon. He's got his own cadre of allies. He's even got his own Kholben Shiar!' Meaningfully, he stared directly into Seilloah's eyes. 'And he knows why I lost at Denathere. He knows what I was after.'

The witch went paler than Audriss' gnomes. 'Corvis . . .'

'I know. But he can't know where I've hidden it, so we're safe for the time being.'

'Would someone be kind enough to fill in the new hire?' Losalis asked.

'Me, too,' the ogre added. 'You never even told *me* what you were looking for at Denathere.'

'All right,' Corvis said, his voice strangely soft. 'I think maybe you'd better know all of it.'

/*I'm not certain this is a good idea.*/

'What, are you afraid someone'll try to steal it?'

/*I would.*/

'Yes, but you have issues.' Then, shifting his focus back toward those in the room who *weren't* currently hanging from his neck, Corvis rose to his feet. 'What I'm about to tell you,' he demanded, 'does not leave this room. No one – not your men, your lieutenants, or the priest at your deathbed – hears a whisper of this. Other than Seilloah, I've never told another soul – not even my wife.' His eyes crept across Davro and Losalis both like a spreading frost; each found himself repressing a shiver.

'But what if—' Davro began cautiously.

'No. Nothing drags this out of you, ever. I'll have your oaths, the both of you, or this conversation is over now.'

'I'll swear to it,' the ogre said, somewhat sullenly. 'You know to whom.'

Corvis nodded. 'And you?' he asked the dark warrior pointedly.

'I swear,' the man said simply, 'in the name of my honour, my ancestors, and the gods of my homeland, that I will never repeat what you tell me.'

'All right.' Unconsciously, his hands clasped behind his back, Corvis paced what little space the room allowed. 'I assume both of you have heard the name Selakrian?'

'It rings bells,' Losalis said with a brief frown, 'but I can't quite place—'

'He was a wizard, wasn't he?' Davro asked. 'Fairly powerful?'

'Fairly?' Seilloah stood, fists clenched, glaring at the lot of them with a sudden anger *almost* powerful enough to over-shadow her obvious fear. '*Fairly* powerful, Davro? Selakrian was the most powerful spellworker ever to set foot on the Maker's world! He not only breached the secrets of the Tenth Circle, he mastered it! Selakrian, until the day he died, was the nearest thing to the gods that any mortal-born creature could hope to become.' She spun toward the warlord, her teeth grinding. 'This is a horrible mistake, Corvis. It was a bad idea twenty years ago, and it's a bad idea now. You're going to kill us all.'

'I don't understand,' Davro admitted. 'I mean, this Selakrian lived hundreds of years ago, right? He's got to be long dead. So what's the danger?'

'The danger,' the witch growled, 'is his legacy.'

'What I searched for,' Corvis said, 'in those catacombs beneath the streets of Denathere, was Selakrian's spellbook.

'And I found it.'

The emptiness of death itself could not have rivaled the silence that fell over the tiny storeroom.

'How – how powerful *are* these spells?' Davro finally whispered.

'Ungodly,' the Terror of the East said simply. 'If legend is to be believed – and everything I've seen suggests that it should – there are spells in this book capable of wiping out whole cities or enslaving entire populations. Selakrian was reported to have summoned creatures so terrible, they make Khanda look like a kitten.'

/*You just* had to *say it, didn't you?*/

'But you're not that powerful,' Davro protested, more hopeful than certain. 'Could you even use these spells?'

'Davro,' Seilloah explained patiently, 'have you ever seen me study a spellbook?'

'Well, no. But you're a witch, not a sorcerer.'

'Two aspects of the same thing, my friend. Most of us don't use spellbooks. Once you've learned or created a spell, it's a part of you. The only reason to create a spellbook is to pass your spells along to others. And most masters teach their pupils verbally. Few of us create spellbooks, because it's too easy to steal them. Like Corvis is trying to do,' she added bitterly.

'The point that Seilloah is not-so-gracefully dancing around,' the warlord told them, 'is that with the spells in written form, I don't have to be an adept of the Tenth Circle to use them. Assuming one is careful enough, studies them hard enough, and has no small amount of luck, anyone with even the most rudimentary magical knowledge can cast from the book.'

'But why would Selakrian leave such a thing just lying around?' Losalis asked, horrified.

'That's just it,' Corvis said resentfully. 'He *didn't* just leave it lying around. The entire damn thing is written in some unique cipher. Without the key, the book is so much dead-weight.'

'Which is why you didn't use it at Denathere,' Davro exclaimed in sudden comprehension. 'You gambled your entire campaign on this stupid book, and when you couldn't use it, everything fell apart!'

'Not tactically sound, my lord,' Losalis commented. 'A good commander always leaves himself a fallback option.'

'And, of course, rehashing my old failures is of *far* greater importance than planning our next step of *this* campaign.'

/*More fun, anyway.*/

'Shut up, Khanda.'

'Corvis!' Seilloah said sharply. 'Listen!'

They paused, each unconsciously holding his breath. 'I don't hear anything,' the warlord said finally. And then it struck him. He *didn't* hear anything. The taproom was silent.

As quick as Corvis was, Losalis was faster. Before the Eastern Terror took three steps toward the door, his massive lieutenant had nearly ripped the portal from its hinges and dashed out into the common room.

The chamber was in shambles. Tables and chairs were strewn about the room, many toppled and some smashed.

Puddles of ale, beer, and wine skulked treacherously here and there on the floor, lurking in wait for an unwary foot. Tankards lay overturned, mugs dropped and shattered – and everywhere, twitching erratically on the dusty floorboards or flopping spasmodically across the broken tables, lay Corvis' men. Their eyes bulged as though the pressure of a mounting storm built up within their skulls, and their tongues protruded, yellowed and swollen, several bloodied or even chewed completely through by gnashing teeth. Even as the four of them watched, one of the men jerked as though he'd been run through with a jagged blade. His teeth clacked together, and his diseased tongue flopped to the floor where it spasmed twice before falling still in a growing pool of blood.

'Urthet,' Seilloah said clinically as she surveyed the carnage.

'Excuse me?' Corvis asked, his voice hoarse. Had they lost the war already?

'Urthet. It's a rare herb, very dangerous.' She was already moving toward the bar, grabbing a large pitcher and filling it from a cask of mild wine.

'Seilloah, this is hardly the time—' Davro started.

'Corvis, I can save some of these men. I'll need them laid out, made comfortable. They have to be kept warm, and you need to get something between their jaws to keep any more from losing their tongues.'

'Losalis, go,' Corvis ordered at once. 'Bring as many men as you need.'

'At once, my lord.'

Losalis was halfway to the door when Seilloah said, 'You'll find more in the streets. In small doses, urthet can stay in the system for hours before it takes effect. Anyone who's drunk here in the past twelve hours is at risk. When you're gathering your men, make sure you bring any more victims here; if I have to go out searching for them, we'll never get to them in time.'

The warrior nodded once and was gone. Even from within, they could hear his deep voice booming out over the town, and soldiers begin trickling in to help.

'Corvis,' Seilloah said brusquely as she crumbled several kinds of dried grasses into the pitcher, 'come here.'

'The bastard was never planning to attack us,' he snarled as he approached. 'This was his plan from the beginning. I'll wager that if we were to search those woods, we'd find he never even used the lumber we heard his men cutting. It was all a bloody distraction.'

'That's nice. Corvis, listen to me. There's another step to this that I need you to handle personally.'

'*That* doesn't bode well. What do you need?'

'The reason Audriss chose urthet, I'm sure,' she said as she stirred the rapidly thickening concoction with a convenient ladle, 'is that, as far as most people know, there's no antidote. It takes longer for some people than for others, but once you've taken a sufficient dose, it's *always* fatal.'

Corvis felt his blood run cold. 'But you *can* help them, right?' he asked plaintively.

'No, Corvis, I'm sitting in the midst of a tavern full of dying men stirring random leaves into bad wine because I've been looking for a new hobby. There *is* a remedy for urthet, one very few people know about. It involves, among other things, a goodly number of herbs and powders, and not a small touch of magic. But it also requires a small quantity of urthet itself.'

'Someday, you'll have to explain to me how you can use a poison to cure a poison.'

'Someday, but not now. The problem is, as I said, urthet is pretty damn rare. I don't have any of it.'

'So then what—'

'I need you,' Seilloah said, very slowly and succinctly, 'to find anyone in this tavern beyond saving. Anyone who's already dead. I need you to take them into one of the back rooms, and I need you to bring me back their blood. As much of it as you can.'

For all the horrors he'd seen, all the horrors he'd *perpetrated,* Corvis blanched. 'Seilloah, I—'

'Do it, Corvis, or Audriss wins right here and now.'

He did it. With the help of several of the mercenaries, several dozen bloated corpses were laid out in the Pixie's main storeroom. And then, after he'd sent the men back to assist the others, the warlord grabbed a knife and several basins, swallowed heavily once, and bent to work.

He was sweating when he emerged some moments later. He carried a number of bowls, basins, and bottles, stacked precariously, and all covered in whatever spare cloth he could find. Balancing them carefully, he stepped back behind the bar and laid them down beside the witch.

'Is that all?' she asked curtly; then, before he could reply, continued, 'Never mind, it'll have to do. Start adding it to the mixture.' She gestured toward a number of bottles filled perhaps halfway with the thick substance she'd concocted. 'No more than two spoonfuls per bottle, though.'

'If the men knew what was going into this cure of yours,' Corvis told her, doing his best not to really think about what he was doing, 'we'd never get them to drink it.'

'That's why we're not telling them, Corvis.' She frowned briefly at the sound of one of the victims trying to retch around a bloated tongue. 'Not that any of these poor fellows would understand a word you said to them right now, anyway. We may have to force-feed them.'

'Hmm.' The warlord kept working, his mind racing. 'Seilloah,' he began, a thought occurring to him, 'should we give this stuff to the healthy soldiers as well? Sort of a precaution in case they're poisoned later on?'

'Not a good idea, Corvis. This stuff we're making counteracts urthet, but it's also extremely toxic in its own right.'

Corvis froze. 'What? But then what's the antidote for this stuff?'

'Pure urthet, of course,' she replied in a tone that implied that he'd been foolish even to ask.

'You mean—'

'I mean that what I'm making here will cure anyone already poisoned, but it'd probably kill anyone else. Shall I explain to you the exact principles behind it, or would you rather just assume I actually know what I'm doing?'

'I'm just going to sit here and mix this stuff.'

'Good boy.'

In the end, only about two hundred of Corvis' men died, though more than four times that number had fallen victim to the deadly herb. Several of Losalis' most trusted men were scouring the town, searching both for the perpetrators of this attack and for any further victims. The tavern was full of men laid out side by side and head-to-toe, wrapped in blankets and groaning in constant pain, but most would eventually recover.

'How long will they be sick?' Corvis asked after hearing the prognosis. Fairly near exhaustion, Corvis leaned with both hands on the bar, staring grimly out over the new carpeting of living flesh.

Seilloah shook her head, collapsing onto one of the stools across the bar from him. Her hair hung down in listless tangles, and she was splattered with the blood several patients spat on her in their agonised throes. 'I can't say. If the stronger men got only a moderate dose, they'll probably sleep off most of the after-effects by tomorrow evening. Others may take as long as three or four days. And that's just taking the poison itself into account. More than a few of the men injured themselves during their convulsions, broke bones or bit their own tongues off. If you're asking me how soon we can be ready to move or fight at full strength . . . I'd say probably five days, maybe a week.'

'Damnation,' Corvis muttered.

'Can we stand up to an attack now?' she asked anxiously. 'A fifth of our soldiers are down.'

'Audriss won't attack us,' the Eastern Terror told her. 'These are mercenaries, Seilloah. If the bastard had actually managed to kill a thousand of them, we'd probably have lost twice that many to desertion. Fighting and dying in battle is one thing to these men, but falling to poison . . .' Corvis shook his head. 'As far as he knows, I don't have enough of an army left to be any threat to him. He's just going to go around

Vorringar and continue on his merry way. And there's not a damn thing I can do to stop him!'

'But you still have your army, Corvis. And weren't you telling me earlier that the larger the force, the slower it moves? We can catch him if we have to.'

'It's not *quite* that simple, Seilloah. Besides, at the moment I'm not sure what we'd do if we *did* catch him. But you're right, it's not over.' He sighed wearily. 'We both need to get some sleep, first and foremost. Then we need to meet with Davro and Losalis again. We've got to decide our next move, and I don't particularly care for our options.'

Though Corvis slept deeply the following morning didn't find him feeling particularly well rested. The black-and-bone armour grew heavier every time he donned it, and the pendant around his neck weighed him down, a stone around his soul.

He'd clanked loudly as he stepped over the recovering mercenaries, muttering encouragements and promising bloody retribution for the dishonourable assault.

'What we need to know,' Davro said as soon as they'd gathered in the storeroom, 'is how Audriss poisoned the ale in the first place. If we can't figure out how he did it, we can't defend against it if he tries again.'

'I don't know that there's anything particularly mysterious about it,' Losalis said thoughtfully, scratching at his beard. 'As many men as we've got here, it wouldn't be too hard for a few outsiders to slip into the crowd. No one here could possibly know everyone by sight.'

Corvis, however, disagreed, 'I don't think so, Losalis. Audriss wouldn't risk letting a human agent fall into our hands. I've got ways of getting information from them they wouldn't be able to resist.

'No, Audriss has stolen yet another page from my book, it seems. He's got the gnomes working for him.'

Even Davro shuddered at that. 'Creepy little buggers, aren't they?'

'They are. They're also nigh undetectable by magic and just a little bit sneakier than a hunting owl when they want to be. It would require pretty much zero effort for one of them to have snuck in here and poisoned the drinks.' Corvis frowned. 'Given their other penchants, it's also likely that it was they who killed our missing soldiers.'

'So if they're so undetectable,' the hulking lieutenant asked, 'how do we keep this from happening again?'

'Tedious as it is,' Corvis said, 'we have Seilloah or myself check over the food and drink stores on a regular basis. Magic may not detect the gnomes, but it should do just fine for detecting any contamination of the food.'

/Speak for yourself, fragile one. I don't have the first notion of what might or might not poison you. You're all so damn easy to kill, it's a wonder you didn't all keel over dead two minutes after the gods spat you out into the world like so much phlegm./

'How colourful. I'm sure Seilloah can explain to you what to look for.'

'I can do what?' Seilloah asked suspiciously.

Corvis sighed. 'Later, people, later. As it happens, while I don't intend to take any chances, we probably don't have to worry about Audriss trying this again. It didn't work, and he won't waste any time reusing old tactics. The trick is to figure out what he's going to do next.'

'He's going after the key,' Losalis said simply.

The warlord blinked. 'He's *what*?'

'The key. The one to decode that spellbook you were talking about. He's going after it.'

'How could you possibly know that?' Davro demanded.

'Think strategically,' Losalis replied. 'So far, Audriss has shown a substantial – one might even say impossible – level of knowledge of your previous campaigns. Correct, my lord?'

Corvis nodded with a scowl. 'He has. The fact that he even knows about the spellbook has me stumped.'

'However he knows, he knows. I think we have to assume that he also knows about the necessity of the key, yes?'

'Your logic's getting a little fuzzy there, Losalis,' Seilloah told him. 'We didn't know about the key until Corvis actually held the book in his hands.'

'Audriss knew that Lord Rebaine found the book,' the warrior pointed out, 'but he didn't ask why it wasn't used at Denathere. That book would have made the difference between victory and defeat. Had I been in his place, I'd have tried to find out from Lord Rebaine why he didn't use the book. Unless, of course, I already knew.'

'It's possible that he simply didn't think I'd tell him,' Corvis suggested, absently drumming his fingers on the wooden crate.

'I suppose it is. Still, I think we have to assume that he knows about the key, if only so that we can plan for the worst.'

'All right, I'll buy that,' Davro said. 'But how do we know he hasn't already got the key?'

'Because he didn't tell Lord Rebaine that he had it. If Audriss was serious in trying to talk you over to his side, my lord, he'd surely have enticed you to bring him the book by presenting himself as the only person who could make it work.'

Corvis blinked twice. 'Losalis, are you sure you're a warrior and not a politician?'

The dark-skinned warrior winced. 'Please, my lord. There are limits.'

Corvis once more began to pace, the clack of his boot heels resembling the sardonic applause of a single, mildly amused observer. 'It took me years to narrow my research to the point where I was *almost* sure the book was at Denathere,' he said slowly, his mind racing. 'I couldn't even begin to guess where to find the key.'

Unnoticed by the others, Davro pivoted slowly and strode to the nearest corner, staring absently into the dust and cobwebs and dusty cobwebs that hugged the walls and ceiling. Something was nagging at him, as though he'd picked up a mosquito bite somewhere between his brain and the inside of his skull.

'My lord,' Losalis began, his arms folded, 'who else knows about the spellbook?'

'Ha! If you mean who else has heard of it, the answer is pretty much anyone who has ever read any tome or treatise written about magic.

'On the other hand, if you want to know who knew where to *find* the book, or knows that I have it now . . . well, everyone in this room, of course, and Audriss. He might have told someone, I suppose, but I don't think it likely.' Corvis shook his head in frustration. 'I don't see how anyone else could know, but I don't see how Audriss can possibly know, either, so take that for whatever it's worth.'

Seilloah smiled bitterly. 'Well, so far we've narrowed the possibilities down to anyone. Anyone covers a substantial number of people, Corvis.'

/*My word, but she's helpful, isn't she?*/

'What, you're the only one permitted to be sarcastic?' Corvis asked.

/*It's just that most of you aren't very good at it.*/

'Oh, gods!'

Everyone jumped, then stared at the ogre. One of Davro's hands rested idly atop a heavy barrel, the forefinger and thumb of the other clasped tightly on the bridge of his nose. His single eye squeezed shut.

'Davro?' Seilloah asked, concerned. 'Are you all right?'

'That depends,' the ogre said with a disgusted sigh. 'If you mean physically, yes, I'm just fine. I am, however, an idiot.'

/*I—*/

'Shut up, Khanda.'

/*Wow. Quick reflexes there, friend.*/

'Davro,' Corvis said carefully, 'what is it?'

'I think someone else knows, Corvis. I'm sorry I didn't think to mention it before, but it didn't seem all that important at the time. And it was so long ago, there was so much else going on, I didn't—'

'Davro,' the warlord said again, a bit louder. '*What* happened so long ago? *What* didn't seem important?'

'It was right after you left Denathere,' the ogre said. 'We were pulling out, a fighting withdrawal as it were. Anyway, some of my tribe and I were holed up in one of the buildings across from the Hall of Meeting, keeping an eye on things, watching for an opportunity to get the hell out. We were there when Duke Lorum and his entourage arrived, Corvis. When they got there, they were wary, but relatively upbeat. You'd disappeared, the army was falling apart, and there was no real cohesive resistance. At least, that's how they all looked when they got into the Hall. Maybe half an hour later, though, one of them storms back out into the street, and she's sure as sunset irked about something. All kinds of rants and curses and words that, no offense intended, I really didn't think humans had the wherewithal to use. So she keeps this up for a good five minutes, blows up a few nearby piles of what's already pretty much rubble, and stalks back inside. I didn't think much of it at the time – maybe she got some bad news, or found a friend among the dead – but now I'm not so sure.'

Losalis raised a hand. 'I'm sorry to interrupt, but did you say she "blew up" a few piles of rubble?'

But there was no confusion at all in Corvis' expression. He knew of whom the ogre spoke; had known, in fact, since his first use of the word *she*. He wondered briefly if the past seventeen years were anything but a brief intermission in some stage play he performed for the amusement of uncaring gods, and if he was destined to continue every little thing left uncompleted so long ago.

'I hadn't heard that she had all that much of a temper,' Corvis mused, speaking to no one in particular. 'For something to anger her that badly, it must have been pretty important.'

'My lord,' Losalis interjected again with just a bit less patience, 'I don't mean to be rude, but might I impose on you to tell me who in the gods' names we're talking about?'

'I'm sorry, Losalis. We're talking about Rheah Vhoune, of course. Personal adviser to the regent, His Grace, the Duke Lorum of Taberness. And also, incidentally, one of the greatest sorcerers alive. Back when we were acquainted, she'd mastered the Seventh Circle at an age when most mages are struggling with the Fifth. She's probably achieved the Eighth by now.'

'Oh,' Losalis said simply. 'Is this really the sort of person that we want getting mixed up in this mess? I think we've got enough wizards and witches and sorcerers involved already.'

Corvis actually laughed. 'I couldn't agree more, Losalis. Unfortunately, our large friend got me thinking with his useful, if somewhat belated, revelations, and I'm afraid that I don't have any choice anymore.'

'You think she knew about the book?' Seilloah asked.

'It certainly appears that way, doesn't it? I'm starting to think that I should have just messengered an itinerary of my entire campaign to anyone who expressed an interest. Obviously, we weren't doing a great job of keeping it a secret.'

/Or,/ Khanda suggested, /she didn't have the slightest clue what you were looking for until after you'd left, and just threw her little tantrum when she found the room and figured out what she'd missed./

'You know,' Corvis admitted reluctantly, 'you may just have a point,'

/Oh! Oh, he acknowledges my humble contribution! My heart palpitates with glee!/

'You don't *have* a heart, Khanda.'

/No? Then what's palpitating?/

'Khanda suggests,' the warlord announced to the others, 'that Rheah may not have learned of the book until after I'd left. She may have initially only realised that something important slipped through her fingers.' Corvis frowned darkly. 'Not that it really matters *when* she found out. If anyone in this whole bloody kingdom could dig up that key,' he acknowledged, 'it'd be her.'

Losalis's eyes narrowed. 'Do we have any reason to believe that Audriss can't figure this out?'

'I don't think so,' Corvis replied. 'We've been assuming that

Audriss has access to the same information we do, if not more. I see no reason he couldn't come to the same conclusions.'

'Then we know where he's going, don't we, my lord? It seems to me that the question now is, what do we do about it?'

Unfortunately, as much as he might wish otherwise, Corvis knew *exactly* what to do about it.

CHAPTER EIGHTEEN

Rheah Vhoune strode through the broken streets of Denathere, but her eyes scarcely saw the damage, her ears barely registered the moans of the injured or the cries of mourning and despair. The smoke in the air swirled around her, but her magics held it at bay. The dirt of the alleys wafted over her boots and rained back down to earth, unable to find enough purchase to stick.

For a time, as ash-stained brick loomed overhead and the occasional sound of lingering skirmishes echoed from afar, her attentions remained focused on the conversation she and Nathaniel Espa had just held with the young regent. Some level of despair was expected, understandable even, given the wound inflicted upon Imphallion's second greatest city and the frustrating escape of the Terror who'd inflicted it. Still, they'd need to keep a vigilant eye on Lorum, make sure that he had sufficient time to recover before he did something foolish. And she wasn't going to have unlimited time, either. When the Guilds regrouped, recovered their authority from the regent, and set out to rebuild, that would be the time to make her own move, to see her own dreams bear fruit. If she was too preoccupied with Lorum, her best opportunity would pass her by like a wild horse, leaving her in the dust.

But soon, thoughts of the Society she sought to construct turned to matters of politics and government and war. Again, as so often in the past hours, she wondered what it was that Corvis Rebaine had thought he was doing, why the Terror of the East had allowed himself to be cornered in this city, scarcely halfway to his goal. And Rheah Vhoune found herself – without the slightest surprise, though she'd no memory of choosing a destination – standing before Denathere's monolithic Hall of Meeting.

With scarcely a glance of acknowledgment, she brushed her way past royal soldiers and Guild mercenaries who, hours after Rebaine's forces had all but disintegrated and Denathere been retaken, still combed the corridors and rooms of the Hall, looking for bodies or survivors. Her soft-booted feet trod along stained carpets, down stone-walled halls, and across bloodstained thresholds. A stair that she'd long known existed but had never had cause to traverse led her ever down, to the deepest cellars of the Hall. And there even Rheah's granite demeanour cracked, for the hole in the floor was still half choked with bodies, the floor around it coated in drying blood. She felt a chill run across her arms, down her back, and sensed the presence of a dozen lingering souls.

A score of workers stood amid the bodies, their steps uneven, their faces pale, arms and torsos drenched in gore. They'd already dug from the tomb of flesh several living survivors, including the infant Braetlyn heir, and the odds of finding others grew more feeble by the moment. Nonetheless, Rheah took a few moments to aid them, directing phantom hands to lift the heaviest corpses and phantom ears to listen for the faintest breath or beating heart. Only when she was certain there were no more lives to be saved did she direct her magics on with greater force, clearing herself a path to walk the scorched passages that had been Rebaine's ultimate goal.

With the aid of a veritable swarm of spells, seeking this way and that, sniffing for any trace of lingering magics, it took her mere moments to find the iron door, peeled back and flush against the wall like a flattened blossom. It took many minutes more – minutes spent sitting cross-legged in meditative concentration on the cold stone floor – for those spells to tell Rheah what had once lain upon the web-shrouded table within.

And many minutes more for Rheah's sobs of frustration to subside. All this time, so close, had she only known . . .

Rebaine had found it, he'd taken it – but he hadn't *used* it. Why? Could he simply be waiting, studying the incantations? It was possible, certainly, but somehow Rheah didn't think so. He'd left his army no path of retreat – surely he'd planned to use the book to make good his victory. That he'd escaped alone, allowing his campaign to crumble, suggested that something had gone wrong.

Rheah Vhoune rose slowly to her feet and stalked back toward the light above, still cursing with every step. First the regent must be informed, for though her instincts screamed at her to keep her discovery a secret from all, she would obey her sworn duty.

But then . . . then she would learn *why*, what had stopped Rebaine within sight of his victory. And damn him, no matter what it took, she would be ready when he appeared again.

One would never know it to look at him, but Rollie Micallec was an easygoing man, softhearted and soft-spoken. At six-foot-six and nearly three hundred pounds, he was dragged into brawls and even duels with unfortunate regularity. His hands, large but dexterous, had been forced to do harm far too frequently.

When such violence could be avoided, he laboured on behalf of others, as his mother had before him, and her father before her. Rollie Micallec, though one of the strongest men in the household of Edmund, Duke of Lutrinthus, was known throughout his master's province not as a warrior, but as one of the most skilled physicians ever to walk beneath the eyes of the gods.

He listened to his patients' complaints with understanding and sympathy, rather than the abrupt veneer many physicians mistake for efficiency. Those powerful hands could set a broken bone, stitch a ragged wound, or merely offer a comforting touch, all with equal facility. As the duke's household physician, Rollie rarely treated the common folk, but his reputation, and those of his pupils, had nonetheless spread far and wide.

Today the famous healer was not in high spirits. He shoved through the crowded hallways of Duke Edmund's estate, pushing through soldiers dressed both in the white-and-silver livery of Lutrinthus and in various other hues as well, not the least prevalent of which was the deep blue and red of Braetlyn.

Rollie didn't like soldiers. He liked even less the fact that his own lord's men were currently outnumbered within the walls of the man's own manor. Intellectually, Rollie knew the warriors were allies, the soldiers of lords and nobles gathered against a common enemy, but emotionally he felt he was playing the part of a lamed lamb amid a gargantuan pack of wolves.

But even worse was the reason the soldiers were present.

Duke Edmund's estate sat just about a mile outside the city of Orthessis, a city currently in the throes of chaotic evacuation. Though much of the populace steadfastly refused to leave, a greater number streamed west, a winding worm of human misery advancing on Pelapheron. Valuables were hastily wrapped and packed into rickety carts, lumbering wagons, or dangling saddlebags. Animals were herded into some semblance of order and driven from their pens onto the dusty road. Friends and family were separated by the slow but steady tide of humanity, valuables were lost or shattered, and fights erupted with appalling regularity. And still the people coming up behind were willing to brave the horrors of this mass exodus, because staying behind was even worse.

The Serpent was coming.

Duke Edmund's scouts had come thundering into town a week before, horses lathered and sweating. Audriss' armies had paused for a day or so, camped just outside Vorringar. But they'd quickly been on the move again, and they'd reached Taiheason's Cross in less than a day. There they had turned, the scouts reported breathlessly to Sir Tyler, current commander of Duke Edmund's forces, down the northwest fork.

Toward Orthessis.

Duke Edmund and Sir Tyler knew they had little chance of defending Orthessis against a determined assault. Edmund had immediately led the bulk of his armies west to Pelapheron, the largest and most defensible city in Lutrinthus Province. He'd taken with them the gathered forces of several of his barons, reinforced by a small detachment of the regent's own armies, led by Nathaniel Espa himself. Tyler was under orders to come west with the remainder of the soldiers once the evacuees were clear — and that was his intention until Jassion, Baron of Braetlyn, showed up with another army at his back and demanded hospitality. Tyler, bound by the demands of noble courtesy and Jassion's rank, was forced to oblige. The two men spent the next week arguing, Tyler insisting they move on to Pelapheron as ordered, Jassion demanding equally as strenuously that, with their combined might, they could hold Orthessis if only Duke Edmund would return with the bulk of the army.

Rollie wished they'd make up their minds, one way or the other. If they were caught before a decision was made and faced Audriss piecemeal, it would be a slaughter.

The healer finally shoved through the main hall, past a large man in a rusty-smelling coif and hauberk, and into a much smaller, and blessedly emptier, corridor. Steadying himself with a few deep breaths, he shifted a bag of herbs and implements to his other shoulder, ran a hand over his bald pate, and moved at a quicker but much steadier pace down toward the room in which his patient lay.

This particular fellow was also a soldier, and not even one of Edmund's. He was an injured man in need of aid, however, and that fact overrode any personal objections Rollie might have regarding either his profession or his loyalties. He'd arrived with Baron Jassion's men, his head bandaged and bloodied, his arms and legs lashed to the saddle to prevent him from falling off. Although his eyes would occasionally open, he'd displayed no indication of speech, or even self-awareness, since his injury. He ate and drank anything put in his mouth, allowed himself to be moved or dressed, and otherwise showed as much life as any other dumb animal.

Rollie was all but convinced that the damage was permanent. Had he been present when the injury was first inflicted, he might have been able to do more. Too much time had passed, alas, and while the men who first treated the wound certainly meant well, their battlefield dressings proved woefully insufficient. It was yet possible he might recover, and Rollie would work to that end as long as the fellow was in his care, but he didn't hold out much hope.

He knew better than to tell that to Jassion of Braetlyn, though.

The heavy door creaked alarmingly as the healer pushed his way in. The room reeked of fevered, sour sweat. His patient lay in the sparsely adorned bed, his eyes shut, breathing softly. His face was sallow and gaunt, pale enough to make the wide scar on his brow all but invisible. His beard, formerly a deep red, had gone grey, and his body, once the paunch-over-muscle common to aging warriors, was a meager shadow of its former girth.

Heaving a sympathetic sigh, Rollie sat on the down quilt beside him and laid his bag on the floor. As had been his practice three times a day for over a week, he removed a small vial of a syrupy concoction and held it to the man's lips.

'Wake up now,' he said softly. 'Come on, friend, I need you awake. Wouldn't want you to choke on your medicine, after all.' He smiled an ironic grin. 'It would sort of defeat the purpose.'

'Yes,' the injured soldier croaked back through the muffling curtains of a voice long unused, 'I suppose it would.'

The gaze of a basilisk wouldn't have frozen Rollie in place more thoroughly. The vial dropped from suddenly nervous hands, and only the fact that it bounced across the mattress, rather than the floor, kept it from shattering.

Could it have been a fluke? His imagination? Rollie leaned closer, trembling slightly. 'Can – can you hear me?' he asked breathlessly. 'Can you understand?'

'I hear you. What . . .' The man coughed once. 'What day is it?'

'Sannos and Vantares, thank you!' the healer whispered, invoking both the Healer and the Guardian of the Dead. Then, his voice awed at the miracle he'd just witnessed, 'It's Queensday, my friend.'

'Queensday,' the man repeated, his voice rough, licking his cracked lips. Immediately Rollie removed from his bag a skin of clear water. With a weak nod of thanks, his patient grabbed it and began to drink.

'Slowly, now,' Rollie cautioned, reaching out for the bag. 'Not too much at once.'

'Of course.' The man's voice sounded a bit stronger. 'Queensday,' he said again. 'I've been out a week.'

The physician smiled sadly. 'A bit longer, I fear,' he said gently, placing a comforting hand on the man's arm. 'It *is* Queensday. And the fourteenth day of the Month of the Crow.'

Rollie would not have thought it possible, but his patient's face grew even paler. 'Has it been so long?' he breathed.

'I'm afraid it has. But you will adjust, my friend. You—'
He jumped with a startled yelp as the soldier's hand clamped tightly onto his arm.

'I must speak with Baron Jassion,' he rasped, pausing only long enough to get over another fit of choking. 'Immediately!'

'I don't know that you're in any condition for that right now,' Rollie objected. 'Perhaps in a few days—'

'No! No, you don't understand! I know – I know who it is! I know whose army it is!'

'Of course,' the healer said calmly. 'Audriss, the Serpent. We all—'

'No. No, please, you don't understand. It's not Audriss! It's Rebaine! Oh, gods, it's Corvis Rebaine!'

'. . . Quite positive he's confused,' Rollie concluded his report before both Baron Jassion and Sir Tyler. 'Probably hasn't a notion of what he's saying. Still, he was so insistent, and so certain, I thought it best to tell you. It won't do him any harm for you to hear him out, and it might help calm him down, speed his recovery.'

Jassion was already on his feet. 'Take me to him. Now.'

They left the lushly carpeted confines of Sir Tyler's office, three separate sets of boots clattering along the manor's stone floors. Although Rollie was ostensibly in the lead, he found himself struggling to keep up with the brown-haired Baron of Braetlyn. Jassion, he'd noted often since the baron's arrival, never did anything in moderation. The severe young man was a bundle of suppressed energy, a tornado imprisoned in the body of a human being. Jassion rarely sat when he could pace, walked when he could run, spoke when he could shout. It would have been a worthy character trait in some people. But in Jassion, it was something to be wary of, perhaps even feared.

Sir Tyler *looked* more the warrior. His own gleaming silver armour was far better kept than the black half-plate over which Jassion wore a tabard displaying his odd, ichthyic ensign. Tyler was disturbingly well muscled – 'a shaved ape', as some of his men described him – and blessed with a grace remarkable in a man of his girth. His hair was cut even more severely than Jassion's own, and his eyes could reflect just as coldly. Nevertheless, Rollie couldn't help but think of Jassion of Braetlyn as the more dangerous man.

The crowds of metal-clad warriors through which Rollie had been forced to push and squeeze parted easily before the steady advance of these two powerful men. Heavy tapestries fluttered in the trio's wake. Only when they finally reached the hallway in which Rollie's patient was quartered did they allow the healer to go first, and only then because neither knew which room they sought.

Rollie poked his head past the creaking door, intending to determine if his charge was asleep, only to be shoved rudely aside to make room for the Baron Jassion. Between the heavy metallic footsteps of the two lords, there could be little doubt the injured man was certainly awake *now*.

'What— who . . .' Obviously, despite his phenomenal recovery, he wasn't completely over his befuddlement.

'Name and rank, soldier!' Jassion barked harshly, looming at the foot of the bed.

Rollie opened his mouth to chide the baron for his callousness, but it proved unnecessary.

'Garras Ilbin,' the patient responded smartly, straightening as much as his prone posture would permit. 'Captain, currently . . . that is, most recently assigned to patrol duty in Kervone.'

'Kervone?' Sir Tyler asked quietly. 'Bit of a trek from Braetlyn, isn't it, my lord?'

Jassion cast the knight a sideways glare and then elected to ignore him entirely. 'This individual here,' he said, waving vaguely in Rollie's direction, 'claims that you have something to report to me.'

'I do, my lord. We've been deceived. This Audriss – if he even exists – is a cover. Our real enemy is Corvis Rebaine.'

Jassion's eyes flashed lightning, but whatever visceral reaction that name spawned in the baron's soul, his voice sounded skeptical as ever when he replied, 'Captain, you've suffered a rather nasty head wound. You've been unconscious for three months. Forgive me if I find your assessment unlikely.'

'I realise it sounds mad, my lord,' Garras told him, refusing to be insulted by his liege's obvious disdain. 'But it's the truth.

You see, we discovered an ogre camped in the trees just outside of Kervone . . .'

In bits and pieces, but with growing detail as it gradually came back to him, the old soldier concisely described the events that had taken place in Kervone a season past. 'I can only assume that Tuvold got there in time,' he concluded. 'I doubt Rebaine would have let me survive, knowing what I did, if he'd not had other concerns.'

'He very nearly *didn't* let you survive,' Rollie interjected from a small chair in the corner. 'That you're alive after such a head wound, let alone recovering your faculties, is nothing shy of miraculous. I have to wonder if—'

'Physician,' Jassion ordered, 'be silent. If Captain Garras here requires any attention, you may provide it. Otherwise, keep to your seat, and keep your lips together. These are matters you wouldn't understand.'

It took a great deal to make Rollie angry, but his face purpled now. Only through several moments of deep breathing and fist clenching did he clear the red from his eyes, the buzzing from his ears, allowing him to concentrate once more on the conversation.

'. . . makes some amount of sense,' Tyler was saying thoughtfully, staring absently at the bedridden soldier. 'Audriss began in Denathere, exactly where Rebaine left off. We've reports of a man matching Valescienn's description – after tacking on a few years, of course – leading some of Audriss' attacks. Hell, we've even heard some unconfirmed reports of gnomes! I'm not entirely sure I believe in those little devils, but, well, Rebaine was said to make use of them, wasn't he? Maybe this *is* all some elaborate charade to keep us from guessing the true enemy here.'

'Why?' Jassion asked darkly, fingering the tip of a broad-bladed dagger. 'The bastard's name strikes fear into the hearts of every weak-willed, knock-kneed, lily-livered so-called soldier from here to the Isle of Kavaley and back again. Why *not* just shout it from the mountain-tops, hmm? He'd probably crush half the resistance by saying *boo*. And I'm not sure his ego would permit him this sort of subterfuge.'

Tyler frowned. 'You may have a point. But it all fits so well, I don't think we can just rule it out. I—'

'Excuse me,' Rollie said mildly from the corner. 'I wonder if I may point out something you worthy gentlemen seem to have overlooked?'

'You?' Jassion scoffed. 'I doubt there's anything you could—'

Tyler raised a hand. 'I suggest we hear him out, my lord. If only out of *courtesy*.' Jassion reddened slightly at the rebuke, but nodded.

'As I understand it,' Rollie continued, 'one of the reasons that Audriss has been as successful as he has is because Duke Lorum and the Guildmasters can't quit squabbling long enough to present a united front.'

'Stupid bastards!' Jassion swore, clearly in agreement. 'They'd rather clutch their privileges to them and die one at a time than risk losing a few of their "sovereign rights". Imbeciles!'

'Well, yes,' Rollie said, his tone carefully noncommittal. 'But, my lord, what would have happened if someone came to them and said, "Corvis Rebaine is back"?'

Rollie could actually see the understanding dawn on them as they stared incredulously at one another. 'The Guilds would have panicked,' Tyler said in a hush. 'They'd have given Lorum full command as fast as they could sign the documents. Rebaine would have faced the combined forces of every army worth mentioning across all Imphallion.'

'I can't believe I didn't think of that,' Jassion said wryly. Then, though it clearly pained him, he nodded to Rollie. 'Thank you.'

'No charge.'

Jassion grinned, slammed the dagger back into its sheath, and began absently to twist the signet of Braetlyn on his right ring finger. The movement was vaguely hypnotic; Rollie forced his gaze from it. 'We've got them now, though,' the baron said happily. 'Once they hear about this, Lorum should find it a lot easier to whip the bastards into line.'

'Maybe, my lord,' Tyler cautioned. 'We have no proof. Only the word of a badly injured soldier who's been down with a head wound for months. I mean no offense to you or your integrity, Captain Garras, but there are many who won't be convinced on the strength of your report alone.'

'No offense taken, sir. But you *must* convince them!'

'We'll do what we can, of course. But—'

'It doesn't matter!' Jassion crowed. 'It doesn't matter if it's true. I'm barely half convinced myself, but as long as the Guildmasters *think* it's true, they'll react as we need them to. It shouldn't be too difficult to whip up a few eyewitnesses if we need them.'

Tyler frowned. 'My lord, I'm not sure that's—'

'And while they're busy assembling their armies,' the baron continued, his voice freezing over, 'I'll go out and look for Corvis myself.'

'You'll *what?*' Tyler shouted, stunned.

'I'll look for him myself. And when I find him, he'll wish he'd died in the war seventeen years ago. I've waited most of my life for this opportunity, Tyler. I'm bloody well not letting it slip by me now.'

'And how will you find him, Jassion?' inquired a new voice.

The baron and the duke's knight both went for their swords, each twisting about, trying to find the intruder. Rollie rose and stepped to the side of the man on the bed, determined to protect his patient.

'Who's there?' Tyler demanded. A quick sweep of the room detected nothing more menacing than dust on the wardrobe and a large spider crawling across the ceiling. 'Show yourself!'

'Why my dear Sir Tyler, of course. How rude of me.'

The spider dropped, dangling by a thin strand of webbing, and began to spin. The web grew quickly, weaving itself into intricately detailed, ornate shapes as it fell. In less than a minute, a life-sized full-body portrait of an attractive woman in a leather jerkin hung suspended, perfectly straight, from the labouring arachnid.

Before their awestruck eyes, the image bulged. Though it had no depth at all, the thickness of a single strand of webbing, it writhed as though a figure moved within.

And then it tore, and from the two-dimensional image stepped a dark-haired woman. She was beautiful, if somewhat more buxom than the current fashion, her bearing regal. She wore a dark leather jerkin and leggings, a red tunic and matching hooded cloak, and an amused smile quivered fleetingly at the corner of her lips.

'I pray you'll forgive the theatrics, gentlemen,' she told them, her voice throaty. 'I'm afraid my sense of style has quite crossed the line into melodrama. One of the dangers inherent in the profession.'

'Who . . .' Tyler shook his head as though trying to physically dislodge his confusion. 'Who are you, lady?'

'Her?' Jassion said darkly. 'That's Rheah Vhoune, Tyler. Did you really have to ask?'

The knight's eyes widened and he loudly crashed to one knee, his armour ringing like a gong. 'My lady.'

'Oh, get up, Tyler. I hold no title, so your genuflection is quite inappropriate. Besides, you'll scuff the floor.' She smiled, a genuine expression of affection, toward the bed where Rollie stood beside his nervous patient.

'Relax, good healer. If I'd intended you or your charge any harm, do you think you'd ever have known I was here?'

'I – suppose that's true, my lady,' Rollie acknowledged, forcing his arms back down by his sides. Though it was clearly contrary to his mood, he plastered a sickly grin across his face. 'You'd not begrudge a fellow *some* bit of uneasiness, would you, my lady?'

Rheah's laughter was light, a refreshing break from the gloom that permeated the manor. Tentatively, the physician's smile grew more genuine.

'Come, my lords,' Rheah commanded, facing Sir Tyler and

the baron. 'We've matters of some urgency to discuss, and I fear our continued presence would tire this good fellow here. Let us go about our business and permit Rollie to return to his.'

Rollie watched the door close from his post by Garras's side, pondering long before he once more riveted his attention on the wounded man before him. So wrapped up was he in caring for the old soldier, so eventful had the day been, that it was only that night, in those last few weightless moments before sleep claimed him, that he thought to wonder idly about one tiny detail.

The colours of the ensign of Braetlyn were deep red and dark blue. It was curious, then, that Jassion's signet ring should be such a brilliant emerald green.

CHAPTER NINETEEN

Lorum, Duke of Taberness and Regent Proper of Imphallion, strode as rapidly away from the assembly chamber as courtesy permitted, literally in the midst of a huge, shoulder-slumping sigh of relief, when the voice called to him from behind.

'Your Grace? A word or two, if you've the moments to spare.'

Gods damn it! He'd thought it was *over*!

Still, he forced a polite smile to split his new growth of beard before turning to face the newcomer. 'Something on your mind, Lord – ah . . .'

'Jassion, Your Grace.'

'Right, of course.' *The new Baron of Braetlyn.* 'I was sorry not to be able to attend your ascension, Lord Jassion. Your cousin had no qualms about giving up his regency?'

'None he expressed to me, Your Grace.' The young baron was a man of intensity, constantly in motion, eyes that gleamed with perhaps an excess of passion and a voice that seemed unable to bear modulation.

'Delighted to hear it. What was it you wished to talk to me about that couldn't be said in chambers?'

Jassion's expression, barely civil to start with, suddenly twisted. He looked less like a man enraged than like a child preparing to throw a tantrum. 'What in the name of all the gods were you *thinking*, Lorum?!'

My, he's a polite one. 'That's still "Your Grace" to you,

Baron.' There was, perhaps, just the slightest emphasis on the title.

'You gave them *everything* they demanded, "Your Grace"! You didn't even *try* to negotiate with them!'

Lorum couldn't quite repress a second sigh. 'Mecepheum needs the Guilds thriving at the moment, Baron. You know full well, if you've studied your history, that I'm no great friend of the Guilds. But if this turns into a mercantile standoff, as they've threatened, well, they're the ones with the resources. They can wait this out a lot longer than the citizens of Imphallion can.' *Or the government, for that matter*, he added silently.

'Well, that's just fantastic, Your Grace. In the interim, your tariff exemptions are going to impoverish the smaller provinces. Many of them *still* haven't fully recovered, you know. Mecepheum was never hit *directly* by the war.'

'Neither was Braetlyn,' Lorum noted mildly.

'You can't shore up the kingdom if you let pieces of it waste away, Your Grace,' Jassion insisted. 'It's like trying to heal a man whose limbs are gangrened.'

'I won't let the Guilds go *that* far, Lord Jassion, I promise. I—'

'May lack the power to stop them, soon enough. I know that you're not a king, Your Grace, but maybe you need to start acting like one anyway. If you don't find the strength to bring the Guilds in line, someone's eventually going to have to do it for you.'

'Someone like you, perhaps?' Lorum's voice remained calm, even, but his expression was suddenly ice. 'Are you threatening my position, Lord Jassion?'

'Of course not,' the young baron replied, finally calming just a bit, 'though I can easily foresee a time where you very well *might* wish someone like me was wearing the regent's tabard. No, I meant someone like Corvis Rebaine.'

'What? What do you know about—'

'I know, Your Grace, that Rebaine came as close to

succeeding as he did because we were too weak to stop him. And so long as we *remain* weak, someone very much like him is sure to try again. I hope that you're able to take control of your own damn nation before it happens.'

Lorum staggered as though physically struck. His face grew flushed; his jaw gaped once, then twice. But Jassion was already gone, leaving only the echoes of his boot heels behind, before the regent could once again draw breath to speak.

'I'm going to assume,' Jassion said as the door to Tyler's office snapped shut behind them, 'that you heard everything?'

'Yes,' Rheah replied, idly smoothing rumples from the left sleeve of her tunic. 'Actually, I was there longer than you were.' She frowned, as though an unpleasant notion had crept up on her. 'You've no idea at all how strangely spiders see the world,' she told them sincerely. 'Those faceted eyes.'

Tyler nodded in sudden understanding. 'You healed Captain Garras, didn't you?' It was almost accusatory. 'Rollie mentioned how unusual his recovery was.'

Rheah shrugged. 'I helped. I don't know that we need to let Rollie know, though. Not that I think he'd disapprove, but why complicate the matter?'

'Why?' Jassion demanded. 'Why help this man, out of so many others?'

'You know, Jassion, you're a positive sinkhole of paranoia. Does everything have to have ulterior motives?'

'Yes.'

She sighed. For a moment she hesitated, her gaze scanning some of the titles on the shelf above Sir Tyler's head. *I may have to ask to borrow that one . . .*

Then, 'The truth is, my mistrustful baron, that I didn't particularly have a reason. I was here, anyway – certain individuals with whom I'm acquainted wanted a first-hand assessment of the situation – and I happened to stumble across Rollie making his rounds. I followed him, from idle curiosity, and he led me to Garras.' Her mouth twisted into a sardonic smile.

'The funny thing about us – sorcerers, wizards, mages, whatever name you care to pin on us like a cheap brooch – is that when you deal with magic long enough, you begin to manipulate the world around you without even realising it.' She paused, as though groping for words to properly express her thoughts. Or, perhaps more accurately, groping for the proper thought to express. 'Sometimes, it seems, the world manipulates us right back. This wouldn't be the first time I've done something on whim, only to learn that it was of no small importance later on. I had no idea when I gave Garras a nudge that he would deliver such a fascinating little tale.' Her smile returned as abruptly as it faded. 'If either of you happens to notice some strings attached to my head and shoulders, you'll be sure to let me know, yes?'

'What about that "fascinating little tale"?' Jassion asked gruffly. 'Is it true?'

'Do I look like an oracle to you, Baron? Even my sight has its limits.'

'I think we'd better assume that the Terror *is* involved,' the older knight suggested. 'I abhor swinging at shadows, but it seems we'd be safer preparing for a phantom threat than ignoring a real one.'

'I don't know much about this Audriss,' Rheah admitted. 'I've found it nigh impossible to scry on him. He's got his own magics to aid him, and they're powerful. And quite similar, come to think of it, to what I felt seventeen years ago . . .' Her voice trailed off.

It was odd, Tyler thought, to hear her speak of the war in such familiar terms. Rheah looked to be in her middle twenties. It took substantial effort to remember that she was far older than she appeared.

'If Rebaine *has* come back,' she said finally, 'we're facing a danger far greater than either of you can imagine. I know something of his objectives the last time he attempted this. If he's accomplished now what he was working on then, he may be unstoppable.'

'No one is unstoppable,' Jassion snarled, a caged dragon pacing the room. 'If it's Rebaine, I'm going to kill him for what he did to—'

The Baron of Braetlyn came abruptly to a halt. His fists clenched inside thin black gloves, and his expression gradually melted, the ever-present mask of anger exposing, if only briefly, the widened eyes of a frightened child.

'Can . . .' Jassion's voice cracked; he swallowed once and licked his lips. 'Can you tell me what happened to Tyannon?'

Gods, how she wanted to! The baron had rarely spoken about his sister in the days after he was pulled, trembling and blood-coated, from the pit of corpses in the Hall of Meeting. After a few months, he never mentioned her at all. For him to open up now, to ask that question, represented a vulnerable spot in the wall he'd painstakingly constructed around his soul.

But Rheah knew that Jassion would not be put off with platitudes or vague utterances, and he would know for certain if she were lying. And so she told him the truth.

'I don't know, Jassion. I'm sorry, but there's no way for me to know.'

Rheah wanted to weep when the windows behind his eyes snapped closed. 'That's too bad,' he said as he began, once more, to pace.

Brighter than it had been in seventeen years, Rheah's hatred of the man called the Terror of the East flared into incandescence. 'There may be a better way,' she said, speaking in a whisper to hide the quavering fury in her voice. 'You may not have to hunt him down.'

Jassion's soulless eyes locked onto her own, and Tyler raised an eyebrow in question. 'What do you mean?' the baron demanded.

Rheah leaned back in her chair. 'If Rebaine is still after – what he was after,' she said softly, 'then he's probably figured out that I know about it.' She smiled once more, but it was no longer a friendly expression. It was angry, predatory, not the housecat's grin but the tiger's snarl. 'People like him, and like me, have ways of learning that sort of thing. That means, Jassion, that sooner or later, he's going to come to me.'

The baron's lips warped into a smile to match her own. 'Are you certain, Rheah?'

'As certain as I can be. Nothing's guaranteed, of course, but I think he'll come.'

'And what then?' Tyler asked, determined to be the voice of reason. 'Can you handle him alone?'

'Well, good sir knight,' the sorceress said simply, 'why don't we talk about "what then"? I have an idea that might just appeal to you . . .'

'Ladies and gentlemen! Ladies and gentlemen, if I could just have – Ladies and – people, *please*!'

Sebastian Arcos, Speaker for the Right Honorable Imphallion and Surroundings Merchants' and Tradesmen's Guild (home office), might as well have saved his breath. The vaulted chamber of the Merchants' Guild's meeting hall in Mecepheum was awash with a crawling, writhing mass of chaos, and trying to shout over that monstrous din was akin to rowing a boat upstream with a salad fork.

The chamber itself was enormous, a man-made cavern. Its ceiling consisted of arches and cupolas, all painted or engraved or otherwise adorned with whatever visual arts that money could buy and style could suggest. Most showed heroes of legend and angels of the divine, but symbols of the gods themselves were interspersed throughout. Here the Scales of Justice, symbol of Ulan the Judge; there the dice, double-sixes, entreating the aid of Panaré Luck-Giver; and hidden away, painted largely in shadow, the hulking and menacing Maukra and Mimgol, the Children of Apocalypse themselves.

The rest of the room was largely empty of furnishings and was currently filled to capacity with Guildsmen, merchants, shopkeepers, and businessmen of all stripes. Sebastian couldn't help but think of the entire assembly as a herd of cattle packed into a barn.

Sebastian himself, along with the others of the Guild's High Council, sat upon a horseshoe-shaped platform towering above the heads of the Assembly's main body. To each side were Guild representatives who'd traveled from other branches to attend this Assembly, and farther beyond them, at the very ends of the platform, sat non-members, honoured guests invited to attend.

The meeting went downhill the moment Sebastian's gavel struck the podium. Many of the attendees were furious that Orthessis had been evacuated and left to fall to the Serpent's advance. A large, relatively prosperous population, a popular duke with moderate policies on taxation, and one of the largest crossroads on the King's Highway all combined to make the Lutrinthus Province a tradesman's dream. And Orthessis, while not so rich or prosperous or well loved as Pelapheron, was still a part of that pecuniary paradise.

They'd grumbled and complained even more darkly when they'd learned Pelapheron itself appeared next on the list, and that no concerted effort was under way to save it. Oh, certainly the Guilds were sending soldiers to aid in the city's defense, and many of Imphallion's nobles contributed men as well, but there was no unified front, no single cohesive force standing in opposition to the Serpent and his armies. That it was in part their own stubbornness that prevented such a joint effort was a fact they seemed either unable to accept or all too willing to gloss over.

And when things finally calmed down a bit from *that* uproar, Sebastian made what could only be described as a tactical blunder. A brilliant businessman and consummate politician, it took a great deal to faze him – but the news he'd just received did the trick handily. Sebastian, for the first time in years, was truly flustered. Thus, after giving the Assembly the *rest* of the bad news, this final detail emerged from his lips before his brain registered the notion that, just maybe, it wasn't in everyone's best interests to make this information common knowledge.

'We also have reason to believe that the entire situation with Audriss may actually be the work of Corvis Rebaine—'

He'd never finished the thought, because the room erupted: a geyser of shouting, a volcanic upheaval of pure, unadulterated noise.

Sebastian, his face flushed, tried for several minutes to make himself heard over the tumult beneath him, shouting himself hoarse to no avail. Finally, he turned toward the individual sitting directly to his left and shrugged sheepishly. In return, he received an icy glower. Then, with a whisk of leather on fabric, the other person stepped to the very edge of the dais, gazing down at the pulsing bedlam.

Rheah Vhoune brushed a few strands of hair from her face, cast a simple spell under her breath, and then shouted, *'Quiet!'*

Her voice thundered through the room, quite literally stunning some of the Assembly as it blew past. The chamber fell into a shocked silence, broken only by a tinkling sound as the cry made its way to the far wall and shattered the window.

'Thank you,' she said in a normal tone of voice. Rheah wore a formal gown, rather than her accustomed tunic and leggings, but she sported her hardened leather cuirass and bracers.

Even the most powerful of wizards finds it difficult to do much about a crossbow bolt in the back.

'I think it's clear,' Rheah told them sharply, 'that we're accomplishing nothing of value. I move we adjourn for the day, early as it may be, and take this up in the morning once we've all had time to assimilate the news we've just heard.' Somehow, without actually moving, she managed to briefly cast another glare in Sebastian's direction.

'Umm, yes,' the Speaker said quickly. 'I second. Motion carried.'

The sorceress nodded. 'Remember, ladies and gentlemen, that what the Speaker has told you is rumour and hearsay. There's no proof one way or the other.' She smiled dourly.

'When you go and blab this particular gossip like lonely fishwives, you may want to be certain you mention that part.'

She waited, unmoving, as the huge crowd, mumbling and whispering furtively, filtered from the hall. Then, her jaw a clenched vise, she faced the Guildmaster.

'Um,' Sebastian began eloquently.

'You *imbecile*! You rat-brained, jaw-wagging idiot! How could you be so stupid?'

'I . . . Rheah, I'm sorry.'

'You're sorry. You're *sorry*? Gods damn it all, you jackass, you'll have this entire city in a blind panic!'

'I'm pretty close to blind panic myself, Rheah! The very idea is terrifying.'

'And that's exactly why you should have kept your flapping mouth shut about it!' Rheah clenched her fist as she ranted, in part to keep herself from casting anything she couldn't take back. 'I ought to transform you into a radish!'

Sebastian blanched. 'You wouldn't actually do that, would you?'

'I don't know. I've never tried it.' She snarled at him. 'In your case, it might actually improve your higher brain functions, though.'

'Now, Rheah, I *am* the Speaker of this council. Whatever power you may have, I outrank you, and I think I'm due a little —' The bearded merchant tried suddenly to retract, turtle-like, into his tunic as the sorceress advanced on him, fingers twitching erratically. She stopped only when she trod on his feet, her nose inches from his. Her breathing was audible, as was the grinding of her teeth, and her face had gone nearly as red as her gown.

'Ah, perhaps I'd best return to my chambers,' Sebastian said hastily.

'That might,' Rheah said very softly, 'be the best idea you've had all day.' She stepped aside, and Sebastian managed – barely – to keep a dignified pace until he was out the door.

Only then did Rheah direct her attention to the rest of the High Council, all of whom sat motionless. 'Anyone who cares to comment,' the sorceress said darkly, 'is welcome to take the floor.'

There were, startlingly enough, no volunteers.

'Good. I'll see you tomorrow.' And then, rather than subject the lot of them to the humiliation of fleeing from the room as their leader had done, she herself turned and strode out.

She was muttering sourly when she reached her private office. The door unlatched itself with a soft click and drifted soundlessly open at her approach. A shimmer passed through the room, and a cheery fire instantly crackled into existence in what had been, mere seconds ago, an empty fireplace. The curtains drew themselves up, allowing an unobstructed view of Mecepheum's main avenue, and the drawers in the ornate mahogany desk unlocked themselves with a rapid series of snaps. The weapons hanging from the wall shone, as though dusted and wiped clean. Several swords, a mace, a halberd, all made not of steel, but flimsy wood. Every one had been wielded against her at some point in the past, and every one had been sharp steel before her magics rendered them harmless.

By the time Rheah Vhoune stepped over the threshold onto the lush fur carpeting, the entire room looked as if a battalion of valets had spent meticulous hours preparing it.

There are, after all, *some* fringe benefits to being a wizard.

Finally running low on worthwhile curses to grumble to herself, Rheah spun angrily around the desk and threw herself angrily into the thickly upholstered chair—

And froze, lips parted in the midst of a final curse, as she saw the figure sitting across the room from her.

He was dressed in dark leathers, worn smooth and dulled with years of use. A heavy cloak fell from his shoulders and wrapped loosely about his arms, a garment well designed to ward off winter's icy winds. The hood was raised, masking the intruder's face in a liquid pool of shadow. His left hand rested idly on a large battle-axe, and his fingers played idly across the flat of the blade.

It was the first time in a very, very great while that Rheah Vhoune found herself surprised by anything. It was not, she decided upon reflection, a pleasant experience.

'How did you get past the wards on the door?' she asked, forcing her voice into a preternatural calm.

'With some difficulty.' The stranger's voice was a bit gravelly, and while she couldn't exactly claim that it was familiar, it rang faint and distant bells in the recesses of her mind. 'You're very good, my lady. One of the best I've ever seen.' The intruder paused thoughtfully. 'Though I must say . . .' Another pause. 'The Merchants' Guild? That doesn't really strike me as being – well, you.'

'And you know me so very well, do you?' Her posture relaxed, Rheah leaned back in the chair, her initial chagrin fading into a murk of anger and curiosity, flavoured with just a pinch of fear. She was more than confident in her ability to handle any normal assailant, but the fact that this man broke into her office without tripping even one of her defenses suggested that he was far from normal.

'Better than you might think, Lady Rheah.'

The sorceress suddenly smiled. 'I might say the same. You might as well lower the hood, Lord Rebaine. You can hardly hide behind it, or your silly skull mask, forever.'

She had the pleasure, then, of seeing the figure in the chair start visibly. His unoccupied hand gripped the armrest tight enough to make the wood creak, and he leaned forward as though pained. Then, with an audible exhalation, he slowly pulled the hood back.

Rheah wasn't certain what to expect, but somehow, this greying, thin-faced man sitting before her – a man whose best days had passed him by years ago – was a far cry from anything she might have anticipated.

Then she looked into his eyes, and knew that this was indeed Corvis Rebaine, the Terror of the East. And it wasn't because his gaze was cold, unfeeling, or cruel, though she didn't doubt that he could be all those things and more. It was, instead, the subtle trace of horror lurking at the very back of those eyes. A lingering revulsion, probably long forgotten by Rebaine himself, at the memory of all the atrocities that he had committed. Only a man guilty of the most foul deeds could loathe himself so much.

It was almost – *almost* – enough to make her pity him.

'How did you know?' he asked, unaware of her intense scrutiny.

Rheah laughed once, sharply, and then stared at him, one hand idly fiddling with a hummingbird-shaped brooch that was the only ornament she wore. 'Your own fault, I'm afraid, Lord Rebaine. You know, you used to do a much better job of killing anyone who might threaten you.'

Corvis looked at her quizzically, not understanding.

'A few months ago,' she explained patiently, 'a guardsman recognised you. In the village of Kervone.'

Comprehension dawned, and Corvis leaned back, smiling bitterly. 'Seilloah told me that would come back to haunt us.'

'Seilloah always was the wise one in your little coterie. So she's doing all right, then? How about Valesci008? And your ogre lieutenant, what was his name again? Dabro?'

'Davro,' Corvis corrected absently. 'You're not impressing me anymore. Everyone knew the names of my lieutenants.'

'Ah. How foolish of me.' A vicious grin spread over her features. Then tell me, how's Khanda?'

Another pause, and then, oddly enough, Corvis responded with, 'No, you absolutely may *not*!' It took her a moment to realise the warlord wasn't speaking to her.

'I see he's here as well. One big demented family.'

'Rheah, we don't have time for this sort of sparring. Audriss is coming.'

The sorceress raised an eyebrow. 'The dominant opinion is that Audriss is a front for you.'

'Audriss? That bug? I hardly think so.'

'If he's such a bug, Lord Rebaine, and if you *aren't* behind him, then what are you doing here?'

Corvis leaned forward once more, face intent. The firelight skittering across his features gave him an ephemeral, ghostly quality, the echoes of a dream that refused to fade. 'He threatened my family, Rheah. I don't take well to that.'

'Family? Who in the world would marry . . . Rebaine, you didn't!'

Corvis smiled sheepishly. 'It was actually her idea, Rheah.'

'Somehow,' she said, her voice cold once more, 'I don't think Jassion's going to see it that way.'

'My point,' the warlord snapped, 'is that Audriss wants something, and it's not just Imphallion itself. If he should happen to get his hands on it . . .'

'Don't play coy with me, Rebaine.' It was Rheah's turn to lean forward, her relentless gaze boring into his own. 'You want to know if I've found the key to the book you stole from Denathere.'

'All right, Khanda swears that you can't be reading my mind, but—'

'Is it his, Rebaine?' The sorceress seemed, in her anxiety, to have momentarily forgotten her hatred for the man before her. Her voice held nothing but excitement, the giddiness of a schoolgirl running home for gifts on the Winter Solstice. 'Is it Selakrian's spellbook?'

Corvis chewed his lower lip for a span, fingers once again drumming on the head of the Kholben Shiar. And then, despite himself, he nodded. 'It is.'

'I knew it!' Rheah crowed happily. 'Gods, Rebaine, you should have just offered it up to the wizards' community. We'd probably have handed you Imphallion on a silver platter in exchange for that book!'

The black-clad intruder blinked. 'I never actually thought of that,' he admitted. Then, with a head shake, he continued, 'No, I don't think I'd have done that. I'd only have been king at the sufferance of whoever finally cracked the code. Being a puppet ruler is worse than being no ruler at all. If there's to be a demigod walking the face of the world, I'd rather it be me.'

'And the great Corvis Rebaine is the only mortal worthy of that sort of power?' she asked sarcastically.

'Worthy? Not at all. I just trust myself to handle that responsibility more than I do anyone else.'

'Of course. Yes, Rebaine, I have the key. I spent thirteen years hunting down bits and tatters so I could piece the rest of it together. And no, you can't have it. If you think I'll put that sort of power in your hands, you're even crazier than everyone thinks you are.'

'My concern,' the warlord said darkly, 'is to ensure Audriss doesn't get it. Nothing more.'

'Oh, of course. And you came all this way – snuck through a city that would be more than delighted to rip you into so much chutney, crept through the halls of the most powerful Guild in the kingdom, and broke into my personal office – to warn me not to hand Audriss the means to becoming a god? Heavens, it's a good thing you got here when you did. I was about to send it to him by carrier pigeon first thing tomorrow.'

'No, I—'

'You know what I think? I think that you haven't changed in seventeen years. I think you saw an opportunity to get your hands on the one thing that would have won the last war for you. I don't know if you're working with Audriss – I think I almost believe that you're not – but you're still a danger to me, my friends, and my kingdom. And not only am I not giving you the key, I don't particularly feel inclined to let you leave this room.'

Corvis stood, Sunder clasped in both hands, Khanda's glow exuding from beneath his leather tunic. 'Do you really think you have the power to stop me, Rheah?'

'Who said *I* was going to stop you?' she asked innocently.

To his credit, Corvis was *almost* fast enough to block the blow. Almost. The heavy cudgel landed like the kick of an angered charger. He staggered, fingers going limp on the shaft of his axe, his concentration far too splintered to bring Khanda's power to bear. The Baron of Braetlyn advanced alongside four of his men, all of whom, it seemed, simply stepped from the wall by the fireplace. The heavy club in his hand and murderous fury on his face, Jassion swung again and again, the hollow slap of wood on flesh soon giving way to the sharper snap of breaking bone. When he finally stopped, cheeks flushed with rage and breathing heavily, Corvis Rebaine was alive – though once he finally woke up, he'd almost certainly wish he wasn't.

'I do not,' the baron said softly, 'want to go through that magic again.'

'I know it was uncomfortable,' the sorceress apologised, absently brushing two fingers against the hummingbird brooch that had activated the magics. 'Slow teleportation is painful, but his pet demon would have detected anything less subtle. The ache should fade by day's end. Tomorrow morning at the latest.'

'I think, however, that it was more than worth it.'

Rheah knelt to examine the warlord's broken form. Swiftly she yanked the pendant from his neck and dropped it on the floor beside her. Then, absently rubbing her fingers as though to clean them of some lingering taint from even so brief a touch, she whispered the words of a counterspell, intended to disperse any lingering sorceries the demon might have cast upon his master. Magics unravelled beneath her will, and the wood beneath the carpet – to say nothing of several of the Terror's broken bones – creaked audibly as Rebaine's unobtrusive garb transformed back into its original form: that of his infamous steel-and-bone armour.

'Did you have fun?' she asked the baron sourly, clearly disapproving. 'The point here was to take him captive, not beat him into some sort of stew.'

Jassion spun to face her, eyes blazing. 'You're damn fortunate I didn't kill him on the spot!' Then, in a calmer tone, 'But then, this may be the best way. We all have questions for him. And I, for one, am eagerly looking forward to making him answer them.'

CHAPTER TWENTY

Audriss wasn't entirely certain, as the hideous shape bowled him over, exactly what he had said wrong.

The cavern echoed with the sudden impact of steel on stone, the bending and snapping of armoured plates, the cracking of bones beneath inhuman fingers. The thing atop him thrashed about, clasping two hands of disparate size around the warlord's throat. Audriss knew well that only the magics of his armour kept him alive, and even through that protection he felt an ache in his muscles, a shortness of breath.

He hadn't even realised the damn thing was coming at him! Mismatched limbs, flailing about at unimaginable angles – it was impossible to tell which way the creatures were moving. They were like nothing Audriss had ever dealt with, a people seemingly stitched together by a blind god who'd heard only secondhand descriptions of men.

Though every instinct fought against it, Audriss released his grasp on the thing's wrists. Immediately the pressure on his throat increased – blood pounded in his ears, the torchlight dimmed before his eyes – but Audriss twisted, turned, subtly shifting the massive weight that crushed him to the floor, until . . .

A gravelly shout bursting painfully through his throat, Audriss yanked Talon from its scabbard and drove it, again and again and again, into his attacker's rigid, inhuman flesh. And though the creature lacked the organs to be found in a human's chest, still the Kholben Shiar found something vital in its violent probing. It shuddered once, this vile thing, and then lay statue-still.

With a second shout – more of an inflated grunt, really – Audriss shoved the corpse away, gasping gratefully as the hands were pulled from his throat. With far more grace than either his armour or his injuries should have permitted, he rolled swiftly to his feet, Talon clasped in one hand, the other clenched in a fist to expose the glowing ring on his finger.

Pekatherosh flashed a nauseating green – sent power thrumming through the cavern – and for a moment, at least, the two sides disengaged. Men and gnomes glared at one another across a pile of bodies that consisted, Audriss was disgusted to note, almost entirely of his own soldiers. The gnome he'd slain with Talon was one of exactly two of the twisted little vermin to have fallen in the sudden melee.

Valescienn drifted up behind, towering over the warlord yet somehow shrinking into his shadow. 'What the hell did you say to them?' he demanded.

Audriss decided to let the impertinence pass without comment for the nonce. 'I offered gold and jewels for their cooperation.'

'That's all?' Then, sensing the Serpent's glare even through the mask of stone, 'Maybe they don't like – uh, money?'

'I *know* they can be bought! Rebaine managed it. He—'

But the gnomes, whatever else they might or might not be, were clearly not hard of hearing. 'It offends him!' hissed the nearest, a hunchbacked creature speaking through a mouth of blocky, broken teeth. 'The Audriss offends him, yes, with insult and vexation, and he will break its neck . . . Break its carapace of rock, yes, and feast upon the sweetmeats within.'

Audriss blinked, trying to translate the foul gnome's speech into something comprehensible. 'I offered you no insult!' he insisted finally. 'I offered you only payment for—'

'Not payment, no!' The gnome was spitting, now, its brethren shifting angrily behind. 'The Audriss offers, yes, to give him things, but not the Audriss' to give, no, not to have or to take! The mans rape the wombs of the Earth, yes, the stone and the dirt and the mountain roots. And from him, from *all* of him, it takes the bones, yes, the bones of all him before, yes, of early days! And then it offers them back, yes, as *payment*? He, all of he, will feast upon the meats and bones of all mans, yes, its bones as it has taken the bones of old from the rock, yes, the earth! He will break the necks of all mans until none, no, not a one remains, and the earth is silent, yes, again silent and peaceful and ravaged no more.'

For long moments Valescienn and Audriss stared at each other, struggling to make sense of what they'd heard, knowing that the wrong word – or even the right word spoken too late – would be disastrous.

/Ancestors, you dim-witted apes,/ Pekatherosh finally interjected. /By offering gold and gems, you've essentially offered them bits and pieces of what they believe to be the bones of their ancestors, raped from the living earth by mankind./ Audriss could almost feel the demon shrug. / Sounds like a fine gift to me, really, but who can account for taste?/

'If that's truly what they believe,' Valescienn whispered, still vaguely bewildered even after his Lord had repeated the demon's explanation, 'what the hell can we offer them?'

But behind his mask, Audriss had begun to smile. 'Why, the same thing Rebaine must have offered, Valescienn. The chance to reclaim whole *cities* of their stolen "bones", and to feast on the meats of *many* mans – uh, men. Come, my friend,' he said, turning once more to the slathering creature before him, 'I think perhaps I can make amends for my previous insult.'

The hesitant sun moved in fits and starts, rappelling down the western wall as moon and stars peeked through the dome of a rapidly darkening sky. The horizon, a mosaic of wavering tree lines and distant mountains, blazed orange, as if the gods planned to incinerate their previous efforts and start over from day one.

If it was a particularly impressive sunset, however, nobody noticed. No eyes watched westward from Pelapheron this eve, save a smattering of sentinels. Those citizens unable to fight from age or infirmity holed up in their homes, doors locked and windows shuttered. Many cried, many prayed, but all waited with a growing sense of desperation.

And as for the soldiers – the lords' garrisons, the mercenary platoons sent by the Guilds, and every inhabitant of Pelapheron able to swing a sword without disemboweling either himself or his neighbour – they all stood atop or behind the eastern wall. Nervously, they fingered weapons, holy talismans, or loved ones' tokens, peering intently into the growing darkness.

From the heavy shadows of the night poured a different darkness: a cancerous, liquid presence, a swelling wave rolling toward Pelapheron. Campfires glowed like fireflies, and even at this distance, the dull roar of thousands upon thousands of voices set the defenders' walls to quivering.

The Serpent had come to Pelapheron.

As the forces behind him dug in and made camp, one man stepped from the crowd. His blond hair cut short, the scars on his face crags of shadow against his pale skin, Valescienn approached the enemy. Two of his soldiers followed a pace behind, the leftmost carrying a lance on which a white flag of parley flapped in the nighttime air. The dark trio advanced until they stood just far enough from the wall to easily gaze at those atop it.

A plethora of hostile glares met their own. Arms crossed casually before him – though one still ached from Corvis' attack of months before – his voice rebounding from the walls, Audriss's lieutenant shouted, 'I will speak with your commanders!'

'I should go,' Edmund, Duke of Lutrinthus, told the older man before him. 'This is my province. This is my duty.'

Edmund was a man on the precipice of middle age, and he wasn't about to plummet over without a struggle. The vain duke shaved his head bald at the first sign of his hair's natural thinning, replacing it with a wig far thicker and blacker than his own ever was. He tried every new remedy for wrinkles and sagging skin he could find like a desperate, aging courtesan. He insisted on wearing only the absolute latest styles – until today, when he'd donned a suit of engraved and fluted armour that had only seen ceremonial use before – and he absolutely refused to attend the other nobles' banquets without first brushing up on the most recent dances.

All of which would have made him, in the eyes of his current companion, an effete snob and not worth so much as a second glance, were Duke Edmund not also a brilliant administrator, a charismatic speaker, a shrewd negotiator, and a man who honestly cared for the welfare of his citizens. For all his personal egocentricities, his duchy was widely considered one of the best homes in all Imphallion for those of lower station.

What Duke Edmund was not, unfortunately, was anything approaching a skilled tactician. That was why he employed Sir Tyler, but Tyler, fleeing Orthessis with the final column of refugees, had been thrown from his saddle when his mount stumbled into a burrow. The knight had fractured a leg and cracked several ribs in the fall, and was in no shape to assist in planning or executing Pelapheron's defense.

Thus had another man stepped forward, a resident of Lutrinthus and simple landowner, though he had once been so much more. And when Nathaniel Espa, hero of the realm, former Knight Adviser to the regent, volunteered to take command of the defending armies, Duke Edmund was only too happy to hand over the reins.

At least until tonight, when he utterly refused to allow Duke Edmund to set one foot upon the battlements.

'You gave me command, Your Grace,' he said, rolling his shoulders in a vain attempt to shift his steel breastplate into a more comfortable position. 'That makes me the man Valescienn wants to speak to. And you, my lord, are too tempting a target. It would be disastrous for morale if you were to be cut down by an arrow.'

'Wonderful. So instead, you ask me to risk the one man who might salvage some modicum of victory from this vile mess! Is that any more strategically sound, Nathaniel?'

'They're less likely to shoot at me. And I'm not *asking* you.'

Edmund cast a glance heavenward. 'Give a man a little authority, and see what he does with it! And you know full well that they may just take a few shots at *whoever* delivers the news we have for them!'

Espa raised a gauntlet. 'I understand your concerns, Your Grace. But as long as I remain in command, the decision is mine to make. You have, of course, the authority to strip me of that command, but I don't think either of us really wants you to do that.'

The duke sighed, gaze cast mournfully at his steel-shod boots. 'No, Nathan, I don't suppose either of us does. Are you quite certain of this, my friend?'

'I am.' Nathan forced a smile and clapped a hand on the duke's shoulder, his gauntlet ringing against the cuirass. 'I'm off, my lord. Wish me luck.'

'Well, it's about bloody time!' Valescienn called when the line on the wall finally parted to allow a looming figure in ice-bright armour to step to the edge of the battlements. 'We've only been waiting out here for the past . . .' He stopped as the man removed his helm. 'You're not Duke Edmund!' he said accusingly.

'How astute of you to notice, Valescienn,' the other man shouted back. 'You said you wanted to speak to the commander. That's me. If you wanted the duke, you should have asked for the duke.'

The blond soldier's lips curled in a silent snarl. 'And who would you be, then, old man?'

'My name is Nathaniel Espa.'

Valescienn froze an instant. The two soldiers behind him muttered briefly to each other, falling silent again only when their commanding officer cast a murderous glance over his shoulder.

Then, 'Espa, is it? It's an honour to finally meet you in person, rather than from opposite sides of the assembled throngs.'

'As I recall, the last time you tried this my "throng" beat the stuffing out of yours.'

Valescienn smiled. 'I have a lot more this time.'

'Go home, Valescienn! There will be no battle today!'

'Oh? And why would that be?'

'Because we've captured your commander, Valescienn!'

Valescienn blinked. 'What?'

'Your leader. We have him!'

The scarred man cursed under his breath. There was no possible way they could have Audriss. None. But the Serpent's soldiers knew less about their master's true powers than Valescienn did, and they wouldn't be so sure. And Audriss *was* gone for the nonce. It was an irritating habit in his commander at the best of times, this tendency to up and vanish for hours or days at a time. He'd departed around midday yesterday and told Valescienn that he would rejoin them when Pelapheron had fallen and his other business was concluded.

But if the armies believed Audriss had indeed been captured – and his ill-timed absence would go a long way, in the minds of some, toward confirming that story – then taking Pelapheron might have become a much more difficult endeavor.

'Really?' Valescienn called back, determined to keep the qualms he felt from emerging in his voice. 'I find that difficult to believe, Espa! I know exactly where Lord Audriss is right now.' The lie was directed more at his own men than the enemy. 'And I can assure you, he's quite free and unthreatened even as we speak!'

He thought he was prepared for any response. Espa's sudden, mocking laughter proved him wrong.

'Audriss, Valescienn? I think we both know better! I mean your *true* commander!'

True commander? Jilahj the Mad take the old lunatic for one of his own, what the hell was he *talking* about?

'Behold, Valescienn!' Espa thundered melodramatically, holding over his head an object nigh invisible in the darkness. 'Proof positive that we speak only the truth when we tell you that we have captured Corvis Rebaine, the Terror of the East himself!'

Something came spinning down from the parapet; Valescienn leapt back, in case this was some sort of attack despite the flag of truce. But what landed in the dirt with a thump was nothing but a shoulder plate of black steel, adorned with a smaller plate of polished bone.

Like a sleepwalker, Valescienn lifted the spaulder from the dust at his feet. Incredulously, he glanced at the two soldiers with him, but they looked even more puzzled than he.

'We'll have to get back to you on this,' he called to Espa, his voice as nonchalant as he could manage. Then, with a curt wave at his honour guard, he stalked back to his own camp.

His first urge was to contact Audriss immediately. This was an unexpected twist, to put it mildly. What, by all the gods, could possibly have given them the idea *Rebaine* was behind all this?

On the other hand, though he possessed the means to contact his lord and master, his instructions explicitly defined the circumstances under which he was permitted to use such methods. Unforeseen and bizarre as this particular twist might have been, it didn't really qualify as either emergency or imminent threat.

'General?' the man carrying the pennant asked quietly.

'What were they talking about, sir? What's all this about Corvis Rebaine?'

Valescienn shook his head. 'Nothing to worry about, soldier. I don't know what sort of herbs they've been smoking behind those walls, but I don't think it much matters. They're expecting us to turn tail and run, or at least dither aimlessly for a spell.

'Start spreading the word. I want no noise, no hint of preparation, but we attack at dawn.'

'Well, this is just fantastic,' Davro exclaimed almost before the tent flap flopped shut behind him. 'What do we do now?' The winter wind swept by outside, not quite powerful enough yet to howl, and a chill sauntered through the tent, wandering about casually in search of a place to settle down.

'The first thing *you* do,' Losalis told him, glancing up from the flimsy table on which lay various reports, 'is duck. This tent won't keep the weather off us if you rip it open with that tusk of yours.'

'Tusk?' the ogre protested, crouching until he reached the corner in which he'd previously stacked several cushions. His single eye gleamed irritably. 'This is a horn, Losalis. You see this big, round thing beneath it? That would be my head. My head, where the horn is coming from. You see this opening in my head, with all the teeth? That would be my mouth – where my horn *would* be coming from, *if* it was a tusk!'

'My apologies, Davro. Perhaps if you stopped talking long enough for me to see anything other than your mouth, I might not have confused the issue.'

Seilloah snorted, and only the ogre's acerbic glare prevented it from growing into a full-bore chuckle.

'Yes?' Davro asked icily. 'Was there something?'

'Why, Davro!' the witch said with false joviality. 'Do you really think I would stoop so far as to mock you under such circumstances?'

'Which circumstances would those be? The ones where we're both awake and breathing?'

298

'Is there any chance,' Losalis asked pointedly, 'that we might eventually get around to discussing the pending, battle?'

As though waiting for just such a cue, the flap opened once more to admit Teagan and Ellowaine, followed by another man nearly as large as Losalis himself.

'I understand you've been wantin' to see us,' the chestnut-bearded warrior said, slumping down into a chair and placing one hand on the table before him. The other, fingers splayed, came to rest dramatically on his breastplate. 'Well, here we are, sir, ready for duty and reportin' to be seen.'

'Stow the melodrama, Teagan,' his female companion snapped at him. 'Let him get to what he's got to say so we can be back in our own tents, by our own fires. It's cold as Chalsene's ass out there!'

The last man to enter was named Ulfgai. A barbarian warrior from frozen lands far to the south, he'd been Losalis's second in command and had taken charge of the general's old company. The polar opposite of his former commander, he was pale bordering on albino: his skin was pallid, his hair and beard some nebulous shade between blond and white, his eyes the light grey-blue of coldest ice. Unlike the others, he wasn't the least discomfited by the chill settling into the air around them. He had, in fact, left his heavy furs in his own tent and come to the meeting wearing only bearskin leggings and a light tunic beneath his breastplate.

'So why *have* you called us out here?' the southerner rumbled. 'Perhaps you've lost the taste for it, but some of us have better pursuits in which to spend our few free hours.'

'You mean getting sloppy drunk and breaking things?' Seilloah asked acidly.

'You speak as though that was a bad thing.'

'The reason I asked you here,' Losalis announced loudly, 'is that we have a decision to make.' He paused to ensure that all eyes were upon him. 'Or rather, I have a decision to make, and I want your input on it.

'As you're no doubt aware – or,' he amended with a

dangerous glance at Teagan, 'you *should* be aware, if you've been paying attention – the Serpent's army is camped just outside Pelapheron. We're looking at a fairly hefty siege. Not a *long* one, given the techniques that Audriss has access to, but a large one.'

'Are you supposing that Audriss might hole up in this place for the winter months?' Ulfgai asked, idly spinning a thin-bladed knife around the fingers of his right hand.

'It makes sense,' Losalis admitted. 'On the other hand, we're already a ways into the cold season. Any sane commander would have holed up weeks ago, and any sane army would have refused to come this far.'

'Hmmph,' the barbarian snorted contemptuously. 'What you lot call winter—'

'However he's doing it,' Losalis continued, refusing to be sidetracked, 'Audriss is keeping his armies fed and moving.' He turned his head slightly. 'Unless you know of any reason why he can't keep it up?'

Seilloah shrugged, frowning. 'Losalis, it's about all I can do to keep *us* fed as winter approaches. It's very difficult to make plants bloom and to call animals when they'd all much rather be hibernating. I can't imagine how he's managing it with so large an army, and since I don't know how he's doing it, I couldn't begin to tell you if he can keep it up or not.'

Losalis nodded. 'I thought as much. So maybe he'll stop for the winter, and maybe he'll keep going. But in either case, I think we have to assume that Pelapheron will fall, just like all the others. Unless we interfere.'

Several shocked stares crossed the tent, forming a lattice-work of incredulity at about the level of Losalis's neck. They'd been trailing a day or so behind Audriss's army for over a month now, and they'd done nothing but harry the enemy's scouts, or ambush the occasional straggler. Those, in fact, were Rebaine's parting orders: harass them, never let them forget that the enemy was on their tail, but do not provoke them. Let him continue to think Rebaine's army was no real threat, until the time came for a decisive strike.

'But is this really the right time?' Teagan asked hesitantly. 'You know how I hate bein' the one spreadin' the doom and the gloom, but the Serpent didn't lose men enough to be worth mentionin' when he took Orthessis. We're still outnumbered by four or five to one.'

'Orthessis,' Losalis reminded them, 'was largely abandoned and completely indefensible. The folk who stayed behind never had a chance, and we all knew it. Pelapheron, on the other hand, is a walled city with a full garrison. Not enough to hold Audriss off, of course, but maybe enough that a sudden strike from the rear could turn the tide.'

Ellowaine nodded. 'A vise, then. Trap them between us and the wall.'

'Pretty much what I had in mind, yes.'

'If ye be wrong, it may just be costin' us our army,' Teagan pointed out.

'But if we *can* make it work, it may just end the war,' the larger man countered. 'I've got scouts ascertaining enemy positions and viable strike points against Pelapheron's walls. You'll all have your specific unit assignments by morning.'

His grin was predatory, splitting his dark beard and making him resemble an unusually mirthful bear. 'Get some sleep, people. We have something of a full day ahead of us.'

Losalis, Davro, and Seilloah were once again alone within the tent's canvas walls. Grimacing irritably, Losalis relit the candle sitting in a shallow brass holder on the table before him, the candle that had guttered out at least four times already that evening.

'This is all well and good,' Seilloah said worriedly from the other side of the table, 'but it doesn't address our other problem.'

'You mean the fact that Corvis has been gone for more than a month now?' Davro asked from the cushions, reclining comfortably and clasping his hands behind his head.

'Of course I mean that!'

'So where's the problem?'

The witch, exasperated beyond any concerns of dignity, actually stamped her foot. 'Listen, horn-head, I don't give a damn about your problems with Corvis! We're all out here because of him, he's our gods-damn leader, and he's missing! What, other than making ever so useful and constructive comments, do you plan to *do* about it?'

Davro merely shrugged.

'Seilloah,' Losalis interjected, 'what options do we have? Either Lord Rebaine was successful in his objective, in which case we have to assume he's got valid reasons for his absence, or he was unsuccessful, in which case he's dead or imprisoned. Since he's beyond our help if he's dead, and he's beyond our reach if he's been captured, I don't see there's much Davro, or any of us, can do.'

'If the two of you will excuse me,' Seilloah said stiffly, 'I believe I'd best retire for the night. We have, as you were so good to remind us, a busy day ahead of us.'

The flap snapped shut angrily behind her, as though picking up an echo of the witch's agitation. Losalis glanced at the candle, which had once more blown out in the sudden breeze, and sighed.

When the sun, bleary-eyed and blinking, rose from his eastward bunk the next morning, it was to observe, with no small measure of surprise, the drastically changed world beneath him. The hardened earth and dormant trees surrounding Pelapheron were wrapped in a heavy coat of white, set to dancing by the light but persistent gusts that trundled through clearings and slid between trees. The world around the endangered community had reacted in advance, spreading a scab of snow across the wounds and scars soon to be inflicted.

Winter, long held in abeyance by the autumn's abnormal warmth, finally stretched its icy fingers across Imphallion, grasping its hard-won prize.

Not that something so insignificant as the weather would alter Valescienn's plans. Pelapheron's defenders were startled out of any lingering drowsiness by the sound of thousands upon thousands of men assaulting the city walls.

The Serpent's forces hadn't been camped long enough to have constructed any large siege engines, and they travelled with only a light complement of smaller varieties. A few ballista bolts lunged upward at the defenders, and now and again a small rock would smack into the wall, but by and large the invaders' tactics were limited so far to frontal assaults with scaling ladders.

Pelapheron's defenders, of course, were not similarly constrained. Catapults dropped bushels of stones upon the heads of the attackers, ballistae thrummed as they launched their missiles, and porcupines lobbed dozens of crossbow bolts screaming through the air to shred armour and flesh alike. The pristine white snow went first a sickly pink, and then a rich red. The shrieks of the injured and the dying swarmed like flies.

Though the torn and mangled bodies seemed endless as the stars, Nathaniel Espa knew well that Valescienn had thrown only a probing force at him. When a single trumpet blast from Valescienn's heralds called for them to disengage, what had felt a full-fledged offensive left only a few hundred dead in its wake.

'Report,' Valescienn ordered, eyes never straying from the blood-soaked wall.

'No exact count yet, sir,' an armour-clad warrior replied, breath steaming like a dragon's in the frosty air. 'Quick estimates would be that we've lost about two hundred and fifty, maybe up to three. Enemy casualties are lower, sir, probably about a hundred.'

'Excellent.' The general's scars writhed as he smiled. 'If you were atop that wall, Captain, you'd certainly judge what just happened to be a probe for weak points, yes?'

'Absolutely, sir.'

'Good. Then they should believe that the next wave is a real attempt on the walls.' His smile grew cold. 'Pass the ready order to Mithraem and the gnomes.'

'Yes, sir!' The soldier snapped off a quick salute, which rang sharply against his helm, and trudged rapidly back through the clinging powder.

It was a tactic Audriss had used often since his campaign began, and it never failed to bring swift victory. The Serpent's entire mortal army, if truth be told, was little more than a combination of diversion and cleanup crew. The highest walls and the most alert defenders were nigh useless against the shadow-clinging gnomes or Mithraem's Endless Legion.

Valescienn gave it another hour before ordering his herald to sound the charge. The Serpent's warriors leapt forward, voices raised in a cacophony of disparate battle cries, weapons held aloft, but it was a slow, faltering charge, as boots pulled against the weight of the rapacious snow. Arrows and stones fell in a deadly rain, and men once again collapsed with split breastplates and crushed helms. It certainly looked bad for the attacking force, but then, it was supposed to.

The screams from *within* the walls, when they finally reached Valescienn's ears, were a beauty to rival the greatest symphony. The sheets of arrows faltered as the defending archers found themselves facing a threat from behind. Valescienn had hoped that the Endless Legion could take down the bowmen with no warning; an archer with his wooden shafts was a far greater danger to Mithraem's people than warriors with their blades of steel. Still, he was more than confident in their ability to do their job with minimal losses. With that distraction to ease their way, the first of his human soldiers reached the top of the wall, and the battle for Pelapheron began in earnest.

Which was, of course, when things fell apart.

Valescienn was one of the first to hear them coming. It wasn't quite thunder, for the snow muffled their footsteps, and the earth did not shake beneath their tread. Nevertheless, Audriss' lieutenant was briefly paralysed by their sudden appearance, his eyes wide and his jaw agape as the army of Corvis Rebaine charged from the ice-encrusted trees.

CHAPTER TWENTY-ONE

The stone-walled hallway echoed – no, shook, really – with the footsteps of half a dozen ogres. Their shoulders hunched and heads bowed, they still barely fit within the corridor built for humans, but they were determined to let neither cramped muscles nor bone-deep weariness slow them down.

Nor the angry, ever more desperate human jogging in their wake, for that matter.

'Davro, you're not listening to me!' Valescienn had to shout just to be heard over the clattering of his flail against the metal of his greaves, to say nothing of the aforementioned marching feet.

Davro rolled his eye ceiling-ward. 'No, Valescienn, I'm listening. You're just not saying anything worthwhile.'

'Damn it, Davro, I told you to *stop*!' Even as his pale-skinned hand reached out to snatch at the ogre's belt, a veritable chorus of low growls sounded from six enormous throats, Valescienn found himself staring up at Davro's narrowing gaze – and at the bristling array of spears beyond.

Swallowing softly, he released his grip and took a step back. Fearless, Valescienn might have been, but not stupid.

'Was there something?' Davro queried politely.

'Davro, *think*! Think of what we can still accomplish! There's no reason to give up now! We—'

'No reason? You haven't noticed the surrounding armies, the complete lack of surviving fortifications, or

305

the abrupt disappearance of one suddenly less-than-terrifying Terror of the East? You're not really all that observant, are you?'

'I'm not an idiot, Davro.'

'Ah. Just practicing, then?'

Valescienn ignored him. 'I know we're in a bad position, but it's *not* untenable. They're not ready yet; they think they can come in and wipe us out at their leisure. A sudden sally, a single thrust through the encampments, and we can be through them before they can react!'

'*Kovul shinak, et,*' Davro marvelled to a handful of ogrish chuckles. Corvis' lieutenant – former lieutertant – didn't need to speak the language to understand that he was not being complimented.

'We'll lose a chunk of the army,' he admitted, 'but not so much that we can't rebuild! They're tired of war, they'll be back to feuding with one another in weeks! We can still—'

'Valescienn.'

'What?'

'Shut up.' Davro hunched down farther still, bringing his one eye on level with the human's two. 'Corvis is gone. The war is over. You want to stay and fight? You go right on ahead. We, however, are going home.'

'Davro, I can't do this without the ogres!'

'Then I guess you have a problem, don't you?'

Behind Valescienn's pale skin, the slow flushing of his face looked almost like a growing forest fire, and he seemed literally unable to catch his breath. 'I will *not* let you ruin this for me, you damn savage!'

'*Me* ruin this? Remember that army we just talked about? I'd think—'

Valescienn's hand dropped to the hilt of his flail; Davro's hand dropped to Valescienn's. The meaty fist snapped shut and the rattling of the chain ceased as abruptly as it had begun. Valescienn fell to one knee, grunting, as the bones in his forearm shifted, threatening to give way entirely.

'Because we've fought together,' Davro whispered to him, 'side by side, you're still alive. Try that again, and you die messy.'

'You took an oath, Davro,' Valescienn whispered through the pain. 'In Chalsene's name!'

'An oath to Corvis Rebaine, Valescienn. Not to you.'

Valescienn collapsed to the floor, gasping in relief, as Davro let loose his grip. Without a word, the ogres turned as one and resumed their inexorable march toward the exit.

'I won't forget this, Davro!' Valescienn shouted after them.

But the only answer he got was the slamming of a heavy door, and the pounding of large feet receding swiftly into the ash-coated streets of Denathere.

Any other time, they'd have posed little threat. Without even counting the Endless Legion or the gnomes, the Serpent's army outnumbered the Terror's several times over. But nothing about these circumstances was normal. Audriss' army found itself, for the first time since they'd taken Denathere, trapped in a defensive battle, crushed between the unyielding stone walls and a flanking foe.

Valescienn didn't even bother calling orders, for no one could possibly have heard him over the surrounding roar. With a furious cry, the scarred man met the enemy, short sword clasped loosely in his left hand, barbed flail whirling from his right.

Expertly, he parried an overhand blow with his short blade, even as he wrapped the chain of his flail around the soldier's calf. Valescienn yanked hard, driving the flail's spines deeper into armour and flesh, jerking his opponent's leg out from under him. Even as the man fell screaming to the snow,

Valescienn's short sword flickered forward and down. The screaming ended abruptly with a wet gurgle.

Snow crunched behind him and he whipped around, rising from his crouch. Flesh ripped as the ball-and-chain tore free and a second of Rebaine's soldiers went down, the side of his head caved in, shreds of his dead companion's leg muscles dangling from his skull where they'd been stuck to the barbs.

But while Valescienn held his own against the surprise assault, his men fared less well. The defenders on the wall, heartened by the unexpected arrival of reinforcements, redoubled their efforts against both the attackers without and the invaders within. Arrows dropped on the Serpent's soldiers with increasing speed, rocks and boiling pitch poured from the ramparts, scaling ladders were shoved back with long poles or else doused in oil and set ablaze (and *then* shoved back with long poles). The Terror's forces harried the armies, attacking at the edges of the battle and then veering off, only to return moments later in a thrust aimed straight at the heart of the melee. Even as Audriss' soldiers tried to regroup, the officers could see that the damage was done. Units were scattered, companions separated, commanders isolated from their subordinates. And still the arrows fell, and still the enemy advanced.

'Valescienn!' It was a primal sound, the roar of a hurricane. It carried well across the tumult, climbing the wind and striding across heads to reach the ears of Audriss' beleaguered lieutenant. Eyes narrowed, stretching his scars into an ugly white line, he turned to meet the source of that voice.

'Davro . . .'

Nor was he alone, gods take him! With a fury to drown the battle cry of Kassek War-Bringer himself, a scream split the frigid air: a hundred inhuman voices, shrieking the Night-Bringer's unhallowed name. Sliding from the snow-coated trees came an entire wedge of ogres, a living, snarling avalanche of muscle and steel. The first of them, taller and broader than Davro himself, carried an iron-headed maul. It rose and fell methodically, and if it was not a speedy weapon, well, it had no need to be. The first man within reach of that crushing sledge, unable to leap aside due to the snow piled around his feet, threw his shield up over his head in desperation. It, along with the arm behind it and most of the man's body from the waist up, disintegrated into a wet smear on impact.

And everywhere the ogres struck was more of the same. Swords broad enough to cleave a horse in twain laughed at such conceits as armour; axe blades the size of body shields cut through men like wheat; and those horrendous mauls pounded everything beneath them – metal, flesh, bone, and blood – into indefinable pulp. Here and there, an ogre who'd somehow lost his weapon laid about him with fists and horn, and more of Audriss' soldiers fell to the ground, torn and bleeding.

Valescienn did not, however, have much time to absorb what Davro's people were doing to his men, not if he wanted to prevent Davro's spear from doing the same to him. The insanely long weapon licked outward long before Davro came within the human's reach, and Valescienn realised, even as he hurled himself from the heart-seeking blade, that he would have to bring the fight to the ogre.

He rolled back to his feet, his entire left side coated in a patina of blood-soaked snow. His brow creased in rage, Davro spun, slicing his spear in a horizontal arc. Unable to dodge a second time, Valescienn braced himself for the coming shock and twisted *toward* the spear, flail and sword crossing in an X-shaped parry.

Though he did indeed prevent the spear from sinking home, the terrible force of the blow knocked him from his feet. His arms aching, his hands ringing from the impact, he heaved himself upright once more, just before Davro's spear plunged down into the snow where he'd fallen.

Valescienn lunged desperately, aware that he might never again find himself so far inside the ogre's reach. The short sword flicked outward, stabbing at the weak spot in the ogre's armour between stomach and waist.

And Davro laughed.

It was a harsh, heavy laugh, ridiculing Valescienn even for the attempt. And even as he recoiled, face red with fury, the human realised why. He'd been too stunned by the force of the ogre's blow to notice earlier, but the short sword with which he'd attempted to gut his opponent was little more than an inch of jagged metal. The rest of the blade had snapped clean off when he'd parried the weighty spear.

Cursing defiantly, Valescienn hurled the useless weapon at his foe and gripped his flail in both hands. For a moment, the two opponents circled, each waiting for the other to move.

'Why are you here, Davro?' Valescienn taunted, buying time. 'I thought you preferred slaughtering sheep and pigs to people.'

If he'd been hoping to stun the ogre with his knowledge of Davro's dark secret, he was destined for disappointment. 'Obviously,' Davro replied, 'you were mistaken.' He grinned maniacally. 'Or Audriss was mistaken. Or Audriss' pet demon, Pekatherosh. Maybe it was *his* mistake?'

Valescienn's scowl darkened, but he, too, was unsurprised at the extent of the enemy's knowledge.

'Loyalty to Rebaine, then?' Valescienn continued, jerking away from an experimental spear thrust, though he knew he was once more beyond reach.

'If I'd known we'd be having such an in-depth conversation, Valescienn, I'd have brought wine and pastries. Since I didn't, do we want to get on with trying to kill each other?'

But Valescienn saw before him a different sort of opening. 'We could,' he admitted. 'But there's no point now, is there? What with Rebaine having been captured and all.'

Finally, *finally* he evoked a reaction. The ogre tried to hide it as quickly as it occurred, but Valescienn knew he'd seen that ugly, single eye go wide, seen the horn twitch with a sudden doubt. 'What are you talking about?'

'Don't even know your own leader's whereabouts? *Tsk, tsk,* Davro. You used to be a lot better than—' Valescienn yelped as Davro lurched forward, and once more twisted wildly aside to avoid gaining an extra orifice.

Even as the shaft thrust past him, he brought his flail spinning up and around. The weighted length of chain wrapped tightly around the spear in a lustful suitor's embrace, the barbs digging furrows in the dark wood.

Valescienn yanked before the far stronger ogre could react, every muscle in his body straining. The spear tilted sideways, and Valescienn lifted a foot and dropped it down in a devastating kick. The haft of the spear, thick as it was, gave way with a deafening snap. Davro pulled back, grimacing in consternation at the splintered wood in his hand.

Valescienn grinned nastily. 'I'd say that makes this fight a *little* more even, wouldn't you?'

Davro's shoulders slumped. 'My father gave me that spear at my coming-of-age ceremony,' he said, almost whimpering. Valescienn's grin grew larger still.

And then, without the slightest change in expression, Davro drove the broken end of the shaft straight through that mocking leer.

For a moment, the ogre held the broken weapon and its gruesome burden aloft, until his single eye settled on the thick trunk of a nearby tree. He lowered the broken spear – allowing Valescienn's feet, still kicking feebly, to once more touch the ground – and then charged, setting the staff under his arm like a lance. The impact rocked the earth around him and torrents of snow shook down from the leaves. When the dust settled, the staff was embedded in the wood and Valescienn's body hung lifeless from the trunk, a large rivulet of blood coursing down his chin.

'That was completely uncalled for,' Davro told the corpse seriously, actually waving a finger at it. 'I *liked* that spear.' Then, drawing his sword with a resigned sigh, the ogre tromped back toward the battle. Valescienn's pale eyes followed his killer in an eternal, empty stare.

*

'Something's not right.'

Mithraem's head rose from the now bloodless body of another defender: a teenage boy whose primary duty had been to carry arrows to the bowmen on the ramparts. His eyes were tinged red with his victim's stolen life, and a thin trickle ran red from the corner of his lips, but his clothes were spotless as ever, and not a strand of his slick black hair was out of place. He looked like a nobleman dressed for a semi-formal event, not a participant in a brief and bloody siege.

Or at least, one that was *supposed* to be brief. But while the gnomes and his own Legions were doing their usual magnificent job of slaughtering the mortal fools who held the city, Valescienn's soldiers weren't following the plan. The defenders were distracted; the wall should have been swarmed under by now. And yet, after the initial wave of attackers, there was no sign of the invading force.

And now that he listened – truly *listened*, with senses only vaguely comparable to what humans thought of as hearing – Mithraem could detect the sounds of a pitched battle on the far side of the wall.

Something had changed, and he needed to know what it was. The lower half of his body already dissolving into a pink-tinged mist, Mithraem's disembodied head spoke to another of his kind.

'The gnomes can handle this from here,' he said, fog pouring from his mouth as he continued his transformation. 'Something's happening outside. Gather as many of the others as you can find, and follow.'

And then there was nothing human left at all, merely a serpentine haze swiftly whipping its way through the streets toward the main gate and whatever lay beyond.

'Fog! Fog from the walls!'

With a bitter curse in his native tongue, Losalis smashed his enemy's blade aside with his saber and drove the razored edge of his shield into the soldier's throat. Then, ignoring the muffled thud of another body dropping to the thick snow, he looked toward Pelapheron with growing trepidation.

Losalis knew, thanks to Corvis' warnings, exactly what sort of inhuman creatures he might be facing that day, and he'd posted lookouts, men specifically ordered to watch for just this troubling sign. The problem, of course, was this: now that he had his forewarning, what the bloody hell was he supposed to do with it?

'Fall back and form up!' he ordered in a bellow audible even over the din of battle. Inwardly, he winced. Letting up now would allow the Serpent's army to recover from the initial assault, and he begrudged every second his own men weren't pressing the enemy. But he knew, too, that what was coming was beyond the experience, even the comprehension, of most warriors. If they hoped to survive, let alone salvage a victory, they had to fight as a unit, even if it meant giving the enemy opportunity to do the same.

'Defensive lines!' Losalis shouted, squelching his own doubts the better to deal with theirs. 'Shield walls where terrain allows! Archers to the rear!' He stabbed an imperious finger at the ogres' commander. 'Davro! Form up your people by the archers! You're floating backup!' Davro nodded and roared his own orders in the sharp, guttural tongue of the ogres.

Men dashed across open ground and crunching snow, hearts pumping, sweating despite the blue nip in the air, shivering with more than cold as voluminous clouds of mist, advancing against the prevailing wind, poured from the palisade. It frothed as it came, the leading edge splitting and tearing and bubbling in agitation, curling at the corners. A wave of malice swept ahead of it, unholy herald of its master's deathly advance. Here and there, not quite masked by eddies in the swirling fog, appeared blood-gleaming eyes or pale grasping hands. Several of Losalis' slower men vanished with a terrifying abruptness as the mists rolled over them, their fear-filled, earsplitting shrieks dragging on and on and on . . .

They began to emerge, then, humanoid shapes coalescing

from the mists. Pale-skinned with reddened eyes, trailing streamers of fog as they walked, leaving infinite ranks of bloody footprints behind them in the snow. Mist took on the shape of shadow, shadow the substance of man, as they appeared, each after each, from the thinning mists, the ones in back stepping over the rent and bloodless bodies of the men they'd slaughtered. Tall and short, gaunt and stout – all manner of men and women, but all dark of hair and pale of skin.

In the ranks behind Losalis, someone whimpered, someone gasped. Even the general himself had to grit his teeth, clench his fist tight about the hilt of his saber, and command his feet with muscles of stone and will of iron that they *would not run*.

When Corvis, Davro, and Seilloah had battled one of Mithraem's minions previously, they were fortunate indeed to face it alone. Here, the Legion was massed. Massed, their power was dominant. The terror they rode into battle, bucking and lashing out in rage, was no mere emotion but a physical thing, a foe no less real than the undead themselves. The men who stood, trembling as they held their ground, could no more have shrugged off that fear than could a young deer simply choose to ignore the instinct for flight at the sudden baying of the wolf.

He was aware, suddenly, of Seilloah beside him, her own face twisted in fear, though she, too, held her ground. Her fingers twitched, her lips moving silently. When the first of the enemy was a mere handful of yards away, she stepped forward and allowed a dull powder to sprinkle from a clenched fist, dusting the snow with a light coat of black.

Instantly the fear lessened. Oh, certainly the men still gazed at the implacable foe with no small amount of consternation, but the mind-numbing crush of terror was gone, allowing Rebaine's army to think clearly once more. A protracted howl – heard not in the ears or even the mind but as a flutter of the heart and a chill of the blood – arose from the advancing horde. It was a call of fury, not despair, for if the vanguard of fear was indeed their first weapon, it was far from their last.

'Can you do anything else?' Losalis hissed anxiously.

'Not really.' Seilloah's voice, rock-steady when she cast the spell, now shook with the fear they all repressed. 'I might manage one or two, but there's just so many . . .'

And then the Endless Legion was upon them.

They were fewer than they first appeared. As all but a few residual tatters of haze melted away, Losalis saw that these 'Endless' soldiers numbered, in fact, only a few hundred. It gave him a brief, flickering hope that his men might stand a chance.

And then the first appeared before him, and there was no more time for thought or hope or anything but battle. She was a bone-thin woman in thick furs, with blood-reddened lips and a thin-bladed short sword clasped before her. Though not unclean, she reeked of blood and rot and things long gone and forgotten from the world of man.

The she-thing hissed, an angered beast, and Losalis blinked in surprise – apparently, the precise reaction she'd wished. With a gleeful cackle at the gullibility of mortal foes, she stepped forward in a perfect lunge, her thrusting blade seeking the fleshy vitals of the fool before her.

But Losalis, too, could feint and switch, and where the creature expected a startled opponent and an easy kill, a heavy downward chop with his shield sent her short sword careering into the snow. A sharp cry of defiance, a stab upward and outward, and the tip of his saber slid neatly through furs and flesh, prying ribs apart with a wishbone crack and plunging deep into desiccated organs.

Screeching wildly in agonised fury, she thrashed about on the end of the sword, claws reaching hungrily for the man who'd dared do this to her. Blood – black, viscous, and thick with congealed and clotted chunks – belched from the wound to fall, steaming, to the frozen ground.

Nor was Losalis finished. With a grunt he pivoted on a single foot. The snow slowed him, threatened to trip him up, yet he muscled his way through. The saber, yanked free, whistled around again as he completed his spin and cleaved cleanly through the monster's neck. Her head, jaw sputtering silent imprecations, landed crookedly at his feet.

Even before the rest of the body hit the ground, it was putrefying into black, hideous sludge. Despite himself, Losalis retreated a pace as the thing he'd just slain decayed into a thick morass that refused to mingle with the surrounding snows.

A tendril of fog flowed from the rotting form, skimming low over the white-shrouded earth, and then shot arrow-swift to the nearest corpse, the bloodless husk of one of Losalis's own men. He watched, pulse racing, as the mist slammed hard into the body, sending the corpse tumbling and rolling. Another instant, and it ceased thrashing, rolling smoothly to its feet, eyes open, mouth quirked in a malevolent grin. Haze hovered beneath its feet as it slowly, deliberately, advanced toward Losalis, a familiar spark of hell in its eyes. Losalis saw the skin tightening across its bones, growing pale as the remaining blood in the corpse was consumed by the thing that rode it.

The Endless Legion. Finally, Losalis understood.

With no shame in his heart, Losalis called for a full retreat.

It was not entirely a rout, though. At least one advantage came from their first encounter with Mithraem's people.

Far from Losalis, fighting madly to hold the flank, Ellowaine's hatchets were a wall of razors, her hands blurring in complex and ornate patterns that delivered dismemberment and death to anyone within reach. Already two of the foul monstrosities had fallen to her whirling blades, only to rise again in the nearest corpses. Her assault did not falter, her axes did not slow, but a shroud of futility fell upon the golden-haired mercenary. Already to her right, the line was broken. The archers, unable to loose even a single volley of arrows before the Legion was upon them, would have been slaughtered to a man had Davro's ogres not charged in to fill the gap in the lines.

The creature she battled now was one of the most hideous

of the lot. A twisted hunchback of a man, it stood but five feet tall, but it must have weighed upward of 250 pounds. The morningstar clenched in its gnarled fists bristled with heavy spikes, and its pale skin stood out markedly against the thick black cloaks that wrapped it.

Slowly, step by step, Ellowaine fell back. Despite her opponent's twisted form – or, perhaps, because of it – it possessed an iron strength that even its fellows could not match. Its hideous club smashed aside anything in its path. Still, she couldn't just keep retreating. Many more steps, and she'd open a hole in the defensive line through which anyone could simply saunter. If she—

She yelped despite herself as her heel snagged on a root concealed beneath the snow. Her arms pinwheeled in a wild attempt to maintain balance, until she sensed her foe's sudden charge. With a grace more feline than human, she shifted her weight, allowing herself to tumble backward after all. Her back and shoulders smacked into the snow, and Ellowaine kicked both legs up as she rolled, going completely over and landing in a crouch. Though a simple tumble, it was, under the circumstances, an impressive feat that few on the battlefield could have duplicated.

It was barely enough. Any human warrior would have been thrown by the move, left a few feet behind, allowing Ellowaine opportunity to regain her feet, her poise, her balance. The hunchback, however, never hesitated. Even as she gathered her bearings, Ellowaine saw her misshapen enemy closing fast. As Valescienn had done against Davro, she raised her weapons in a parry she knew could not suffice.

The wicked morningstar crashed into her hastily raised weapons with a resounding clang. Her arms thrummed in agony, and her left hand bled freely where one of the weapon's spikes proved long enough to punch through flesh despite the intercepting hatchets. And again echoing Valescienn's duel with Davro, one of the parrying weapons simply wasn't up to the task. Ellowaine glanced unhappily at the foot-long handle that was all that remained of one of her favourite weapons.

The hunchback spun, its feet churning up the snow like a digging dog, its weapon already raised for another strike. Ellowaine, out of options and growing ever more frantic, fell back on the last refuge of the hopeless: superstition.

Mithraem's Endless Legion weren't precisely what folklore made them out to be. The mists, the blood, the inhuman strength and speed – these were certainly all too real. But Ellowaine hadn't once seen them shapeshift into some animal; nor did the daylight appear to cause them much difficulty. So inaccurate had it proved thus far, she balked at trusting to folklore now. But she had no other way to turn.

With a sudden, piercing shriek, Ellowaine lunged forward, but not with her remaining hatchet. As she'd previously echoed the actions of the doomed Valescienn, so now did she unknowingly mimic the ogre who'd slain him. With every bit of strength in her battered and tired body; she thrust with the broken shaft clasped in her other fist.

Whether Ellowaine was the first on the field to remember her folklore and attack the Endless Legion with wood rather than steel, none could say. But it was she who first reported to Losalis, after the battle, that the tactic was as effective as myth proclaimed.

A high-pitched keening, scarcely audible, burst from the hunchback's parted and gasping lips. Now it was her opponent who retreated, morningstar held loosely in one hand, the other feebly plucking at the broken shaft protruding from its chest as though he was afraid to actually touch it.

Ellowaine might not have understood exactly why the tables suddenly turned – she'd assumed that either her stroke would slay the monster or else have no effect at all – but she recognised the fear in its eyes when she saw it. She lunged again, this time with her remaining hatchet, smashing the beast's collarbone and carving down into its torso with a series of snaps like a crackling campfire.

That same black, viscous, oily blood pumped forth, and the

creature putrefied into a puddle of corruption. But things changed when the liquefying corpse, the wooden shaft still protruding from its sodden flesh, hit the ground. The mist began to emerge, as it always did, but something was clearly wrong. Tendrils of haze stretched out, anxious to be on their way to a new body, but the bulk of the mist clung stubbornly to the wood as though held by some magnetic attraction it couldn't understand. Over the span of several infinite seconds, the mist seeped into the shaft, which darkened from a deep, rich brown to a sickly black. And then, with a faint wail that reverberated forlornly in the back of the warrior's mind, the rotted stake crumbled to black dust. The creature did not rise again.

Only then, as she stood panting heavily in an island of relative calm, did she realise that one of the sounds she'd heard moments before, during the height of her deadly struggle, was the call of the herald's horn.

Sucking in her breath, sliding her remaining hatchet into its ring at her belt, Ellowaine ran to catch up with her retreating companions.

'Well,' Losalis said thoughtfully as the flap once more closed behind the departing backs of Ellowaine, Teagan, and Ulfgai. 'That's certainly – ouch! – interesting. It'll be useful, if we have to face those things again, although that's still – ow! – not a prospect I'm looking forward to. And it might – damn it! – explain why they didn't chase us back to camp.'

Seilloah snorted as she worked on a crooked but shallow gash on the large warrior's arm. 'It wouldn't hurt now if you'd let me numb it first,' she reminded him mercilessly.

'Sorry,' the general muttered, though his tone was unrepentant. 'I don't like it when I can't feel what people are doing to me.'

'Losalis, you're looking right at me.' She pulled the sutures tight, the wound twisting so that it appeared to be grinning sardonically up at her, and once more worked the curved needle through flaps of flesh. 'You'd have to be blind, deaf, and possibly dead not to know what I was doing to you.'

'But I wouldn't *feel* it. It wouldn't be the same.'

The witch sighed. 'It's your pain.'

'Thank you.'

'I wish I had the strength left to do this magically,' Seilloah told him more softly. 'This will hurt for a while, and it's certainly going to scar.'

Losalis shrugged, drawing a mild curse from the witch as the needle was nearly tugged from her hand. 'I can live with a few more scars, Seilloah, and there were those who needed your magics far more than I.'

They lapsed then into exhausted silence, punctuated occasionally by Losalis's exclamations. It was odd, Seilloah noted in the back of her mind. This was a man who could take a sword in battle without so much as a complaint, yet he couldn't stop muttering and flinching as she sewed that same wound shut. If she lived to be a thousand, the witch decided crossly, she would never understand people. Especially warriors. Especially men. Can't live with them, can't eat all of them.

Only when Seilloah tied off the sutures and slumped back with a fatigued sigh did Davro nervously clear his throat. Warily, the others looked his way.

'Umm.' He cleared his throat again. 'There's something you should know. I . . . that is, before I killed Valescienn—'

Seilloah sat up sharply, and Losalis's eyes widened. Then, as one, they both cheered.

'Davro, that's fantastic!' the general told the ogre, wide-grinned and chortling. 'If I were the one paying you, I'd give you a bonus.'

'Thanks,' Davro said drily.

'We've got to tell Corvis as soon as he gets back,' Seilloah added. 'It'll be some of the best news he's heard in months!'

The ogre's face went flat. 'That's what I was getting to.' Seilloah and Losalis fell silent. Davro shook his head. 'I'd be lying if I said that I didn't consider not telling you this,' he admitted. 'But whatever else I may be, I'm no oathbreaker, and I swore to help him to the best of my ability.' He paused.

'Corvis has been captured.'

The only sound in the tent was the occasional spark from the burning candle. Slowly, as though terrified he'd miss something, the general leaned forward. 'How do you know?'

Davro repeated to them, verbatim, the conversation he'd held with Valescienn while they were circling, and he shook his head when Losalis suggested the scarred warrior might have been lying.

'I don't think so. I admit it's been a while, but I knew the man, fought beside him. It wasn't his kind of bluff.'

'Then why wouldn't they use him as a hostage to force our surrender?' Seilloah asked softly.

'I don't think Audriss is the one who's got him,' Davro explained, 'precisely because Valescienn didn't do just that. I think it's the regent, Seilloah. Duke Lorum, Rheah Vhoune. Them.'

'Sodomy and damnation!' It was, to the best of her knowledge, the first time Seilloah had heard Losalis curse. He was up from his chair, pacing the small tent. 'What do we do now? We've neither the time nor the manpower to go hunting for him.' He spun violently toward Seilloah. 'What about magic?'

The witch shook her head sadly. 'I don't know where he is. And even if I knew or could guess, distance might well prevent me from accomplishing anything. There are very specific boundaries on the kind of magics I can invoke, Losalis.'

'Then we're royally buggered, aren't we?'

Seilloah frowned. 'Maybe not I think I'm getting an idea.' She looked up at them. 'It's absolutely the most harebrained, asinine thing any one of us has ever thought of, but I don't think we've got much choice.

'Losalis, pass me that parchment and ink from the table, please? Thank you. Gentlemen, I'm going to explain my idea to you. Kindly try not to scream too loudly.'

CHAPTER TWENTY-TWO

The sword whistled as it arced, high and across, a wild and overeager swing. Corvis ducked beneath it, lashed out with the hilt of Sunder and felt it impact nice and heavy against the fellow's gut. The mercenary's hauberk took the brunt of the blow, but still the breath burst from his lungs in a painful grunt. He didn't double over so much as simply bow ever so slightly, but it would do. Corvis twisted back the other way, raising his right hand as though delivering a vicious uppercut, and Sunder's blade cleaved clear through the man's jaw. A rush of warmth that Corvis didn't really want to think about washed over his fist and forearm.

/Oh, I've missed this!/ Khanda cackled shrilly even as Corvis whirled, readying himself for the next attack.

For a moment, it failed to materialise, as the survivors regrouped to reconsider their prey. Corvis straightened, ignoring the tearing ache in his shoulder and wishing briefly that he'd had his armour to turn the blow aside. It wasn't slowing him yet, but it was only a matter of time before the wound grew too bad to ignore; already he could smell little over the scent of his own blood. He had to wrap this up.

They stood in the midst of a muddy street, in a tiny town whose name Corvis couldn't even recall at that moment. There were five of them now, whittled down from the original seven, all clad in mail and leathers, all armed, and all with at least some reasonable knowledge of what they were doing. Corvis didn't know if they'd somehow tracked him down, or had simply found themselves lucky enough to stumble onto the biggest bounty in Imphallion's history, but either way was bad for him. Other than these – and Tyannon, who stood to the side with a peculiar expression and seemed uncertain whom she ought to be rooting for – the streets were empty, doors locked and shutters slammed as the townsfolk fled the sudden eruption of bloodshed in their midst.

/If you're through playing,/ Khanda reminded him, / now might be a good time to burn the lot of them down./

Corvis, for once, agreed with his mouthy accoutrement. Sunder clenched tightly in a gore-splattered grip, he raised his other hand, fingers splayed, felt the warmth begin to grow in the amulet against his chest . . .

And with a speed that Corvis could only marvel at, one of his foes – the man, in fact, who carried the broadsword stained with the Terror's own blood – lunged across the road and swept up Tyannon in a fearsome grip. The girl uttered a quick squeak, then grew wide-eyed and deathly silent at the press of steel beneath her breast.

/Perfect! We can get all of them at once!/

But Corvis clamped down on his will, snuffing the spell he'd been ready to throw, ignoring the demon's indignant squawk.

'She means nothing to me,' he growled coldly, locking his gaze with the mercenary's own.

'Then attack us and see what happens, Rebaine.'

Each stared at the other, while the remaining thugs shuffled their feet and spread out, ready either to lunge in attack or dive away from whatever monstrous spell the Terror of the East might unleash.

Instead, Corvis frowned and allowed Sunder to tumble to the earth from a slackened fist.

/Are you completely insane?!/

'Possibly,' Corvis muttered. Then, more loudly, 'All right. Let her go and I'll come quietly.'

'I don't think so. I think it'd be better if aauggch—!'

Corvis never did find out what would be better, since it was then that Tyannon grabbed the man's crotch and squeezed like she was juicing an orange. It wasn't really all *that* painful, given the fellow's protective padding, but it was sufficient to loosen his grip. Tyannon bent forward and straightened, slamming the back of her head into his face. Even as formerly solid bits of anatomy crunched flat, she allowed herself to fall from his grip and scramble away, trying to ignore the warm blood, mucus, and occasional tooth that now matted her hair.

Between one bloody cough and the next, the mercenary saw Corvis hook a foot beneath Sunder's shaft, saw the demon-forged axe take to the air and land solidly back in the Terror's waiting fist. And then the amulet around the warlord's neck flashed, and the mercenary's world was washed away beneath a wave of crackling fire.

Two of them managed to dive aside in time to avoid Khanda's burning wrath. Sunder split one of them efficiently down the centre, but the other was long gone, leaving both his weapons and his footprints in the muddy road.

Blood dripping from his axe and a truly peculiar expression marring his face, Corvis stepped over to Tyannon, who crouched against the side of the nearest house. 'We're going to have to move on,' Corvis said. 'I don't *think* the fellow's likely to come back, but if he does, it'll be with reinforcements.'

'I figured as much,' she told him dully. Mechanically, he reached out a hand to help her up. Equally mechanically, she accepted.

'We, uh, probably have time to get washed up first,' he offered, glancing with strange distaste at the smear her hair had left along the wall.

'I'd appreciate that.'

/Oh, just kill me./

For a few moments they walked in silence toward the inn in which they'd been staying, unseen by the villagers who still refused to open their windows, the only sounds the squelch of their feet in the mud. Until, finally, 'Tyannon? Why in all the gods' names did you help *me*?'

'You weren't the one with a sword to my ribs, Rebaine.'

'Well, no, but . . . Once I'd dropped Sunder—'

/*Like* a complete *moron*,/ Khanda interjected. Again, shockingly, Corvis ignored him.

'—you probably weren't in any further danger.'

Tyannon drew stiffly to a halt and stared ahead at the waiting inn, refusing to look at the man beside her. 'Why *did* you drop Sunder?'

/*An excellent question.*/

'Because I made you a promise, Tyannon. I said no harm would come to you.'

/Not *such an excellent answer.*/

'Maybe you had no reason to believe that promise when I made it,' Corvis continued, 'but I meant it all the same.'

'That,' she said, her voice flat as parchment, 'is why I helped you.' Still refusing to so much as turn and look at him, Tyannon marched ahead and vanished through the inn's front door.

The darkness hurt.

No. No, that wasn't quite right, was it? Wasn't the dark his sanctuary, his salve? For when it was dark, he remained blessedly alone. When he was alone, the pain throbbed, oozed through him, permeated flesh and bone, but at least it didn't grow any worse. It was when the dark fled before the burning touch of torches and lanterns, when the voices echoed through the chamber, when he *wasn't* alone . . . *that* was the true source of his constant agony, the beginning and ending of his world.

The dark should have been his comfort. But it was not, for it was there, in the blind silence, that he was left to imagine, what new horrors would be birthed in the light.

So he suffered for more days than he cared to count. More days than he *could* count, for he'd been permitted to see no light but the flame since they'd brought him here, never felt the touch of the sun on his skin in this chamber of the deepest hell. Through it all, he saw no other people save the leering Baron Jassion of Braetlyn and the muscle-bound, empty-eyed cronies assisting him in his 'work' – and, far too rarely, the healers who would mutter a few words, apply a few poultices and herbs, ease his wounds *just enough* to ensure that the prisoner wouldn't succumb before his next 'session'.

When they'd dragged him down here, nearly naked, broken, and bloody, he'd already suffered perhaps two or three cracked ribs, bone bruises and at least one fracture in his left arm, a near break in his left leg, and uncountable con-tusions. And he'd thought – with a foolishness he'd have laughed at now if laughter hadn't made him cough up blood – that he'd been in pain.

The beating he'd taken in Rheah's room was the heights of ecstasy compared to what he'd endured since.

His face, swollen and purple from the constant beatings, resembled a malformed eggplant. It was easier, now, after so many fists had landed, to count *unbroken* ribs. His limbs were nothing but deadweight dangling from his battered body, sluggish, weak, reluctant to obey his commands. Black skin flaked from where they'd applied reddened pokers – and, in one case, the flaming end of a torch – and other patches of skin were scraped or sliced away, exposing a gaping maw of raw, bleeding flesh to the open air. Wounds festered, caked in the dirt and dust and rat excrement that made up the carpet-ing of his new home. The sweat and dried blood of endless days encrusted his face and his body.

Though others often lent a hand, Lord Braetlyn performed most of the work himself, delivering blows to crush flesh and crack bone. He took no small amount of perverse pleasure from the suffering he inflicted on the 'great' Corvis Rebaine, a fact he announced loudly and often. It was he, Jassion bragged, who had struck the warlord down in Rheah

Vhoune's office. It was he who had stripped the Terror of his possessions and locked them away with his own hands. It was he who had inflicted more damage on Corvis Rebaine than the man had suffered his whole life through.

It was a cliché that Corvis had never more than half believed but now knew to be manifest truth: there was, indeed, a point at which death was not a threat to be avoided, but a comfortable end to suffering, a final draught of cool water to quench an agonising thirst.

But he did *not* wish for death, though all of life seemed nothing but pain. He did not want it, would not ask for it, would fight against it with all of what little strength remained within. Even though, at times, he could scarcely remember why he fought at all.

When he could, when he remembered there was a world beyond this tiny pocket of malicious night, he saw their faces dancing about him, heard the laughter of children at play in the fields or the soft whispers of his wife breathing passionately in his ears. To surrender now, however tempting, would not merely cost him himself – it would cost him them.

And even when he could not remember, when the pain of the here and now was all he knew, he would not yield. Gods damn them all, he was Corvis Rebaine! The Terror of the East, the scourge of Imphallion, and he'd willingly be damned to an eternity far worse than this before he'd let himself succumb to scum like Jassion of Braetlyn!

There were questions, of course.

'Why have you come back?'

'Are you the power behind the Serpent?'

'How strong is your army?'

'What is your plan?'

'What the hell have you done with *my sister*?'

He'd answered truthfully enough – some of the time, anyway – but the young baron didn't much care for his answers. The notion that Corvis could have emerged out of seclusion to *stop* Audriss was so diametrically opposed to everything Jassion believed that the words scarcely even registered. He'd already been judged: everyone already knew he was indeed the man behind Audriss, and all his captors required now was that he admit it.

He'd declined to reveal the strength of his army, and his refusal had earned him many a bruise or a burn but it was as nothing compared with the baron's reaction when Corvis answered his final question.

He could have lied. He could have told Jassion what he expected to hear, that Tyannon was long dead. He could have told Jassion that he'd let her go after a few weeks of captivity, that something else must have happened to her.

But even now, even when Tyannon would have begged him to say whatever he must to save himself, the idea of lying about her was a repudiation of everything he'd worked for. If he denied his family now, he might as well have stayed at home and let Audriss march unopposed.

So he'd told Jassion the truth, and the baron exploded. His frothing lips no longer spat anything resembling a sentient language – primal animal sounds echoed through the room, crashing against the stone walls. Corvis didn't doubt that his life would have ended then and there had not one of the baron's own men dragged his liege off the bloody pulp. There were others who wanted the opportunity to 'speak' with Corvis Rebaine. And so, raving and spitting, Jassion was dragged away until he'd calmed down.

But from that point forward, Jassion stopped caring about his answers. He asked questions in a dull monotone, a formality, and reached for a gauntlet or a club or a knife even before he'd finished speaking. It was an excuse, now, and a challenge: how much agony could one man take before his body gave out?

The rag-wrapped figure lying splayed across the filth-encrusted stone flinched at the scrape of footsteps in the hall, at the flicker of torchlight under the door. Peeling himself painfully off the floor, he backed into the cell's farthest corner.

His eyes – his left eye, actually, as his right was swollen shut – twitched as the lock turned over. There were voices outside, Jassion's among them. But the other proved a mystery. It struck a dim and distant chord in Corvis' memory, but he'd not heard it recently enough to place.

'. . . wasting your time,' Jassion was saying angrily. 'He hasn't spoken a word of truth since we got him down here! You questioning him personally is absolutely—'

'Essential,' the other interrupted. 'Strange things are happening, Lord Jassion, and I'm hearing unusual reports. Especially regarding the fall of Pelapheron. If—' The intractable lock finally clicked open, and Corvis could not help but flinch from the light.

Jassion, clad in his accustomed black armour without regard for the dungeon's chill, entered first. The man who followed was handsome, his face emphasised rather than hidden by a well-trimmed blond beard. His outfit was largely white, embellished with navy blue. Corvis may have failed to identify him by voice, but he certainly knew the man by description.

The newcomer's gaze met that of the filthy, bloodied tatterdemalion who stood as straight as his injuries would allow. Then, his voice the very embodiment of courtesy, he nodded. 'Lord Rebaine.'

Though his neck ached at the effort, Corvis returned it. 'Your Grace.'

Lorum smiled slightly. 'You know me?'

'I know *of* you.' The prisoner coughed, a tearing hack that moistened the fist he'd raised to his mouth with a thin layer of blood. 'You'll forgive me if I don't bow, and for my informal attire.'

Jassion, fists clenched tight, grew livid that Corvis had strength and spirit enough for sarcasm. He stepped forward, arms raised, but Lorum's extended hand halted him.

'When I require your assistance, Jassion, you'll be the first to know.'

Face twisted and eyes burning, Jassion reluctantly stepped back.

Lorum strode fully into the room and stood beside the

caged Terror. Grimacing in disgust, he looked over the shredded, filthy rags and open wounds.

'You aren't frightened to be so near me, Lorum?' Corvis asked only half sarcastically.

'Should I be? Will the Terror of the East kill me with his bare hands? Hold me hostage for his freedom?' Lorum smiled. 'At your best, Rebaine, you might possibly have done it. In your current shape, it's not even a contest. No, Rebaine, I'm not scared of you. If anything, I think you're the one who's afraid.'

Though his entire face throbbed, Corvis raised a sardonic eyebrow. 'Of you?'

'Of this.' Lorum gestured around him. 'This isn't a pleasant place, Rebaine, and what's happening here even less so.' He leaned in and whispered, resembling a schoolboy spreading a salacious rumour. 'Between you and me, I think Jassion's getting just a bit more enjoyment from this than he should be. The man's got something against you, Rebaine. More so than rest of us, more even than his sister, I think, could account for.'

Corvis nodded slowly.

'In any case,' Lorum continued, straightening, 'I thought you might prefer to speak to me. I've got much the same questions Lord Jassion does, but perhaps I can phrase them more to your liking.'

The former warlord chuckled through raw and bloody lips. 'You come sauntering in here, Your Grace, show me forty-five seconds of what vaguely passes as kindness, and I open up to you? Is that the plan? Because if so, I think it's tactically unsound.'

Jassion shook visibly, struggling to hold himself in check. Lorum continued to ignore him.

'Not really, no,' Lorum said, his voice still calm. 'This isn't a game, Rebaine. We're not playing "good guard, bad guard".' Absently, the duke toyed with his signet ring, a purple stone set in a band of gold. 'I simply thought to make it clear that, whatever personal grudge Jassion holds against you, I don't share it. Talk to me, and I will treat you in the exact manner you earn, no more no less. If you do not . . .'

His fist lashed out, a sledgehammer of flesh slamming into Corvis' swollen face. The prisoner's skull snapped back against the wall and he dropped, coughing loudly and bleeding from a nasty gash in his cheek where Lorum's ring had sliced his skin.

'If you do *not* choose to cooperate with me, I will again treat you in the exact manner you've earned. While I may not take the same pleasure in your pain that my young companion does, I assure you that I will be just as methodical in inflicting it. And I've learned tricks in my time to make even Jassion blanch.'

Jassion grinned maniacally as Corvis struggled to regain his feet.

'Give him a few minutes to think it over,' Lorum ordered. 'And I mean make him think.' The regent turned away. 'Not too hard, though,' he admonished. 'I want him able to ponder the wisdom and generosity of my offer.' He stepped from the room, idly wiping the blood from his signet with a handkerchief.

His jaw twisted wolfishly, Jassion reached down and helped the struggling prisoner to his feet. When Corvis glanced at him, puzzled, from beneath swollen lids, the baron shrugged. 'I wouldn't want to start with you already on the floor,' he explained. 'You'd have nowhere to fall.'

As Jassion began punching – fists blasting the breath from Corvis' lungs, bruising his stomach, pounding his face – a portion of the prisoner's mind simply stepped back into the corner, where the rain of blows was something to be observed rather than felt, and watched the proceedings with clinical detachment.

He noted for the first time that the reason Jassion's lefts hurt more than his rights was due to his own signet ring, similar to the one that had opened Corvis' cheek. It was green, rather than the royal purple of the regent's own, and the band was a dull pewter rather than gold.

He knew that ring. He'd seen it before . . .

At last, through a haze of agony, in a mind dulled by countless days of torment and deprivation, he finally made the connection. And everything fit into place with a resounding click.

'*That*,' that same, distant sliver of his consciousness observed in a voice so calm it infuriated the rest of him, '*would at least explain his excessive animosity, wouldn't it?*'

Oh, it certainly would. Corvis' hands twitched, as though prepared to leap, of their own accord, for the throat of the man before them – and then he chose the path of least resistance and passed out.

/*Audriss . . . oh, Audriss . . . rise and shine, time to get up. The barbarians are at the gates! Setakrian's back from the dead, and he wants a word with you about a book. The Dragon Kings are knocking on the door. Wake*—/

'I'm awake, you infernal nuisance! Damn you, I'm awake!'

/*Infernal . . . Oh, I get it. It was a joke. Forsooth, 'tis to laugh.*/

Audriss groaned, rolling over and blearily rubbing the sleep from his eyes. He cast an irritated glance at the nearest window and grew even angrier at the sight that greeted him.

'It's the middle of the night, you cretin!'

/*My, but you're cranky. No wonder you haven't got married yet.*/

'Pekatherosh—'

/*Oh, relax. Someone's trying to contact you.*/

'What? Valescienn? I gave him strict instructions—'

/*Not Valescienn. Mithraem.*/

Mithraem? *That* was a surprise, and one, Audriss felt by the sudden churning in his gut, that probably did not bode well. He allowed himself one last moment to shake the dregs of sleep from his skull before replying. His first act was to erect a shield of silence around the room. It wouldn't do to have a passing guard or late-night wanderer overhear his end of the conversation. Then, another moment of concentration . . .

'What is it, Mithraem?' he asked once he felt the other's mind. 'I left strict orders with Valescienn that I was to be disturbed only in case of dire—'

'Emergency?' Mithraem's silk-smooth voice replied from empty air. 'I'm certain your lieutenant would be only too happy to accept any reprimand you'd care to give him. Why don't I just dig him up and let you talk to him?'

'Dig him up?' Audriss asked softly.

'Rebaine's army hit us from behind while we were assaulting Pelapheron's walls,' Mithraem said succinctly. 'The Legion disengaged from inside the walls and drove them off, but not before they'd wreaked considerable damage.'

Audriss' left hand came down on the bedside table, actually cracking the wood. 'Define *considerable*, Mithraem!'

'Between Rebaine's people and the defenders, we've lost over four thousand. Including Valescienn. I doubt Rebaine's army lost more than three or four hundred, and Pelapheron still stands.'

The end table hurtled across the room, smashing into a bookcase with a crash that sent books tumbling to the carpet and would, had Audriss not deployed his spell, have alerted the entire floor to his tantrum. Even before the furniture came to rest, the warlord was on his feet, pacing angrily and cursing obscenely in three languages.

It wasn't so much the loss of Valescienn that disturbed him. The man was an able second and quite useful, but hardly essential to the Serpent's plans. Nor was it the loss of men, though he'd feel their absence well enough when the time came. What disturbed him above and beyond all else was a pair of facts that stuck in his craw and left a hideous taste in his mouth.

One, Pelapheron was the first city to successfully stand against the armies of the Serpent. True, he could try again and probably take it easily, but they'd fought off his first real effort, and the news of that victory would spread like a plague across Imphallion. This defeat struck Audriss' reputation for invincibility a devastating blow.

And two, even locked up and battered in the depths of the dungeons, Corvis Rebaine was still causing him untold problems, and he was no closer to getting what he needed than he'd been weeks ago. Especially since it would give too much away to just come right out and *ask*.

'All right,' he said, finally calming himself. 'The first thing we need to—'

'So sorry for interrupting you,' Mithraem said, his tone suggesting nothing of the sort, 'but there's more.'

'Oh? And what might that be?'

'A few hours ago, shortly after the battle, we were approached by a messenger from Rebaine's camp.'

Audriss snorted. 'This should prove interesting. What did they want?'

'They want to make a trade. Apparently, Valescienn told Davro – before the ogre drove a large stick through his face – that Rebaine was a prisoner. I imagine they think *we* have him.'

Audriss nodded thoughtfully. 'Do they now? And what are they offering in exchange?'

'Something about a book.'

The warlord froze in midstep. 'A book?'

'A book. They claim you've been looking for this book, and they're willing to give it to you in exchange for Rebaine. Alive, of course.' Mithraem paused. 'You haven't been keeping things from me, have you?'

'It's a spellbook,' Audriss rattled off instantly. 'Nothing special, as such things go, but one I've wanted for some time. Rebaine acquired it somewhere, which is one of the reasons I met with him. I didn't mention it because it's not worth mentioning. Personal obsession, nothing more.'

Silence fell, and Audriss found himself fidgeting. Mithraem was an invaluable ally, but if he should discover what his 'partner' truly sought, he could become a far deadlier adversary than even Rebaine himself.

'As you say,' Mithraem offered blandly. 'So what do we do about it?'

The warlord resumed his pacing, less angry now, face clenched in contemplation. 'I've an idea,' he said slowly, 'but I need to work out some of the details. I'll get back to you shortly.'

'I wait with bells on.'

'That would be a sight, wouldn't it?' Audriss stumbled slightly as the connection was severed. And then, when he was absolutely certain Mithraem's presence was well and truly gone, he began to laugh outrageously.

/I fear that, for the first time in our working relationship, I seem to have missed the joke./

'My dear Pekatherosh, it's absolutely perfect!' the Serpent cackled.

/Enlighten me, mirthful one./

'Don't you see? Davro and Seilloah want to trade Selakrian's spell-book for Rebaine!'

/Yes, I eavesdropped that much, thank you. But the Rebaine situation isn't exactly a simple one, and you already know where the damn book is!/

Audriss scowled. 'Pekatherosh, I've known since the beginning where the book is. But I still need Rebaine to tell me himself. If I were to come up with that particular bit of knowledge on my own, he – and others – would start wondering how I knew, and I can't have them figuring it out just yet. Without the key, it's as useless to me as it was to him. Let it stay where it is until we need it.'

/Ah. But if it's traded to you in exchange for him . . ./

'Then he need never know about my foreknowledge. You know, you're quite clever for a piece of jewellry.'

/You're too kind. So what do you have in mind?/

'Corvis Rebaine is going to make a miraculous escape from the dungeons of Mecepheum,' Audriss said slowly, working through the scheme as he went. His pacing feet set up a monotonous thump, thump, thump, on the hard floor beneath the carpet. 'Of course, he'll be aided the entire way by agents of his "ally", Audriss. That ought to mortar a few thoughts into the heads of the rest of these idiots.' A leer curled across his face. 'And once we're clearly part of a team, with Selakrian's spellbook in our hands, Rheah Vhoune will have no choice but to act against us. Facing the combined power of the Serpent and the Terror of the East, she'll realise she needs the book herself to stop us. How she reacts will tell me if she truly has the key, and where.' His laughter resumed, softer than before.

'Tell me, Pekatherosh. Have you ever served a god?'

'What? Huh . . .'

'Quiet, Lord Rebaine! We're here to help.'

Squinting through his one good eye, his entire world muffled in a shroud of agony and exhaustion, Corvis peered at a blurry figure. He was, as best the battered warlord could determine, human and light-skinned. Probably. One eye swollen shut, the other refusing to focus, it was nothing short of a miracle he could see at all.

His splintered ribs screaming at him, digging viciously into flesh, Corvis used the wall to prop himself into a sitting position. His tattered rags left a dark stain smeared across the stones in a profane shadow of a rainbow.

'Easy, my lord, easy,' the voice admonished. 'You're in bad shape, Lord Rebaine, and we've got a way to go.'

'Go?' It was happening too quickly, whatever 'it' was. Corvis' head was spinning and screeching at him like a crow in a tornado.

He leaned toward the floor, tried to push himself up, collapsed with a muffled gurgle of pain as the broken bones of his left arm ground together and refused to support him. His face, puffy and swollen, barely even registered the pain as it bounced off the floor.

Pressure on his shoulders and his upper arms, the blood-encrusted stone falling away from his bleary gaze. It took him a moment to realise he was being lifted, powerfully but gently, to his feet. He stumbled, his legs refusing to lock, his weight sagging against the other's grip. Then, with a defiant effort, he forced his knees to cease their shaking, demanded his abused and aching muscles to quit slacking and get back to work. It took a moment, and if someone had flipped through a book too swiftly the breeze would be enough to send him tumbling, but he stood, finally, on his own.

'Where . . . ,' he gasped, and immediately fell into a spasm of choking. His liberator waited for the fit to pass, reacting only with a sideways glance as Corvis hawked up a mouthful of semi-congealed blood and spat it vigorously onto the floor.

'Out,' the other said softly, peering suspiciously out into the hallway beyond the door. Corvis, even with his blurred vision, could see the lock had not been picked, but wrenched open by main strength. Even in his prime and at full health, he would have been hard-pressed to duplicate such a feat.

'How many?' the warlord wheezed. His vision was clearing slightly, though his head throbbed in time to his wildly beating heart. His entire body threatened to dissolve into a wave of pure agony and flow out from beneath him.

'I see none at the moment. But these dungeons are not well patrolled, as they are believed secure—'

'No.' Another brief cough. 'I meant how many . . .' A wheezing breath, panting.

'How many men do I have?' the other asked, finally understanding.

'Yes . . .'

'Myself and two others, Lord Rebaine.'

The Terror started, one eye wide. 'Three? Three of you infiltrated . . .' Corvis' legs chose that moment to collapse, noodle-like, beneath him. Only his rescuer's astounding reflexes saved him from tumbling again to the floor.

'We will be enough, Lord Rebaine.' Carefully, maintaining his grip until the warlord could once more stand under his own power, he propped his charge up beside the nearest wall. Nodding gratefully, Corvis leaned on it with his good – or, more accurately, less bad – arm.

'A larger force would be detected,' the man continued.

Corvis could now make out further details. The fellow wore black, of course, for an operation of this sort. A leaf-bladed short sword hung at his waist, but he otherwise appeared unarmed. He was, as the warlord noted, quite fair of skin, and his hair was crow-feather black. 'Stealth is essential if we are to win free of this place before your absence is discovered. My companions are currently keeping a watch along our intended route. There is an old sally port not far from the dungeon. It will mean a quick run across an open garden, I fear, but I think we can manage you for that long if—'

'My weapons,' Corvis rasped, shaking his head. 'Need . . . Sunder and Khanda.'

The dark-haired man shook his head. 'Too risky, Lord Rebaine. We need—'

'Not . . . asking you.' He took a tottering step from the wall, and remained standing. Dust and cobwebs coated his arm, his back, the side of his face, but he wasn't leaning now. 'This will go a lot faster,' he said, forcing himself to speak clearly, 'if you just accept it. Do you know where they keep the confiscated equipment?'

The other man glared, then shook his head with a sigh. 'I believe we know the general vicinity,' he said discouragingly, 'but not the exact location. The best we can do is get you into the proper hall.' He frowned thoughtfully. 'Can you call upon your demon at that distance?'

'I don't know,' Corvis said, a strange, enigmatic half smile stretching his cracked lips. He winced as one of them split under the pressure and began, again, to bleed. 'I can speak to him without direct contact, but it's difficult. In my condition, I'm not sure I can reach him.' He shrugged, then gasped in pain as bones that weren't hanging exactly as they should moved in unison with his shoulders. 'On the other hand,' he said, face pale where it wasn't mottled by bruising, 'we don't seem to have any other options.'

'Of course we do. We can move straight toward the exit – as we should have been doing for the past five minutes, instead of arguing – and get out of here. No weapon is worth—'

'Oh, spare me the act,' Corvis growled. 'If I'd wanted a show, I'd have bloody well paid for a ticket.'

'What? My lord, you're delirious. I—'

'Why does Audriss want me free?'

To his credit, a brief blink was the only sign of the fellow's shock.

'How did you know?' he asked simply.

None of my people but Seilloah, Davro, and Losalis know what Khanda is, he could have said.

But he did not. Instead, he said simply, 'We don't employ your kind.'

'My kind?'

'Come on, now. Pale skin, black hair . . . Yes, some humans fit that description. But it was enough to make me wonder, and there *are* signs, if you know what to look for.' Corvis smiled again, though it hurt more than he would admit. 'And if you really didn't want me to retrieve my stuff, you wouldn't have given me the option. You'd have just carried me. So not only does Audriss want me out of here, he wants me out of here fully armed. Why would that be, I wonder?'

The other man scowled. 'You're doing so well,' he said, just a bit petulantly. 'Why don't you tell me?'

'Because if I were making a real escape,' Corvis told him, 'I wouldn't leave without them.'

'Very good, Lord Rebaine.'

'So if we're through playing our little games, shall we get moving? Someone's bound to come along sooner or later, and I'm not exactly at my quickest right now.'

'You'll cooperate?' The tone was, to put it mildly, incredulous.

'Friend, I don't know why the Serpent's helping me, and I'm certain I won't like the answer. But I'm *quite* sure I'll prefer it to spending any more time in *this* hole!'

Of course, if his suspicions were correct, and not merely the product of fevered delusions, Audriss *was* the same man who was keeping him down here, beating him, torturing him. But no sense in playing that particular ace until he held a better hand to go with it.

And so, doing his best to maintain the stumbling, shuffling pace that was all he could manage – and trying very hard not to think about what accompanied him – Corvis followed the unholy creature toward the light.

CHAPTER TWENTY-THREE

'Everything's ready, Lord Rebaine.'

Corvis waved a black gauntlet at the guard. 'All right. Prisoners first.' Without waiting to see if his orders would be followed – they always were – the Terror of the East spun, cloak flowing like a wave, and heaved his armour-clad bulk into the great stone chair.

It was a throne, really, in all but name. It was here that the baron had formerly held his audiences with the leading citizens of Hollecere. It was clear from the great throne, the raised dais on which it sat, and the towering windows beyond that split the rays of the midday sun through stained glass that 'm'lord' had clearly held aspirations higher than his station.

Now he was dead, of course, his head stuck on a pike beside the gates of his city, and he didn't aspire to much of anything. But his arrogance had left Rebaine the perfect site for the show that the citizens of Hollecere were forcing him to put on.

First through the doors were a dozen of Corvis' guards, fully armoured, naked broadswords glinting evilly in gauntleted fists. Valescienn led the pack, his lips compressed into a grim line – whether because even he couldn't stomach the thought of what was to come, or to prevent himself from grinning maniacally, Corvis couldn't say, but for a brief moment he absolutely loathed his cold-blooded lieutenant.

Shuffling amid the guards, clad only in rags and leg irons, their hair matted and their skin filthy from days without bathing, came more than a score of prisoners. Their steps faltered, more than even the heavy manacles could account for, and their eyes glazed, for each and every one of them had been given heavily drugged wine. It was vital, for what was to come, that they remain unfocused, their minds unable to react to any event.

Unable to prepare.

Corvis felt a surge of nausea and forced it down. These were some of Hollecere's surviving military officers, community elders, priests of Kassek and Panaré and Sannos – and all were leaders in a resistance that had formed the moment the city fell to the invading armies. Their attacks had been well planned and, worse, unexpected. The Terror's armies had grown lax, accustomed to the instant obedience they'd acquired after their prior conquests. Already, Rebaine had lost more than a hundred men, including several officers, and almost a week of time to the Hollecere underground, and he could afford no more. Not with the end so near.

So it was time to make a statement, to remind Hollecere – indeed all of Imphallion – what it was to defy the Terror of the East.

Another wave of his hand, and the prisoners were lined up on the dais before the throne, turned to face the room, and forced – rather easily, given their befuddled states – to their knees.

'The others,' he ordered hollowly.

Again the door opened. More soldiers and several ogres – including Davro, now chieftain of the tribe since Gundrek had fallen to resistance assassins – ushered in the audience Corvis required. These were several dozen more of Hollecere's citizens; some were also priests of various gods. They, too, were necessary for this to work. They would recognise what was to come from religious tales, and would confirm for any skeptics among the populace that the Terror had indeed done what he claimed.

Corvis gave them just a few moments to recognise the faces of those who knelt, drugged and chained, upon the dais, allowing their horrified murmurs and whispers to reach a fever pitch before rising to his feet. The room fell silent, as every sober eye stared into the impassive face of the Terror's iron-banded skull.

'I didn't wish this,' Rebaine intoned, voice echoing once within his helm, a second time between the room's stone walls. 'I had hoped that the blood I was forced to shed in taking this city would be enough. Alas, Hollecere has proved me wrong, proved itself far less wise than its sister cities. The deaths of your leaders and your soldiers, displayed for you atop the gates and from the guttering streetlights, has proved insufficient deterrence.

'Maybe you feel that your deaths are worth it, that bravery in the face of hopeless odds will somehow aid your families, or grant you a greater glory in the afterlife. But make no mistake: this is no bravery, it is stupidity. And you have forced my hand. If you don't value your lives enough to remain obedient, to leave me and mine alone to do what must be done, then perhaps you value your *souls*.'

Ignoring the sudden fearful cries from below, Corvis turned his attention inward, lowered his voice lest it be heard beyond the confines of his helm. 'Khanda?'

/*Yes, O bone-headed one?*/

'The leaders are drugged – too drugged even to recognise that they're in danger. They're yours, Khanda. All of them.'

/*For me? Oh, Corvis, you shouldn't have! You know, my birthday's not for a couple of months . . .*/

'Gods *damn* you! Just *do* it!'

The crowd erupted into a single, multi-tongued scream as the leaders of the resistance simply collapsed, their eyes and mouths leaking a hellish red luminescence before their features vanished utterly in a shower of gore.

A raised hand was enough to silence them. 'Spread

your stories through Hollecere. Let everyone know that *this* will be the fate of any still foolish enough to rise up against me.' Corvis turned to face Davro, who stood across the room with pale, clenched fists and an unreadable expression. 'Show our guests out.' He lowered himself once more into the stone-backed chair, stared across the room at nothing at all until everyone else was gone.

/*That was* fun, Corvis. Can we, do that again?/

The warlord ripped the iron-and-bone helm from his head and bent over the side of the chair, his entire body convulsing, yet his heaves brought nothing up. It seemed that his gut had become as hollow as his soul.

But at least, thank all the gods, it was almost over. No more cities stood between his armies and Denathere. No matter how low he had allowed himself to fall, soon, so soon, it would finally be over . . .

/*Well, old boy, I can't say as how I'm entirely pleased to hear your voice again. But I'll acknowledge that it's not altogether a bad thing under the circumstances. That bitch Rheah kept poking and prodding at me for hours!*/

Corvis, breathing heavily, slumped with his back to the iron-banded door, grinned through his exhaustion. 'Why, Khanda,' he whispered at the keyhole, 'did you just say something nice to me?'

/*Not at all I said something a bit less nasty than normal. It only seems nice by comparison.*/

'I'll take it.' The warlord quickly brought both hands up to his mouth, trying to muffle another fit of choking. The thing that had come to rescue him, who currently stood over the body of two *very* dead guards, glowered at him, then returned to watching the hall for any further interruptions.

Corvis ran his eyes over the heavy portal on which he leaned: thick oak, banded with three separate strips of iron, possessed of a heavy black lock. Shaking his head, he painfully dragged himself back to his feet. 'Hey, you! What's-your-name!'

The creature again spun, lips clenched angrily. 'Lord Rebaine, if you *want* to call the entire castle guard down on our heads, that's your business. *I* can just become mist. I don't believe you'd appreciate the consequences, however.'

'Sorry. Any chance you could just mist yourself under the door and retrieve my stuff?'

'No chance at all. Neither the Kholben Shiar nor your demon would make the transformation with me.'

'Ah. Well, can you deal with the door, then?'

A sudden kick slammed into the wood beneath the latch with roughly the force of an enraged rhino. Wood splintered, iron bent, and the door ceased, by all meaningful definitions, to be a door at all.

'Well,' Corvis said softly as the dust and debris settled at his feet. 'That was certainly – vigorous. But . . .' He coughed again, triggered by the floating particles that formerly constituted part of the mauled portal. 'I thought you were the one who wanted us to be quieter?'

'And how, then, would you have wished me to "deal with" the door?'

'Uh . . .'

'Precisely. May I humbly suggest, Lord Rebaine, that you do whatever you came to do, so we can move on?'

Corvis limped into the storeroom, his entire body shuddering with pain at even the simple effort of lifting his feet high enough to clear the rubble.

The room was relatively well ordered, though some of the articles had tumbled off their shelves when the door burst. Various chests, boxes, weapons, scroll cases, books, and other curiosities cluttered the racks and cupboards, but it was Sunder that first caught Corvis' roving eye. Though it currently wore the form of a two-handed greatsword, the style of the hilt and the needle-thin engravings that rode up and down the blade like errant travellers made the weapon unmistakable. But even as the beaten warlord stretched forth his hand to reclaim the Kholben Shiar, another, rock-hard grip slapped down on his wrist.

'You'll forgive my paranoia, Lord Rebaine, but I think I have to insist on carrying your weapon for the time being. Wouldn't want you getting any unfortunate notions in your current condition.'

'No, of course not,' Corvis said drily. 'Can't have that.'

He was, however, fascinated to discover that Sunder didn't shift when his 'companion' lifted it from the shelf on which it lay. The Kholben Shiar *always* changed to fit the wielder.

Unless, of course, the wielder possessed no soul to read.

/*Corvis! Are you going to stand around all day admiring your shaft, or are we getting out of here?*/

All right, so where . . . ah. Corvis just barely spotted a few tiny links of chain, jutting from a chest in a far corner. He shuffled over, ignoring the worsening pain as he forced the lid all the way open, the ribs on that side gleefully chewing away at his insides. There the pendant lay, atop a heap of bone and black steel that Corvis had grown to truly despise over the past months. His fingers weakly closed around the chain an instant before he collapsed with a muffled sob into the corner of the room.

/*You're* really *not in good shape, are you?*/

'So good . . . of you . . . to notice,' the Terror gasped, choking for breath.

/*I aim to please. Umm, you* are *aware that your compatriot over there is a*—/

'Yes, I know.' Again using the wall as a crutch, Corvis once more struggled feebly to his feet. 'We should hurry,' he said toward the figure looming in the shattered doorway. 'Our luck can't hold out much longer.'

'You're not healing yourself?' the other asked, with a gesture toward the dimly glowing pendant.

'I'm surprised you don't know,' Corvis replied. 'Demons can't heal. Hell, it's damn near impossible even to magically heal a demon-made wound. It's fire and water. They're sort of at opposite ends of the karmic continuum, as it were.'

/Has anyone ever told you that you get obnoxiously verbose when beaten into a bloody pulp?/

'Shut up, Khanda.'

The warlord's companion shrugged. 'Why would I know? What need have I for magical healing?'

'Granted, but—'

'It does, however, leave me in something of a quandary.'

Corvis tensed, an act that in and of itself caused him no small amount of discomfort. 'Oh?'

'Yes. You see, I expected you to be rather better off before we departed. I'm not entirely certain you're currently capable of outrunning a lethargic sloth.'

'Well, if I got the drop on him . . .'

'I'll have to carry you, I fear.'

You fear! I don't want you that close to me! I—'

'In addition to which,' he continued, ignoring Corvis' growing annoyance at his inability to complete a sentence, 'is the fact that I don't believe that either I, or Audriss, particularly wants you to have access to any real power at the moment. Since Khanda can't heal you, there's no need for you to keep hold of him.'

'Oh no you don't! I—'

By which point the other had already sidled up to him and cracked him across the jaw with a closed fist.

At full health, the Terror of the East *might* have reacted fast enough to stop it. As it was, he barely registered Khanda's sudden */Oh, sh—/* before he collapsed, unconscious, once again.

The journey to the Serpent's encampment was less unpleasant than Corvis' stay in the regent's dungeons, which was to say that it was only the *second* most miserable event of his life. His trio of liberators tossed his semi-conscious body onto a saddle, lashed his hands to the pommel to keep him from sliding, and rode swiftly into the night. They'd acquired for him a cloak, boots, tunic, and pants, and cleaned the worst of the filth off him, but made precious little further effort to make him comfortable. Now and again he spotted Sunder and a few spurs of bone jutting from the saddlebag of one of his so-called companions, and he assumed Khanda and the other component pieces of his armour could be found within as well. They did him no good at all where they were, though, and the Terror wasn't yet so irrational as to believe he had a chance of getting to them.

The constant pounding of hooves on the ground, the rise and fall of the horse beneath him, sent constant javelins of pain through him. Aggravated by the perpetual stretching and abuse, his wounds refused to close, vomiting fresh crimson whenever the ride grew rough. Shards of broken bone stabbed him from within at every step. One night, Corvis dismounted to find blood soaking through his shirt where there was no wound before. Upon examination, he realised, with no small amount of disgust, that a sliver of rib had actually cut him open from within. He'd grown so inured to the pain he hadn't even noticed it happening.

They rode through the heart of winter. It only snowed lightly, and that was something to be grateful for, but it was a small favour at best. The cold made him lethargic, and the frigid air set his wounds to aching, throbbing in time with the steady plodding of his horse.

They rode for perhaps a week, passing snow-coated woods and villages lying largely abandoned, maintaining a pace Corvis would have found trying at the best of times. He could no longer differentiate one injury from another, and he found himself maneuvering through the day in a daze, the road fringed with visions that had no place beyond the confines of his dreams. The trees, though sparse and scattered beside the road, suddenly grew thickly around him, looming dangerously, and he was once again riding through the ever-tightening tunnel in the forest of Theaghl-gohlatch, the sidhe cackling madly from all sides.

'Not a pleasant place,' Tyannon said from where she walked casually beside him, clad in a light summer dress despite the frost coating the road. She didn't leave any footprints behind her. 'I'm glad I didn't bring the children.'

'You're not here,' Corvis said, trying to blink her away.

'You're probably right,' his wife replied with a shrug that set her brown hair dancing in ways that always captivated him. 'On the other hand, you're not really here, either,' she added, pointing to the darkening trees. 'Or maybe it would be more accurate to say that here isn't you.'

'I know that. I think. So, since you're sort of here, what do you want?'

'A million gold nobles and the meaning of life.' It was an old joke, one they'd shared since before they were wed. Hearing it now cheered Corvis considerably.

'Maybe,' not-Tyannon said seriously, 'I ought to ask you that question.'

'At this point? I just want to lie down and sleep for a month or three. I hurt, Tyannon. I hurt more than I ever thought possible.'

'You'll get through this, Corvis,' she told him seriously, her soulful eyes staring into his own, and the warlord found himself wanting to believe his wife truly stood before him. Gods, he hadn't seen her in so long! 'You'll get through it, and you'll come back to us. I love you.'

'Will you, though?' he asked, voice cracking. 'Will you love me after I kill your brother?' It was the first time he'd put his reluctant conclusion into words.

'Jassion? Why would you kill Jassion?'

Corvis sighed. 'He's Audriss, Tyannon. I don't know how it happened, or why, but Jassion is Audriss.'

'Oh.'

They walked in silence for a few moments. Then the hallucination frowned. 'If it's true, Corvis, then you do whatever you have to do. I'll understand.'

'I hope you will,' he said sincerely.

'I have to go soon,' she told him. 'You're almost there.'

'We can't be,' he protested. 'Audriss is supposed to be at Pelapheron! We've only been travelling a week or so.'

'Good-bye, Corvis. Do what you must, but remember something, sweetheart. Things change. Sometimes when you want them to, sometimes when you don't. But things *do change*. Remember that. And remember, we love you.'

And then it was all gone: Tyannon, the woods, everything. He was once again riding his horse, his body screaming at him, on a frost coated road with the sun dipping into the west and the first fires of a huge encampment appearing on the horizon.

Corvis, the Terror of the East, buried his mottled face in his aching hands and wept.

The same tent, enormous enough to encompass an entire cottage and to house a large family in comfort. The same long table, spread with what might as well have been the same papers, accompanied by the same chairs, the same bed, the same iron maiden. The leader of Corvis' 'rescuers' led the mangled prisoner into the tent, bowed once, and departed.

He'd been abandoned just inside the flap – what would, were the canvas dwelling a more permanent structure, have qualified as the foyer. The chairs were well beyond reach. He had nothing even to lean upon, let alone sit in. But whatever it took, however deeply Corvis dug into the dregs of his strength, he *would* stand tall. He would show no weakness here, not in front of . . .

'By the gods, Lord Rebaine, you look positively dreadful. I'm afraid the months since our last encounter have not been kind to you.'

'Audriss, with all due respect – which is to say, none at all – can we please cut through the crap?' The warlord's voice was strong, steady, far more so than it should have been. *No weakness.* 'You and I both know that my condition comes as no surprise to you at all, seeing as you were the one who caused it.'

'I? It wasn't I who . . .' The flat-black mask tilted as the man within examined his adversary. 'Ah, the hell with it. Whatever conclusion you've come to, you're welcome to it. I don't care.' The tendrils of his cloak floated behind him, ghostly streamers wavering in unconscious mimicry of Mithraem's mists, as he advanced on his prisoner. 'Tell me, Rebaine, do you know why you're here?'

'Absolutely.'

'And why is that?'

Corvis smiled through battered lips. 'Because I don't, at the moment, have the strength to run the hell away.'

The stone helm tilted. 'Are you trying to be funny, Rebaine?'

'What can I say? I've been hanging around with Khanda too long. While we're at it, what are *you* doing here? From what little I overheard during my stay in your duke's dungeons, I'd have figured you'd still be trying to take Pelapheron.'

Despite the obscuring mask, Corvis could actually *hear* the man scowl. 'Yes, I'll have to admit you won that one on points, Rebaine. Very neat. You cost me more men at Pelapheron than I'd lost in the entire campaign.'

'So why aren't you there?'

'Because Pelapheron isn't worth it. Oh, I could've taken it the next day with little difficulty. The defenders were thinned out and demoralised by Mithraem's Endless Legion, and your ragtag little army wasn't about to face them again, either, I assure you. But it would have cost more men, and I think I've lost quite enough as it is. We simply moved on.'

The ache in Corvis' face couldn't prevent his jaw dropping in astonishment. 'You left an enemy stronghold behind you? Intact? I've been battling an idiot!'

'Hardly.' With a deliberate show of nonchalance, the Serpent strode to the table. He pulled out the nearest chair and sat. 'I'd offer you a seat,' he said magnanimously, 'but it's such a chore to clean bloodstains from the upholstery. I'm sure you quite understand.'

'Quite' was the strained reply between clenched teeth.

'I'm so glad. Rebaine, Pelapheron is no danger to me. Its forces are shattered, in disarray. They've plenty to do without harrying me. Assuming they're not too busy celebrating my departure, they have rebuilding to do, and it is, after all, the heart of winter. They're short on food and supplies as it is. No, my friend, I've left nothing at my back that could possibly pose a real threat.'

He didn't say as much, but Corvis was fairly sure Audriss included *his* army in that assessment as well.

'It's getting late, Audriss, and I'm just a bear if I don't get a full night's sleep these days. Why don't you just get to the point?'

The Serpent pressed the tips of his fingers together, the green-and-pewter ring flashing in the dancing firelight. 'Such bravado, Rebaine. You and I both know it's taking everything you've got to keep from keeling over. Why should I not just keep you standing there until you collapse?'

'Because you've got other entertainments at your disposal. You didn't waste your time and effort bringing me here to watch me suffer. You could have done that back in the dungeons.'

'I haven't the first notion of what you're talking about,' Audriss said in a monotone, clearly indifferent as to whether the prisoner believed him. 'But you're right. You're here now for the same reason you were here the first time.'

Corvis forced a grin. 'You're offering me a partnership again?'

'Not exactly.' Audriss sighed. 'This would have been so much easier if you'd agreed then, Rebaine, but at this point, I don't need you anymore. What I want from you now is Selakrian's spellbook.'

'You wanted it then. Why do you think I'd change my mind now?'

'Because, my dear Terror, I can do things to you here that will make your experiences over the past few weeks positively joyful by comparison. I have – shall we say, *unique* – tools and techniques at my disposal. I can assure you, and I mean this in all modesty, that I will get what I want from you. It is entirely a matter of when.'

'You're not impressing me, Audriss.'

'No, I imagine not.' The warlord snapped a black-gloved finger, and a pair of heavily armoured soldiers appeared at the flap. 'Take our guest someplace secure. I want to give him the remainder of the night to think.' Audriss' eyes locked on Corvis' own. 'Rebaine, understand something. I would enjoy nothing better than to see you spend your last days in torment. You've caused me no end of problems, and the idea of paying them back in full is more than a little appealing. But I want that book more than I want your blood. You know the power I have available.' He clenched his left hand and held out his fist in emphasis – Corvis' gaze was drawn, unwillingly, toward the emerald ring. 'Work past your bravado, and consider what I – what *we* – can do to you.'

Despite himself, Corvis shuddered.

The Serpent nodded. 'Good. I'll expect an answer by morning. Do try to have a good night, yes?'

'Corvis!'

He struggled upward through a sea of dreams, fighting currents determined to drag him back into the depths of sleep and worlds of the mind, where the light could not reach and the constant pain was nothing but a fading memory of past lives.

'Corvis!'

'No,' he mumbled through swollen lips. 'Lea' me 'lone.'

'Corvis, wake up!'

Didn't they understand? He didn't *want* to wake up! This and only this – submerged in the dreaming – was all he had left, his final refuge from the agonising wounds that were, if Audriss could be believed, merely a prelude to far more unpleasant things to come.

And besides, the Serpent had promised him until morning, and while the heavy canvas of the tent lacked windows, it was thin enough to show the difference between night and day.

A tent. The part of Corvis already awake scoffed in disgust. It was a humiliating notion, the thought he was so broken and beaten that Audriss considered a tent, with a single pair of guards outside, sufficient to hold the Terror of the East.

Almost as humiliating was the fact that Audriss was absolutely right. His wounds still refused to close. Bruises grew darker, rather than fading. Broken bones, aggravated by constant movement, abraded one another as they moved within him, and would not heal.

He'd begun to wonder if he wasn't dying. And, finally, to wonder if it wasn't for the best.

And then, that voice, tugging at him through the layer of slumber into which he'd deliberately burrowed. He tried to swat it away, like an offending bug, and the pain lancing through his arm did more to awaken him than the constant urgings of the invisible stranger.

'Corvis! Gods damn it, Corvis, wake up!'

'I'm awake!' he finally hissed, curled tightly around his aching arm, teeth clenched against the scream of pain trying to burst from his throat.

'Gods, Corvis, you look awful! What did they do to you?'

'What didn't they do to me?' he grumbled bitterly, eyes dancing as they struggled to pierce the darkness within the tent. 'Where are you? *Who* are you? What the hell do you want with—'

'Corvis, it's me!'

The voice finally sank into his sleep-fogged brain. 'Seilloah?'

'In the flesh. Umm, so to speak.'

'Gods, how did you get here? Where—'

'I'm not actually here, Corvis. And don't step back. You'll crush my proxy.'

'Your . . .' Corvis froze as something small and hairy brushed his ankle. 'You're talking to me through a rat?'

'Best I could do, Corvis,' Seilloah whispered via the rodent. 'It needed to be small and inconspicuous, and I don't have Rheah Vhoune's way with bugs.'

'Seilloah, rats can't talk. How are you—'

'Corvis,' she replied patiently, 'listen to yourself. Are you telling me you've no problem accepting the fact that I can mind-control a rat, but it bothers you that I can make it speak?'

'I guess,' he rasped around a bloody cough, 'it is sort of silly, isn't it?'

'Gods, Corvis,' Seilloah said softly, 'you're a mess. I'm so sorry you—'

'Don't. It was my choice, not yours.' He took a deep breath, hawked, and spat the last of the clinging gunk from his throat. 'What happens now?'

'Now we get you out of here.'

Corvis shook his head, wincing as the movement brought a new surge of agony. 'Seilloah, we can't risk the men it would take to stage a rescue.'

'I'm not talking about a rescue. I'm talking about an escape.'

'Seilloah, look at me. I don't even know . . .' He swallowed as the thought well and truly hit home. 'I don't even know if I'll survive much longer, even without Audriss' tender ministrations. I can barely stand. There's not a chance—'

'I can heal you.'

'What?' In his incredulity, Corvis allowed his voice to rise. He collapsed, feigning sleep, as the flap shot open and one of the guards thrust a head and a small lantern into the tent. The man, flat-featured and ugly as an ogre's wedding, glared irritably at the prisoner, who appeared to be mumbling and crying out in his sleep. Grinning a browned and gap-toothed grin at the misery within, the guard withdrew.

Corvis watched the flap through narrowed lids until he was sure the ape was gone. 'Seilloah,' he resumed, whispering softly, 'how? These injuries . . . well, lesser wounds have proved beyond you in the past, and that was when you could actually touch your patient. Trying to do this while you're channeling through a proxy is insane! You'll hurt yourself!'

'I did not,' she told him simply, 'have you dragged all the way back here to let you die at the Serpent's feet. We'll take it slow, we'll take it careful, and we'll make do.'

'Have me dragged . . . Seilloah, what are you—'

'Later! Now don't move.'

Corvis opened his mouth to protest, and froze as he felt something warm and furry with sharp claws crawling down the back of his shirt. 'Seilloah—'

'I need contact, Corvis. Just relax.'

'You're joking, right?'

There was a pause. 'Corvis, I'm afraid this won't be pleasant. I have to be slow and methodical about this, heal one injury at a time. Things are going to *move*.'

'Fabulous.' Corvis took a deep breath, held it, exhaled slowly. 'Let's do this.'

The process was 'not pleasant' in the same way Sunder was 'a little sharp'. Over the next two hours, some mad sculptor among the gods shoved his hands through Corvis' body, rearranged the damp clay of his innards, and then proceeded to jump up and down on them. Splinters of rib embedded in the flesh of his chest gradually worked themselves free, sliding back into place like homesick worms and melding together with sudden bursts of heat. Scabs and scars forming over improperly treated wounds shredded themselves as flesh and muscle flowed around them. And he not only felt, but *heard* the tectonic grinding as the broken bones worked themselves around to their normal positions, to bond with neighbouring fragments. Had there been any source of light in the tent, Corvis was certain he would have seen bulges and protrusions writhing across his limbs. His cheeks spasmed as the bruising and swelling faded; his eye, swollen and crusted shut for so many days, finally opened.

Fists clenched and teeth gritted, gurgling in the back of his throat, Corvis endured.

Finally, it was done. Corvis Rebaine lay on the canvas floor, the contours of the ground below him uncomfortable beneath his weight. He was exhausted, as tired as he could ever remember, and his whole body ached terribly.

But for the first time in what seemed an eon, he could breathe without pain. He could move without agony as his constant companion. He could see with both eyes – or could have, had it not been pitch black around him – and hear with both ears. Tentatively, he stood, and when he stumbled half-way up, his body threatening to fall, it was due only to fatigue. Tears – the only ones he'd cried in years, save for those he'd shed during his fever-induced hallucinations – gathered in the corners of his eyes as he fully registered that the pain was gone.

'Seilloah,' he said softly, 'I thought I'd never—'

'Corvis, don't.'

He smiled quietly in the darkness. 'Thank you.' Then, a bit more urgently, 'Are *you* all right? The strain of that spell . . .'

'Is beyond your imagination,' she told him, and Corvis couldn't ignore the tremour in her voice. 'I'm going to miss muster tomorrow morning,' she told him. 'I assume you don't have a problem with that?'

'Uh, no. No problem.'

'Good. I'd hate to have to kill whoever you sent to find me. Corvis, Khanda and Sunder are in Audriss' tent. I don't think you'll be able to—'

'Without Khanda, we've no chance. Relax, Seilloah. You've done your part. Now I have to do mine.'

'Corvis, you're not exactly at your best. You're tired, your body's been through some incredible stress, and—'

The warlord yanked open the tent flap and reached out. From the rat's point of view, a sudden burst of movement was followed by two gasps of shock, and then a single wet crunch as the guards' skulls met and made every effort to merge. Framed in the light of the moon, the silhouette turned back to the wide-eyed rodent.

'No, Seilloah, I'm not at full strength. But I'm a bloody sight closer than anyone expects me to be. I'm not going to do anything stupid, but I am going to make damn certain that Audriss recognises his mistake.'

'And what mistake would that be?'

'He got the Terror of the East very, *very* upset.'

CHAPTER TWENTY-FOUR

Marching beneath the bear-and-crown flapping weakly in the errant breeze, Lorum, Duke of Taberness and Regent Proper of Imphallion, passed through the broken gates of Denathere. Surrounded as he was by scores of soldiers, most of whom likely thought he was an idiot for entering the city at all, he found it difficult to see the devastation around him, even from atop his spirited mount. Nathaniel Espa rode to one side of him, Rheah Vhoune to the other, and all seemed subdued into silence by the weight of what they saw.

For hours that felt like minutes – or perhaps minutes that dragged like hours – Lorum surveyed the broken, ravished, and desecrated body of what had been Imphallion's second greatest city. Men, women, and children who would never again rise, never laugh or cry or work, lay scattered about the wreckage of once magnificent temples and ancient halls that were very nearly as irreplaceable.

And Lorum, who had already seen too much of the horrors of war for his age, found his tears evaporated by the growing heat of his fury. Soldiers and emissaries appeared and disappeared through the wall of guards, delivering reports and making requests, and the regent's expression grew ever harsher, ever more brittle. Abruptly he spun his warhorse with a terribly cry and broke into a gallop, practically trampling his own guards before they dived desperately from his path. Espa ordered the soldiers to remain while he and the sorceress followed.

Some streets away, in an alley almost blocked by Lorum's anxious horse, they found him. He stood at the end of the filthy byway, where even the stench of human misery nearby had not overwhelmed the reek of rotting garbage, slamming his fist over and over into a broken stone wall until blood began to leak through the joints in his steel gauntlet.

'Your Grace?' Rheah began, sliding from her horse and moving down the alley, Espa two steps behind. 'I know that this is horrible, but you need—'

'Horrible, Rheah? Is that what this is?' The young regent spun, and where the sorceress and the knight expected tears, they found a jaw clenched in murderous rage. 'I think it's a damn sight more than horrible!'

'I understand, Your Grace,' Espa said gruffly. 'This is among the worst I've seen. But it's over. Rebaine's fled. He—'

'You don't understand.' Lorum sighed and slumped back against the wall, staring at something over their heads that only he could see. 'This isn't about the bodies and the burning and the destruction, Nathaniel. I've seen enough of that in this gods-damn war.'

'Then what—?' Rheah began.

'It didn't have to happen!' Lorum leaned forward, gesticulating with his right hand before clutching it painfully to his chest. 'We've known he was heading this way for weeks, maybe months! If the damn Guilds hadn't dragged their feet, if they'd bloody well let us – let *me*,' he corrected with a glance at Espa's glower, 'take command when we should have, we could have intercepted him before now!'

'You don't know that, Lorum,' the knight said gently. 'And if we'd faced them before Rebaine fled, before they were demoralised and disorganised, there's no telling—'

'And that, too,' the regent interrupted. 'Word of Rebaine's disappearance is only just now spreading through the armies – and I've *already* had two Guild emissaries demanding I return command of their forces. We haven't even *secured* the damn city, let alone started to help the people rebuild, but do they care?

'Maybe . . .' Lorum sighed and looked down at his feet. 'Maybe Rebaine should have won.'

He heard the both of them gasp, looked up into Rheah's horrified eyes and Espa's furiously furrowed brow. 'At least someone would damn well have been in charge,' he growled. 'It can't have been worse than the Guildmasters' games, can it? Maybe then all this death would at least have meant something.'

'He's young,' Espa said swiftly as Rheah spun away. 'He's angry. He'll learn better.' But the sorceress was already gone. With a glare, Espa waved the regent toward him. Not speaking, neither meeting the other's gaze, they rode slowly back toward Lorum's soldiers.

Nathaniel Espa, as it turned out, had been *mostly* right. Lorum had calmed down quickly enough, and he'd come to truly understand, in the weeks, months, and years that had followed, why the Eastern Terror could not have been allowed to win, that a warlord like Corvis Rebaine could never be permitted to rule. The regent had swallowed his distaste and worked alongside the Guilds – though it had been a near thing – even learning to argue against those nobles, like Jassion of Braetlyn, who believed as he once had.

But even to this day, Lorum didn't think he'd been *entirely* wrong, and wondered how much better things might be if *someone* – the *right* someone, not someone like Rebaine – were truly able to rule.

And right now, the Guilds certainly weren't doing a whole hell of a lot to change his mind.

'Can I have your attention please? Can I . . . ladies and . . . Ah, the hell with it. Rheah, would you mind?'

As she'd done once before, Rheah Vhoune stepped to the front of the dais, traced several intricate patterns in the air with her fingers, and spoke her words of power. And as before, the shock wave blasting through the crowd – setting flesh to stinging and ears to throbbing – instantly grabbed the undivided attention of what was previously an unruly, unlistening mob.

Where she'd last been forced to take such measures in the hall of a single Guild, she stood now upon the podium in Mecepheum's great Hall of Meeting. Where she'd previously addressed the disorderly mass of humanity that was the Merchants' Guild, she now faced an entire pack of Guild-masters and nobles, representing every Guild of influence and every major territory throughout Imphallion. And where she'd once come near to deafening a similar crowd for the sake of a single Guildmaster, she now drew their attention to the Regent Proper of Imphallion, His Grace, Duke Lorum of Taberness.

When the sudden booming finally rebounded off the far walls and faded away, Lorum nodded politely to Rheah and stepped to the fore. Dressed again in formal navy, the great bear and broken crown gleaming gold upon his tabard, he looked every inch the noble.

To his right sat Rheah Vhoune and Nathaniel Espa, to his left, Baron Jassion of Braetlyn and Duke Edmund of Lutrinthus. Before him, crowded into various chairs, benches, and pews, was the hostile and unwavering sea of men and women, all of whom were determined that, regardless of what was happening outside these city walls, the regent himself was the real enemy.

Only a single chair, deliberately pushed apart from the rest of the room, remained vacant in the otherwise congested chamber. A ceremonial seat, coated in dust, it had lain empty at every meeting of the Guilds for hundreds of years. It stood as a symbol, intended to remind them that they were incomplete, that even the power of the Guilds was not unbreakable. Most of them considered it a misuse of space.

Once upon a time, it housed the representative of the Sorcerers' Guild, until the day Selakrian threw down that organisation, declaring that such a gathering of powers was dangerous to all, wizard and common man alike. Some thought it heroic; others felt that the greatest magic user ever known had simply considered the Guild a threat. Whichever the case, that day saw the last attempt at organisation among the wizards' community.

Lorum watched Rheah Vhoune's eyes flicker, as they so often did, to the old and decrepit red cushions. It was, she'd once told him, why she had joined the Merchants' Guild, why she was so determined to master the ins and outs, the nooks and crannies, the tiniest details of Guild operation. Soon – when this nonsense with Audriss and Corvis Rebaine was over – she intended to seat herself in that chair, the first members of a fledgling Sorcerers' Guild around her.

Lorum wasn't entirely certain how he felt about that idea, but that was for later. The stubborn, mule-headed morass of Guildmasters and lords was *now*.

'Now that I have your attention,' Lorum said, hands clasped behind his back, 'I have something to say. We—'

'Why are you bothering, Lorum?' a voice shouted from the rear. Salia Mavere, priestess of Verelian the Smith and councilwoman of the Blacksmiths' Guild, rose to her feet. A large woman, with the heavy musculature common to the profession, she wore her dark hair short, and dressed in the formal robes of her religious office, emblazoned with the hammer and anvil. 'You know damn well the Guilds won't hand over our armies to you. You've asked us about three dozen times now over the past months, and you still refuse to accept our answer. I've worked with solid iron bars less dense than you seem to be.' There was general acclaim and no small amount of chuckling from the crowd.

'And the fact that Audriss is nearly here, his armies no more than a few days' march from our gates, isn't enough to make you reconsider?' Lorum asked calmly.

The laughter died away, and Salia's face grew tight, but she shook her head. 'Lorum, no one here denies the need to defend ourselves. But we can do it without granting you full command over the armies. We made that mistake once, remember? You took three years to give us back our rightful authority.'

'And if I had not done so at all,' Lorum snapped, his patience giving way, 'we wouldn't be in this predicament now!'

With a deliberate exhalation, he forced his features to relax, clasping his hands once more behind him. 'But that's behind us,' he said more calmly. 'So even the threat of the Serpent will not make you reconsider?'

'As we've told you time and time again, Your Grace,' Salia told him.

'Then what of Corvis Rebaine? Surely you acknowledge the need for a unified authority to defend against the Terror of the East!'

'Rebaine,' the priestess scoffed, her sentiments once more echoed in the mumbling of those around her. 'We've all heard that particular rumour, Lorum. There are those,' she continued slyly, 'who have accused you of making it up yourself to give some extra weight to your case. I'd never believe such a thing myself, of course, but I felt you should know. If you continue to insist on this, it may erode what support you *do* have. I . . . What's that?' She gaped, as did the entire assembly, at the dull black object Rheah Vhoune produced from nowhere and placed in the regent's hand. Smiling grimly, Lorum held it over his head for all to see:

A dark metallic shape, with a yellowed bone spike protruding from it, the mirror image of the spaulder Espa hurled from the battlements at Pelapheron.

'Is there anyone here,' Lorum asked simply, 'who does not know what this is?'

Had the silence grown any thicker, the duke's ears must surely have burst from the pressure.

'Is there anyone here,' he began again, his voice suddenly harsh, 'who truly believes I, or Lady Rheah, would fake or forge something of this magnitude?'

Surreptitious gazes danced through the assembly. A few

present were suspicious enough to believe just that. But none was willing to speak out on his or her own, and none willing to be the first. So each turned from the imploring glances of compatriots, and the chamber remained silent.

'Rebaine was *here*!' Lorum told them, his voice thundering through the room. His right hand gestured violently, chopping downward in cadence with his words as though he would batter the very air into submission. 'Imprisoned in the cells beneath my own castle!'

The silence finally shattered as the throng erupted into disjointed exclamations, oaths, questions, and demands. Like a wall, Lorum stood, letting the confusion and rage and fear of the crowd wash over him. Then he signalled, a simple crook of a finger. Rheah Vhoune rose once more, hands raised.

It was, as the duke anticipated, sufficient. The throng quieted once more, glaring balefully at the sorceress.

'Rebaine *was* held here,' he reiterated, speaking calmly but clearly. 'He is here no longer. He escaped.'

The crowd buzzed angrily but restrained itself from another full outburst.

'Escaped, with outside help.' The regent's piercing gaze swept the room. Several of the onlookers could have sworn they felt their hair rustle as it passed over. 'A small group of men — we don't know exactly how many. But we *do* know they killed several guards on the way out, guards found drained of blood.' He scowled darkly. 'I think we all know what that means. And who was behind it.'

'Then it is all true!' The voice belonged to Bidimir Vrenk, a scrawny, whiny-voiced scarecrow of a man. Dressed to make even a rainbow look subdued, he carried a gold-engraved harp slung over his shoulder. Vrenk represented the Minstrels' Guild, and as much as for his skill with harp and lute, he was known for his unfortunate habit of speaking as he believed the heroes of yore spoke, inspired by the hundreds of ballads and epics he'd read in his time. Vrenk either failed to realise he sounded the idiot, or simply didn't mind. 'The Terror and the Serpent are in league, one with the other! Can we do nothing to avert the doom creeping upon us from the long night?'

Lorum rolled his eyes. 'Audriss has been spotted leading the main body of the troops. Rebaine himself travels with a smaller division, less than a day behind the main force. An elite division, we assume.

'The bulk of the army will be here in a matter of days. We are facing not only a force numbering upward of twenty thousand, accompanied by ogres, gnomes, and the Endless Legion. We are facing the combined might, the combined magics, and the combined knowledge of Rebaine and Audriss.'

The regent slammed a fist upon the lectern, and the old wood cracked audibly beneath his blow.

'We've no more time for this!' he shouted. 'No more bickering! No more politics! *No more*! We stand as *one*! *One* army, *one* authority, *one* community!

'Or we die.' Once more, the duke grew quiet, speaking so softly that the assembly now strained to hear. 'Mecepheum will fall. We will fall. The Guilds, the nobles, all of us. And Imphallion . . .' His voice trailed off, then resumed. 'Imphallion, too, will fall.

'We survived the Terror of the East almost twenty years ago. We did so *only* because we provided a single, cohesive front. If we are to survive him now, we must do the same.

'I call for a vote of this Assembly. Think hard on your choice here today, my friends. Think very hard. This will be the last time I ask this of you. Choose well, and there will be no need to do so again. Choose poorly, and go to your graves, content with the knowledge you have maintained the "sovereign rights" of your Guilds, and your houses – and all it cost you was your homes, your kingdom, and your lives.

'Let us vote.'

'Damn him!'

Fingers clenched in impotent fury, Audriss peered through the thinning smoke that hung across the dawn like morning mist. Around him, men tiredly trod from the nearby stream, a line of ants feeding their colony, buckets clasped in white-knuckled grips. Before him, atop a small hillock, lay the charred and sodden remains of what was once his massive tent. From the ashes of the canvas climbed occasional serpents of smoke, spawned of a few smoldering flickers not yet extinguished. Here and there protruded the scorched leg of a table or chair, the blackened corner of the iron maiden. His papers, his plans, his notes – all gone.

/*It could have been worse,*/ Pekatherosh noted clinically, /*It could just as easily have been you, not merely your furniture.*/

'Hardly. It takes more than a simple fire . . .' The Serpent trailed off into dark mutters. 'This is *very* upsetting. All the things I'd prepared for him over the next few days . . . such a waste!'

/*So tell Corvis. Send a messenger or something. He's a reasonable fellow. I'm sure he'll come running right back once you've explained the situation to him.*/

'You saw him, damn it!' Audriss erupted, gesticulating contentiously. 'He couldn't *move*, let alone escape! He killed . . . How many men did he kill?'

/*The guards on his tent, another who apparently stumbled over him while he was creeping up on* your *tent, and three more on his way out. Or rather four, since it's unlikely Evral will survive another day.*/

'Six or seven men. Not to mention stealing his equipment back from *my own tent* and setting the bloody thing on fire!' Behind featureless stone, Audriss scowled furiously. 'He had help, Pekatherosh. He must have.

'They lied to me. This is why they wanted him back here in the first place: so he'd be near enough for them to work their magics.'

/*You didn't suspect it might be a trick when they made their offer in the first place? You're not exactly the brightest star in the firmament, are you, Twinkles?*/

'I underestimated them,' Audriss admitted in a low growl. 'Look at everything we've built here, Pekatherosh. Imphallion has never seen an army such as mine, not even during Rebaine's own campaign. No one has come close to what we're about to accomplish.

'But I have no illusions, demon. This isn't about a cause. This is about me, and the fact that I can pay or otherwise compensate those who follow. If I fell on the field of battle tomorrow, this entire army would evaporate like so much steam.'

/And you assumed Rebaine's people were the same. That they would fall apart before they could make any real effort at retrieving him./

'I did. It is not a mistake I intend to repeat.'

/I'm so glad. There are so many new mistakes you've yet to make, I'd hate to see you wasting your time on old ones./

The Serpent glared at the gleaming ring. 'I don't suppose you'd care to say something useful for a change, instead of just being a bloody nuisance, would you?'

/That would be a novel experience, wouldn't it? Might be interesting./

'Good. I—'

/On the other hand, there's something to be said for consistency./

A pause, punctuated only by the gnashing of teeth and a subaudible murmur that might, or might not, have qualified as speech.

/I'm sorry, I don't believe I caught that./

'Never you mind.' Without warning, Audriss lashed out and grabbed the nearest soldier, dragging the wide-eyed fellow by his collar. 'Find my heralds,' the warlord said coldly. 'Tell them to call for general assembly and then to break camp. I want to be at Mecepheum before the month is out.'

'Yes, my lord!' the man acknowledged, grateful to have escaped the dozen unnamable dooms that flashed through his head when the Serpent seized him. Except . . .

'Um, my lord?' he asked tentatively, mouth dry, palms sweating.

From the midnight hood, a gloss black mirror stared at him. 'Yes?' The warlord's voice was calm, neutral, inhuman.

'I . . . I'm sorry, my lord, but you're . . . that is, you're still . . .'

'Ah.' Audriss released the soldier's tunic, taking a moment to pat the worst of the wrinkles from the material. 'Is this better?'

'I . . . Yes, my lord, much better.'

'Then I suggest you make haste.'

'At once, my lord!' He all but sprinted into the encampment, knocking over breakfast pans, stepping on feet, and drawing a veritable retinue of curses in his wake.

'As soon as we're fully assembled, Pekatherosh, he's all yours.'

/Really? Not to sound ungrateful, Audriss, but may I ask why?/

'I want my people scared of me, but not so much so that they can't function. Any man that nervous around me is useless.'

/If you say so./

'I do indeed. I say, too, that it's about time we began the last phase of this little endeavour, Pekatherosh. We'll be standing at the gates of the capital in two weeks. It wouldn't do to be unprepared. Contact our friend; tell him it's time.'

/Are you sure? You yourself said it might raise unfortunate questions./

'Doesn't matter anymore, Pekatherosh. It doesn't matter at all. In two weeks, the Serpent's army will be camped outside the walls of Mecepheum.

'At that point, let Rebaine question whatever he wants. It won't help him now. And if he shows up at Mecepheum, well, he was the first to go after Selakrian's spellbook. Since it means so much to him, I'll be happy to show him what it can do.'

Corvis Rebain was clad in *most* of his infamous armour. The confining helm leered at him from atop the table, along with the heavy gauntlets, and the missing spaulder had been replaced from a standard suit, transforming his left shoulder into a single spot of bright and burnished silver amid the unrelenting black. He sat on a heavy stool and stared at the parchment reports scattered across the table without really seeing them. As had become unconscious habit, he rubbed absently at the fresh scar that pulled at the skin of his left cheek.

'Are these numbers accurate?'

'As best we can determine, my lord,' Losalis told him. 'I have only the scout's estimation to work with, but I've known the man for years. If he told me the grass was purple over the next rise, I'd be inclined to believe him.'

The warlord grimaced, the fingers of his right hand drumming miniature hoofbeats on the wood. 'Then Lorum's finally done it. He's forced the Guilds and the houses to cooperate.'

'So it would seem. I don't see any other way he could have fielded a force that size.' The looming man grinned through his beard. 'And all it took was an army camping on the doorstep. Threaten a man's home, it always brings out the protective instincts.'

'You've seen Audriss' army in action. How do you see it playing out?'

Losalis frowned thoughtfully. 'Without our interference, it'll be close. Once the Guilds finally hopped on board, they held nothing back. As it says there,' he gestured at the report, 'our best guess is that the regent can muster thirty thousand men. He won't field them all – he'll want to keep a good many back to defend the walls. Between numbers and fortifications, if all else was equal, I'd say Mecepheum could hold.

'But Audriss cheats. Considering the *types* of soldiers he can call on . . . well, he may find Lorum the toughest nut he's ever cracked, but he'll still come out ahead.'

'Then we'll just have to intervene, won't we?' Corvis observed. 'We wait until the battle's joined, and then hit their flank. Hard.'

'Umm, my lord, you *do* remember what I told you about Pelapheron, don't you?'

Corvis laughed. 'Relax, Losalis. I've been through a lot, but I haven't gone insane or senile. Not quite, anyway. Yes, I know it's the same tactic you utilised at Pelapheron. Audriss may even be expecting it. But so what? If our numbers are accurate, he can't afford to hold anything more than a token force back from the main battle. Even if he knows we're coming, he can't throw much at us to stop us. He doesn't have the manpower.' His smile grew tight. 'Go get some sleep. It's midnight, and I doubt Audriss plans to spend any longer camped on Lorum's doorstep than he has to. I imagine we'll see the first attack tomorrow morning. I want to be ready the instant our opportunity presents itself.'

Losalis departed with a swift salute.

'Well,' Corvis said to the empty room, 'you've been awfully quiet tonight. What's the matter? Not feeling well?'

I feel like hell.

'Oh, ha. Ha, ha. And, in case I forget to mention it later, ha.'

/*You're the one who asked the question.*/

'Seriously, Khanda. You didn't make a single comment the entire time Losalis and I were talking. For that matter, you haven't said much since we escaped from Audriss.' Corvis absently tapped a finger on the breastplate, close to where the pendant rested against his chest. 'If I didn't know any better, I'd think something was bothering you.'

/*And what, my porcine-brained companion, could have given you the impression that you* do *know better?*/

The warlord blinked and leaned back slightly in his chair.

'You mean something *is* bothering you? I thought you didn't let *anything* get to you.'

/*I doubt that.*/

'You doubt that I thought nothing got to you?'

/*That you thought.*/

Corvis scowled. The demon was, if anything, even more pugnacious than usual. Utterly alien as the idea sounded, something really had upset Khanda. But it seemed unlikely that he'd admit it, and even less that he'd talk about it.

The Eastern Terror decided, reluctantly, to let it go. What else could he do?

So what he said instead was, 'Well, as utterly stupefying as the notion may be to you, Khanda, I've got another idea.'

/Will wonders never cease? Or will I merely cease to wonder?/

'Right. Anyway, after what I've been through for the past few months, I think it best to minimise the possibility of us being separated again.'

/You enjoy having me around. I'm touched./

'You're not going to make this easy, are you?'

/If I was easy, you wouldn't respect me in the morning./

Corvis, who felt as if he'd just danced six or seven times around the tent, sensed that he was rapidly losing control of the situation. Determined to stay on track, he cleared his throat. 'My point,' he said firmly, 'is that it's too easy to lose a necklace, or to have it taken off. I think it's time we – and by "we," of course, I mean you – expand our options.'

/What did you have in mind?/

'A bracer, I think. Something thin enough to fit under the armour. No clasps, either. I don't want it to be possible to remove without your cooperation. One solid piece.'

/That just means anyone who wants me badly enough will simply cut off your arm./

'Khanda . . .'

A humming sounded from beneath Corvis' armour. He felt a spot of heat form against his chest, then slither across his body and down his left arm, where it settled just above the wrist. Swiftly the heat faded, and he could feel the unfamiliar pressure of a thin metal band.

/Is this what you had in mind?/

'Actually, I was wondering if you could bring the heat back for a minute. I'm not as young as I used to be, and this weather is murder on the joints.'

/You want heat?/

'Umm, no. Now that I think about it, I believe that maybe

you're not the best person to ask.' Corvis unfastened the straps holding the metallic sleeve of his armour in place, and let it fall to the table.

The blood-red jewel was now fastened not to a thin chain of silver, but to three narrow bands encircling Corvis' arm. It boasted no latch, no clasp, and the bands would never fit over his hand. As he'd wished, the bauble couldn't be removed without taking part of the arm along with it.

Of course, quite a few people would be delighted to do just that.

Corvis Rebaine finally fell asleep. His right hand clenched in slumber about the unaccustomed pressure on his left arm, he dreamed quiet dreams of dismemberment.

Maintaining an unbroken stream of curses, Corvis ducked beneath the first sword, knocked the second aside with an armoured forearm, and slammed Sunder into the chest of the man before him. Armour, flesh, and bone split as one, and the soldier fell back, blood pouring from him in a thick torrent.

The second warrior – a large bearded man who resembled a shorter, lighter-hued version of Losalis – tried to thrust forward with his own blade before the warlord recovered from his killing stroke. The Terror dropped to a crouch, left hand palm-down in the snow behind him, as the razor-edged blade passed over his head. Leaning most of his weight on that arm, he lashed out with a kick. The bone spines on his greaves punched through the soldier's leather leggings, shredding the skin and muscle of his calf. Corvis scrambled to his feet even as the crippled warrior fell screaming to the ground. A single, efficient stroke with Sunder, and the screaming stopped.

/Left!/

Corvis' curses grew even more profane as another band of soldiers, half a dozen of them, charged doggedly from the flank, swords held high.

It was just possible that Corvis was good enough to take on all six, despite the fatigue of two solid hours of battle. It was also possible, and substantially more probable, that he wasn't.

Wishing it hadn't come to this, Corvis gave a subvocal command and obliterated all six in a burst of hellfire. When the smoke and the steam finally cleared, twelve charred legs, seared clean at the knees, lay amid a huge circle of ash and molten steel.

/Smells yummy./

'Shut up!'

Through the nearby trees and atop a winter-white rise, Corvis saw Davro and several ogres battling a squad that outnumbered them four to one. Those odds probably didn't bother the ogres, but there was a real danger of losing at least one or two of them. Realising that he'd probably feel guilty if it was Davro who fell, the warlord sprinted toward the hill, smashing foes from his path with great sweeps of Sunder.

One of the ogres heard the crunch of footsteps, lowering his weapon only when he saw who it was. '*Davro!*' he called out in the cyclopean giants' native tongue. '*Nev raheth, ukrahkan Rebaine ma et!*'

'*Che,*' Davro answered, jamming his blade through his enemy's defensive parries and into the soldier's skull.

'Fancy meeting you here,' Davro said neutrally as he moved to fight back-to-back with the man who'd dragged him into this whole mess. Corvis could feel the enormous muscles tensing and flexing behind him as they each faced down an opponent, axe and sword rising and falling in unison.

'Silly me,' the ogre continued, yanking his blade from a stubbornly clinging rib cage, 'but I thought you and Losalis said something about Audriss not having enough men to intercept us. Obviously, I misheard you. We ogres don't hear very good.' He paused to decapitate a chain-mail-clad warrior trying to edge around them. 'Comes from only having one eye, I expect.'

Corvis ignored the comment in favour of handling the endless flow of enemy soldiers.

Sunder parried a stroke that would have cleaved Corvis' skull in two, helm or no helm, had it connected. A quick thrust sent the butt-cap of the axe into the groin of the man who'd tried to split him, and a twist of the weapon finished the job. Corvis reached down with his left hand, grabbed the edge of his cloak, and tossed, so the next soldier charging up behind the first got a faceful of heavy wool. The soldier batted it aside just in time to see Sunder coming up at him. His head bounced into the snow even as Corvis twisted to slam the axe into yet a third soldier . . .

Who crumpled *toward* Corvis rather than away from him. The man's feet spasmed out from under him, and his weight, augmented by the chain-mail hauberk he wore, hung entirely across the Kholben Shiar. Corvis' fingers clenched, strained . . . released. The dead body tumbled into the snow, Sunder efficiently buried beneath him.

'Oh, hell.'

Maybe there was no one in immediate striking distance. Maybe the ogres were keeping everyone busy enough he'd have time to recover the weapon. Maybe. . .

Corvis glanced around furtively, and then hurled himself aside, barely avoiding the edge of a broadsword.

His attacker was a coarse-featured man, his face made up entirely of crags and angles. A coat of chain protected his trunk, heavy leathers his legs and hands. Broadsword held high, a triumphant grin playing across his jaw, he advanced on his unarmed foe.

He was too close for Khanda to burn him without Corvis feeling the flames as well. The warlord dived forward, shoulder tucked into a roll. The armour's spines churned dirt and snow from the earth, and he came to his feet with his fist clenched tightly around the hair of the man he'd just decapitated.

The advancing soldier froze as Corvis twirled the head, a grotesque flail of bone and flesh. The gruesome weapon moaned eerily, air flowing through the mouth and gaping throat, as it spun once, twice, and then collided with sickening force against the soldier's own skull.

It might or might not have been a crippling injury, but the

point became moot as Corvis stepped forward, grasped the dazed man's throat in the tips of his fingers, and twisted. The soldier dropped, thrashing and very quickly dying, to the ground.

/I see you'll do just about anything to get ahead./

Corvis, who finally stood in a spot of calm, went to retrieve his axe. Shoving the ruined body aside with the toe of his boot, he reached for Sunder, surreptitiously taking the opportunity to kneel down and rest for just a few precious seconds.

I'm really, really *getting too old for this*, Corvis thought.

Fortunately for Corvis and his advancing age, the struggle had receded, leaving the flotsam of dead bodies heaped in piles where the tide of battle deposited them. Only one of the ogres had fallen, laid low by a pike through the midsection, but more than two dozen of the enemy had paid with their lives. The sphere of quiet now encompassed Davro and the others as well, and for a time, they could stop and breathe. The fighting flowed around them, never drawing near, as though they stood atop a single tiny island in some rough and deadly sea.

Davro knelt, cleaning the worst of the gore from his sword with handfuls of snow. Corvis merely shook Sunder twice and watched in morbid fascination as the blood and solids easily slid from the blade and splashed at his feet.

'Well, Davro,' the warlord began, 'I've got to say—'

He saw the sudden shock on Davro's face, heard Khanda's shout of */Look out!/* Even then, he wasn't quite fast enough.

He tried to duck, succeeding well enough that the heavy sword slammed into the side of his helm rather than cleaving through the softer armour protecting his neck. Blazing lights erupted before his eyes, and the world bucked under his feet. He heard a clattering sound from nearby, slowly realising it must have been Sunder falling once more from his grip. He staggered, mind reeling, eyes blinking. Two steps back, three, and Corvis found himself sitting in the snow, staring stupidly ahead. Stunned, he couldn't quite comprehend the significance of the heavy white cloak and hood his attacker wore, until he saw a dozen men, similarly garbed, rise from where they'd belly-crawled across the winter carpet.

Even as the ogres surged forward, calling upon Chalsene Night-Bringer while they moved to protect their fallen leader, the men charged to meet them, bellowing war cries with steaming breath. It was a suicide run, eleven humans against four maddened ogres. But they'd slow the ogres long enough for the remaining man to finish the job he'd begun. Unable to shake the lethargy and confusion caused by his head wound, Corvis watched through his iron-banded helm as death advanced on him, broadsword in hand.

And then something flashed past him, a blur of chain and leather and blonde hair. The oncoming soldier stopped short, his seemingly inexorable tread suspended by the whirlwind of sharpened steel in his path. Hatchets, one shinier and cleaner than the other, blazed in intricate patterns, a constantly moving yet unbreachable wall. The broadsword, never intended as a defensive weapon, parried desperately as, slowly but steadily, Ellowaine forced him away from the helpless Terror. The air resounded with the constant clatter of metal on metal, so swiftly it seemed to be snowing steel. Every time the sword intercepted one of the wicked hatchets, the other was already in motion, seeking the gap in the man's defenses, that mere instant of delay.

And then that instant was upon them both, and the clatter ended in a sudden meaty thunk.

Ellowaine decided the ogres had the situation well in hand – already more than half the camouflaged warriors were dead – and then briskly wiped her weapons clean on the dead man's cloak. She strode through the snow to stand beside Corvis, who finally shook off the worst of his bewilderment, though his head ached something fierce. He looked up gratefully as the thin mercenary crouched before him, carefully examining the helm to be certain it was undamaged and safe to remove.

'Thank you,' Corvis began sincerely, looking into her sharp features. 'I . . .'

'Teagan's dead,' she reported simply, her voice quavering briefly with the grief she forbade her face to show. 'An arrow. He never even had the chance to fight back.'

Corvis closed his eyes in a moment of respect. Annoying he may have been, but the man was one of his best field commanders. 'I'm sorry. I know you'd become friends.'

Apparently satisfied that the skull helm was indeed safe to remove, Ellowaine unfastened the straps. She glanced up once as Davro and the ogres approached.

'Can I help?' Davro asked.

'Do you know anything about battlefield medicine?' she asked him.

'I—'

'On humans?'

'Ah, no.'

'Then go find Seilloah. I'll do what I can in the meantime.'

The ogre nodded once, horn bobbing, and ran.

'Ellowaine,' Corvis began as she lifted the helmet up and set it roughly aside, 'this isn't necessary. It wasn't that bad a—'

'Shut up . . . my lord. We've already lost Teagan. If *you* die here, the army falls apart.'

/*So when did she become a convert to the cause?*/

'All right, Ellowaine,' Corvis said, ignoring the demon, 'do what you think best.'

He winced, biting his lip to keep from crying out, as she proceeded to poke and prod. 'Can you see all right?' she asked professionally.

'Fine. No concussion, I'd say.'

'Don't say. When I'm convinced, *I'll* say.'

Despite the pain, Corvis couldn't help but smile. 'Yes, ma'am.'

Ellowaine smiled, too, just a little.

'What I don't understand,' Corvis continued, as much to take his mind off the pain as anything else, 'is how Audriss managed this. He should barely have had the manpower to keep an eye on us, let alone stop us in our tracks. I—'

'It wasn't Audriss.'

'Beg pardon?'

Ellowaine scowled. 'You must have been hit harder than I thought. Lord Rebaine, Audriss did the same thing you did: he hired mercenaries. A lot of them.'

'Right,' Corvis agreed, still not catching her point. 'And?'

'Look at the bodies around you, my lord.'

He saw it as soon as he started looking, and if he hadn't been sitting he'd have kicked himself. These men were equipped identically: the same chain hauberks, the same leather pants, gauntlets, and boots, the same broadswords. None of the patchwork, 'use what you can afford or what you scavenge' gear he'd expect of mercenaries.

Further, these men willingly threw their lives away to ensure Corvis' own demise. Hardly the behavior of soldiers-for-hire.

'Military,' Corvis breathed, frowning. 'Audriss didn't send them. Lorum did.'

Ellowaine nodded curtly. 'He must have thought we were a separate unit of the Serpent's army. Maybe a special strike force or something.'

Corvis shivered. The snow-covered ground had leached the heat from his body, but he knew Ellowaine probably wouldn't let him up yet.

'Any idea who led the force?' he asked her.

'Some guy in black armour with what looked like a bloody fish on his tabard.'

'Jassion,' the warlord hissed. 'I wonder why he didn't come after me personally?' *And what, for that matter, is he doing here at all?* he added silently.

'Probably couldn't find you in the chaos,' she suggested.

'Maybe.' But Corvis, glancing down at his left wrist, didn't seem convinced. 'Any idea where he is now?'

'I imagine he's retreated with the rest of his men, assuming he's not dead in the snow somewhere. Why?'

'Just curious.'

'Well,' Ellowaine said, standing up and brushing snow from her knees, 'I think you'll be fine.' She reached down, helped the Terror of the East to his feet. 'It'll bruise up right nicely, but I doubt anything worse will come of it.' She poked a finger at his cheek. '*That's* going to leave a nasty mark, though. Where'd you pick that up?'

Corvis thoughtfully prodded at the scab on his cheek, the wound he'd been noting absently for days now, and frowned. Where *had* he picked it up? During his escape from Audriss' camp? No, he'd snuck up on most of the guards he'd killed, and the one he'd actually been forced to duel never landed any blows. He'd fallen several times on his way back to his own people, but never face-first. So when . . .

Corvis' eyes grew so wide that Ellowaine spun, expecting to see a horde of the enemy charging her unprotected back. 'What? My lord, what is it?'

But if he heard her at all, his face showed no sign of it.

It couldn't *be that. Could it*?

'Khanda?'

/*Oh, so you've finally deigned to remember that I'm here, have you?!*/

'Stow it. Why red?'

/*Excuse me*? And *she says that head wound isn't serious?*/

Through gritted teeth, Corvis asked again, 'Why are you red?'

Somehow, he got the impression the demon shrugged. /*That's the colour of the stone I was imprisoned in. Kind of fitting, in a way. I—*/

'Could you change it? Could you decide to be – oh, say, green?'

/*I don't like green.*/

'But could you do it?'

/*Well, sure. Why, have you decided I clash with your wardrobe?*/

Corvis closed his eyes and exhaled. *Of course . . .*

'Things change. Sometimes when you want them to, sometimes when you don't. But *things* do *change*.' That's what he'd hallucinated, what he'd told himself in Tyannon's voice. A part of him, apparently, had already figured it out, was just waiting for the rest of his brain to catch up.

They were in very deep trouble.

'We have to find Losalis and Seilloah,' he snapped at a truly puzzled Ellowaine. '*Now*.'

CHAPTER TWENTY-FIVE

'Not too bad,' Corvis acknowledged, his tone somehow conveying both *impressed* and *mildly disgusted* with equal faculty. He directed his mount to shift aside, clearing the dusty road so that yet another caravan of lumber and stone, smelling of sweat both human and equine, could trundle on past.

Tyannon raised her hand to her eyes, shading them from a sun that poured a cascade of brilliance over the world despite autumn's rapidly growing chill. For the length of several deep breaths, she stared at the outer wall of the city. It was, so far as she could tell, just a wall like any other.

Which might be why she finally responded with, 'It's a wall. Like any other.'

'My point exactly!' Corvis seemed almost to pounce on the comment, like a ravenous cat. 'Just a few months ago, these walls were so many heaps of broken rubble. The buildings beyond weren't much . . . better . . .' His commentary trailed off at the sharp narrowing of her eyes.

'My point,' he continued quickly, determined suddenly to move the topic away from his prior activities, 'is that the place looks pretty damn near to normal, doesn't it? They've done a remarkable job of rebuilding. Maybe Lorum actually grew enough of a spine to keep the whip on the backs of the Guilds.'

'Did you ever think that maybe the Guilds are financing the recovery on their own?' she asked darkly, her brow still furrowed and her gaze still clouded. 'Why would you just assume that, if they're doing something helpful, it *has* to be because the regent's forcing them?'

'Tyannon, do you know what city this is?'

Again she shaded her eyes to examine the looming structures. 'No,' she admitted finally. 'I can't say that I do.'

'And that, again, is my point. You're a nobleman's daughter, Tyannon, highly educated, yet this city isn't major enough for you to even know its name. When was the last time the Guilds voluntarily spent this sort of coin anywhere that wasn't a major financial centre?'

Tyannon grumbled and turned away, unwilling to concede the point but unable to argue it.

The sun coasted slowly overhead as they stood within the shadows of the walls, waiting for the day's traffic to subside before making their own entry through the narrow gates. And finally, Tyannon's curiosity wrestled her irritation into submission.

'Why does it matter to you, anyway?' she asked softly.

Corvis had to physically wrench his gaze off the city's gates. 'Because,' he told her slowly, his eyes as expressionless as the death's-head mask he no longer wore, 'if someone's actually, finally in charge – if it's the *right* someone – maybe everything I've done hasn't been entirely in vain.'

'With all due respect, my lord,' Losalis intoned in his deep, rich voice, 'you have gone absolutely stark-raving mad.'

Corvis, Losalis, Davro, Seilloah, and Ellowaine hurriedly assembled on a small rise overlooking Mecepheum. The battle raging below them was enormous, two opposing tidal waves of blood and steel crashing one against the other. Clouds of steam rose where hot blood splashed into cold snow, and the field was already thick with the dead and the dying.

'I know it sounds a bit reckless,' the Terror of the East

assured his second in command. 'It's not a decision I've come to lightly. But it's the only way. I have to get inside the city.'

'My lord,' Losalis pressed, 'every last person in Mecepheum, native or otherwise, would be more than happy to kill you on sight. They think you're behind all this, remember?'

'And you're not exactly inconspicuous,' Davro added, grasping one of the bone spikes between his thumb and forefinger and wiggling it. Corvis grimaced as his entire body shuddered.

'Believe it or not, I'd figured that much out for myself. I don't intend to wear the armour. Not at first, anyway.'

'You're carrying that monstrosity with you?' the witch asked incredulously. 'Corvis, you haven't been hiding a spare pack mule in your coin purse, have you?'

The warlord cast her a scathing glance. 'You, Seilloah, have been hanging around with Khanda and Davro too long. No, I'm not going to carry it. I'll just have Khanda shape it into something inconspicuous until I have need of it, like he did . . .' Corvis couldn't quite repress a shudder at the agonising memories. '. . . last time I came here.'

/Your wish is my command, Master./

'Thanks ever so.'

'I don't understand,' Losalis said gruffly. 'What do you hope to accomplish with this?'

'Audriss is already inside Mecepheum. I'm going after him.'

Ellowaine looked up sharply from where she'd stood brooding off to the side, a sudden spark in her eyes. 'How do you know that?' she demanded.

'I know what he's after.'

'He's after the whole city,' the ogre protested.

'True. But something else as well, and he can't afford to wait for the city to fall to get it. I'm going into Mecepheum, finding him, and killing him.'

/Hey, Corvis. Do you know what cities have a lot of? People. All Audriss has to do is follow your example and take off his

armour, and you'll never find him. It'd be like looking for a needle in a whole bunch of other needles./

'Not at all. I know who Audriss is.'

Before any of his stunned companions could find the presence of mind to speak, the Terror of the East moved on to other subjects.

'All right,' he told them, either missing or ignoring the various widened eyes and gaping jaws, 'here's how it'll play out. I'm going inside. Losalis, I wish I could take you with me. I can't easily think of anyone I'd rather have at my back. But I need you in command out here.'

The large man scowled, one hand idly scratching at his beard. 'I'm not happy with it,' he admitted. 'But you're in charge.'

'Good.' Corvis nodded. 'Seilloah, you're with me. I know they'll miss your healing out here, but I need all the magic assistance possible. We don't know exactly what Audriss and Pekatherosh are capable of, and Rheah Vhoune's around somewhere, too.'

The witch nodded in turn. 'Just give me a few minutes. I want to make sure Losalis's healers have a good stock of my salve before we go.'

'Make it quick. Ellowaine, you're with me, too. I need *someone* watching my back, and you're just about the best we've got. Hell, you saved my hide once today already.' Deliberately, Corvis locked his gaze with her own. 'But Ellowaine, until and unless I say otherwise, your job is to keep Audriss' goons off me. The Serpent himself is mine.'

'But—'

'Swear to that, or I find someone else.'

Sullenly, she swore.

Corvis faced the last member of the motley little band, and a strange, sad smile crossed his face. 'Davro, as you yourself pointed out, some of us aren't entirely inconspicuous. There's no way I can take you with me.'

'See how disappointed I am.'

'Davro, it's entirely possible I won't have the chance to say this later.' The ogre found himself mildly taken aback at the sudden sincerity in Corvis' voice. 'I'm sorry. I'm sorry I forced you into this. I'm sorry I risked destroying the life you'd built for yourself. Win or lose, whether I live or die, this battle is the last I'll ask of you. When it's over, regardless of the outcome, I release you from any and all vows. You're free.'

'Just like that?' Davro asked suspiciously.

'Just like that. When we're through here, you can go home. For good.'

The ogre was clearly trying to fight off the enormous, cat-and-canary grin growing ever larger on his jaw. 'Thank you, Corvis,' he said simply.

Oh, gods. Can we get moving already? If this gets any more cloying, I fear I may just have to vomit. And believe me, you do not *want to see a half-digested soul. And the* smell!/

'All right, all right, we're going.' Corvis closed his eyes in concentration for a moment, muttering under his breath the words of a simple transformation spell. A sudden surge of power flowed from the demon on his wrist, and the spell swelled, expanded, and strengthened. It wrapped around him in a phantom embrace. Metal and bone shrank, shifted, folded, and Corvis Rebaine stood in the snow, dressed in a hefty cloak, fur wraps, and thick leathers. Sunder hung loosely at his right hip, and Khanda perched tightly on his wrist, but every other detail of his garb had changed. Nothing about this lean, grey-haired warrior separated him from a hundred other mercenaries past their prime.

'Lord Rebaine,' Losalis said, 'I hate to bring this up, but if you don't come out of there alive, how are we all getting paid?'

'Oh, that little thing.' Corvis smiled, putting on his most reassuring face. 'If I don't make it out, Davro knows every-thing about your fee. He'll handle it.' Then, ignoring the murderous glare the one-eyed giant hurled his way, he clasped Losalis's good arm with his own. 'Luck and Kassek's favour, my friend.'

'And to you, my lord.'

'Ladies? Shall we?' And they were off, trudging through ankle-deep drifts of clinging snow.

'My lord,' Ellowaine began, 'I—'

'Ellowaine, as of right now, don't call me that. Let's not draw attention.'

'We can't exactly call you by name, either,' Seilloah pointed out.

'Oh, *now* you realise this?' Corvis asked sourly. 'You couldn't have thought of that back in Kervone, before you exposed me to that damn guard?'

Seilloah's glare was almost vicious enough to hide the slow flush of embarrassment in her cheeks.

'All right.' The warlord shrugged. 'Call me Cerris. I'm used to it.'

'All right, Cerris,' Ellowaine said hesitantly. 'Tell me how we get inside a besieged city without being noticed.'

'Why, simplicity itself, Ellowaine. We'll climb a tree.'

'Oh, of course,' she retorted sarcastically. 'How could I possibly have missed that? Seilloah, how did I miss that?'

Seilloah just shook her head.

'There,' Corvis announced cheerfully after an hour of leading his increasingly irritable companions around the perimeter of the raging battle. 'That one should do.' He gestured at a towering, snow-coated conifer with a discouraging dearth of low branches large enough to support a corpulent pigeon, let alone a trio of encumbered climbers.

Corvis had a solution for that, too, of course. He made liberal use of Khanda's magic to levitate them, one by one, to the higher branches, where Ellowaine and Seilloah found themselves clinging to the trunk with quiet desperation.

'What do you think, Khanda?' Corvis asked softly, standing atop a large limb. He peered, squint-eyed, across the bloodstained snow and crowded parapets, into the distant streets of Mecepheum. 'It's not very clear, but it is in line of sight. Can you do it?'

/If it was just you, no problem. With your two tagalongs . . . Yes, I can do it, but I won't be good for much immediately

386

afterward. It'd help if I had a snack waiting for me on the other side./

'No chance. We're not here to kill the population. Besides, it'd draw attention.'

/Fine, but if you get into a scrape I'm too exhausted to pull you out of, it's your funeral./

'You know, you're really obnoxious in the face of danger.'

/It's that whole immortality thing. Makes one a bit blasé about it all./ A moment passed. */Say, are you going to tell them ahead of time what you're planning to do?/*

Corvis concentrated once more, and they were swept by a sudden sense of falling, atrociously fast. The world blurred around them, and then they were standing inside the mouth of a dark and filthy alley off Mecepheum's main boulevard.

'Nope,' Corvis replied. 'Gives them less time to worry about it.' Then, repressing a chuckle at the slackened expressions on the faces of his companions, he set out at a brisk pace.

Even here, far from the walls, Mecepheum was clearly a community under siege. The street bustled with activity, the calls of vendors and the pervasive buzz of conversations replaced by grimly determined voices, shouted orders, and calls for help. The scent of the marketplace – that strange but universal mixture of bodies, meats, vegetables, and dyes – was absent, smothered by sweat, steel, and leather. Most of the citizens dashing back and forth carried water, bandages, and spare arrows for the soldiers on the walls. The snow, inches deep outside those walls, was almost nonexistent on the streets within, kicked aside and trampled into slush by the constant stir. On occasion, a gnome rose up – seemingly from solid stone – and darted from a darkened byway to drag away some unsuspecting soldier or citizen.

Corvis, Seilloah, and Ellowaine went largely unnoticed in the hubbub.

'My lo . . . ah, Cerris,' Ellowaine hissed, nudging him slightly to draw his attention from the crowd around him. 'You still haven't told us where we're going. Or what we're doing. Or who we're looking for.' She waited expectantly, and

Seilloah, striding behind them, stepped up her pace to be certain she could hear.

'You're right,' Corvis agreed. 'I haven't.'

Seilloah snorted once, and Ellowaine began turning a vegetative shade of purple.

'Ladies, listen to me.' Corvis dragged them to stand beneath a small awning protruding from a nearby shop. His voice cut through the bedlam of the surrounding throng despite his hushed tone. 'Audriss has his demon, remember? I don't *think* Pekatherosh is telepathic – Khanda's not. But I don't *know*. Khanda can warn me if I'm being magically probed in any way, but the two of you don't have that defense. If I tell you what I know, and he sees us coming before we see him, it might warn him off. Trust me when I say this isn't something we want him to know that we know.'

Ellowaine frowned unhappily but nodded. Seilloah just shrugged. 'Whatever you say, Cerris.'

'Right.' Somehow, he wasn't precisely reassured.

/You know, Corvis, you could just ask me if Pekatherosh can read your minds./

The Terror of the East coughed once, embarrassed. 'I, um, I guess I didn't think of that. All right, Khanda, can Pekatherosh read our minds?'

/How should I know?/

With an inarticulate gurgle, Corvis lunged once more into the street.

The minutes fled in droves as the trio maneuvered, wiggled, and shoved through the crowds, drawing glowers and curses as they passed. And then, abruptly, Corvis drew to a halt. 'I realise you can't do much with what I've told you,' he said to his companions. 'But any preparations you feel the need to make, make them now. We're almost there.'

Ahead, looming from the surrounding structures, was the Hall of Meeting. His face radiating determination, one hand resting atop Sunder, Corvis stepped into the building's shadow – and the shadow of a past he'd thought he'd left many, many years behind him.

/*How perfectly karmic,*/ Khanda commented as though he indeed read Corvis' thoughts. /*You lost your* last *war in a Guild Hall, too. If this was any more symmetrical, I'd have to rethink my assessment of the gods. It seems they have a sense of humour after all.*/

'You find this funny, do you?' Corvis asked angrily.

/*Corvis, my boy, you've absolutely no idea.*/

For a brief instant, Corvis' eyes closed in supplication to he knew not which gods, and then he deliberately pulled open the huge door and walked inside.

The nobles and guildmasters were meeting not in the audience chamber downstairs, but within the confines of an upper-level room, large enough (albeit barely) to seat them all comfortably. The horseshoe-shaped table within was enormous, with sufficient chairs for all. The room possessed but a single door, a heavy hardwood monstrosity with iron bands and multiple bars, and the walls were twelve-inch stone. It was, put quite plainly, practically impregnable, and the various nobles and Guildmasters felt far safer making their plans here than they would downstairs.

At the moment, however, they weren't making many plans at all.

'Absolutely impossible!' Rheah Vhoune stood beside her chair, white-knuckled fists pressed against the table. 'I don't believe it!'

Duke Lorum, face covered in a thin sheen of sweat, his armour caked with dirt, leaned back in his own chair and shook his head. 'I understand, Rheah. Jassion's a friend of mine, too, remember? But the facts fit.'

'Like hell they do!'

Ignoring the outburst, Salia Mavere, the priestess of Verelian, shifted in her own chair, idly playing with the head of a massive hammer. 'How reliable is this information, Your Grace?'

Lorum smiled sadly. 'As reliable as any battlefield report, I suppose. According to the few who made it back, the unit

Jassion took to engage Rebaine's elite force was largely wiped out, despite the element of surprise.'

'And the baron did not return with them?' That from Sebastian Arcos of the Merchants' Guild, who sat as far from Rheah as courtesy and acoustics permitted.

'No.'

'It proves nothing!' Rheah insisted. 'Maybe he fell in battle! Gods, we're sitting here condemning the man, he could be dying as we speak! Why—'

'Rheah,' Lorum's tone, though gentle, cut succinctly through her protests, 'you've heard the full report. Several of his own men saw him vanish into a sudden bank of fog, fog that rose with no warning and, faded as quickly. And we all know what that means.'

'So who's to say,' Duke Edmund asked, 'the Legion didn't just kill the poor young man? Not that I would wish for such a thing, of course, but it might be a more reasonable explanation.'

'No.' Nathaniel Espa, who held no official position but attended as personal adviser to the regent, stood and leaned across the table. 'No, I've seen the Legion in action, at Pelapheron. They kill quickly, efficiently, and I've never seen them take anyone with them before.' He sighed. 'I fear Duke Lorum's theory, however distasteful, may be correct.'

'No!' Rheah insisted again, though her conviction wavered. 'Damn it, I know Jassion! I've known him since he was a baby! He's headstrong, stubborn, violent, obsessive . . . But he's no traitor! I cannot believe he'd willingly serve Audriss.'

'You're supposed to think he *is* Audriss, actually.'

Every head in the room turned toward the door, now gaping open. No one should have been able to enter the chamber: the door was not only locked and barred, but enchanted by Rheah Vhoune herself. Yet now, without so much as a sound of movement or a flicker of the wards, the portal swung wide, framing three people within.

The man – tall, wiry, and grey-haired – moved to stand at the center of the U formed by the table, where he could address the entire assembly. His companions, both female, spread out to either side. One, as gaunt as he, held a pair of hideous hatchets, and the gleam in her eyes suggested she was all too ready to use them. The other was dark haired, older than the first, and appeared to be unarmed.

'Who are you?' Espa demanded, hand falling on the large sword at his waist. 'How did you get in here?'

'Rheah,' the man said, 'please tell your friend that if he pulls that sword, he'll be dead before the scabbard stops wobbling.'

Her jaw clenched tightly, Rheah nodded. 'He means it, Nathan. All of you. Your weapons are useless.' She raised an eyebrow. 'Mine aren't, though,' she continued. 'You know I can stop you. I may not match your pet for sheer power, but you can't channel it all at once.'

'Possibly true. That's why my companion over there looks so edgy. If anything unnatural happens to me, her orders are to take those hatchets and start killing.'

Rheah cursed under her breath.

'As far as who I am,' the man said, 'let me make it more obvious. Khanda?'

He rippled very much like a watery reflection into which someone had hurled a stone. And then he was dressed not in fur and leathers, but in the black-and-bone armour known to everyone within the room. He wasn't wearing his helm, but then, he didn't need to be.

He'd expected, truth be told, to have to curb the subsequent commotion, to browbeat everyone back into their seats long enough to listen to what he had to say. For whatever reason – quite possibly utter shock – it didn't happen. Instead, most of the assembly simply gaped at him with fearful eyes and made no sound save for uneven gasps.

'Good,' Corvis said succinctly. 'That makes things easier.' Slowly, purposefully, he took in the entire gathering, one by one. Few of the Guildmasters and nobles were courageous enough to meet his gaze. Fewer still could hold it.

Despite his best efforts, he couldn't keep a sneer of

contempt from crossing his features. These were the men and women who ruled Imphallion? Cowering weaklings and squabbling politicians, fools for whom even the threat of a conquering army was insufficient motivation to work together. They weren't worthy to govern. A part of Corvis wondered if they were worthy even to survive.

'What are you doing here?' Duke Edmund finally burst out, clearly hovering at the precipice of hysteria. 'What do you want with us?'

'I assure you,' Nathaniel Espa added more calmly, 'that if you seek to hold us hostage in exchange for the city, you're sadly delusional. The safety of our citizens—'

'Oh, put a cork in it, you windbag,' Corvis snapped at him. 'Gods, are you people naturally this dense, or have you been stuffing rocks in your ears? *I'm not working with Audriss!*'

A moment of silence, and then Corvis could feel the weight of their disbelief come crashing down upon his head. Undeterred, he pressed on.

'Shocking as this may be to everyone concerned, myself included, I'm trying to *help* you people!'

'Ha!' Duke Lorum rose – slowly, so as not to aggravate the fidgety lady with the hatchets – and glared at the greatest nightmare of his time. 'With all respect, Lord Rebaine, do whatever it is you've come to do and get it over with, but spare us the lies. It's obvious what's happening here!'

'Is it?' The warlord began, methodically, to pace. 'I wonder.'

With that he fell silent, save for his boot heels clicking across the cold stone. Various councilmen traded glances, frightened, confused. Whatever they'd expected of the Terror of the East, this wasn't it.

Slowly, at the far end of the table, Nathaniel Espa shifted in his seat. Stealthily, his fingers stretched downward, closing about the pommel of the throwing dagger in his right boot.

'Baron Jassion of Braetlyn,' Corvis said abruptly, continuing to pace, 'is many things. As the Lady Rheah pointed out, he's violent, short-tempered, brutal. Trust me on this last one, he's as brutal a man as you'll ever meet.' He winced in remembered pain. 'But he's not Audriss, although I was supposed to *think* he was.' The warlord smiled, his stride unwavering. 'The fact that you've been deceived into believing the same thing is entirely secondary. The evidence was aimed at me. A fallback plan, as it were. Audriss seems to be good at those.'

'What evidence?' Rheah asked softly. Her lips bent downward, as though the question itself tasted sour. Clearly she recognised that *something* was afoot here, something she just knew she wasn't going to like – and just as clearly she'd decided, though she might have choked on the very notion, that Corvis might just know what it was.

The dagger was halfway from its sheath when Espa felt a grip on his shoulder. 'If she were the closer to you,' Seilloah told him in a whisper, indicating Ellowaine with her free hand, 'you'd be dead. I'm a *little* less bloodthirsty, so I'm giving you the opportunity to hand me the knife before I carve you into steaks with it.'

'Do you really think you could stop me if I wanted to use it?' the old knight challenged, equally quietly.

The witch shifted her grip just slightly, so that her thumb rested against the exposed flesh of the man's neck. 'In my palm,' she told him, 'I'm holding a thorn tipped with a fascinating combination of herbal extracts. If I prick you with it, you'll be quite paralysed. You won't be able to move, but you'll be quite conscious when I start to carve.'

Scowling, he handed her the dagger.

'Good. Now pay attention.'

'. . . very subtly done,' Corvis was saying, without breaking stride. 'It was smart, skillful. Nothing obvious, just enough to make me think I'd figured it out for myself. Remember, I've met Audriss face-to-face, so I've seen him in pretty clear detail. He wears a ring – emerald on pewter – that serves as the host talisman for the demon who grants him his power. I saw the ring again, in the dungeons beneath His Grace's castle. It was Jassion's signet.'

A low murmur stalked through the assembly. Rheah frowned, but Corvis continued before she could speak. 'Furthermore, Jassion always seemed to hold a personal grudge against me. Granted, this can probably be attributed to, let's say, past transgressions. But if I was interfering with his plans – Audriss' plans – it made so much more sense. Then, of course, there's the fact that Jassion vanished off the battlefield just now in a cloud of fog, a last-minute addition to the picture, as it were. And Audriss knows too many things only a man in Jassion's position should know. Including the fact that you,' and here he looked directly at the sorceress, 'have in your possession a certain item we've discussed in the past.'

Rheah blanched.

'That's why he's come here personally, in secret, rather than attacking the town with his soldiers and the Endless Legion, as he normally does. He wants to get his hands on it first, rather than risk it being lost in the chaos.'

'Even if we believe all this,' Rheah asked, 'all it does is suggest that Jassion really *is* Audriss. What makes you so sure he's *not*?'

'Because Audriss isn't stupid, Lady Rheah. I've dealt with enough demon-inhabited baubles in my time to know how they operate. They're more than capable of changing shape. *And colour*. If Audriss and Jassion are wearing the same ring, it's because Audriss *wants* his ring to look like the baron's.'

Things change. Sometimes when you want them to . . .

'Then there was this.' Without quite drawing it – no point in panicking the council when they were actually listening – Corvis half lifted Sunder from his belt. 'Most of you have heard of the Kholben Shiar. You've heard the legends that they change their own shape to best match the persona – the soul, if you will – of the wielder. It's not something you can choose. Any one of the Kholben Shiar that I pick up becomes an axe, even if I'd prefer, say, a spear at the time.' Corvis allowed the axe to fall back into its clasp. Once again, he swept the entire table with a deliberate gaze. 'When I was a prisoner here, Jassion made a point of bragging that he'd been a participant in every part of my capture. He attacked me, he brought me here. And he, *with his own hands*, stripped my equipment and weapons from me and stuck them "in a safe place". When I retrieved Sunder during my escape, it wasn't an axe, but a rather hefty sword. But I'd seen Audriss pick up a Kholben Shiar before – as a dagger. If Jassion was the last one to touch Sunder, as he claimed, then he couldn't be Audriss.'

. . . sometimes when you don't.

'This is ridiculous!' Duke Lorum snapped with a dismissive wave of his hand. 'This man is the enemy and a known liar! He's just trying to protect his ally! Magic shapeshifting jewelry and weapons. I hardly—'

'He may be telling the truth,' Rheah interrupted, a clenched fist resting against her chin. 'At least, it's possible. What he's said, about bound demons and about the Kholben Shiar, is accurate.'

'Oh.' Lorum didn't seem impressed. One hand ran idly through his growth of beard. 'Well, then, Lord Rebaine, if you're so bloody positive Jassion *isn't* Audriss, why don't you tell us who *is*?'

Like an iron trap, Corvis' gaze locked onto the regent's own. The sheer intensity of his stare, the sudden ice in his expression, was enough to silence the room. Nothing moved, nothing at all.

'It's rather presumptuous for *you*, of all people, to be asking me that,' the Terror of the East said slowly to the Regent Proper of Imphallion. 'Don't you think . . . Audriss?'

CHAPTER TWENTY-SIX

'No! Absolutely not!' Lorum leaned across the desk, fists planted on heaps of parchment strewn across the surface. Had he turned his gaze downward, he might very well have set them all ablaze.

'Your Grace . . . Lorum.' Nathan shrugged his broad shoulders, trying to settle his formal garb more comfortably across his chest. Damn, but even his armour was more comfortable than this nonsensical getup! 'Lorum, please. Be reasonable—'

'Reasonable? *Reasonable?*' Fists clenched, parchment crumpled. 'Tell me what's reasonable, Nathan. Tell me why I should give in to the whining demands of a bunch of corpulent, useless pigs!'

'Maybe because the Guilds are the economic backbone of Imphallion, Your Grace? You can't afford to make enemies of *all* of them.'

'Watch me.' Lorum turned, pacing beneath the crossed swords that hung on the brick-faced wall, blades that – thankfully – had seen no use since the Terror's war. 'They're *not* the power in the kingdom anymore, Nathan. I *am*. And you can't possibly tell me that the past years haven't been better for it!'

The knight shook his head, moved around the desk, and took his young protégé by the shoulders. 'It's not your power, Lorum.'

The regent merely snarled and smacked the older man's hands aside.

'It's not,' Nathan continued, his own eyes going flinty.

'So far, they've cooperated – no matter how grudgingly – because you keep throwing the specter of Corvis Rebaine in their faces. And yes, I'll be the first to admit that you've rebuilt a lot more of Imphallion than the Guilds would have, left to their own devices.'

'Then why—'

'Because this can't continue! You've already almost exhausted their resources, and it's not going to do you any good to rebuild the cities if they can't support themselves. You can't rule a nation when there are no taxes to collect. There's only so much capital available, Lorum, and the Guilds generate more than the rest of us could dream of doing.'

'Then they'll operate under my control.'

'And you're going to enforce that how, exactly?'

Lorum stared, jaw going suddenly slack. 'You're not serious.'

'Very serious, Your Grace. There's been talk, for months now. You don't have anywhere near the military might to stand up to the Guilds. And remember, you're the regent, not the king. As long as they get even a little noble backing, it's not even treason.'

The young regent slumped back toward his chair and missed it entirely, finding himself sitting, legs sprawled, on the thick carpet. Slowly, he allowed his face to sink into his palms.

'All right,' he said finally, voice muffled by emotion as much as by his trembling hands. 'All right, Nathan. Tell the Guildmasters I'll be in to see them shortly. Tell them they can have their damn Guilds back, free and clear.

'But you tell them, too, that they damn well better not make me regret it.'

Duke Lorum threw his head back and laughed as though he hadn't a care in the world. Every last individual in the room, save Corvis, gaped as tears of mirth ran down his face to vanish into his faded gold expanse of beard. The regent looked as though he might be forced to sit, lest he topple over completely.

Finally, however, the fit died away in a final burst of chuckling.

'Are you quite through?' Corvis asked.

'Rebaine,' Lorum said through gasping breath and reddened face, 'you're absolutely mad!'

'Well, one of us is.' Corvis grinned, and Lorum's own smile vanished. 'It was a brilliant scheme, Audriss. I almost didn't see it. But you made just a few tiny mistakes, enough to tip your hand.'

'What, exactly, are you talking about?' Rheah asked, ignoring Lorum's murderous glare.

'Lorum held on to his power seventeen years ago, remember. It took the Guilds three years to recover the authority they'd handed over. For a brief span, Imphallion had a king again, in fact if not in name.' Corvis pointed a black iron finger at one of the assembly, a scrawny fellow who wore the latest finery, now absolutely drenched in sweat. He blanched visibly at the sudden attention. 'You. What's your name?'

'Ah . . . Bidimir Vrenk, O dread lord. I represent the august yet humble assembly of the Minstrels' Guild.'

/Dread lord?/ Khanda snickered.

Corvis ignored him. 'Tell me, Master Vrenk, how exactly has Duke Lorum dealt with the current crisis? What is it he's been trying to accomplish since the moment the Serpent appeared over the horizon?'

'Why, he's been trying . . . Trying to consolidate power.' Vrenk's eyes narrowed thoughtfully. 'Under his authority.'

A low mutter swept through the Guildmasters.

'So what?' Espa demanded, rising to his feet (after a careful glance at Seilloah, who was blandly cleaning her nails with his dagger). 'Combining our forces was the best way to deal with the crisis!'

'But we *offered* to join forces!' Salia Mavere announced, armour clinking beneath her robes as she shifted in her seat.

'We were more than willing to have our troops fight beside his own! But that wasn't good enough! It had to be under a single authority! Your Grace, I'd very much like to know why.'

'It prevents confusion,' Lorum said, his voice rising. 'It's more efficient! It—'

'It puts power back in your hands,' Corvis told him flatly. 'I'm not going to sit here and guess at your motives. Maybe you just enjoyed the taste of power you got after the last war. Hell, maybe you actually thought you were doing your best for Imphallion, at one point or another. But either way, you hit on the perfect way to go about it. It was a win-win situation for you, Audriss.'

'*Stop calling me that!*'

'After all, whether you succeeded in conquering Imphallion as the Serpent, or whether you talked the Guildmasters into handing over control, you end up in command. And because the nation's just gone through a massive war, nobody would remain with strength to oppose you.'

Lorum drew himself up, his expression frosty. 'Unless you purport to have some evidence to back up these ridiculous claims, I refuse to hear any more of it.'

'Oh, but I do.'

The regent seemed to deflate.

'I've already explained why Audriss has to be someone in power in Imphallion. Someone in this room, in fact. He – you – knew too much. You knew of Rheah's acquisition. You were too well able to avoid the patrols that *were* put out to intercept you.

'Tell me, how else could Jassion's team have got through Audriss' forces to attack my little army this morning? I seriously doubt the Serpent's scouts just *happened* to miss an entire battalion sneaking past them. Unless they were ordered to let it pass. And Audriss would only have given that order if he *knew* they were attacking me, not him!'

The stares aimed in Lorum's direction subtly shifted: less shock, less confusion, and substantially more anger.

'I still see no evidence, Rebaine.'

'How about this?' Corvis ran a finger over the recent scar on his cheek.

'What about it?'

'Look at me, Lorum. You saw me after you and Jassion had me beaten and tortured—'

'Interrogated!'

The warlord scowled. 'Beaten and tortured,' he repeated. 'I could barely walk. Do I look injured to you at the moment?'

'Magic, I assume,' Lorum spat.

'True. Except this. This one little wound the magics wouldn't heal. I finally remembered where I got this scar, Lorum. It's where you hit me. Once. Your signet ring cut me.

'It's not a deep wound, Audriss. The spell should have utterly erased it. But you see, as I explained to one of your cronies who "rescued" me: Demon-inflicted wounds don't respond well to magic. Demons, such as Pekatherosh.'

Corvis cast a questioning glance at Rheah Vhoune. 'Lady Rheah, I know you've no reason to trust me. But a simple detection spell on that ring will prove whether I'm telling the truth.'

The sorceress blanched, her face torn with indecision. And then, with a deep sigh, she nodded. 'You're right.' She stepped forward. 'I apologise, Your Grace. I realise this seems disrespectful, but we have to be sure.'

'Of course, Rheah,' Lorum said stiffly, raising his hand so she could see the purple-stoned ring. 'I fully understand.'

A burst of power blasted from his outstretched fist. Rheah, her clothes smouldering, slammed into the far wall with a bone-bruising thud.

The entire assembly was on its feet, some crying out, some frozen, some running pell-mell for the door, and others drawing whatever weapons they carried.

Corvis beat them to it. Even before the glow of Audriss' attack faded from the room, the Terror of the East vaulted the conference table, Sunder in hand. Mere inches from his target, however, an invisible fist knocked Corvis from the air. The warlord struck the floor hard, the breath knocked from his lungs. Doggedly, he dragged himself to his feet, just in time to see Ellowaine advancing on Audriss, hatchets blurring.

'No!' he shouted. 'Ellowaine, back off!'

The mercenary snarled, a growl more animal than human, but she obeyed.

And it *was* Audriss they faced, now, not Duke Lorum. The impossible stone armour was back, the featureless mask once more in place. One hand glowed with a sickening aura of green and purple, the other held Talon low and ready to strike. Sporadically, a flash of purple and green appeared, not around the Serpent's hand, but in the air around him. It was that, Corvis realised, that thwarted his attack.

'Damn you, Rebaine!' Audriss hissed at him in a hate-filled voice.

Corvis shrugged. 'I have to admit, the height thing was a nice touch. You really are shorter when you're wearing the armour. It must have been a terrible strain, working that kind of magic into the outfit.'

'You've no idea.' Audriss shook his head. 'You realise you've forced me to alter my plans somewhat.'

'That was sort of the point. You can't win now. The council knows the truth.'

'Indeed. It's too bad. They would have been useful in the coming months. There's going to be a great deal of rebuilding to do. But I suppose I'll make do without them.'

The councilmen who'd attempted to flee had long since discovered that the door was quite firmly sealed against any escape. Many moaned or cried out, now, at Audriss' horrifying pronouncement. Those with a bit more courage, led by a determined Salia Mavere, hammered away at the infernal shield surrounding their former leader, with no more success than Corvis had had.

'Rebaine,' Rheah hissed, limping to his side. A thin trickle of blood ran down the side of her chin from a split lip, and she was clearly favouring her left leg. 'You can't let him do that!'

'I wasn't planning on it,' he told her. 'Between the two of

us, we should have no problem taking down his barrier. And then . . .'

'Droll, Rebaine,' Audriss hissed at him. 'But I'm afraid that you'll do nothing of the sort. Khanda, now.'

Corvis froze. 'What?' It was barely a whisper as he glanced, despite himself, down at his left wrist.

/*Sorry, Corvis. Change in plan.*/ And just like that, the armband was gone, fading from Corvis' wrist and reappearing on the Serpent's own. The green and purple surrounding Audriss were joined by sparks of deepest red.

The Terror of the East felt a sudden overwhelming urge to sit down on the floor and sob.

'Rheah—' he began through clenched teeth.

'Forget it, Rebaine. *Maybe* I could have taken down his shield when he had only *one* of those things. Against both, no human alive today could do it.'

'Rheah,' Audriss said, his voice suddenly silky, 'I have a favour to ask you.'

'Go to hell!'

'Now, that's not very nice. I believe you have something I want. Give it to me, or I kill them all. Now.' He raised a hand, and another great moan escaped from the huddled mass.

'You'll kill them anyway,' Rheah protested.

'Perhaps not. Once I have the key, they'll no longer be a threat, no matter what they know.'

'I—'

Audriss snapped his fingers, and a surge of red surrounded his newly acquired armband. Bidimir Vrenk shuddered once, coughed, and then showered everyone around him in an explosion of bone shards and brain matter. The headless body stood upright for five full seconds before landing with a wet slap on the floor.

Several more thumps followed as a handful of councilors fainted dead away.

'Yum, yum,' Audriss said coldly. 'A snack for my new friend. Seems with the power of *two* demons, even a wary soul can be consumed. I think Pekatherosh is hungry, too. Three . . . two . . .'

'Here!' Rheah cried, yanking a small ivory scroll case from a pouch at her belt. 'Take it, damn you!' Tears in her eyes, she hurled the tube at the Serpent.

It stopped halfway, snagged in tendrils of purple light, and drifted slowly toward him. He popped the cork with a thumb and glanced curiously at the contents. 'Ah, yes. This should do nicely.'

'It doesn't do you any good, anyway,' Corvis snapped at him. 'You don't have—'

And then the Serpent raised his right hand, giving them both a good look at Khanda. 'Don't I?'

'Oh, damn . . .'

Audriss sheathed Talon and held forth his hand. A heavy, leather-bound tome, steaming at the sudden temperature change, now occupied his fist.

'Careless of you, Rebaine,' Audriss chided him as he wiped a layer of moisture off the heavy cover. 'Hiding this in the ice. Why, if this were any other book, the damp would have destroyed it!' Safe behind his infernal protection, the Serpent unrolled the key scroll and flipped idly through the pages, glancing occasionally at the key as he went. The assembled throng gazed in helpless consternation at the man who quite literally held their lives in his hands.

'Oh, Rebaine, you'd have loved some of these,' Audriss cackled. 'The spells in this book, they're like nothing anyone's ever seen before! Shall I curse you, Rebaine? Not just any curse, but one that extends to all your descendants, and anyone they so much as speak with? Or shall I raise up a mountain from the very earth and drop it on you? Summon a storm to wash away a continent? Or this one you'd especially like, my Terror. A charming spell to control *dozens* of people, so long as you have the proper foci. Or perhaps—' And then he froze, his breath catching in his throat.

'Oh, yes,' Audriss breathed, and Corvis could have sworn that the man's hands actually shook. 'Oh, dear gods.' Slowly, the Serpent raised his head. 'I'll be leaving you now,' he announced. A sudden blinding flash, a deafening thunderclap, and the building's roof exploded into hundreds of fragments, showering down onto the panicked populace outside. 'I think I'll kill you lot after all,' he told the terrified council as he rose into the air. 'If it's any consolation, though, you won't die alone.' Hanging a full two dozen feet above them, he rotated so that he looked down at Corvis. 'Enjoy the theatrics, Rebaine. I learned from the best, after all. When this is over, my name will be legend after the very gods have faded in the mists of time! No one will dare challenge me after today!' And then, as though he stood on the thickest stone, Audriss strode through the air above Mecepheum, spell book and key open before him. His voice rang out in a sonorous chant, audible to those left behind despite the growing distance.

Corvis dashed across the room, up onto the table, and leapt. His hands clamped down upon the top of the walls that once held the ceiling. Hauling himself up, he attained the vantage to watch as his enemy moved across the city. Random citizens collapsed to the ground, heads bursting. Either Audriss was allowing his pets to feed indiscriminately, or . . .

'He's fueling something,' Rheah said from beside him, floating easily at his level. 'Whatever that bastard's about to cast, it's going to be huge.'

'You think so?' Corvis muttered.

'I can probably protect us from having our souls eaten, if he doesn't catch me by surprise. We have to stop him, Rebaine.'

'I'd sort of come to that conclusion myself, actually. If you have any ideas how to go about doing it, I'd be delighted to hear them.'

Rheah remained silent.

Furniture scraped as several heavy chairs were placed upon the table, and then Seilloah, Ellowaine, Nathaniel Espa, and Salia Mavere stuck their heads over the wall to watch in helpless fascination as Audriss continued his spell, invulnerable and unopposed.

'So,' Corvis said conversationally, though his eyes never wavered from his enemy, 'where's the *real* key?'

'Pardon me?'

'Come on, Rheah. I'm not a *complete* cretin. After all the trouble you went through to prepare your little surprise for me earlier, am I supposed to believe you were caught flat-footed today?'

'Excuse me,' Ellowaine interjected, 'but what are you talking about?'

'Rheah developed this key through her own research. She then proceeded to create a fake, just in case either the Serpent or the Terror of the East got his hands on it.' There was no small amount of self-mockery in his tone.

'I'm impressed, Rebaine,' she said simply.

'Flattered, I'm sure. So when does the spell fall apart on him?'

The sorceress frowned. 'I wish I knew. It needed to be convincing, Rebaine. It had to fool you, Audriss, Seilloah, or even your demon. So it's not dissimilar to the real key. Just a few pronunciations here and there are a little off.'

'Are you telling me,' Seilloah demanded, voice shrill, 'that you've just handed Audriss the most powerful spells in the world, with a cipher that may cause them to *misfire*?'

'Relax, witch. You should know that most spells just collapse in on themselves when they go wrong. Only a few specific types ever actually go awry . . .'

And then, standing above the city's centre, Audriss halted. His voice rose farther, overpowering the bedlam of the citizens below, and the noise of the war raging beyond the walls. In a single instant, dozens of people on the streets below collapsed in pools of blood, a final burst of power to break through whatever natural barriers prevented the travesty in which Audriss was now engaged. From the nearby alleys, Corvis spotted a flicker of movement amid the shadows. A handful of Audriss' gnomes – who'd been happily butchering several of the army's couriers as they carried orders this way and that – glanced upward and then vanished bodily into the earth, fleeing from whatever they sensed building in their master's magics.

Silence fell, complete and utter. Corvis listened to himself swallow, twice, to be certain he'd not gone deaf. At the edge of town, some miles from where the Serpent stood, the clouds in the sky shuddered, grew dark, blacker than any cloud could ever be. They hardened, as if they formed a solid ceiling above the heads of the soldiers on the ground. And then that ceiling *cracked*.

From that rift in the world came a furious, freezing wind. It blew across the field, across the walls, across the city, and it carried with it the voices of the damned: not hundreds, not thousands, but millions upon millions of souls shrieking in unwavering, endless torment. It carried on it a charnel air, a draft from the houses of the dead, and strong men and women collapsed, retching and gagging, to their knees.

The crack widened further, the wind grew stronger. And they were there. They had not climbed from that tear in the sky but simply appeared beneath it, as though carried on the winds. They stood, screaming, towering over the city and battlefield, and both armies threw down their weapons and ran, for they knew the end was upon them all.

The end of everything. The death of the world. Fire and Flood. The Children of Apocalypse.

Maukra and Mimgol.

Maukra, the Dragon, spawn of flame. Hundreds of feet long, it raised its fire-enshrouded head over the buildings it crushed by mere presence, set ablaze through simple proximity. Its serpentine body undulated to the pulsing of some hideous, inhuman heart. Higher that head rose, and higher still. The neck flared, a cobra grown to monstrous proportions, and within that hood, writhing beneath the skin, were the pale and featureless faces of the damned. They reached with ghostly arms toward those who would soon join them, a loving embrace they would never, ever release, and all the while screaming, screaming. . .

Mimgol, the Spider, child of flood. Smaller than its sibling, yet still over thirty feet in height, more than thrice that in width. Like a tarantula, thick-limbed and furry, it scuttled over the roadways with a sickening, alien pace. From mandibles large enough to crush castles, and from the underbelly of the beast, ran constant rivulets of watery venom, poison and pestilence that trickled over the cobblestone streets. A stray dog, tail curled between its legs, sniffed tentatively at the flowing substance, then howled, pawing at its snout as the entire front of its face simply sloughed off its head. People fleeing the flames of the Dragon splashed through the streams of corruption raining from the Spider. They collapsed, dead or dying, vomiting organs or drowning on internal fluids. Mimgol surveyed it all, head darting back and forth in true arachnid spurts, and in each and every facet of those giant spider's eyes, a wide and unblinking human iris wept.

'That,' Corvis said, his face gone preternaturally pale, 'does not look like the result of a failed spell.' His hands were sweating profusely inside his gauntlets, and his gut curled into a ball and crawled up into his chest.

'He's mad,' Salia whispered, hands tracing the holy icon of Verelian over and over in the air before her. 'He's absolutely mad!'

'Rheah,' Corvis asked, 'what went wrong?'

The sorceress stared over the city, listening as the cries of the dying grew audible over the screams of the damned. 'I didn't know – couldn't know . . .'

'Know what?' Ellowaine demanded, her voice tinged with lurking hysteria.

Seilloah shook her head, though she, too, could not look away from the primal creatures stalking through the city, obliterating anything and anyone in their way. 'That's the problem with summoning spells,' she said softly, fists clenched tight. 'Actually calling something up is bloody easy. It's controlling them that takes real skill.'

'In other words,' Espa rasped from behind them, 'the only thing Rheah's false key may have accomplished—'

'Is that Audriss can't control them, either,' Corvis finished for him. 'But since he *wants* them to tear the city apart until they reach us, he hasn't realised anything's wrong.' He swallowed once. 'Nice job, Rheah.'

'Shove it, Rebaine!' Rheah snapped, rage blazing in her tear-reddened eyes. 'How could I have known he was mad enough to attempt a Grand Summoning? I did the best I could under the circumstances, which is more than I can say for some people involved in this mess!'

'Those *can't* be the Children of Apocalypse!' the priestess insisted, still tracing her deity's rune before her as though she would never stop. 'The gods themselves imprisoned those abominations! No mortal, however powerful, could have created a spell to free them!'

'Maybe they're not,' Corvis told her. 'Maybe they're just demonic essences inhabiting projections of the Twins. And you know what difference that makes to us?'

'None at all,' Rheah acknowledged, her gaze shifting from Salia to the warlord. 'All right, nothing's changed. We have to stop this. The city's dead within hours if we can't do something.'

Corvis nodded. 'Rheah, many spells collapse if the caster dies. Do you think this is one of them?'

'I honestly don't know.' She frowned thoughtfully. 'I can't imagine Selakrian would have wanted those things running around uncontrolled if something happened to him. So he *might* have built in a safeguard.'

'Why would he create that spell at all?' Ellowaine shrieked.

'Because he could?' Rheah shrugged. 'Rebaine, I have no idea if killing Audriss will stop this or not, but I don't see any other alternatives.'

'Right, then.' Corvis peered carefully at Audriss, forcing himself to ignore the massacre taking place at the edge of town. Though it sickened him to admit such a thing, the Twins' personalities – regardless of whether they were the true mythic entities or mere demonic fakes – were actually working *for* them. The monsters' insistence on slaying *every-thing* was slowing them down, as they sifted through burned rubble and drowned and diseased bodies to be sure nothing survived. Had they simply covered as much ground as possible, they'd have been halfway to the Hall of Meeting already.

It wouldn't be long before Audriss realised something was wrong. They had to move quickly. Corvis continued his examination of the Serpent, trying to make out details despite the distance and the smoke, looking for . . .

There. Barely visible in the flickering, vicious glow of the ravenous inferno spreading, a tiny gleam of silver around the wrist of the black-clad warlord standing in the air above Mecepheum.

'Rheah,' Corvis asked quickly, 'I need to talk with Khanda. Can you make that happen?'

'What?' Seilloah screeched before Rheah could do more than draw breath. 'Corvis, are you insane? Khanda betrayed you! Betrayed us all! Who the hell cares what he has to say? Especially now!'

'I do,' Corvis said simply. 'Trust me, it's important. Rheah?'

The sorceress frowned, trying to concentrate past the horrible screams. 'What's your normal range of communication?'

'Physical contact is optimal,' he told her, 'but I've spoken to him from six feet away through a door.'

Rheah shook her head. 'Not from here, then. If we could get within, oh, twenty-five or thirty yards, I might manage something.'

'Then we'd best get moving.'

This time, it wasn't just Seilloah who stared at him. 'You want us to go out *there*?' Salia gasped hoarsely at him.

'Us, no. *Some* of us, yes.' Corvis refused to back down under the weight of their combined gaze. 'Listen, if we sit here and cower, or argue about it, they're going to tear this city out from under us and kill us anyway. Then Audriss wins. Period. I have exactly one idea, and it's a bad one, but it's all we've got, and it means I *have to speak with Khanda*. So yes, I'm going out there, and yes, some of you are coming with me, or we might as well just fall on our swords now, because I bloody well guarantee it's an easier death than the one coming for us!'

It was, strangely enough, Rheah Vhoune, rather than Seilloah or Ellowaine, who first nodded her assent. 'What's your plan, then?'

'Not much,' Corvis admitted. 'You're with me, to help me talk to that damn traitor. Seilloah, Ellowaine, and Espa are coming along to keep any trouble off us while you work your magic. I—'

'I beg your pardon,' Nathaniel said coldly, 'but I don't recall agreeing to any such thing. As far as I'm concerned, you're just as big a threat as—'

'Nathan, shut up!' Rheah snapped, her hair practically whipping Corvis' face as she spun to confront her old friend. 'As of right now, Rebaine's the best chance we've got of stopping this, seeing as how he's the only one here with even a single idea! So either propose something else, or shut the hell up and cooperate!'

The old knight actually recoiled, clearly taken aback. 'But . . . but Rheah—'

'What part of "shut up" didn't you get, Nathan?' Another turn. 'All right, Rebaine, we're with you, at least for now.'

And a good thing it is, too, Corvis noted, watching as the cowed Espa climbed his way back to the floor, grumbling under his breath, and went to retrieve his sword. 'Salia,' he continued, 'you're in charge here until we get back. There's not much you can do against those things, but if any of Audriss' soldiers make it this far, it's up to you to organise a defense. You up to it?'

'I believe I can do that, yes.'

'Good. Rheah?'

The sorceress chanted a low, discordant verse, and then Corvis, Seilloah, Espa, Ellowaine, and Rheah swiftly floated up and over the broken walls to touch down softly in the street. The citizens in the vicinity, already dashing around in mindless panic, took one look at the warlord's armour and scattered. Audriss, the Children of Apocalypse, and now

Corvis Rebaine. If the Day of Judgment truly had come upon the city of Mecepheum, its heralds could have been no more frightening than those who fought over the capital today.

Weapons drawn and faces determined, the motley band moved across the cobblestones, directing their path toward the centre of town and the megalomaniac demigod striding through the air above it. Audriss probably wouldn't see them coming – he seemed enraptured by the devastation wrought by his summoning.

But Audriss was not the only one guilty of tunnel vision.

The faintest stream of mist, cloaked by the smoke of burning buildings and heaps of rubble and bodies, paralleled their path. It had no eyes to see them, yet it paced them perfectly, never drawing more than a few yards ahead or behind. It had no ears to hear, yet their words had struck like a physical blow.

Although he currently lacked features with which to express it, Mithraem seethed with an overwhelming rage. So powerful was the fury of this most ancient and most powerful of the Endless Legion, it was all he could do not to materialise, to rip into the nearest mortals whoever they might be, to rend them limb from limb, and to gorge upon their blood until even his eternal thirst was satisfied.

How dare he? How *dare* that delusional little fool keep this from him! 'Not that big a deal' indeed! Selakrian's tome, by all the darkest gods! And Mithraem had let his best chance at it slip right through his fingers! If he'd known which book Rebaine's sycophants were offering for trade, he'd never have told the Serpent word one of it. With that book in his hands, he wouldn't need Audriss, or *any* mortal allies, ever again.

Which was, he knew, why Audriss *hadn't* told him about the book, but that knowledge didn't make the situation any less infuriating.

Audriss, Duke Lorum, the Serpent, whatever he called himself today . . . Even with such power at his beck and call, his dreams of godhood were just that: dreams. No spell could make him more than inherently human. Long life he could have, but never immortality.

Mithraem, though, was forever. With Selakrian's power, he *could* rule as a god among men, and he could do so until the end of time itself. Nor was he troubled with the slightest tugs of morality to which even Audriss was susceptible. The Serpent had seen a few decades in which to purge himself of the weakest and most frail of human emotions. Mithraem had seen over a hundred, more than enough time to smother the final flickering embers of such nonsense.

All of which made him far more worthy of this power than Audriss was or could ever be.

But this would do, for now. Audriss trusted Mithraem, thought himself in control. Let him think it. Let him grow complacent in his newfound power. Mithraem's patience was that of a true immortal; he could wait. *He* could wait.

Right now, though, he must make certain Audriss didn't lose the tome to someone else, someone less susceptible to Mithraem's future machinations. And that meant stopping whatever pathetic scheme Corvis Rebaine and his ilk hatched.

Perhaps he could even work this to his advantage. This might even inspire the warlord to trust the Endless Legion more than he already did.

His unseen expression shifting from a snarl of rage to a self-satisfied smirk, Mithraem drifted closer to the unsuspecting party, and the cobblestones in his wake gleamed slick with blood.

CHAPTER TWENTY-SEVEN

It is an old, old legend, found today only in the most ancient, most ragged of books, forgotten by all save the most learned sages and storytellers. It tells of a small city, a community called Sanvescu. No Imphallion name, this, but a name – indeed, a city – that rose and fell long before the successful crusade of Imphalam the First. Sanvescu stood deep within a mountain range, low on the slopes and sheltered from all but the worst of the winter storms by the heavy darkwoods that grew nearby, thick as wool on an unsheared ewe. The folk there were simple, serious and hardworking, religious, and superstitious. They believed in the virtues of simple garb, simple fare, and companionship with one's neighbours.

Sanvescu, the legend tells, was also a community beset by horror. A trio of brothers holed up for several nights in the temple of Chalsene, gorging their eyes and minds on the most ancient and secretive teachings of the Night-Bringer – including those that most civilised branches of the Church had long since excised. Tales of sacrifice, of atrocities, of power granted in exchange for blood and the rights of the strong over the weak – these were their intellectual provender. Was this merely curiosity gone wrong? Or were these a criminally minded family seeking divine permission and holy absolution for the horrors they were already inclined to perform?

Whatever the case, these brothers became the collective nightmares of Sanvescu. Families were slain, their bodies laid carefully in occult symbols. Men, women, and

413

children disappeared off the streets, their blood found adorning the altars of Chalsene. For months, the citizens of Sanvescu huddled in terror, unsure even if their tormentors were mortal, or something from beyond life's flimsy veil.

It was Sanvescu's sheriff, by the name of Harlif, who finally ended the town's nightmare – and in turn unleashed one upon the world entire. For Harlif finally recognised, through tracks and bloodied smears, that each atrocity was committed by three men together, a piece of knowledge that led him eventually to the trio of siblings. The men were bound and, without ceremony or trial, hanged until dead and buried in shallow graves. Atop each grave, the townsfolk planted a heavy oak – unearthed from the nearby forests – to symbolise the cycle of the gods, the life that must always sprout from death.

And had Harlif left it at that, accepted the victory and the city-wide acclaim that he had well and truly earned, that would have been the end of it. But Harlif was angry, Sanvescu was angry, and the relatively swift dispatch of their tormentors had not assuaged them.

Some nights later, Harlif led a throng of angered citizens against the temple of Chalsene, blaming the Night-Bringer's priests and their teachings for all that had transpired. Chairs and tables were placed against the doors, wooden planks across the windows, and – in the midst of services, when the score or so of Sanvesans who revered Chalsene all prayed within – Harlif set the building to the torch. There he stood, basking in the warmth, watching the greasy smoke rise skyward, and drinking in the screams of the dying as gladly as he'd accepted the townsfolk's gratitude.

Some variants of the legend claim that Chalsene's priests pronounced a dying curse; others that it was the Night-Bringer himself who took offense at the sheriff's actions. But whichever the case, Harlif awoke that night to a room bathed in the chill of deepest winter. Mists poured through his windows from the outside, leaving a trail of blood to soak into the boards of his floor. And as his eyes grew accustomed to the dark, he stared up, horrified beyond measure, into a face as pallid as death.

And that face spoke, saying 'Every drop of blood I shed, every life I claim from now until the end of days, is upon your soul, not mine. For I have none left to damn.'

Harlif was found by the townsfolk, his corpse as white as snow, drained entirely of blood. Suspecting the worst, the superstitious folk turned immediately and raced to the triple grave, if only to reassure themselves that, once again, they faced a purely mortal adversary.

Two of the graves remained, the towering trees growing straight and tall. But over the third, the bole had rotted, curling in on itself like a weak old man. The grave itself, when they exhumed it, lay empty; nothing remained of the body save a few shreds of dead heart, caught in the roots of the dying tree.

The missing brother's name, so the legend says, was Mithraem.

'There,' Corvis hissed, pointing at a hastily abandoned tavern. 'Is that close enough?'

Rheah squinted upward, trying to judge the distance to the airborne warlord. 'It'll be a near thing,' she said at last, 'but I think I can make it work.'

The door was quite firmly locked, which slowed Sunder down not at all. Five pairs of feet dashed through the common room, kicking up clouds of sawdust and setting the floorboards to creaking. They pounded up the flimsy wooden stairs, shaking dust from the banister. Corvis chose a room at the far end of the corridor and barreled into it, shoulder-checking the flimsy door as he went through.

He'd chosen well. Sure enough, the window allowed an

unobstructed view of the hovering Serpent, as well as the horrors beyond.

Even as Corvis and Rheah took up positions by the window, crouched beneath the sill, the others took what precautions they could. They propped the door back into place, shoving the bed and dresser across the room to barricade the entrance. It was hardly a solid defense, but it might at least slow down any attackers.

Well, anyone human. Maukra and Mimgol would rip the building apart and then set the remains on fire, but they hoped to be long finished before the Children reached this part of the city.

'Ready?' Rheah asked breathlessly, clearly not as calm and collected as she tried to appear. That was all right, though: it distracted Corvis from his own barely leashed panic.

'I suppose so. What's going to happen, exactly? Do I just talk to him? Do I have to keep staring out this window, or is it enough that I see him when the spell starts?'

Rheah grinned weakly. 'The truth is, Rebaine, I can't bring him to you. This sort of communication, as you pointed out, requires proximity. What I *can* do is send *you* to *him*.'

'And you don't think it'll be a little obvious, me floating out there next to Audriss? Not to mention that damn shield he's thrown around himself! If I could get through *that*, I wouldn't need to do this in the first place! I thought you—'

'You misunderstand me, Rebaine. I'm not sending all of you.'

Corvis blinked. 'Huh?' he asked intelligently.

'Projection, Rebaine. I'm sending your essence into Khanda's pendant.'

The warlord actually shrank away from her. 'You said *what*?'

'It's the only way, Rebaine. I promise you, it's safer than it sounds. The amulet's not enchanted to hold you, so there's no danger of being trapped. You'll just pop in, have your discussion, and pop back out again.'

'You're mad! There's no way—'

'You're damn right!' Rheah shouted, leaning forward so her nose was mere inches from Corvis' own. 'If you won't do this, there *is* no way! It's put-up or shut-up-time, Rebaine. You were the one harping about our one and only chance to stop what's happening out there, to turn Audriss' plans around before he walks all over us. You don't get the option of backing out now, you bastard!' Rheah raised her hands and rose from her crouch, muscles tensed. Seilloah took a step back from everyone, her own fingers twitching, and Ellowaine and Espa both drew steel.

'I am going to cast a spell now, Rebaine,' the sorceress said simply. 'If we remain allies, it will be the sending spell. If we're not, I fully intend to burn you down where you stand for crimes against the kingdom and the Guilds. Which will it be?'

Corvis, too, rose to his feet, his hand hovering casually by the infernal weapon at his side. 'If I decided not to let you cast that spell, Rheah, do you think you'd have the chance to do so?'

'Which is it, Rebaine?' she asked again, unwavering.

No one moved. Even the dust filling the room, kicked up and swirled around by their presence, froze as the very building held its breath.

Then Corvis smiled and let his hand fall from Sunder's haft. The witch and the warriors released their tension in three explosive sighs. Rheah merely nodded. 'Are you ready, then?'

'I doubt it. Let's do this before I have one of my rare fits of common sense.'

'Very well.' Rheah relaxed her arms and straightened. 'I should warn you, your destination may seem odd.'

'Odd?'

'You're entering a place – well "place" isn't really the right concept, but it'll do – designed and enchanted to imprison a demon lord. There is nothing in any way, shape, or form natural about it.

'You won't see the worst of it. Chances are, your mind will

interpret what you see in whatever way is necessary to keep you from going stark-raving mad. Even so, it'll look like nothing you've ever seen.'

'Terrific. Can we get this over with already?'

The sorceress nodded, then glanced at the others. 'This is where you earn your keep,' she told them. 'It's absolutely essential you keep any- and everyone off us for the duration. Rebaine, for all practical purposes, won't be here, and I've got to monitor and make sure nothing goes wrong.' She looked back to the warlord, wiped the sweat off her hands with a swipe across her now filthy skirts, and began to gesture.

'Wait a minute,' Corvis began, tense once more, 'what do you mean "make sure nothing goes wrong"? I thought—'

'Relax, I'm just taking precautions. Projection rarely goes awry.'

Corvis probably would have said something to that, but Rheah began her chant. Instantly, he felt the life drain from his limbs, his arms and legs suddenly falling asleep.

The lethargy spread through his chest, his head. He could have sworn he actually heard his heartbeat slowing . . .

And then he was *elsewhere*.

Corvis Rebaine, helpless. Rheah Vhoune beside him, her attention focused on the subject of her spell. The others distracted and concerned, far too intent on the condition of their companions to properly pay attention.

There would never be a better chance.

Thinning himself to transparency on wafting currents of air, Mithraem seeped beneath the door and the pitiful barricade, steadily pooling into one shadowy corner of the room.

Nathaniel Espa, former knight, former adviser to Duke Lorum, forcefully locked his legs into place to keep from pacing. He was more than a little agitated and his body, accustomed to the rigours of warfare despite his advancing age, demanded movement.

His eyes flickered constantly to the motionless, mismatched

pair at the window. He took in the witch who'd stood behind him in the council chamber, and the wild-eyed woman with the hatchets.

It would be so easy. Yes, he'd die in the aftermath, but neither could stop him if he decided to end the Terror's life here and now. A single stroke of his sword and boundless suffering would be set right. It was worth the price of his own life, so much so he actually felt his hand twitching with eagerness to see the job done. Hell, he was barely half convinced by this whole ludicrous idea that Lorum was Audriss. He'd practically raised the regent from a boy, supervised his education in all matters military and political. He *couldn't* be so blind, could he? This could all be some trick of Rebaine's, and they were standing around, letting him get away with – with whatever he was getting away with.

But Rheah, at least, believed, and Nathan had never known her to be wrong. If she trusted, did he not have to as well?

Of course, there was a first time for everything, including the infallible sorceress proving woefully fallible after all. If this was it, Nathan was determined to see the Terror of the East lying in a pool of blood, regardless of the consequences.

Nathaniel Espa continued to stare, at his friends, at his enemies, and not at the pale, long-fingered hand sliding from the darkness behind him, reaching from the depths of the shadows, stretching far longer than any human arm could have stretched, reaching . . .

Oh, great was Corvis' first thought. *Just what I need. More forests.*

His second thought was, *If the only thing about this place bugging me is the fact that it is a forest, I've lost whatever grip on sanity I once had.*

The sky burned red above him, the bloody radiance coming from all directions, for there was nothing remotely resembling a sun. Clouds of bubbling liquids drifted past, leaving smudges and stains in the air, as though that sky was a solid surface.

Which, upon further consideration, it very well might have been.

Thunder roared in the distance, or at least Corvis decided to pretend it was thunder, even though most storms didn't howl like they were in quite so much pain. A hot wind blew through the trees, making him sweat. Not only hot, but moist, and with an acrid odour that suggested it might just be the breath of something far away but very, very large.

Corvis started walking. As one direction seemed as good as any other, he simply set off in the way he was facing.

He was somewhat surprised to note that he was clad not in his armour, but the simple tunic and well-worn pants that were his favourites for helping Tyannon in the garden or playing with his children when the chores were done. He hoped that said something good about him.

The trees appeared normal: brown, rough trunks, green leaves, about the right size. Theaghl-gohlatch had been a lot more disturbing. These were comforting, in a way, an anchor to normality in this alien realm.

That perception lasted exactly as long as it took Corvis, hair standing on end, to think to look behind him.

Protruding from the backside of each and every tree were human limbs. Arms and legs and heads reached beseechingly from the wooden embrace, fingers stretched wide in supplication. Each head was missing its face, as though something had simply peeled the visage off the front of the skull. Blood ran freely from the exposed muscles and sockets, fingers clenched and flexed as he passed, and jaws hung in mute agony.

And then, despite the lack of faces, Corvis recognised a few of them. The big one there, the sheer bulk of the man and the tattered furs that covered his arms, could only be Grat, the trapper from the Terrakas Mountains. That one there was the bartender. And Sah-di. And the young whore who'd propositioned him in the common room . . .

These were the souls Khanda had consumed in his millennia of life, souls trapped in endless torment in this tiny pocket of hell. And many of them, Corvis himself had put here.

The Terror of the East, the scourge of Imphallion, dropped to his knees and retched.

It was several moments later, after he'd struggled back to his feet and staggered weakly on his way, that he thought to wonder just what a spiritual projection held in its stomach to vomit up. He decided quite firmly not to go back and check.

And then the trees simply stopped, and Corvis was staring across a flat plane of gleaming obsidian, brilliantly polished. Had there been a night sky above, it would have been impossible to tell where the horizon ended, to be certain which stars were real and which were reflection. As it was, the darkness merely reflected the dull red hanging above it, creating the illusion of a motionless lake of blackened blood.

In the exact centre of that lake stood a rickety wooden structure bearing more than passing resemblance to a gnarled human hand. As Corvis drew closer, his footsteps careful on the near-frictionless stone, he saw that each finger was, in fact, a cobbled-together extension of ropes and wooden beams, each ending in a thick but fraying noose.

It was a gibbet, conceived and designed by someone who'd never known sanity. The 'palm' of the hand, cupped ever so gently, was the platform on which the condemned must stand. The fingers, curled back over the platform, hung over rusty-hinged trapdoors, squeaking and screaming in the breeze. The nooses were currently unoccupied, gods be thanked, but enough dried bones lay in ungainly heaps beneath the gallows to suggest it saw substantial use.

From behind the horrendous structure came the sound of heavy breathing. Ignoring the hackles rising across the back of his neck, Corvis stepped around it.

An enormous throne, made up entirely of red crystal, stood with its back to the gibbet. It was, in light of its surroundings, surprising in its simplicity. No decorations, beautiful or horrifying, adorned its surface, no tools of torture protruded from its back and arms. It was just a throne.

A young man sat idly in the chair, one leg stretched out before him, the other slung over the side. He was naked save for a bracer made up of three thin silver bands. His body was marble white, and shaped as though sculpted by a student of the classical arts. His hair, light brown, could have belonged to anyone. Only the creature's eyes – each of which possessed a pair of irises, side by side – and the utter lack of humanity in his expression indicated that this thing, whatever it might be, was entirely alien.

The sound of breathing, louder now that Corvis drew near, came not from the chair's occupant, but from something beneath him. For the moment, the warlord could not make out what it might be.

'Corvis!' the figure in the chair crowed. 'How decent of you to come visit!'

An indigestible mix of emotions churning in his gut, Corvis forced a smile in return. 'I always wondered what you actually looked like, Khanda.'

'What, this? Meaningless. Nothing you see here is real, not as you understand the term. Rheah – it *was* Rheah who arranged this little visit, yes? – Rheah should have warned you of that before she sent you here.' Khanda leaned forward, his unnatural eyes narrowing. 'And since it's come up, why *are* you here? We have plenty of time – without your body, in this place, it moves a lot faster than it does outside – so feel free to indulge in the details.'

'I'm so glad you asked,' Corvis said, steeling himself to step closer to the throne and the unholy *thing* that sat upon it. 'Perhaps I should ask you that same question.'

It was eons since Khanda had dealt with anyone who could actually see his reactions. Though, he tried at once to hide it, scowling, imperious, haughty, Corvis saw the demon flinch at his words. 'I haven't the slightest clue what you're talking about, Corvis. And here I thought that seeing you face-to-face might help cut through your tightly wrapped shroud of idiocy, but it seems—'

'Let me tell you a story.' Corvis stood directly before the throne. He lifted up a single booted foot, resting it on the chair mere inches from Khanda's exposed genitals. It didn't make the demon as nervous as it would a mortal, but it did put Corvis in a position to meet Khanda's gaze without leaving the demon room to retreat. 'It starts . . . Well, I'm not sure exactly how long ago it starts. A few years, maybe a decade. It's not really important.'

Khanda blinked. 'Excuse me. What are you—'

'In this story,' the Terror continued, refusing to be interrupted, 'there's a demon. His name is Khanda, and he's trapped inside this itty-bitty little amulet. But even more frustrating is that he's *also* trapped inside this great big cold wall of ice. He was put there by a mean, nasty man who'd used him for years and then just thrown him away.'

'I wonder who that might be?'

Again, Corvis refused to go off-course. 'But after years of being trapped, Khanda made contact with someone, someone who called himself Audriss.' The warlord shrugged. 'I don't suppose you'd care to tell me exactly how you accomplished that, would you?'

Khanda sneered. 'If you must know, I sensed Pekatherosh when Audriss first made use of *his* power. We can talk to each other at much greater range than we can speak with your kind.'

'I thought you hated each other.'

'We do. Some things are bigger than that.'

'Ah. In any case,' he continued, 'Khanda contacted Audriss – through Pekatherosh, then. Eventually, he learned that Audriss planned to pick up where the first bad man left off. This was perfect for Khanda, since he had something to trade, something Audriss would want.' Corvis smiled grimly. 'In retrospect, I shouldn't have hidden the book anywhere near you.'

'Hindsight is a virgin in a chastity belt,' the demon snapped at him. 'Beautiful but useless. Are you going somewhere with this, or is this a bedtime story? Because you're about to put me to sleep.'

'Oh, it's definitely going somewhere. You see, Khanda, I

know *why* you betrayed me. There's only one thing Audriss could have offered that you would possibly want.'

'Sod off, Corvis!'

'So I ask you again: why are you *here?*'

Khanda pulled back against the crystalline throne, drawing away from Corvis' piercing eyes, but the warlord left him nowhere to go. With an enraged bellow, Khanda shot to his feet, shoving the human back. Corvis found himself airborne, and then crashed painfully to the unyielding ground.

'It's temporary!' Khanda screamed at him. 'Just until he's finished with Mecepheum! Then I'm free, Corvis! I'm free! Just a few more hours! Just a few . . .' His face falling, the demon slumped back into his chair, head cradled in his hands.

Corvis clambered to his feet. 'He won't free you, Khanda.'

'You don't know that!' But it was a knee-jerk objection, reflexive, with no conviction behind it.

'I do know that. What amazes me is that *you* believed him.'

Khanda smiled sadly. 'What did I have to lose, Corvis? My other option was to stay trapped in this gem, and that wall, for eternity.' The demon shook his head. 'It's not as if he needs to keep me around, damn him! He's got Pekatherosh, he's got the bloody book and the key. He's already as near a god as any mortal could hope! What good does it do him to keep me here?'

If not for the soul-trees, Corvis might have felt a glimmer of sympathy for his infernal companion. Instead, his voice was cold, clinical, as he said, 'You got too used to dealing with me, Khanda. Whatever faults I had, I did what I did in pursuit of a specific goal. Audriss, though, is mad with power. He'll not let go of even an inch, no matter how much he's got. Good gods, he tried to ally with *me*, remember? Even after he threatened my family, tried to kill me, he couldn't let it end without trying at least once to fit me under his thumb along with everyone else. You're trapped more tightly now than you were a year ago.'

Khanda's head rose. 'Unless I help you now. Is that it, Corvis? Is that why you've come?'

'Fill in the blanks for me, Khanda. Since we *do* have time, finish the story for me. And then I just *might* have an offer to make you.'

'And why should I trust you not to betray me as Audriss did?'

'Because you know me.'

Khanda laughed. 'Better than you do, I expect, and that's as good a reason as any *not* to believe a word you say. But what the hell, I've got no more to lose now than I did then. What do you want to know?'

'I want to know why it went down this way, Khanda. Why didn't Audriss just come and grab you, and the book, from the cave? Why involve me at all?'

'Ah . . .' Khanda actually blushed a bit. 'The uncomfortable truth, Corvis, is that I wasn't entirely certain where I was. You made such an effort to make the teleportation quick and confusing, so I wouldn't realise what was happening in time to stop you, that you skewed with my bearings. You used *my* power to imprison me in the ice, and I didn't know where I was! Bloody irritating, let me tell you what!'

Laughing aloud at the moment would, Corvis knew, be a poor tactical decision. He coughed twice to cover it up, and then asked, 'And Pekatherosh couldn't track you down?'

'We've been enemies for thousands upon thousands of years, you lackwit. We've spent most of those casting spells to *avoid* detection by each other. Besides, you think I'd trust him to do it right, even if I could?'

An avalanche of understanding crashed down upon him. 'So you used me, threatened my family and my home, just so I'd eventually have to retrieve *you*!'

'That's the long and short of it, yes.'

Corvis squelched his rising anger with a near-superhuman effort. Time enough for it later. 'And afterward? Once you knew where you'd been, you knew where the book was. Why not leave me out of it then?'

'You were already fully involved. Besides, Audriss knew that the threat of the Terror of the East might force the

Guilds to submit to him. I think he really wanted to rule as Lorum, not as Audriss, given the choice.'

'I'm so horribly sorry to have disappointed him.'

'I'm sure. Also, he suspected Rheah might have developed the key to Selakrian's book, but he couldn't very well come right out and ask her, could he? Letting you and your so-called army remain involved brought the Guilds in line – though not as soon as he'd hoped – and it was you who confirmed for him that Rheah had decoded the book.'

Corvis felt the urge to glance at his shoulders in search of strings. 'I've been a puppet. Every last godsdamn thing I've done—'

'Well, not all of it. You pretty well bollixed up his primary plan when you exposed him. It didn't stop him, but at least you can say you drew blood.'

The Terror of the East let out a sudden, explosive breath. 'All right, Khanda,' he said, his voice astoundingly level. 'Here's what we're going to do.'

Nathaniel Espa lay on the floor, fetched up in the corner. Huddled and spotted with blood, he struggled to focus past the pain, to blink the tears from his eyes. His right arm was broken in two places, his left leg literally wrenched around at the knee so that it was nothing but dangling deadweight. So covered was he in bruises and lacerations, he looked as though he'd leapt naked into a briar patch. His sword, his armour, his vaunted skill, all proved less than useless against the sudden, inhuman assault.

In the centre of the room, a tornado had struck. Furniture and bits of furniture lay strewn about the room, cadavers made of planks and splinters. The dust fluttered in endless circular clouds, dancing with cruel delight at the unfolding scene of carnage.

Mithraem stood amid the wreckage, a nightmare granted flesh and blood. Mostly blood. He held a relaxed fencer's stance, his thin-bladed sword dancing with simple, idle strokes. Before him, Ellowaine raged, hatchets spinning, but not a single strike could penetrate his casual defenses. Behind them, Seilloah lay crumpled on the floor, trembling and blood-drenched hands clutching tightly around the shaft of wood protruding from her stomach, a stake she'd intended for the creature attacking them. Thick, black blood flowed from the dreadful wound, and the agony goaded her to the very edge of madness. To a witch of Seilloah's skill, the wound need not be fatal, but only if she had access to her powers and her herbs, only if she had the time to treat it properly, only if she could concentrate past the pain . . .

And by the window, Rheah Vhoune and Corvis Rebaine. The warlord stood, a statue of pale flesh and black iron, staring out the window with sightless, unblinking eyes. The sorceress hovered nearby, torn with indecision.

If something went wrong, and she wasn't there to stabilise Rebaine, they could lose him. On the other hand, Mithraem was tearing through her allies like so much parchment, and if he wasn't stopped, Corvis and the rest were *certainly* lost. Reluctantly, Rheah directed her attention away from the entranced man.

Even as she made her decision, the master of the Endless Legion tired of his sport. A contemptuous flick of his sword sent one of Ellowaine's hatchets across the room. A swift kick followed, and the mercenary collapsed to the floor, accompanied by the sound of snapping bones.

Espa writhed in the corner, helpless rage nearly blotting out the pain as he struggled, and failed, to find his feet. A thick trail of blood stretched across the floor, as though left by some gargantuan crimson slug. Seilloah, one hand pressed tightly to her gaping abdomen, collapsed from her crawl only feet from where she'd begun and curled tightly into a fetal position, helpless against the agony. And Ellowaine lay stunned, a dramatic angle to her left leg that shouldn't exist in any animal less flexible than an eel.

Not counting the currently vacant body of the Terror of the East, only Mithraem and Rheah remained standing in that beat-up little room. Outside, twin horrors from the depths of legend ran amok, and if they did not truly signify the end of the world, they were certainly the end of Mecepheum. Inside was a foe that should have been far less terrible, yet the idea of facing him alone was almost enough to make the normally unflappable sorceress seize up into a useless, gibbering mass.

It was his eyes, empty, soulless, endless tunnels into an infinity of nothing at all, tugging at her soul. Even in the vilest of men, a spark of unalterable *something* made them, at their core, human.

Mithraem, to his core, was not.

Even as the thing approached, the wizard's hands rose and syllables older than civilisation rumbled from her lips. The air around her crackled, the room filled with the smell of smoke and ozone. Desperate to stop the advancing nightmare, Rheah pulled no punches. The most powerful offensive spell she knew coalesced before her, stabbing at her foe, the dagger of the gods.

It was a bolt, but this was no lightning. Energies of all hues, from blinding whites to subtle blues and greens, raced the length of the stream. It slammed into Mithraem's chest, hurling him into the far wall hard enough to crack the surrounding brick and shatter the glass. His sword fell from his fist, landing unnoticed by the window. Smoke rose from the floorboards as the heat radiated outward, yet frost formed on the walls as the energies of the arcane assault vied for dominance. A strike of pure elemental power, it contained all that was – earth and air, fire and water – and nothing of this world could stand against it.

But Mithraem, of course, was not of this world. For long seconds, she leaned into the bolt, covered in a sheen of sweat. On the energies flowed, wave after wave, pinning her target to the wall. And then her reserves simply ran out. With a final crackle, the spell dissipated, and Rheah collapsed to her knees, sucking in great gasps of air.

Stone and wood and plaster shifted, dust cascaded from the wall, and Mithraem pulled himself from the wreckage.

His tunic hung in rags, disintegrated by the spell. Ash

coated his torso and face, burns spotted his chest, and half his hair had burned away to reveal a horribly charred scalp. But still he stood, and still he neared, mouth gaping in a taunting smile that showed his white, gleaming, perfect teeth against the blackened canvas of his face.

Too exhausted even to run, Rheah could do nothing as the creature bent down beside her, brushed his lips sensuously across her throat, and began to drink her life away.

CHAPTER TWENTY-EIGHT

Tyannon stood at the room's only window, the shutters open just enough to offer a clear view of the stables, and idly tapped a finger on the sill. It wasn't that she was particularly anxious to *be* anywhere in particular. Rather, she'd found herself generally impatient of late, and had no clear idea why.

The heavy snows of midwinter had kept them in town for weeks, far longer than they'd planned to stay. They also, however, kept travel on the nearby roads to a minimum, so Corvis had told her that he wasn't too concerned about the possibilities of pursuit or attack.

Now that spring was beginning to draw its first shallow breaths, rather like a newborn babe, they'd be moving on shortly. Corvis had gone down to the stables to make some sort of arrangements, while Tyannon gathered their possessions from around the room. Had he left her alone like this months before, she'd have been gone so fast that even the gods would've had trouble keeping up.

Now, though? Tyannon knew she wasn't a prisoner anymore, not really. She told herself that she simply had nowhere else to go, but she knew that wasn't true, either.

No, the truth was that it was growing harder and harder for Tyannon to reconcile the warlord she'd heard of with the man travelling beside her. She knew his crimes, still occasionally shuddered at remembered horror stories, and of course there were still those memories of that day beneath the Hall. But the man she knew – the man who seemed vaguely beaten down by the world around him, the man who had thrown down his weapon to keep her from harm, the man who clearly had no real idea of what to *do* with her – that man seemed someone else entirely. Someone *better*.

And Tyannon found herself unduly curious as to which one was the 'real' Corvis Rebaine.

The door flew open as Corvis heaved himself, and his burden, into the room. With a loud clatter and a grunt of strain, Corvis lifted the saddlebag and set it upright against the wall. Tyannon's eyebrow rose as he took just a moment to massage his back.

'Did you need help with that?' she asked archly.

'You couldn't have offered at the *bottom* of the stairs?'

Tyannon's lip-twitched. 'What fun would *that* have been?'

Corvis grumbled something unintelligible and drew open the bag's ties. There seemed to be nothing within but a collection of cheap and rusty tools; Tyannon knew it to be an illusion, one of the magics that Corvis could manage without the aid of that *thing* that used to hang around his neck. With another grunt, he upended the bag, allowing its true contents – a suit of armour, constructed of black steel and bone spurs, smelling, strongly of oils – to spill across the floor.

Tyannon couldn't quite repress a gasp of revulsion.

'I'm not wearing it,' he assured her swiftly. 'I just . . . I wanted you to see this for yourself.'

'See what?'

He didn't answer, not immediately, Instead, Corvis dug into the pile of pieces, retrieving two that clearly didn't match the others. One was a heavy tome, its ancient leather covers warped and bent. The other was the ruby-red pendant on its innocuous silver chain.

Grimacing, as tense as though he were sticking his hand into a serpent's den, Corvis reached out and clutched the amulet. 'Hello, Khanda.' Then, 'Cute.

Funny as always,' and 'I'm not sure. Almost two months, maybe.'

Tyannon could not, of course, hear the other side of the conversation. Part of her wanted to grab the pendant away, hurl it out the window, or simply to scream her fury at its mere presence. She did none of those things, though, simply watched, and listened . . .

And she could have sworn that, just perhaps, she heard the faintest trace of an enraged scream from deep within the ruby as it, and the ancient codex, suddenly vanished in a pulse of crimson light.

Corvis stood, his shoulders straightening, and damn if he didn't look years younger than he had only moments before. Not yet certain what she'd seen – or perhaps simply unprepared to believe – Tyannon stepped forward. Tentatively, she reached out a foot to prod the spot on the floor where the book had lain, and even poked a finger into the palm of Corvis' hand.

'They're gone,' he told her, his voice softer than she'd ever heard it. 'For good.'

'Why, Corvis?'

Did he actually blush as he turned away? 'Because I know it's what you wanted.'

Tyannon considered once more the two different men she knew as Corvis Rebaine – and she wondered, for the first time, if just maybe she herself might have a hand in determining, once and for all, which of them was real.

His expression thoughtful, Khanda rose from his throne, the muscles beneath his flesh flowing with unnatural grace and precision. As he stepped aside, Corvis finally saw the surface of the throne on which the demon sat, the source of that laboured breathing. Even after his exposure to the horrors of this hellish realm, the warlord sucked in his breath. The crystalline seat and backing of the throne was padded, for Khanda's comfort, with a cushion stitched together from the missing faces of the souls within the forest. Flattened mouths panted desperate, horrified breaths, moaned silently in torment. Tears ran from the corners of blinded eyes long squashed and dried.

It was definitely time to leave.

'It might work,' Khanda finally admitted, thumb and forefinger slowly stroking his chin in a mockery of human contemplation. 'We'll have to be bloody quick about it, though, or Audriss will figure it out. And he holds the pendant, Corvis, which means he's technically in control.'

'Didn't stop you from turning coat on me at the drop of a hat, now, did it?'

'No, I imagine it didn't.' The demon scowled. 'I have your word on this. When this is over, I go free. You release me from this damn prison!'

'That's the deal.'

'If you renege on me, Corvis . . .'

'Have I ever lied to you, Khanda?'

If anything, the scowl grew deeper. 'I suggest you get moving. Even as slowly as time's going by outside this place, you don't want to dillydally. Big snakes and spiders eating people, and all that.' Another pause. 'Rheah Vhoune *did* tell you how to get back, didn't she?'

'I sort of figured it was just a matter of concentration, actually.'

'Right. So why aren't you concentrating?'

Corvis concentrated.

A small corner of Rheah's mind peered through the haze of exhaustion and the clouds of numbing panic, observing, almost clinically, the process slowly killing her. Her skin stretched as the pores on her face gaped wide, as her blood welled up in those pools of flesh. What little strength remained seeped from her, leached out with her stolen blood.

The greater part of her, the part not even remotely calm, sobbed once reflexively at what was happening to her. For a moment, Mithraem pulled away, blood-drenched teeth exposed in a mocking leer.

'It's been a long time,' he whispered in a hoarse caricature of passion, 'since I've had a sorcerer. And you, if it means anything, you're one of the best I've tasted.'

For that single instant, when the blood stopped flowing, Rheah rallied her self-control. She retained enough for one last spell; she *had* to have enough!

Nothing offensive. Her body couldn't take the strain, and if this walking corruption had survived the elemental lightning bolt, nothing she could throw at it would do any better.

But there was a way. In her studies and experiments, Rheah had learned much about the human form, things most common folk didn't know, couldn't understand. And one of those obscure little facts – about the nature of the liquid pumping through her, that Mithraem now stole in his own peculiar brand of rape – might just be enough to save her.

It was a simple spell, one of her favourites, designed to ruin an enemy's weapon. But she must cast it now, exhausted, weakened nigh unto death, with greater precision than she'd ever before attempted.

Under her breath, Rheah began to chant.

Mithraem bent forward once more, his lips returning to the side of her face, as she'd known he would. And then, with the last of her rapidly failing consciousness, she spat the spell's final syllables.

Skilled as she was, it proved nearly impossible. The enchantment was intended for a sword, an axe. Her office was decorated with just such weapons. Now she cast it upon something much smaller, something completely unseen.

But she was Rheah Vhoune, Initiate of the Eighth Circle, and by all the gods she *would* make it happen! The spell's energies crept out, invisible and undetectable, insinuating themselves into the fluids passing between her and the enemy, from her flesh to his lips.

And even as it passed through those lips, the iron in her blood transformed to wood.

So fast was Mithraem drinking the life from Rheah's body that, even as his tongue detected the sudden, grainy taste of the blood, he'd taken three full swallows before he could stop.

A mouthful of strange, watery blood splattered across Rheah's face as Mithraem spat. His expression fell slack as he rose, retreating from his 'helpless' victim. Desperately he hacked, coughed, trying to clear his system of the unnatural substance he'd taken in. The blood – or what had originally been blood – swept through his flesh, permeated his bones, fed life to dead and desiccated organs that belonged deep in the earth.

And then it reached his heart. There was oh so little of it, scarcely the tiniest fraction of the blood that had been transformed. But in this body that should not exist at all, it was enough.

For the first time in generations, the first time since he'd truly lived, eating and breathing as mortals eat and breathe, Mithraem screamed. It held no menace, this high-pitched shriek, nothing predatory, no great font of evil. Only fear and despair, the last hopeless cry of a dying immortal.

Seilloah rose from the bloody floor. From collar to knees, the front of her dress was drenched with blood, clammy and sticky against her skin. The tattered cloth gaped open where she'd yanked the stake from her stomach. Pink and fragile flesh, already bruising, sealed the wound like a patch upon the hull of a sinking ship. It would keep her from bleeding to death until she could do a more thorough job.

Emotionless, remorseless, the witch stepped around her flailing foe, scouring the room. *There*. Seilloah lifted Mithraem's own sword from the floor and raised it high.

Mithraem, lord and master of the Endless Legion, eldest of his kind, ceased abruptly to scream. His head, mouth agape, landed not with a percussive thump but a liquid splash. Black rot and viscous corruption splattered the room, accompanied by the fetor of a dozen corpses splayed in the summer sun. Mist poured from the decomposing sludge, barred by the permeating wood from seeking a new shell, new life. A single sob, harbinger of endless grief and childish fear, echoed throughout the room. And then the mist faded into the floor and was gone.

A heavy hand clamped down on Seilloah's shoulder from behind. With a startled shriek she spun, Mithraem's sword raised in a marginally competent grip.

'Sorry,' Corvis said.

'If we hadn't just gone through nine kinds of hell to keep you alive,' Seilloah snarled, gasping heavily, 'I'd seriously consider running you through.'

With slow, drowsy movements, the warlord surveyed the room. His expression grew puzzled when he saw Nathaniel Espa lying in a heap, shifting to true concern when his gaze fell upon the crumpled forms of Ellowaine and Rheah.

'Mithraem,' Seilloah answered his unspoken question. 'He's gone now. For good.'

Corvis nodded. 'How are they?'

'Espa and Ellowaine are in no immediate danger, though some of those limbs may never work properly again. But Corvis, there's nothing anyone can do for Rheah. She's lost too much blood.'

Softly, the Terror of the East knelt down beside the supine form of the woman who was once his most dangerous enemy. Almost tenderly, he took her pallid hand in his own iron-clad grip.

'This . . . isn't exactly the way I expected . . . to go,' she whispered, voice so soft he could barely hear it. 'It's a good thing . . . nothing went wrong with . . . the spell. I . . . couldn't have . . . helped you. Was it . . . worth it?'

'I spoke to Khanda,' Corvis confirmed. 'He'll help. I'll save your city, Rheah. I don't know if my word means a damn to you, but I give it anyway.'

The sorceress shuddered once. 'Then hadn't you better . . . get moving?'

'Rheah, where's the key? The real key?'

Weakly, the sorceress laughed. 'Rebaine, do you think . . . I'm delirious? We may be on the same . . . side right now, but you're still . . . you. It's far from here, safe . . . safe from you, from everyone. No one will . . . threaten my city again. No one . . .'

One breath. One more.

'I really wanted . . . to see a Sorcerers' Guild . . .'

Rheah Vhoune, Initiate of the Eighth Circle, sighed one final time, and didn't breathe again.

Gently, Corvis closed her eyes. And then, with no hesitation, he reached into the pouch on Rheah's belt and removed a small scroll case, similar to the one she'd given Audriss.

'There's no way she wouldn't have kept it on her,' he replied to Seilloah's questioning look. 'On the off-chance she wrested the book away from Audriss, she'd have wanted to be able to use it against us.

'Take care of Ellowaine,' he said, rising to his feet and sticking the case into his own pouch. 'If I'm not back within half an hour, get her out of here, and tell Losalis to get the men the hell away from Mecepheum.'

'Corvis, I should go with you! If you need help, I—'

'Won't be able to provide it.' The Terror of the East yanked Sunder from his baldric. The blade gleamed, despite the absence of any direct light. 'This is between Audriss and me now, Seilloah. If I lose, this city goes down with me. Don't be here when that happens.'

He reached out a hand, placed it gently on the shoulder of his old friend, and squeezed. Tight-lipped, Seilloah nodded once.

Corvis turned on his heel and departed.

Her face marred by pain, Seilloah surveyed the room. Her eyes fell upon the injured, supine form of the great Nathaniel Espa, and despite her agony, a feral grin slowly crept across her face.

Behind the blank and barren stone, the first traces of puzzlement flickered across Lorum's face. His new pets were causing untold destruction, slaying all who stood in – anywhere near – their path, and that was good. But they were *dawdling*!

They moved forward only slowly, stopping frequently to ensure that everything around them was laid waste, that no spark of life escaped their unquenchable fury.

Growing angrier by the minute, the Serpent actually shook the tome he held in his hand. The Twins should have made a beeline for the Hall of Meeting, as he'd commanded! If the council survived this little exercise, things would be substantially more difficult for him later on.

He'd wanted to make a definite impression, to cast himself into the pages of legend, but he'd also intended to have a capital city left afterward. That was looking less and less likely with every subsequent street engulfed in flames or swamped beneath rivers of diseased ichor.

His steps thoughtful, the warlord called Audriss marched across the air toward the nearest building, a wide, three-story tenement. As though the swirling eddies of smoke formed the most solid of stairs, he descended from his lofty perch to stand instead upon real stone, his formerly silent boots now crunching on the gravel. From this new vantage, he once more flipped through the book, searching for clues as to why he'd lost control.

'Oh, it's not the book, Audriss. It's just that you're an idiot.'

The Serpent actually jumped, so startled was he to hear any voice, and this voice in particular, on the rooftop. But sure enough, there he stood, encased in that ridiculous spiked armour, his hair hanging limply around his ears, Sunder grasped in battle-weary hands.

'Corvis,' the warlord purred, teeth clenched in a predatory grin that his enemy couldn't see, 'how good of you to join me. Pray tell, to what particular aspect of my idiocy do you refer? You might want to make it snappy, mind. From the looks of things, this building won't be here in another, oh, five minutes.' He gestured with his free hand at the Children of Apocalypse, currently demolishing the Weavers' Guild Hall not three hundred yards distant.

'You actually thought Rheah would give in that easily, Audriss?'

The Serpent abruptly began to laugh.

'She switched keys, didn't she?' Far from the consternation Corvis hoped for, his enemy continued to chuckle, actually shaking his head. 'Well, congratulate her for me, Rebaine. She's just unleashed Maukra and Mimgol on the city without the slightest measure of control. Not, I suppose, the result she intended.'

'They can be stopped,' the Terror of the East told him grimly.

'Oh, of course,' Audriss sneered. 'Tell me, Rebaine, is this the part where you suggest we put aside our differences and work together for the common good? I use the book, you use the real key – assume you have the real key, or you'd be miles away by now – to stop the monsters? Is that it?'

'Not at all. This is the part where I kill you and take the book to do with as I please.'

Audriss remained unworried. Without his precious Khanda, Corvis Rebaine was merely a two-bit, apprentice-level wizard. The only thing dangerous about him was Sunder, and even the Kholben Shiar was no threat if he couldn't get near his foe.

'Khanda,' the Serpent said casually, raising an arm to point, 'get me the key and get rid of him, would you?'

A glow surrounded the silver-ringed wristband, an accumulation of power that may have been the demonic equivalent of a man taking a deep, preparatory breath. Khanda gathered his energies . . .

And then, accompanied by a shriek of rage and sheer, malevolent hatred from Pekatherosh that only Audriss could hear, both demons, the wristband and the pewter ring, vanished in a swirl of blood-red sparks.

'Oops,' Corvis said conversationally. 'I bet that wasn't supposed to happen.' And then he leapt, Sunder raised high.

The Serpent, overwhelmed, had no chance to react. The axe slammed into his rib cage, hurling him backward, a rag doll bearing the brunt of a spoiled child's tantrum. The enchanted stone held, though it was once more split in a cobweb of cracks. They'd both learned, on their first encounter, that the Serpent's armour could withstand at least one blow from the Kholben Shiar.

Nor had Corvis forgotten it. His attack wasn't meant to kill. What it *was* supposed to do, and accomplished quite nicely, was send the warlord over the edge of the roof.

The Serpent slammed onto the cobblestones with a resonant crash. Pieces of the magic armour, already weakened by Sunder's bite, lay scattered through the street, rough fragments that crumbled swiftly into powder. Audriss lay stunned, limbs splayed around him.

Selakrian's tome, covers spread and pages crumpled beneath it, lay fetched up against a building across the street. Windows nearby erupted as Maukra's hellfire, herald of the Dragon's approach, ignited the opposite end of the structure, consuming everything within.

Bereft of any other option, Corvis leapt from the rooftop.

He had an uncomfortable amount of time to think as he dropped to the waiting earth. His own armour, though not without its own eldritch enchantments, was not as tough as Audriss', and his own physical prowess was hardly what it once was. If he could just . . .

Ground.

Corvis rolled as best he could, but still pain shot through his leg, throbbing in time with his rapidly beating heart. He clattered as he rumbled, spines digging into the stone.

His breathing laboured, his body covered in a colourful collection of bruises and contusions, the Terror of the East came to his feet, wincing at the pain in his ankle. Not broken, he determined as he gingerly leaned into it, but badly twisted. He wouldn't be doing much running in the near future.

A monstrous shadow fell over him, many-legged and dripping, cast by a horror blocks away. Spurred into action, ignoring his fallen foe as the lesser priority, Corvis divided once more, coming again to his feet beside the blazing building, Selakrian's spellbook clutched in his hands.

It didn't look all that special, but then it never had. Simple leather covers, dried and cracking, bound perhaps a hundred pages of brittle parchment that would have crumbled into memories long ago without the arcane protections laid upon them. Audriss was the first person to actually use the book in centuries, and his careless treatment had already bent the ancient, stiffened spine. Thus, when it tumbled from his grip, it fell open to the very pages of the summoning spell that had unleashed Armageddon upon Mecepheum.

It required no key to decipher the notes Selakrian wrote beside each spell; only the actual casting of the rituals required that tiny, invaluable scroll. His eyes quickly scanning the page, Corvis felt his throat tighten. Selakrian had indeed worked a fail-safe into this Grand Summoning, a condition under which the spell would collapse, sending the twin horrors back to the deepest netherworld. But did 'destruction of the source' refer to the *caster*, or the *book*?

And before he dealt with that, there was something else he needed to do, something he had to find. Desperately Corvis leafed through the book, scanning pages. Even as the horrors drew nearer, when the shrieks of the dying resounded in his ears, in harmony with the piercing, otherworldly cries of Maukra and Mimgol themselves, he flipped madly, searching, searching.

There it was, exactly what he needed! Now if he could just . . .

'*No!*' His featureless mask abandoned, his armour crumbling in chunks and slivers, Duke Lorum slammed into Corvis from behind, grabbing for the ancient tome. Sunder, knocked from Corvis' grip by the impact, went skidding across the flagstone in a shower of sparks. 'The book is mine, do you hear me? *Mine!*' A thin worm of spittle dangled obscenely from the corner of his mouth, his hair was plastered to his cheek with blood, and his eyes were devoid of anything resembling sanity.

Like common barroom brawlers, the two most feared men in the entirety of Imphallion fell heavily to the ground, rolling in the street. Fists flew and fingers grabbed. Here, Corvis held the advantage, for his armour was mostly intact. But Audriss was utterly mad, ignoring the thunderous blows Corvis drove home again and again, uncaring that his nostrils bled freely and his teeth rained to the cobblestones in a miniature hailstorm.

And then Audriss, in the midst of another grab for the tome, suddenly reversed his stroke and drove his elbow into Corvis' chin. The Terror of the East felt his teeth clack together like a portcullis, pain blazing across his face. He struggled to shake it off, but it bought Audriss precious seconds to drop a hand down to the scabbard at his waist.

At his best, Corvis might have grabbed the wrist holding the dagger, or perhaps tried to hurl Audriss away and make a dive for his own weapon. But Corvis was bruised, battered, exhausted, and not as spry as he once was. The best he could do, as the gleaming blade of Talon rose to strike, was to scuttle away like a terrified crab. Before he could even rise to his feet, Audriss lunged and stabbed again. Desperately, Corvis twisted.

And gods be praised, it worked! One of the spines on his shoulder, those foolish, ridiculous ornaments, slammed into Talon in a perfect parry. The blade skittered across the steel beneath those spikes, marring its jet-black sheen, but otherwise harmless.

Corvis had perhaps a full half second to marvel before Audriss slammed the weapon's pommel into his head.

The world dimmed and flashed before Corvis' eyes, and the ground tilted. He tightened his grip on the book, felt parchment crumple beneath his fingers even as the Serpent grabbed once more for the prize. A fierce tug, a brief ripping, and the book was gone.

A sudden heavy kick against the side of his ribs, and the world spiraled yet again. As he rolled, he heard a second, louder tearing noise, and he felt the heavy purple cloak, already holed and tattered, finally tear completely from his shoulders.

He slid, flipping completely over before skidding to a halt, and wondered for a moment why it had grown so damnably hot.

Through the throbbing in his head, Corvis forced his eyelids apart.

Every building around them was engulfed in apocalyptic fire, and the harsh cries of the Dragon and the Spider rose to a deafening crescendo. Even as he watched, Maukra's serpentine shadow fell over them from an impossible height, blotting out the sun.

Before him, oblivious to the coming danger, Lorum stood with his back to the blazing building. In his right hand he clutched Talon, in his left, Selakrian's spellbook. And he laughed – a laugh devoid of humanity, let alone sanity.

There was nothing Corvis could do. His head pounded, Sunder lay beyond his reach, and Audriss, now alert and armed with Talon, could easily counter any further attempt on the book. The realisation that he could have come so far, suffered so much, only to fail here, at the end, left a bitter taste in the warlord's mouth. He felt a sudden overwhelming urge to throw himself into a last suicidal attack, to die now rather than live to see the results of his failure.

And then – despite the winds, despite the fire, despite the screams, despite the pain – Corvis swore he heard the laughter of his children, the whisper of his wife telling him to live. To live.

To look.

His gaze dropped, perhaps at that command, perhaps in despair. For a long moment, until it was very nearly too late, they didn't register the sight before them. But then Corvis looked, really *looked*, at Audriss' feet.

He forcibly bit back a hysterical cackle. It *couldn't* be that easy! It was a joke, a cliché, not something that ever actually happened! But there it was, exactly where it fell when Audriss kicked him, exactly where Audriss stood now.

Arms and knees aching, Corvis crawled toward the

Serpent, ignoring the fire, ignoring the nightmares rising above those greedy flames. Audriss held his dagger high.

'I see you've finally learned to crawl, worm!' he exulted, shouting to be heard over the crackling inferno.

Forcing his face into a mask of despair, Corvis nodded, surreptitiously tightening both fists around his objective. 'Yes, Audriss!' he called sadly. 'You've won! I beg of you now only a single favour!'

'Oh?' the Serpent asked magnanimously. 'And what might that be?'

Corvis smiled abruptly, and Audriss' own expression fell.

'I want my cloak back, you greedy bastard!' the Terror of the East shouted. And with that, Corvis rose to his feet, oblivious to the pain, and yanked at the tattered purple cloak on which the warlord stood.

Now it was Audriss' world that lurched. The building across the street tilted away from him, and the loud crackling in his ears and acrid scent in his nostrils told him, even before he felt the heat, that he'd lost the ends of his hair to the raging fire behind him.

Still he teetered, arms flailing for balance he could not find. The flames licked at his back, heated the bits of armour hanging from his body, seared his skin first red, then black.

But he *would not fall*! He was Lorum, Duke of Taberness, Regent of Imphallion! He was Audriss, the Serpent, the most feared man since – no, including – Corvis Rebaine himself! He held in his hands the spellbook of Selakrian, the power to make himself a god among men! He . . .

. . . still ranted internally, struggling to right himself away from the flames dancing joyously across his back, when Corvis planted a foot in his chest and shoved.

Audriss landed flat on his back, engulfed in the hellish flames dripping from Maukra's scales. Tongues of fire dug into his flesh, parting skin and slipping between dark and cracking bones, lapping thirstily at fluids that bubbled and steamed. And Audriss, even as his eyes boiled away, as smoke flowed from every orifice of his rapidly disintegrating body, laughed. He laughed until there was no more air to carry the sound, until no lungs remained to give him breath, nor mouth to release it. Even as the flames abruptly faded away, as the horrors called Maukra and Mimgol vanished, banished to whatever Pit they'd come from, the Serpent's laughter drifted upward on heated currents. It drifted out above the ruined city like a bird in flight, circled once, and then it, too, was gone.

In the sudden silence, unseen amid the charred rubble, the ancient pages of Selakrian's spellbook burned away into embers and ash. Had anyone looked closely, they might – just might – have seen the whirling eddies of smoke coalesce, take on a not-quite-abstract form that could, from the proper angle, have been a face. They might have seen that face nod once in satisfaction at the pile of cinders that had been his greatest creation. And then they would have seen the smoke break apart and fade away into the breeze.

But no one did.

EPILOGUE

A heavy boot landed on the ash-coated gravel. The curtain of smoke parted and Corvis Rebaine, Terror of the East, knelt down by the side of a great stone structure. His face was masked in grime, streaked through with trails of sweat. His hair lay plastered to his neck, and he walked with a pronounced limp. Sunder hung once more at his side. The armour, dirt-encrusted, presented a truly odd appearance without cloak or helm; it made him feel like a large and bedraggled porcupine.

Carefully, Corvis pushed aside a few bits of rock and other detritus, seeking something – two somethings, more accurately. They'd talked this out ahead of time, arranged for him to go to the base of the building nearest the confrontation, but that was still a lot of area to cover.

But no, here they were, ring and bracelet both, gems dulled by the soot coating the city. Corvis reached first for the bracelet.

'Hello, Khanda.'

/Corvis. Would it surprise you to learn that you've looked better?/

The former warlord actually found it in him to grin. 'I'd be rather astonished if I hadn't.' Corvis shook his head, as though trying to shake out some unpleasant thoughts. 'No trouble with Pekatherosh?'

/I wouldn't say that, precisely. Caught him by surprise, though, just as we planned. We've been sitting here ranting at each other ever since, since we can't do much without a wielder. Sort of makes me wish I were a monkey. At least I could have hurled a nice gob or two of faeces his way, something to pass the time./

'My, but you're colourful.'

/Right. Enough chitchat already, Corvis. You have a promise to keep./

'I do. And shocking as it may be, Khanda, I intend to do just that.'

Using the tips of his fingers, Corvis lifted the silver bracelet from the dirt. Clenching his fist only partially around the bauble, he began to concentrate.

/Oh, yes! It's going to be so nice to get out and . . . Corvis? Corvis, what are you doing?/

'I'm setting you free, Khanda. Just like I promised.'

/But – but then what . . ./ The first stirrings of real panic crept into the demon's voice, and it sounded as though he were shouting from farther away than normal.

'I'm sending you home, Khanda. You'll be completely free there!'

/No!/ Corvis could feel the imprisoned entity struggling against his will, but even had Khanda possessed the necessary strength to break his control, it was already far, far too late. /Corvis! Corvis, I wanted to be free here! Here!/

'I never promised that, now did I?'

/Corvis!/ The voice was tiny now, as shouted across a widening gulf. /Corvis, we have to be summoned by name! I've been trapped in that stupid gem for years! Nobody but you even knows who I am! If you do this, I may never be able to come back!/

'Noticed that, did you?' Corvis asked casually.

/Corvis! You bast—/ Then nothing. The blood-red gem flared once, dulled, and cracked. Corvis let the worthless bracelet fall.

'Now you,' he said darkly, carefully lifting the purple-stoned ring. 'Are we going to have to go through the whole contest-of-wills shenanigan?'

/Ah,/ Pekatherosh said hesitantly. /No, I don't think so./

'Good.'

/You're sending me back, too, aren't you?/ The demon sounded almost resigned.

'Actually, no. I probably should. But if I've learned nothing else from these past months, I've learned you can never be too prepared for the unexpected. I promised Khanda I'd free him, and so I did. But I think I'd prefer to have access to one of you, if the need ever again arises.'

/*So then what. . . Rebaine, you wouldn't—*/

With a purple flash, the ring was gone.

'Oh, I most certainly would,' Corvis corrected the empty air.

In an ice-filled cave in the peaks of the Terrakas Mountains, Pekatherosh cursed vilely, loudly, and for a very, very long time.

There was, of course, no one to hear him.

'. . . The perfect opportunity, Lord Rebaine,' Ellowaine explained as she limped behind her commander. 'The city's essentially defenseless!'

Corvis nodded as he approached the soot-stained doors of the Hall of Meeting, though his expression remained enigmatic. He hit the doors without slowing – they rebounded from the walls with a pair of synchronous crashes. The trio crossed the room and set foot upon the wide stone stairs before the echoes faded.

Seilloah picked absently at the heavy green wool as she walked, one hand pressed to her magically treated (and now quite full) but still aching stomach. She'd grabbed this new garment from an open window in an abandoned house, as the last was far too shredded to meet modesty's demands. It covered her well enough, but it was a sickly shade of green, not unlike a dying plant, and it couldn't have itched any worse if it were woven of living insects.

'Ellowaine's got a point,' Seilloah finally said as they left the staircase and turned down the hall. The wind was now free to roam with impunity through the upper floor, thanks to the absence of the roof. It whipped joyfully around them, unconcerned that this remained a somber situation and that a certain degree of sober behaviour would have been more seemly. 'You've never had a better opening than you do now. The nobles and the Guildmasters are all gathered in one place. Yours is the only army left on the field with any trace of leadership or discipline. You could do it, Corvis. One word from you and you would finally rule, just as you've always wanted.'

For a moment, standing before the final door, his ears filled with the frightened whimpers and whispers of the people within, Corvis paused. Exhausted as he was in body and soul, his mind raced ahead, poring over the possibilities.

They were right. For years, he'd worked toward a single goal, and he'd been thwarted by nothing more than bad luck and insufficient knowledge. For twenty years, now, he'd listened to the goings-on of the world around him, watched as the nation's fortunes rose and fell, and he'd wondered: would things have been different if he'd ruled? Would things have been better? Could he have given his family a better life? Something more than a tiny hut on a small bit of property, looking constantly over his shoulder on the off-chance that the next stranger might somehow recognise him? Could he give his children a home where they would never again have to fear the bad men hiding over the hill, in the trees at the edge of the woods?

Could he forget the promises he'd made to himself, when he and the nation were so much younger?

The Terror of the East began to draw breath to speak, and exhaled it in a single, mournful sigh.

He'd made other promises in more recent days, and they'd been made to someone far more important than the man he used to be.

The Terror of the East died with that breath. Corvis Rebaine turned to face the women behind him.

'Ellowaine,' he said, wiping a filthy strand of hair from his face, 'I want you to head out. Find Losalis, tell him to assemble the men beyond arrow range of the walls – or what's left of the walls, anyway. I want a complete casualty report. And I mean *complete*, from death down to bruises and hang-nails. I want a full equipment inventory as well. And then I want Losalis to wait until I order otherwise.'

449

The blonde mercenary stared through narrowed eyes. 'You're stalling, Lord Rebaine.'

Corvis smiled. 'Have I let you down before, Ellowaine?'

For a moment more she stood, motionless, unblinking. Then, muttering under her breath, she headed back toward the stairs.

'You're not going to give "the word" at all, are you?' Seilloah asked once she'd gone.

The former warlord shook his head. 'No, Seilloah, I'm not. I promised Tyannon this was the end of it. No more blood-shed. I think I'd like to start making a habit of keeping my promises.'

The witch's mouth quirked ever so slightly. 'What about your promise to pay this rather sizable army?'

'Well, *some* of my promises.' He frowned. 'You might want to see about sending Davro a message. It's probably best if he's well on his way by the time Losalis and Ellowaine figure out I'm not coming back and they're not getting paid.'

'I can do that. You think they'll attack the city anyway? Try to make up their pay with looting?'

'Possibly. I think the city might prove more than they can handle, though. I hope they're smart enough to cut their losses and go home.'

Seilloah's hand absently picked at the heavy wool. With a conscious effort, she forced it back down to her side. 'You're not making any friends today, Corvis.'

'You might be surprised. And you're one to talk about making friends. *I* didn't *eat* one of the city's greatest heroes!'

'He wasn't doing anyone any good, anyway, Corvis. And I'd just used a lot of healing magic. You know how hungry that makes me.'

'Hmph.' He threw open the door.

The room was no less a mess than when he'd left. Chunks of brick lay where they'd fallen when Audriss obliterated the ceiling. Tables and chairs were overturned, some to provide a vantage point over the walls, others as some small measure of cover should any hostile forces storm the room. Several dozen pairs of eyes peeked at Corvis over the edges of those tables as he entered.

Smiling internally, Corvis made a point of putting on his business face as he surveyed the haphazard defenses. For a full moment he just looked, allowing the fine representatives of the upper classes to look back.

Then, 'Well, I suppose your instincts were in the right place. But this wouldn't stop a determined stable hand with a rake, much less professional mercenaries. And the Children would have just burned the building out from under you and sucked the souls from your falling bodies.'

Hammer clenched in a white-knuckled fist, Salia rose from behind the barricade. 'Duke Lorum?' she asked, voice shaky.

'Dead. And his pets are gone.'

The entire room – the walls included, or so it seemed – breathed a huge sigh of relief. More than a few sobs of joy were heard from behind the table.

'And you?' the blacksmith-priestess asked, the mood again growing cold and brittle. 'What are *your* intentions now?'

Slowly, each footstep clear and distinct, Corvis strode toward the edge of the table. Stepping around, he found a young noblewoman staring up at him, face slack with terror. Her gown was dust-covered, her makeup long since washed away by tears and sweat, her fanciful coif of hair unravelled.

She flinched as this monster of her childhood reached out toward her, and then blinked as his hand stopped, palm-up.

The world paused, watching.

It took every bit of courage she possessed, but her hand finally, hesitantly clasped his. With a smooth effort, Corvis helped the young woman to her feet.

'I came here,' he told the stunned assembly, 'to stop Audriss. I succeeded. Our business is complete.' As he spoke, Corvis moved down the line, helping the astonished council members from the floor on which they'd lain or crouched. A hand here, a shoulder for support there. By the time the rest gathered their wits and regained their feet, more than half the assembly had actually been physically assisted by the greatest nightmare of their lives – well, perhaps second greatest now – and felt the simple touch of human flesh.

'Audriss yanked Baron Jassion off the field,' Corvis told

them. 'I imagine you'll find him in the duke's dungeons. Lovely place. I vacationed there myself recently. Personally, I couldn't care less if you left him there to starve, but you'll need every hand you have to rebuild this place, and if there's one thing you can say for Jassion, he's determined.'

And with that, Corvis moved to leave.

'Rebaine!'

Corvis locked eyes with a shaken but determined Salia. 'Yes, priestess?'

'What about you? Whatever else has happened today, you're still responsible for your actions of years past. Are we to just let you go?'

'Salia,' he said softly, 'I'm not a young man anymore. My days of fighting are over, as of right now – *unless* you force me to do otherwise. I can walk out of here, in peace, and we can never trouble each other again. Or you can try to stop me.' Sunder clanked as Corvis' hand rested upon the blade. 'Which will it be, Salia?'

The priestess forced a smile, though it was weak and sickly at best. 'Have a safe journey, Rebaine.'

'And for a change,' Corvis finally finished, 'that's exactly what happened. Davro and Seilloah travelled with me part of the way. She's back in Theaghl-gohlatch, probably chatting it up with the sidhe. Swapping recipes for wayward travellers, I imagine. Davro as much as told me that he'd kill me on sight if I ever came near his valley again, but to tell you the truth, I think a part of him enjoyed the whole thing.'

Tyannon lay next to him, far more beautiful than he remembered, eyes wide as she took in the entirety of the tale. The kids, excited beyond measure to see their father again, had exhausted themselves into slumber hours ago. They'd hear a heavily edited version in the morning.

Corvis and Tyannon were curled up in bed, where they'd spent hours talking. Lying in a heap at the foot of the bed, its fate largely undecided, was a battered suit of black-and-bone armour.

'It's so incredible!' Tyannon breathed, one hand tightening on his. 'Even knowing what happened seventeen years ago, it's hard to believe.'

'Believe it,' Corvis said simply. 'I'm not proud of it all, but it's all true.'

'And you really saw me? When you were . . .' She choked, just as when he'd described to her his condition at Jassion's hands after his capture. 'Seeing things?' she finished lamely.

'Tyannon, you're all I've seen since I walked out that door last summer. It was just a little more vivid that time, that's all.'

For a time they lay in near silence, each pretending not to notice the other's occasional tears.

Finally, Tyannon stirred. 'I'm so sorry about Jassion, Corvis. About what he did. I—'

'Hush. It's over now. And at least you know he's alive and doing well for himself.'

She frowned. 'He's not the kind of person I'd wanted him to be.'

'I don't think any of us are.'

'You know, you're right,' Tyannon said brightly with a sudden, unexpected grin. 'I think we'd better work on improving you – right now!'

The next hours passed with no conversation at all.

Softly, with a stealth he'd lacked months before, Corvis closed the door to the kitchen and sat down at the table.

It was the darkest hour of night outside. The moon had long since sunk beneath the horizon, but the sun would not rise to take its place for some time yet. Tyannon and the kids slept soundly, content for the first time in ages. Corvis – Daddy – was back, and everything was all right again.

He'd see to that himself.

Corvis was tired, a weariness that saturated muscle and flesh, down to his bones. He wanted nothing more than to sleep, perhaps for a week or three. To forget the events of the recent past, to awaken to Tyannon's face, her smile outshining the dawn itself.

But Corvis Rebaine was never a man to leave things undone, and though his last remaining task could have waited days, or weeks, or longer, he would do it now, this night, and have it done with.

Moving slowly, smoothly, silently, he lifted the pouch he'd worn at his belt and placed it gently on the table beside the flickering candle. As nimbly as he could, he untied the thong and reached inside.

The first item to emerge from the depths of the bag was a small scroll case, containing Rheah Vhoune's key, pieced together from fragments of ancient lore. The key to a spellbook that had burned to ash in a storm of apocalyptic flame.

Mostly.

Next came a handful of parchment, ragged and torn at one end where the pages ripped from the book when Audriss grabbed it. Thank the gods he'd had the time to find the proper place, to get a solid grip on the pages before the Serpent recovered! He wondered, briefly, if Audriss had even heard the sound of tearing as he'd wrested his prize away and, if he did, if he'd been sane enough to understand the repercussions.

Finally, from the depths of the pouch, he pulled a jumbled mess. Strands of hair, scraps of cloth, baubles and adornments such as rings and earrings: everything he could surreptitiously gather, palm, or outright steal while he'd helped the nobles and Guildmasters to their feet.

'. . . *this one you'd especially like, my Terror,*' Audriss had gloated. '*A charming spell that flawlessly controls dozens of people, so long as you have the proper foci . . .*'

The new regent – the new *King* – would create a better Imphallion. Exactly the kind of nation Corvis would have created . . .

If *he'd* been in charge.

Slowly, keeping his voice low so as not to disturb the silence of the night, Corvis began to cast.

Turn the page for a preview of the
follow-up to *The Conqueror's Shadow*

WARLORD'S
LEGACY

Coming soon from Gollancz.

The ever-thickening smoke was more oppressive even than the weight of stone looming above. Black and oily, coughed up by sickly, sputtering torches, it swirled and gathered until it threatened to blot out what little light the flames produced, to transform the passageways once more into a kingdom of the blind.

Not that there was much worth looking at. The stones were old: dark and made darker, grimy and made grimier, by the smoke; joined by mortar so ancient it was little more than powder. The corridors smelled of neglect – or would have, were the air not choked by, yes, that selfsame smoke. All along those walls, clad in the sundry hues and tabards and ensigns of half a dozen Guilds and at least as many noble Houses, soldiers stood rigidly at attention, fists wrapped around hafts and hilts, and did their best to glare menacingly at one another. It was an effect somewhat ruined by the constant blinking of reddened eyes and the occasional wracking cough.

At the corridor's far end, an ancient wooden door stooped in its frame like a tired old man. Cracks in the wood and gaps where the portal no longer sat flush allowed sounds to pass unimpeded. Yet something within that room held most of the thick haze at bay.

It might have been the press of bodies, so tightly crammed together that they had long since transformed this normally chilly chamber into something resembling a baker's oven. It might have been the hot breath of so many mouths jabbering at once, speaking not so much *to* as *at* one another in diatribes laden with accusation and acrimony.

Or it might have been the tension that weighed upon the room more heavily than smoke and stone combined. Perhaps one could, as the aphorism suggests, have cut that tension with a knife, but it wouldn't have been a wise idea. The tension here might very well have fought right back.

Gathered within were the men and women to whom those soldiers in the hall were loyal, and they were doing a far better job than their underlings of glaring their hatreds at one another. Clad in brilliant finery and glittering jewels, the leaders of several of Imphallion's most powerful Guilds stood with haughty, even disdainful expressions, and weathered the array of verbal abuse (and occasional emphatic spittle) cast their way. Across the room, separated from them only by a flimsy wooden table whose sagging planks somehow conveyed a desperate wish to be elsewhere, a roughly equal number of the kingdom's noble sons and daughters who, it must be said, had more than a bit of justification for their anger.

'. . . miserable traitors! Ought to be swinging from the nearest gibbets, you foul . . .'

'. . . filthy, lowborn miscreants, haven't the slightest idea the damage you've . . .'

'. . . bastards! You're nothing but a litter of bastards! Dismiss your guards, I challenge . . . !'

And those were among the more polite harangues against which the Guildmasters were standing fast. Their plan had been to allow the initial fury to wear itself down before they broached the topic for which they'd called this most peculiar assembly, here in an anonymous basement rather than Mecepheum's Hall of Meeting. But the verbal barrage showed no signs of dissipating. If anything, it was growing worse, and the presence of the guards in the hallway no longer seemed sufficient to prevent bloodshed between these entrenched political rivals.

Perhaps sensing that precise possibility, one of the nobles advanced to the very edge of the table, and raised a hand. One voice slowly wound down, then another, until the room reverberated only with the sounds of angry, laboured breathing. A red-haired, middle-aged fellow, Duke Halmon was no longer Imphallion's regent – Imphallion no longer *had* a regent, thanks to those 'lowborn miscreants' – but the nobility respected the title he once held.

Leaning forward, two fists on the table, the white-garbed noble spoke to his fellow aristocrats behind him even as his attention remain fixed on the Guildmasters. 'My friends,' he said, 'I feel as you do, you know this. But this is a most unusual gathering, and I'd very much like to hear the Guilds' reasons for arranging it.'

'And they better be damn good ones,' spat the husky Duchess Anneth of Orthessis. Behind her arose a muttered chorus of agreement.

Across the room, expressions of condescension turned to frown's of hesitation. Now that it was time, nobody wanted to be the first to speak.

Halmon cleared his throat irritably, and Tovin Annaras – a trim fellow, master of the Cartographer's Guild – shuffled forward with little trace of his accustomed athletic step. Smiling shallowly, almost nervously, he took a moment to brush nonexistent dust from his pearl-hued doublet.

'Ah, my Lords and Ladies,' he began, 'I realise we've had more than our share of differences of late. I want to thank you for being willing to—'

'Oh, for the gods' sakes, man!' This from Edmund, a grey-haired, slouching fellow who bitterly resented his recent defeat at the hands of middle-age. Edmund was duke of Lutrinthus, and a popular hero of the Serpent's War. 'Our provinces are starving – not least because of you Guildmasters and your tariffs! – Cephira's massing along the border, and many of us had to travel more than a few leagues to be here. Would you *please* dispense with the false pleasantries and just come to it?'

Again, a rumble of assent from the blue-blooded half of the assemblage.

459

A lightning strike of emotion flashed through Tovin's face, from consternation to rage, and it was only a soothing word from behind that prevented him shouting something angry and most likely obscene in the duke's face.

'Calm, my friend.' Even whispered, he knew the voice of Brilliss, slender mistress of the rather broadly named Merchants' Guild. 'No turning back now.'

He nodded, choking on the bitter dregs of his anger. 'None of that matters today, m'Lords,' he said tightly, looking from Edmund to Duke Halmon. 'What we must discuss today is of far greater – or at least far more immediate – import.'

Scoffs from several of the nobles, but Halmon's eyes narrowed in thought. 'And what, pray tell, could possibly qualify as more—'

'Lies,' Tovin interjected without allowing the question to continue. 'Broken promises. Murder. Treason. *Real* treason!' he added, scowling at those who had hurled that word at the Guildmasters mere moments before. 'Treachery that threatens us all, Guild and House alike.'

It was sufficient to quiet the jeers of disbelief, though more than one noble wore an expression of doubt that was nearly as loud.

'All right,' Halmon said, following a quick glance toward Edmund and Anneth, both of whom nodded with greater or lesser reluctance. 'We'll hear you out, at the least. Speak.'

With obvious relief, Tovin turned toward Brilliss, who moved to stand beside him. A deep breath, perhaps to steady her own nerves . . .

And the room echoed, not with her own slightly nasal yet eloquent tone, but with a shriek from the hallway, a scream of such despair as to bring a sudden chill to the chamber, to make even the most irreligious among them contemplate the inevitable fate of his own soul.

More screams followed, in more than one voice. The rasping of steel on leather echoed through the hall, weapons leaping free and ready to taste blood, but it was not quite

460

sufficient to drown out the sound of dead bodies striking the cold stone floor.

Edmund, who had stood beside the great Nathaniel Espa while leading the troops of Lutrinthus into battle, who had been present during the near destruction of Mecepheum at the hands of the crazed warlord Audriss, was the first to recover his senses. 'Back! Everyone, back away from the door! Halmon! Tovin! Get that table up against it!' It wasn't much of a barricade, but it was what they had – and more, it got the wide-eyed and gape-mouthed aristocrats moving.

Not a man or woman present wore armour, for despite the animosity between Guilds and Houses, none had anticipated bloodshed . . . And besides, that's what the soldiers out in the hall were for. Several did, however, carry swords or daggers, if only for show, and these took up a stance between their unarmed compatriots and the sudden violence outside. Halmon and Tovin retreated from the table and each drew a blade – the duke a short broadsword, the Guildmaster a wicked dirk – and stood side by side, mutual antagonism momentarily buried, though scarcely forgotten.

From beyond the door, battle cries melted into screams of agony, and a cacophony of many voices faded with terrifying swiftness into few. Like the chiming of old and broken bells, blades clattered as they rebounded from armour. A horrifying roar shook the walls until mortar sifted down from the ceiling. The smoke that poured through the cracks in the door grew horribly thick, redolent of roasting flesh.

'Dear gods,' Duchess Anneth whispered, dagger clutched in one hand, the linked ivory squares that were the symbol of Panaré Luck-Bringer in the other. 'What's *out* there?'

And to her an answer came, though clearly sent neither by Panaré nor any other of Imphallion's pantheon.

A sequence of lines etched themselves across the door, as though it burned from the inside out. For the barest instant the portal split into eight neat sections, each peeling back from the centre like a blossoming flower, before the wood gave up the ghost and disintegrated into a thousand glowing embers.

Without the door to lean against, the table slumped forward, clattering into the hall to lie atop corpses and bits of corpses.

More than two score soldiers had stood guard in that hall, drawn from the various Guilds and Houses of those who met within this basement chamber. Only one figure stood there now, a hellish portrait framed in that smoldering doorway, a figure that owed fealty to none of the frightened men and women within.

Whimpers rose from what few throats hadn't choked shut in mortal dread, and more than one blade scraped itself dull upon the stone floor where it had fallen from nerveless fingers. For nary a Guildmaster or noble present failed to recognise the man – the *thing* – looming before them.

Plates of steel armour, enamelled black as the inside of a closed casket, encased him from head to toe, showing only thin gaps of equally dark mail at the joints. Across the chest, the shoulders, and the greaves were riveted plates of pale-white bone. Spines of black iron jutted from the shoulder plates, and from those dangled a worn purple cloak. But it was the helm, a gaping skull bound in iron bands, to which all eyes were drawn.

It was a figure out of nightmare: the nightmares of an entire nation, dreamt first more than two decades ago, and again six years past. Nightmares that should never have been dreamt again.

'You promised us . . .' It was a whisper as first it passed through Duke Edmond's lips, but rose swiftly into a scream of lunatic terror. '*You promised!*'

And the unseen face behind the skull laughed, laughed until he could scarcely breathe, even as he strode forward to kill.

A vicious clatter, a sullen clank, and the grotesquely armoured figure stepped through a very different doorway, entering a wood-walled room several streets away from that cellar-turned-abattoir. Soot and crimson spatters marred the armour, as did the occasional scrape where a soldier's blade had landed in vain. Without pause he moved to the room's only chair and slumped into it, oblivious to any damage he did the cheap furniture.

And there he waited, so motionless within his cocoon of bone and metal that the armour might have been utterly vacant. The sun drifted west, its lingering rays worming through the slats in the shutters, sliding up the walls until they vanished into the night. The room grew dark as the armour itself, and still the figure did not move.

A latch clicked, hinges creaked, and the door drifted open and shut in rapid succession. This was followed by a faint thump in the darkness, which was in its turn followed by a sullen cursing from the newcomer and a brief snigger from the armoured figure.

'Gods damn it,' the new arrival snapped in a voice made wispy with age, 'is there some reason you didn't bother to make a light?'

'I'd rather hoped,' echoed from within the horrid helm, 'that you might trip and break something. Guess I'll have to settle for what sounded like a stubbed toe.'

'Light. *Now*.'

'As you demand, oh ancient fossil.' Fingers twitched, grating slightly against one another as the gauntlet shifted, and a dull glow illuminated the room's centre. It revealed the newcomer to be a tall, spindly fellow clad in midnight blues, with an equally dark cloak thrown over bony shoulders. His bald head was covered in more spots than the face of the moon, his beard so delicate that he appeared to be drooling cobwebs, his skin so brittle it threatened to crack and flake away at the joints.

'Better?'

The old man scowled. 'Better, *what*?' he demanded in a near screech.

The sigh seemed to come from the armour's feet. 'Better, Master Nenavar?'

'Yes,' the old man said with a pleased – and surprisingly toothy, for his age – grin. 'Yes, it is.' He looked around for another seat, spotted none, and apparently decided not to give his servant the satisfaction of asking him to move. 'I assume it's done?' he said instead. 'You smell like someone set fire to a butcher's shop.'

'Nope, not done. Actually, I explained your entire plan to them and led them back here. He's all yours, gentlemen.'

Nenavar actually squeaked as he spun, arms raised before him in a futile gesture of resistance – only to find nothing more threatening behind him than cheap paint slowly peeling off the walls.

'I imagine you think you're funny,' he growled, crossing his arms so as not to reveal the faint trembling in his hands. The man in the armour was too busy chortling to himself to answer – which, really, was answer enough.

'Of course it's done,' he said finally, once he could draw sufficient breath to speak. 'They're all dead.'

'All?' Nenavar asked, his brow wrinkling.

Another sigh, and somehow the helm conveyed the eye-rolling within. '*Almost* all. A few guards survived. I actually *do* know how to follow a plan, *Master* Nenavar.'

'You could've fooled me.'

'Very likely.'

Nenavar glared. 'You stink. Get rid of that thing.'

The skull tilted upward, as though the wearer were lost in thought, and then it, and the armour, were simply gone.

Every man, woman, and child in Imphallion had heard the description of that armour, heard the horror stories of the warlord and wizard Corvis Rebaine, who had come so near to conquering the kingdom. But the man who sat revealed by the disappearance of the bone and steel – now clad in mundane leathers and a cloak of worn burgundy, his features shadowed in the feeble illumination – appeared far too young to be the infamous conqueror.

'You know what you have to do now, Kaleb?' Nenavar pressed.

'Why, no, Master.' Kaleb's expression slackened in

confusion, and he somehow managed to unleash a single tendril of drool as his lips gaped open. 'Could you tell me again?'

'Damn it, we've gone over it a dozen times! Why can't . . .' Nenavar's fingers curled into fists as he realised he was being mocked. *Again*.

'Well, it appears you were right,' Kaleb told him. 'I *could* have fooled you.'

Nenavar snarled and stomped from the room. Or at least Kaleb *thought* he was stomping; the old man was so slight, he couldn't be positive.

He rose, stretching languorously, and stepped to the window. Pushing the shutters open with one hand, he stared over the cityscape, the winking starlight more than sufficient for his needs.

Yes, he knew what he had to do next. But he also knew that he wasn't expected until after dawn, and that left him plenty of time for a little errand that Nenavar needn't know about.

Whistling a tune just loud and obnoxious enough to wake anyone in the neighbouring rooms, Kaleb climbed the inn's rickety stairs and out into the Mecepheum night.

The heat of the day had begun to dissipate, its back broken not merely by the setting of the sun but by the falling of a faint summer drizzle. Kaleb flipped up the hood of his cloak as he went, more because it was expected than because he was bothered by a bit of rain.

Through the centre of town, through the city's most well kept streets, he made his way. Glass-enclosed lanterns gleamed at most intersections, burning cheap scented oil to keep the worst of Mecepheum's odours at bay. The capital of Imphallion was a witch's brew of old stone and new wood, this neighbourhood far more the former than the latter. The roads were evenly cobbled, the rounded stones allowing the rain to pour off into the cracks rather than accumulate along the lanes. All around, wide stairs and ornate columns, some in fashions that had been ancient when Mecepheum itself was new, framed the doorways to edifices that were home and workplace to the rich and powerful – or those rich enough to *appear* powerful.

Despite the hour, Kaleb was far from the only traveller on these streets. The many lanterns illuminated all but the narrowest alleys and deepest doorways, and patrols of mercenaries, hired to police the roads and keep the peace, gave even the most timid citizen sufficient confidence to brave the night.

So it had been for some years now, ever since the Guilds had effectively taken over the city. Tight-fisted they might be, but keeping the shops open and commerce running into the hours of the evening was well worth their expense.

Kaleb kept his head down, sometimes nodding slightly to those he shoved past on the streets, or to the occasional patrols, otherwise ignoring the shifting currents of humanity entirely. And slowly, gradually, the traffic on the roads thinned, the lanterns growing ever farther apart until they were replaced by simple torches on poles, spitting and sputtering in the rain. Gaps appeared in the cobbled streets, missing teeth in the city's smile, and the great stone edifices vanished, edged out by smaller buildings of wood.

On the border between Mecepheum's two separate worlds, Kaleb briefly looked back. Looming high over the inner city, the great Hall of Meeting itself. Here, now, it looked magnificent, untouched by time or trouble. Only in the brightest noon were its recent repairs visible. Despite all the city's greatest craftsmen could do in six years, the new stone matched the old imperfectly, giving the Hall a faintly blotchy façade not unlike the earliest stages of leprosy.

Kaleb smirked his disdain and continued on his way.

Six years . . . Six years since the armies of Audriss, called the Serpent, and Corvis Rebaine, called the Terror of the East, had clashed beyond Mecepheum's walls. Six years since Audriss, gone mad with stolen power, had unleashed eldritch horrors on Mecepheum in an apocalyptic rampage that had laid waste to scores of city blocks. Six years, more than enough for the Guilds to patch Mecepheum's wounds, if not to heal the scars beneath.

Oh, the citizens had avoided those mangled neighbourhoods for a time, repelled by painful memories and superstitious dread. But cheap property near the heart of Imphallion's greatest city was more than enough to attract interest from outside, in turn inspiring Mecepheum's own merchants and aristocrats to bid for the land lest outsiders take it from them. The rebuilding, though slow to commence, was long since complete. An outsider, ignorant of the region's history, might wonder at the abrupt shift from old stone to new wood, from the affluent to the average, but otherwise would never know that anything untoward had ever happened.

The confident footsteps of the richer – and safer – neighbourhoods transformed into the rapid tread of pedestrians hoping to reach home before trouble found them, or else the furtive stride of those who *were* trouble. Coarse laughter staggered drunkenly through the doors and windows of various taverns, voices argued behind closed shutters, ladies (and men) of the evening called and cooed from narrow lanes. Still Kaleb ignored it all. Twice, men of rough garb and evil mien emerged from doorways as though prepared to block his path, and twice they blinked abruptly, their faces growing slack and confused, and continued on their way as Kaleb passed them by.

The rain had grown heavier, threatening to mature into a true summer storm, when Kaleb finally reached his destination. It was just another building, large, ungainly; he wasn't even certain what it was. A storehouse, perhaps? It didn't matter. Kaleb hadn't come for what was, but for what *had been*.

Ignoring the weather, he lowered his hood and glanced about, his magics granting him sight beyond what the night and the storm permitted anyone else. Even in brightest day, no other would have seen what he did, but there it was:

scorched wood and ash, the last remnants of the lot's former edifice, mixed in with the dark soil.

He knelt, digging his hands deep into the earth until he was elbow-deep, first through clinging mud, then drier loam the falling rains had not reached. It smelled of growth and filth, things living and things dying.

Very much like Mecepheum itself, really.

Kaleb tensed in concentration, closed himself off from the world around him. As though he had melted in the downpour, he felt himself – the essence of what he was – pour from his eyes like tears, flow down his skin and meld into the welcoming soil. He cast about, blind but hardly unaware, seeking, seeking . . .

There.

He rose, the soil sliding in chunks and muddy rivulets from his arms. He moved several yards to his left, knelt once more. But this time, when his hands plunged into the soil, they did not emerge empty. He carefully examined his prize: a skull, cracked and broken, packed with earth.

And then, without hesitation or hint of revulsion, Kaleb lifted it to his mouth and drove his tongue deep into a socket, probing through the dirt to taste the essence within. It was not a technique his 'master' Nenavar would have recognised. For all the old wizard's skill, there were secrets of which even he remained ignorant.

Six years, but there was just enough left to work with. Just enough for Kaleb to taste, and to know that this was not who he sought.

No surprise, that. The dead from Audriss' rampage, lost amidst burnt ruins and collapsed buildings – buried by nature, by time, and by the rebuilding – numbered in the hundreds if not more.

Kaleb, frankly, had no interest in taking the time to search them all.

With a grunt, he planted the skull before him and began to trace symbols in the mud. Twisted they were, complex, unpleasant even to look at, somehow suggesting memories of secrets never known.

He was chanting, now, his words no less corrupt than the glyphs accompanying them. Sweat poured from his face, a sticky film that clung despite the pounding rain.

Until, audible to none but him, a dreadful wail escaped the empty skull.

'Speak to me,' Kaleb demanded in a voice nigh cold enough to freeze the surrounding storm. 'Tell me what I need to know, and I'll return you to your rest. Refuse . . . refuse, and I will bind you to these last of your bones, here to linger until they've decayed to dust.'

A moment, as though the risen spirit hadn't heard, or wasn't certain it understood, and then the wailing ceased. It was all the answer Kaleb received, and all he required.

'You did not die alone,' he told the skull. 'Hundreds perished even as you did, burned by Maukra's fires, drowned in Mimgol's poisons, or crushed as the buildings fell. From here, your ghost made its way to the Halls of the Dead in Vantares's domain. You must have seen the others as well, and it is one of your fellow dead whom I seek.'

'*A name* . . .' It was no true sound, a mere wraith of a voice for Kaleb's ears and Kaleb's mind alone. '*His name* . . .'

Kaleb spoke, and the spirit howled as though the worst agonies of Vantares's deepest hell had followed it even into the living realm. But the necromancer would not relent, and finally it spoke, told him where he must dig.

And dig he did, in another lot some streets away. Again his senses plumbed the earth, revealing to him the broken bones. Again he drew forth a skull, his tongue flickering out to taste of whom it once had been.

But this time, Kaleb drew no sigils in the mud. He had no use for the spirit that had gone below. From this one, he needed knowledge possessed while living, not sights seen beyond the veil of death.

For hours he sat, fingers and tongue flitting across the interior of the skull, seeking every last trace of lingering thought and dream, every remaining sliver of what had once been a living essence, desperately seeking, desperately hoping . . . And only as the eastern sky began to lighten, dawn transforming each falling raindrop into a glittering jewel, did Kaleb hurl the skull to shatter against a nearby wall, screaming his frustration to the dying night.

ACKNOWLEDGMENTS

Thanks and accolades . . .

To the many eyes that have analysed *Shadow* in its earlier sundry incarnations: Gary, Chung, Joe, Cortney, Erin, Brian, and Laura; and especially to my dear wife, George, and my sister, Naomi. (And also to Dad, but you already got a dedication earlier in the book. Leave some for everyone else.)

To Brendan, for 'You know, that looks interesting.'

To David, for agreeing with Brendan.

To C.A., who's been waiting patiently for his misplaced acknowledgment since 2004. (It's a little dusty, but it's still good.)

To Justin, who started the whole thing. (Well, *my* whole thing.)

And to my mother, Carole, because failing to thank Mom is always a bad idea.